SENGALI

A Cat's Tale

CHRISTIS JOY PINSON

SENGALI, A Cat's Tale

Copyright © 2016 by Christis Joy Pinson

Published by Tiny Seed Media
P.O. Box 91
Fall Rock, KY
40932
www.tinyseedmedia.com

All rights reserved. This book or any portion thereof may not be reproduced or used in any manner whatsoever without the express written permission of the publisher except for the use of brief quotations in a book review.

Cover design: Tiny Seed Media
Cover illustration: *SENGALI* © 2017 Christis Joy
Author bio photography: Jennifer Combs

www.sengali.com

Printed in the United States of America

Library of Congress Control Number: 2017910100

ISBN 978-0-692-91093-1

To **Jesus Christ**

Apart from You
I can do nothing

SENGALI

A Cat's Tale

PROLOGUE

THE SMELL OF INCENSE was strong and bitter as the young man strode silently into the darkened room. Thick tapestries lined the walls where mourners gathered in somber huddles, their red, tearstained faces made visible by the dull glow of golden lamp stands burning without a flicker. As the man passed by, a strange change came over each face looking his way—a cold change. No one spoke to him, but their narrowed eyes and bitter glances communicated far louder than words. His sharp ears heard the whispered slander of women behind his back, while men made sure he saw their hateful looks when they spat in disgust. The young man barely noticed. None of that mattered anymore. His eyes were fixed on a frail form laid out on an oversized bed at the far end of the room.

As he drew near, a sudden trembling came over him. The sight of the old man's body so close, stiff and mangled nearly beyond recognition, was almost more than he could bear. The covering over the thin chest still rose and fell, but ever more slightly; the old lungs wheezed as each breath came harder than the last. Tears rushed to the young man's throat, but he clenched his teeth and forced them back down.

Not now! He thought. *Not when we are so close!*

Straining to keep his own hand steady, he tenderly reached for the scarred, wrinkled one resting limp on the bed. At the touch of those strong, familiar fingers a shiver of life passed through the fragile body. The old man's eyes slowly opened. Though wracked with age and pain a look of pleasure passed over his ancient face.

"My boy," he mumbled weakly.

The young man went to his knees and leaned in closer, clutching the dear, frail hand in his. "Yes, Great-Father; I'm here."

The old man strained a few moments, working up the strength to speak. "So, this is it," he managed at last, a weak smile lifting the lines of his mouth, "the end of the journey."

The other's brown eyes were locked in determination not to weep, yet his lips trembled and his deep voice cracked as he replied, "No, not here. You still have a journey before you—the greatest of your life. Your eyes will yet see the deliverance!"

The white head shook faintly at the young man's words. "No, my son; do not deny death when it comes at the end of many years. My days have been long and hard. I welcome their end. For me deliverance has come early." Pride and pity shone from the wise eyes as he continued, "The journey remains for you. And for your family." With great effort the old man moved his other hand, stained red and black with bruises, to slowly draw the covers away from his neck. He winced with pain as his brittle fingers ran over many wounds. Once they found their object, however, a surge of strength seemed to course through him. He pulled himself up on one elbow. "Take it," he commanded, placing the small object into his great-grandson's hand, "it is the symbol of the covenant of your fathers." Though his body shook his voice burned with a force no weakness could diminish, "Bear it well—with honor and with fear. Return with it to your father. He will still comfort us concerning the toil of our hands but you *must* strengthen his. Promise me! Promise you will strengthen your father's hands."

The tears would no longer be suppressed; they flowed freely down the young man's cheeks even as his jaw fought hard not to quiver. "I promise, Great-Father," he choked in sorrow but his voice did not falter, "*Before God*, I promise!"

A look of satisfaction washed over the old man for a moment, removing all his years of cares. Beaming with pride he grasped the shoulder of his great-grandson with a strong grip: a grip of both affection and blessing. His noble eyes shone gray and clear as a winter sunrise. But it did not last. As a smoldering wick will blaze one last time only to fade to cold blackness, so the old man faded as if all the fire in him had finally been snuffed out. He sank back onto the pillow, strength utterly spent. Minutes passed. His breath became very labored. An air of expectant grief hung in the room. Some of the mourners even stole away quietly, unable to face death in such close quarters. The young man never moved. Silently his eyes searched the face of the man before him, committing to memory every feature of one whom he loved so desperately but would never again see in this life. One whose wisdom had always guided him, whose presence had always steadied him, whose integrity had inspired him to be the man he now was—and whose loss might prove unbearable.

At length the old eyes appeared again, pale and weak. He spoke, but his voice was thin and very faint.

"One...more...thing..."

None of those standing around heard the patriarch's final words; none except the young man, who bent brokenhearted over his great-grandfather's dying whispers, and the keen ears of a large gray wolf, whose head rested sadly upon the foot of the bed.

A CAT'S TALE

PART ONE

"Dreams"

ONE

IT ALL BEGAN one particularly hot, still day. Early spring afternoons could be like that in the jungle. The cool morning mist had melted into a hazy vapor rising through the thick tree tops like heat from an oven. The horizon looked wavy, bending and twisting where the green forest met the blue sky. Hazy green and blue, blue and hazy green was all you could see for miles in any direction, except for the occasional yellow and black of a flying toucan, or the bright orange breast of a bluebird nearby. Few other creatures ventured up so high on my mountain: an eagle or two, a few hawks, some winged reptiles, fruit bats, and one very loud owl living in the hollow shell of a dead pine tree. Then there were the fish: rainbow trout, shimmering salmon, delicate minnows, living out their wet lives in one crystal stream flowing from a lake at the mountain's summit all the way down to its roots. But besides fish and fowl I was mostly alone. Solitary. No friends or neighbors to speak of. *Alone*. And that was the way I liked it.

But allow me to introduce myself. My name is Sengali and I am a cat—a *big* cat. Orange fur covers my body, fading to white on my eyebrows, cheeks, and undersides. Black stripes running across my back, neck, and face become black spots on my legs and the tip of my tail. I run faster than an antelope and jump farther than a kangaroo. My roar can echo for miles, but my prey never sees me coming. I hunt by night, rest by day, and cannot stand the presence of a dog unless I consider him my equal. As for water, I still have yet to make up my mind about the stuff: nice on a hot day, but what a mess it makes of a sleek, dry coat! There are other cats who have certainly had more reason to dislike it than I do, but I am not sure they had much of a choice in the matter. Then again, perhaps they did. But I am getting ahead of myself.

It was one of those days when everything moved slower: the clouds in the sky, the wind in the trees, the water in the streams. All of nature seemed to flow at a lazier pace. The animals were no exception. Elephants and emus, crocodiles and crickets, marmots and mice found their own quiet place and stayed there till nightfall. I myself had followed their example and lay stretched out on the surface of a flat, stone cliff high above the crowded jungle floor. Below, the heat was thick and sticky; above, the air was clear and open, the shade of an outcropping rock over my head making things quite comfortable. The view wasn't bad either. Not far away the ground dropped off in a steep cliff, opening up to a sea of treetops: fluffy, green tufts rolling on in every direction, so close together it looked like you could walk right out on top of them without falling through. Drowsily I surveyed the exotic landscape. This mountain had been my home for many moons: my own domain in a vast, lush forest. Other predators claimed other parts of the jungle. One lion in particular (a hulking beast who called himself Mantos) ruled all lands north of the Great River as his personal empire. Except my mountain. Oh he wanted it, but had never yet been able to take it by force, even with his army of lionesses. With them, Mantos had spread his iron rule across the jungle crushing everything in his path (except the giant lizards who could have easily crushed him if they felt like it). But not my mountain. Here life remained the same: easy, abundant and peaceful. Panting from the heat, I laid my heavy head back on the cool rock and began to drift off. At some point a swarm of noisy mosquitoes disturbed me and I glanced up at the sky. Not a cloud was in sight. A welcome breeze had begun blowing gently and the shelter of the rocks was now quite comfortable, even pleasant. All else remained lazy and quiet; the perfect day for a catnap. With a great yawn, I again closed my eyes.

Suddenly there was a sharp squeal! I jolted up and looked around, groggy and irritated. Nothing seemed out of the ordinary. The sun had moved a little towards the west; all was quiet. I lay still. Nothing but the wind in the trees and the hum of the mosquito swarm met my ears. That was it. Even the birds were silent.

That's odd, I mused. With a stretch and a moan I stood to my paws and sniffed the wind.

All at once another shriek split the air, high pitched and very frightened! It seemed to come from somewhere beyond the cliff. Moving to the edge of the stone I peered into the forest far below. Something was happening down there. My ears caught the sound of a small creature crashing its way through the woods and several larger ones right on its heels. Not unusual; the sound of a chase through the jungle was common place. But my nose caught something that made my eyes narrow and my talons flex. A scent flew up on the hot breeze—one all too familiar and not at all welcome. A growl rumbled inside of me. Deciding to investigate, I leapt quickly off the hot rock to a grassy hillside on my left. Carefully but swiftly my paws descended the steep bank, every stone and hole in the path as familiar as the spots on my legs. With each step the noises came closer; whatever they were seemed headed straight towards me! Up ahead a group of large boulders rose from the ground, standing right between the foot of my mountain and the rest of the jungle. This far down the air was stuffy and miserable; it was hard to see how any creature could even breathe in such an atmosphere! Yet from all the snarls and crashes I heard there were obviously several of them closing in fast. I could smell fear and hunger. Staying low to keep my own scent hidden, I climbed up onto the topmost boulder and waited. It did not take long. Bursting suddenly from the underbrush, a streak of gray fur ran into the quarry of boulders, squealing as it realized it was trapped in a dead end. *A wombat!* I observed in surprise. I had seen the fat creatures before, but much further to the west. *What on earth brought a wombat this far from home?* Before I had a chance to think about it several masses of yellow flesh came right behind: five lionesses, muscles bulging, fangs barred. Slowing to a stalk they closed in on the wombat, cutting off all hope of escape. But the little creature had courage. It dug its long claws into the ground and acted like it would charge, hissing with all the menace a wombat can muster. I had to smile in admiration. Yet it was decidedly outnumbered.

Now usually in such a situation I would have let nature take its course, calmly walked away, and left predator and prey to fend for themselves. But this was different. I knew this pack of ravenous females. One in particular. She was gliding at the head of the group: a powerful huntress, lean and poised. Every movement she made was deliberate and controlled with incredible intensity. Her green eyes flashed with delight as she observed her prey, and her face twisted in a cruel smirk. All sinew and bone, she was the leader of this league of feminine assassins and the most lethal. A virtual killing machine.

Lena!

My eyes narrowed again. I thought I had recognized her foul scent on the breeze; here in the close jungle air it was almost unbearable. With mounting anger, I watched from above as she approached the wombat step by deadly step. Head down, neck rigid, her two fore-fangs dripping saliva under her shaggy chin. She paused, lowering her whole body to the ground. The wombat hissed again but it was no use; one more second and it would all be over.

"LENA!" My voice roared, echoing off the walls of the stone cove. The lionesses jumped in surprise, cowering, looking this way and that. Lena's head darted back and forth glancing around. As her green eyes found me, they turned pale. Then the smirk returned.

"Well," she called coolly, "if it isn't the great King of the mountain! What's the matter, Sengali? Finally get bored of your lonely den? Or are you just hungry? We can leave you the bones if you like." A hoarse chuckle escaped the lioness' mouth.

"You're trespassing again, Lena," I said flatly, ignoring her remarks, "I warned you last time what would happen if I found you in my territory." Cautiously I sat on a boulder not twenty feet away from where she stood.

"Did you really?" The tawny shoulders shrugged. "That's funny; I don't remember any such warning. Do you ladies?" But the females behind her were too shaken up to respond. Pretending ignorance she looked back at me with big kitten eyes and cooed, "You mean *this* is your territory, too?"

I did not flatter her with a response.

"Oh come on," Lena huffed, "Don't be so dramatic! Surely the Great Sengali does not fault poor, hungry cats for following their instinct and getting a little carried away in the heat of the chase?" Her gruff voice dripped with sarcasm, "How were we supposed to know the rat would run straight into your 'territory'?"

A spitting sound escaped the wombat, apparently miffed at being called a rat. I glanced over. The little creature might have passed as just another rock except for two beady eyes, four flat, padded feet, and a coat of short fir. Its plump body was about the size of a small pig and its gray sides were heaving deeply in and out from running so hard; the big leather nose was wet and flared. I looked back at the lionesses. "You have a whole jungle to follow your instinct in," I said to Lena, "Just stay out of mine."

The green eyes smoldered but the lioness held her composure. "How long do you honestly think you can hold out up here, Sengali, all alone like some proud turtle who won't come out of its shell? Or don't you realize every other inch of land—far as your eyes can see and farther—belongs to Mantos now? Anytime he wants, my father can overrun your tiny little hill. Then where will you be: you and all your bold words? The Great Emperor always gets what he wants in the end; if you were smart you'd realize that and join him." Suddenly she lowered her voice almost to a purr. "I could make it worth your while. My father can be very generous. He could give you whatever you desire!"

"Except the only thing I want, which I already have. You can save your bribes, Lena. I know why your tyrant-father wants this mountain. It is the only thing standing in the way of him ruling everything from the Great River to the open plains as his personal empire. He's already ripped and slaughtered his way through the rest of the jungle until nothing has the courage or the life left to stand against him." I growled low, "Tell Mantos this: anytime he thinks he is cat enough to challenge me himself Sengali will be waiting for him. But if you, or anymore of his females, sets so much as a claw on my mountain again he's going to have a hard time finding you because you'll be scattered through the jungle in tiny, little pieces!" I smiled, "That should be easy enough—even for *you* to remember."

The lioness' composure was quickly evaporating. "Who do you think you are, Sengali," she lashed, "some kind of benevolent protector-of-the-woods or something? The Righteous Benefactor, too good to be seen with cats who actually admit they *enjoy* killing their prey? I suppose you cry every time you eat a deer."

"No, but neither do I bring down a whole herd of them to sharpen my claws on, only to leave their carcasses rotting for the buzzards. There are rules about that sort of thing."

"*Rules?*" The feline jeered, "Oh, don't make me laugh! *This*," she held up a scarred, powerful claw, "is the only rule I live by! The law of fang and claw. Those with the biggest rule those with none." A cruel smirk pulled her face, "The strong live; the weak die. It's that simple."

I smiled right back, "If you can understand it, Lena, it has to be simple."

That did it. The yellow teeth flashed again and her deadly glare locked on my face. The lioness crouched with such a look of rage I expected her to spring up the rocks any second. "Are you prepared to die for that remark?" She growled.

Slowly I rose, making the most of every muscle, standing to full height. With complete control I thrust out each of my claws. "Are you?"

That stopped her. She hesitated, allowing her better judgment to think twice. Though Lena was a formidable opponent in her own right, she was also no fool. Obviously the cowards behind her would be no help, and though her strength was without equal among her peers it had never been pitted against mine. She was at a disadvantage and she knew it. Her temper melted as quickly as it had flared. "Very well, Sengali," she said with a forced smile, resorting back to fighting with words, "you win for now. After all, it *is* only fair you should be able to enjoy your sense of power for a little while. It won't last much longer. Come, ladies," she called to her comrades, "we'll leave our prey to the King of the Mountain. Apparently he needs it worse than we do." Glancing from the wombat back to me her smile became a mocking grin, "Try not to eat it all at once!"

"Goodbye, Lena."

"And 'good riddance', I know. But if you ever change your mind about leaving your lonely den, you know where to find me." And with that she turned and sauntered away into the forest, followed by the dejected pack of lionesses. I stood unmoved and watched their tan forms get lost in the thick underbrush. When sure they were gone, I dropped to the ground and turned to head back up my mountain, having had enough stuffy air and bad company for one day. The breezy cliff was calling my name.

"Wait!"

I turned and, to my total surprise, saw the wombat running up after me! Huffing and grunting, it came within a few feet then stopped abruptly. "Y,y,y,ou won't eat m,m,me?" Its voice was somewhat squeaky but still deep enough to show the wombat was a male. Caution was etched across his little sloping face. I just stared back, mouth open and speechless, not exactly used to talking with prey animals.

"Y, y, you won't eat m, m, me?" He repeated, looking anxiously through dark, buttonhole eyes.

I managed to snap out of my astonishment long enough to say, "No."

"You p,p,promise?"

It seemed like an odd request, but "Yes," came out of my mouth.

The wombat's muscles were still tense, "You won't break it—break your p,p,promise?"

What's wrong with his speech? I wondered while answering out loud, "No."

The shiny black nose twisted back and forth, as if the creature was weighing whether or not he could trust me. But after a few moments the little animal heaved a great sigh. His whole body relaxed. Then he did something that took me even more off guard: he smiled—a grateful, trusting smile—and stuttered, "Thank y, y, you!" Hearing gratitude from an animal I might consider as breakfast was unusual, to say the least. I cleared my throat and started back up the trail, eager to leave the awkward situation behind.

"W, w, wait!" he called again, and when I looked back I saw the plump, furry ball waddling in my steps up the rocks. The wombat was actually following me! "Where are y, y, you going?"

Oh no! Instead of fear on the little face there was curiosity. Nothing could be more obnoxious than a curious prey animal! "Away," I grumbled then sprang over the rocks and up the mountainside.

The whole afternoon he followed me at a distance, though never out of sight. At last I stopped on an overhanging bank to see the clumsy plant-eater only a few feet below, scampering up the path I had just taken. "Stop following me!" I growled loudly.

"Y, y, you won't eat me! You p,p,promised!" He called back.

This was getting ridiculous. "That doesn't mean I won't kill you!" The wombat stopped dead in his tracks—for the moment anyway. "Now go home!" I shouted and bounded up the rest of the grassy trail. By the time I reached my den, the sun had already begun to sink in the western sky behind the mountain. Its warm light seemed to gild the whole countryside in a breathtaking display of color. Every green leaf turned gold, every sparkling stream flowed pink as a grapefruit, and the steamy atmosphere was transformed into a sauna of amber air. I stood on the brink of the high platform and searched the hillside. No sign of the wombat, though I thought I caught his musky smell on the gentle breeze. More than likely he had decided to seek refuge for the night somewhere on the mountain. "Well, so long as it stays away from me," I mumbled. Sitting on the edge of the cliff, I watched for a long time as stars slowly began to appear in the deep blue eastern sky. My stomach started to growl. Soon it would be time to get to work. But not just yet; I hadn't gotten my nap out and my body knew it. Overcome by drowsiness, I stretched out upon the cool, hard stone and fell asleep.

TWO

FALLING. Senseless falling. Sound swirled around me like a funnel in the dark.

"Oomph!"

With a thud I landed on my side, smacking against prickly leaves, thorny twigs, and cool, hard ground. I stood to my feet.

Where am I?

Looking up, a thick black canopy of trees nearly choked out the sunlight from above. I blinked.

Sunlight? I thought it was night time. And why am I down in the jungle again?

My legs felt shaky; trying to walk was like balancing on a floating log. Everything felt wobbly and all the wind seemed to be knocked out of me. *I must have fallen from a tree,* was my first thought—until I remembered I had not gone to sleep in a tree. Then I noticed how incredibly loud the forest was; it hummed, whirred, and buzzed so much I wondered if I had fallen into a giant hornet's nest. Yet, I didn't see any insects—or any other creatures, for that matter. Only trees and plants standing completely still; not even a breeze stirred their drooping branches. Slumped and frozen, they looked like scolded children awaiting their punishment.

Something's wrong.

Suddenly all noise stopped, cut off as abruptly as if someone had sliced it with a knife. For one horrible minute there was nothing—only dead silence. The thud of my own heart was so loud it felt like it was echoing for miles around. Then it came.

"Sengali."

A voice from behind, a whisper, breathing my name. I spun around but saw no one.

"Who's there?" I called. But I wasn't prepared for what answered. A huge BOOM shook the ground, erupting from far below my feet and high over the trees at the same time. The earth I stood on gave a massive lurch and jerked out from under me like a pulled rug! Everything started to move. The earth heaved and churned like boiling water, flipping over everything on its surface. The trees that had stood so still just seconds before now toppled rapidly, ripped up from their roots. Crashing down they sprawled on the ground in growing piles, rolling around like dead corpses. Terror overwhelmed me as I lay on the boiling ground tossing about like a leaf in a whirlpool.

"*Sengali.*" The Voice called again, louder and more distinct. In the midst of the chaos, it sounded deep and strong—even calm. I struggled to my feet and instantly ran for it—feeling even more than thinking the Voice would lead to safety. Leaping over fallen trees, digging my claws into sliding dirt, I ran as hard and fast as I could. I ran till I felt like my lungs would burst. Yet, no matter how hard I tried, I never seemed to move. The ground under me churned so quickly I couldn't go any further. The more I strove the worse it got, but if I stopped the earth threatened to swallow me whole!

"*Sengali!*" It called from ahead of me.

"Help!" I gasped with what air was left in my lungs, "Help me!" Suddenly there was an awful flash like a crack of light in the sky, and water started pouring on my head. It stung my face and beat onto my back like thousands of tiny needles. The ground became a swirling mass of mud, heavy and thick. Running was impossible now. I started sinking—first my paws, then my legs, then my shoulders. I was being buried alive!

"*Sengali!*" Above the noise, beyond the chaos, the Voice found me. I leapt towards it, struggling, urging every muscle to shake free of the sinking death pulling my body down. I had to break free! Kicking, grappling, fighting with everything in me, I started to emerge. A few more strokes and I would make it! Then suddenly a shadow fell over the earth. It blocked out the sun. It smothered all light. A sound rose behind me like nothing I had ever heard before. A roar, unbelievably loud and full of fear. I froze in the mud, unable to turn around, yet somehow my mind's eye still saw a wave of darkness rise like a mountain into the sky. Higher and higher it towered: a swirling mass of pounding blackness. I heard what sounded like millions of voices united in one hellish scream.

Then it swallowed me.

THREE

I JOLTED AWAKE. Overhead the night sky was thick with stars. In front lay the vague outline of my cliff and the tops of the trees stretching on for miles. Nothing seemed out of the ordinary. Nearby the owl had started his nightly "whoo-hooting", accompanied by a concert of crickets and tree frogs. The air was still and sleepy. Everything was peaceful—except me. My heart pounded like a hammer. Thoughts scrambled like rabbits in a panic and my emotions were worse. With a groan I forced myself to concentrate. *Get a hold of yourself, Sengali!* My body trembled and my chest was heaving like I had just chased a herd of wildebeest and lost. *Was that just a dream?* With a jerk I swatted my face and wobbled up to all fours. Shivering from head to tail I forced myself to breathe deeply, trying to shake the racing emotions inside. Of course it was a dream! The night around me was as still and peaceful as you could hope for. There had been no booming earth, no falling trees, no black wave about to kill me. No strange Voice calling my name. I was on my mountain; everything was fine. I was safe, secure, and in control.

So why could I not stop shaking?

For some time I stood lost in my own thoughts, gazing silently at the lush mountain range to my left, then over the treetops before me and past them towards the far off eastern plains. Yet the more I looked around the more anxious I became. The nightmare had been so real, so vivid that everything my eyes fell on felt more like a dream than it had. Over and over the thing played in my mind: the chaos, the fear, the screams. The Voice.

My eyes narrowed.

That Voice!

Perhaps more than anything else it was what had gripped me the most: soothing and terrifying all at once. Never before had I heard my name called with such power. Yet somehow it was also filled with pain. I had not known where the Voice came from or what it meant, but I had bolted after it without thinking almost like it drew me towards itself. Like a moth to a flame. Even now, as I stood on the brink of the cliff, the longing was so strong inside of me to hear the Voice again, to follow it, I had to keep reminding myself it wasn't real. "Just your imagination," I said out loud, "Too much stuffy air this afternoon. Or going to sleep on an empty stomach." My head shook for emphasis, "Voices just don't speak out of thin air!"

"You heard it, too?!"

Nearly jumping out of my skin, I spun around, fangs barred! There against the wall of my cave sat the wombat, eyes big and frozen in fear. "P,p,promise!" he squeaked, pointing a long claw at my face.

I stared. The dream had completely knocked the wombat out of my mind! In seconds I went from shock to disbelief to anger. "What are you doing here?" I growled.

"Waiting."

"For what?"

"Y,y,you." He relaxed a little, "For you to wake up." Getting even braver, the animal shuffled out of the shadows and into the starlight. "Do y,y,you always wake up l,l,like that?" he asked with a friendly smile. I did not return it.

"What are you talking about?"

But instead of driving him away, my anger seemed to bring out the wombat's pity. "Scared; you w,w,woke up scared."

I snuffed, "That's no concern of yours!" though something in the wombat's eyes made me wonder if that was entirely true. But by this point my pride felt too injured to take the blow of actually asking the animal what it meant. So I started giving orders,

"Look, promise or no promise, I'm not going to warn you again: go home wombat—before I lose my patience!"

The little head drooped, its gray fur shimmering with the motion. "Can't," he spoke quietly.

"Why not?"

The dark eyes locked onto mine with surprising intensity, "The Dream."

My anger vanished (along with my ability to breathe). A heavy silence fell filled with the buzz of insects and night birds. In the distance a band of howler monkeys broke out in loud chattering, but my own mouth had gone dry as a bone. "What did you say?" I finally managed to mumble.

The little creature became excited. "C,c,can't," it repeated, "can't go back! The Dream; it called me. Called me by n,n,name! The Voice," he stopped abruptly as if remembering something then violently shook his head, "C,c,can't go back!"

My hind legs folded under me. The shakes were returning. I was not given to spooks as a rule, and it was a very rare thing for me to ever be really frightened. But I was now. The dream I had just experienced was bad enough, yet finding out the wombat had had a dream of his own—complete with a voice calling his name—filled me with a dread I couldn't explain. It just made no sense. *Calm yourself, Sengali!* "Calm yourself," I said out loud to the wombat, who had plopped down and started scratching nervously. *He could be lying*, I thought suspiciously. *He could have overheard me groaning in my sleep and is now trying to manipulate me!* But one look at the frank, open face turned upwards and I immediately gave up that idea. But then what? *What does it mean—if anything?* Just then my stomach let out a terrific growl.

The wombat's soft, pointy ears came forward, "Y, y, you hungry?"

"What?"

"Do you n,n,need some supper?"

Shuddering with a deep sigh, my whole body felt exhausted. "Probably," I finally admitted.

The wombat smiled. "Me, t,t,too: let's find some food!"

By now I was too tired to argue. Forcing myself to move, I found a familiar trail leading mostly in a straight line around the hillside. From the soft shuffle I heard behind me the wombat must have been following close at my heels. The delicious smell of jasmine and lilies, the deep blue and pale silver uniting everything around us, the rhythm of my own paws against the ground, all combined to soothe my troubled nerves—if not totally lift the fear of my heart. Twisting and turning, the path eventually led us to a very familiar place: a mossy green hillside, split down the middle by the sparkling, clear stream that watered the mountain. I took a slow, deep breath. As soon as the wombat caught scent of the sweet rushes growing along the rocky banks he zipped passed me. Burrowing nose first into the wet grasses he flipped over, stuck four padded claws straight into the air, and rolled around in delight. In a moment the happy animal popped up again, sniffed the air and looked my way. "You hungry?" he asked. Digging in the rich dirt, he pulled up some weeds with his front paws. "Here," the wombat urged, holding the smelly things towards me, "have some!"

I tried not to curl my nose too much, "Uh, no thanks. You can have my part."

The stocky shoulders shrugged as he shoved the green stuff in his own mouth. "They're really g,g,good!" he sloshed out through fat cheeks.

With a shake of my head I smiled. "I prefer to get my own." Off to the side there was a quiet pool where the gushing stream took a break from its downward plunge. Crouching on a flat rock overhanging the still water I waited and watched. A brightly colored salmon swam by, fat, juicy, and completely unaware of my presence. Slowly, ever so slowly, I lowered my paw to just inches above the water's surface. One second the fish was swimming right under my claws, the next it was flopping around on the ground wondering what had happened. A fine, quick catch. In very little time a nice pile of slippery meat had gathered and I settled in for dinner. From the rock serving as my table I could see out over the jungle roof, so dark and still to the eye yet buzzing with a hundred thousand different noises. The mountain forest around us whirred and whistled, sang and croaked, till the tall, silent trees seemed alive with voices. And overall the stars gleamed from their frosty heights. By their light I watched the wombat trying to climb the rocks to where I was. All at once he stopped. A distressed look came over the little face, contorted with worry, as he glanced back and forth. Then I remembered wombats are near-sighted; he must have lost my scent in the spray of the stream. As I watched the black nose twist around searching the air for some sign of me, a strange thing began happening. For some unexplainable reason I found myself pitying the wombat—even wanting to protect him. Believe me; that was not a sensation I was used to with prey animals! But it was there, nonetheless—as gripping and strong as anything I had ever felt.

What is wrong with me tonight? I wondered in amazement. Like a lost cub, helpless and alone, the wombat started to whimper.

"Where are y,y,you?" He cried out.

FOUR

"UP HERE," I replied.

His distress turned to joy and the furry creature waddled up without a stumble. When he came to rest beside me the wombat breathed a long sigh. "You have a nice home," he said quietly. "No w,w,wonder you chased off the she-cats. I would t,t,too."

Observing from this close I noticed the wombat was rather young, especially to be so far from his own home. "You're from the western plains, aren't you?" He looked up at me, surprised. "I've been there before, a couple of times," I explained. "Beautiful country."

"Best in the world!" He exclaimed, becoming animated, "B,b,best dirt, best grass, best water! Nice neighbors, t,t,too," suddenly the small ears drooped, "if you t,t,talk right." The wombat fell silent.

"What do you mean?"

"I d,d,don't; talk right, I mean. Never have. They laughed at me; said I was a half—w,w,wi," his stuttering became worse, "a h,h,half—w,w,w—"

"Half-wit?"

"Yeah. B,b,but they're nice to each other. They're normal. People are nice when you're n,n,normal. If I'd been normal they'd've been nice to me, t,t,too." A far-off look came into the wombat's eyes, "Maybe then they'd've believed me."

"About what?"

The black buttons turned on me, "The Dream." My pulse jumped; I pawed at a fish bone to look casual.

"This dream you keep mentioning, what is it like?"

The wombat was quiet for a moment. Then he shivered, "Scary. Very, v,v,very scary! And dark. All d,d,dark everywhere. Can't see—but I can hear," there was a gulp as he swallowed to continue, "lots of sounds, lots of voices. All l,l,loud and scared. Then it happens. I d,d,don't know what, exactly—a big, b,b,big sound far, f,f,far under. I c,c,can't move. They start screaming. Awful screams," he shivered again. "But then a Voice, n,n,not like the rest, calls. Calls me by name." Fear lifted from the wombat's face, replaced by a kind of awe, "I turn and see light—l,l,like a sunrise. The Voice c,c,calls again and I just know."

My mouth was dry again, "Know what?"

"If I can reach it I'll b,b,be safe." Worn out, the wombat collapsed onto the rock, "Then I wake up."

I swatted at the bone aimlessly. The wombat's dream compared to the one I had just had was uncanny: so similar yet different enough to convince me it was true. "So you left your home just because of one dream?" I forced myself to ask.

He nodded emphatically, "But it kept coming! Over and over—every d,d,day—every time I fell asleep. 'It means something', I t,t,told myself. Told others, too, b,b,but they just laughed. Always they laughed. They d,d,didn't believe me." The sadness in the wombat's voice was unmistakable as it added, "Even she d,d,didn't believe; she didn't believe her Womby." He choked up.

"Your mate?"

The young male sniffled, "She was going to b,b,be." I stared at the little, round form, all huddled in the dark, as wet tears dripped from the end of his nose onto the cool rock below. Feelings of disdain and deep admiration kept switching back and forth inside of me.

"But *why?* Why leave everything you've ever known—your home, your mate, *everything*—just because of a bad dream? What did you hope to gain by it?"

With wet eyes and an earnest face the creature known as "Womby" looked up at me. He opened his mouth but nothing came, as if the reason was so strong he could not find words for it. Remembering the incredible pull I had felt towards the Voice, I realized what he wasn't saying.

"So you followed it?" I asked after a pause, watching a cloud of bats whirl overhead.

The furry head nodded.

"How did you know which way to go?"

"The light in the Dream. It l,l,looked like the sunrise, so I just f,f,f,ollowed it—the sunrise."

"For how long?" I wondered.

He twisted his face and tapped his claws on the ground as if he were counting only to finally shrug, "Lots of them. That's how I g,g,got here."

I noticed the stars were beginning to fade in the eastern horizon. "Well," rising to my paws, "the sun will be coming up over that knoll in a short while. Better get some sleep while you can."

I was turning to leave when the wombat started to sputter. "P,p,please," He said in a small voice, "W,w,would I... C,c,could it... M,m,maybe, would it b,b,be..."

"Out with it," I prompted, getting impatient.

"Please, c,c,could I stay here awhile? Just awhile—'till the she-cats are g,g,good and gone?" Fear clouded his face, "They m,m,might get me now." I was going to protest, but then I thought of Lena. Looking out over the jungle I knew the wombat was right. She and her pack were still out there. I could smell them.

"P,p,please?" He asked again. I took a deep breath and closed my eyes.

What am I getting myself into?

* * *

The next few days felt like someone took my calm, routine, solitary life and flipped it on its head. After I agreed he could stay "for *one* day" Womby decided I was perfectly trustworthy and would never eat him. Once that was settled it was easy for him to also decide he was much safer remaining on my mountain than down in the jungle where she-cats were. His Dream still continued, and as I watched him struggle in his sleep I did not doubt it was the same as mine. It was tormenting, yet his fear of the she-cats seemed just as strong. And so I wound up with a neighbor: a gullible, trusting, jolly little male who set about making himself right at home by digging up every inch of dirt he could find, consuming enormous amounts of vegetation, and following me wherever I went. Every place I roamed, the wombat waddled right along with me, and whatever I did he was determined to try and do as well. He had a knack for getting into *everything*. Several times I came so close to either wanting to eat the little nuisance or scare him away, lose him in the forest, or just leave him on his own. But then the wombat would do something helpless or trusting, and suddenly the same protective feeling I felt that first night would well up inside of me. I just couldn't shake it. Whether I liked it or not, the young animal needed help, and for some unknown reason it seemed I had been chosen for the job (at least until a better solution came around). So I tried to adapt to the situation as best I could. All my meals wound up coming from the river, and I learned to wait patiently whenever the wombat stuttered. My name, however, did turn out to be a challenge for him.

"S, s, seng-g,g,ga-l,l,l,i," was the best he could do.

"Perhaps you should just call me 'Li'," I suggested.

With relief the wombat nodded, "Li!"

Along with adjusting to Womby another thing remained constant for the next few days; over and over again the Dream came in my sleep as well. The same terrible darkness, the same numbing fear. Each time I awoke with a jolt, shaking from head to tail, my pulse thudding through my veins like a hammer. But it was not just the death, or the screams, or the fear that haunted me. As awful as those things were, the memory of them would fade after a while, at least somewhat. It was the Voice. Waking or sleeping, it stayed in my mind till I almost fancied I could actually hear the strange call in the sighing of the wind, the humming of the insects, or the rushing of the mountain stream. It was as if something—or *someone*—was calling to me. And as the Dream kept coming—always mysterious, always terrifying—I finally realized I would never be able to rest until I found out who or what was calling my name.

And why.

FIVE

"W, W, WAIT FOR ME!" Womby cried out. I turned to see him waddling in my footsteps and panting hard. We had been traveling since sunset without a rest and his short little legs were beginning to have some difficulty keeping up with my long strides. I stopped and waited for him to catch up. "Y, y, you sure t, t, take b, b, big steps!" He always seemed to stutter more when he got excited. "W, w, where are we g, g, going, anyway?" he managed to ask after a few more moments of wheezing at my feet. I looked up and around. We were standing in a small field of tall, sharp grass and brown rushes—one of the few clearings in the jungle where the trees withdrew and you could actually see the sky. Only once before had I ventured this far from my mountain, but I knew the direction where it lay and was satisfied we were still on course.

"East," I replied.

Womby crinkled his nose. "East? W, w, where is 'east'?"

"East is where the sun rises from the ground," I smiled a little at how accustomed I was becoming to his naive questions.

The wombat's eyes grew wide, "'Where the sun r,r,rises'?" He was getting excited again, but in a different way, "We are g,g,going t,t,towards the sunrise?" The look on his face was enough to let me know what he was thinking. And he was right. This was not a pleasure stroll.

My mind went back to the previous morning. As I had awakened from a late-night nap (gasping in terror once again) a strange thing had happened. Fog was draped over the mountainside like a wet gray veil, obscuring everything beyond the edge of my cliff. Yet through the mist I heard something. A whisper of a sound. Floating like smoke on the air it was gone almost before it came. But it was enough to make me swat my ears. Was I imagining things now? Or had the Voice just actually gone from dream to reality? The fog dissolved, melting before the light of dawn, and still something hung in the air. Whether or not I actually heard it, I could *feel* it. A strange sensation—almost even a presence—seemed to be coming from beyond the cliff. I felt an incredibly strong urge to stand on the ledge, like I was being drawn from the front and compelled from behind. As the ocean of treetops became visible I looked out across their green surface. An eastern breeze began to stir. The rays of the sun were just beginning to climb into view, rising like an opening curtain over the jungle world. I had wondered before why the sunrise had been so important to the wombat. Now I knew. The Voice was coming from that direction. From the east. Morning turned to afternoon, and slowly, gradually my thoughts had gathered themselves into a radical plan. So when afternoon became evening I left the cliff behind and descended the mountain using the same path I had used the day I rescued Womby. Never far away, the wombat had followed me, not noticing we were leaving the safety of the mountain behind. As we passed under the heavy roof of the jungle I had a fleeting impulse to turn back, but instead focused on the steps in front of me.

Just find the Voice, I told myself, *the sooner you do, the sooner you can return: a mountain isn't worth much if you don't have the peace to enjoy it. Not to mention if you die from lack of sleep—*

"W,w,what about the she-cats?" Pulled out of my thoughts I saw Womby looking around with concern—apparently just realizing he was back in the jungle, "You w,w,won't let them eat me, will y,y,you?"

I laughed to set him at ease, "Do you ever think about anything except eating?"

It worked. His smile re-appeared, "Naps!"

I shook my head with a chuckle while glancing up. The white sliver of a new moon had passed over and was now glowing somewhat behind us casting our black shadows on the ground in front of where we stood. "East is that way," I said, nodding to the other side of the glade, "If we keep moving there's a chance we may find what we are looking for by morning." With a wink I added, "We might even get back home in time for supper!"

"Hooray!" Womby cried with delight, "Hooray f, f, for east!"

* * *

But the morning came and nothing extraordinary appeared. And the next morning. And the morning after that. Four mornings came and went with no sign of anything to help solve the mystery of the Voice. Still I drove on relentlessly. In this, at least, the Dream proved to be a blessing in disguise: sleep was no longer something I enjoyed. Staying awake, no matter how exhausted my body was, was better than getting caught in the nightmare again. However, the pace did become a problem for my short-legged companion. Hard as he tried, Womby barely kept up. But he never complained, remaining cheerful and savoring every new sight, sound, smell, and (of course) taste he encountered. To my surprise I was actually glad to have him along—despite his mind-boggling capacity for stopping to eat and his painfully slow pace. But at least we were able to fix the latter problem by having him ride on my back. A strange solution, to be sure, but I was in a hurry. It took some doing, but the wombat finally managed to get his balance by digging his long claws into the fur of my back, latching onto me like a wooly parasite. Once we discovered he could even sleep that way without falling off we finally started to make good time. I barely rested, but whenever I did I always woke up with the Voice ringing in my ear. It became like an obsession, drawing the wombat and me further and further away from anything either of us had ever known. Yet no matter how many miles we traveled, how many streams we crossed, how many forests we passed through, the Voice always seemed just beyond our reach. Always further east. It was like chasing down wind that only blew from one direction.

Less hard to find was evidence of whose territory we were in. Traces of Lena and her female troop were everywhere. Carcasses were strewn along the ground and markings along the trees, combined with a general fear among the jungle's inhabitants. Most of these went into hiding just on hearing us approach, and the few who did stay to show their faces fled in panic as soon as they saw ours. Hunting was a very touchy business. Apparently Mantos kept his lands well patrolled. It struck me as strange, and a little suspicious, that I never saw any of the lionesses themselves. There was a constant feeling of being watched. So we traveled by day as well as night. The heat under the massive trees was oppressive, filling the humid air with a drowsy lull, yet I forced myself to keep moving. It was our best chance at avoiding the lionesses, who were far less active in daylight.

By the fourth sunset, however, I was exhausted. The lack of sleep and emotional strain finally took their toll. While the moon rose far overhead, its ghostly glow dismembered by the black branches of the trees, I stumbled along the tangled ground searching for a safe place to rest. Off in the distance the sound of rushing water met my ears. Through the dark it led to a cool, mossy cove, hidden among giant boulders and fallen tree trunks, where a silver waterfall poured into a misty pool. Around this waterfall on either side were shallow caves dug into the cliffs. With a little probing a small one was discovered nestled behind the sheet of falling water. *Should be safe enough*, I thought as my heavy eyes surveyed the close roof and quiet solitude of the cavern. Womby had already been asleep for quite some time, awaking only briefly as he tumbled off my back. My whole body ached from exhaustion. Lying on the damp, hard floor a heavy weariness overtook me. I was asleep in a matter of seconds.

* * *

"Sengali."

Within the dream world I cringed. *Not again!*

"Sengali, wake up."

I was lost in a dark sea. The angry sky rained fire and hail as I floated in an ocean of purple and black. There was nothing else in sight. No life at all. My throat closed up with terror. The water was sucking all my strength like a leech. *I can't wake up*, was my only thought.

"Wake up, Sengali!" The Voice was louder, more forceful.

"No!" I managed to shout out loud, and in the next moment all of my senses began to sink under the waves. I was drowning.

"SENGALI!"

* * *

Suddenly my eyes opened. Something was different—the voice was no longer the same. With the final call it had changed from something deep, mysterious, and hardly tangible, to a very definite, very familiar tone. It was higher in pitch, colder in feeling, and distinctly female. My senses quickly returned and I knew who it belonged to before my eyes even fell on the lean, powerful frame standing over me.

"Lena!" I mumbled, trying not to sound as off guard as I felt, "What are you doing here?"

"So there *are* some things you don't know!" came the sly response. "It's funny you should ask me that, Sengali, since I came to ask you the same thing." By this time I had raised myself up enough to look around in the dark. She was not alone. Three other lionesses stood at the entrance to the cave, and by smell I determined there were probably more outside. They were not the same lionesses I had seen her with a few days before: these were larger and much more equal to Lena herself. This was obviously not a social call.

Keep your wits, Sengali; you are on their land now! I slowly stood to my feet, "We're just passing through, Lena; we haven't bothered anything."

The lioness smirked, "'We'?"

Quickly I glanced around: Womby was nowhere in sight.

"Well," Lena mocked, "As much as I hate to, Sengali, I'm going to have to ask you and your invisible friend to come with me." Her emerald eyes gleamed in the dark. "Mantos has his own opinion about you 'passing through' his territory."

SIX

THAT WAS THE END of the discussion; to decline her "invitation" would have most likely proved fatal. Without a word I walked out of the cave, escorted by Lena and the three guards. The moon had sunk beyond sight, but the pale stars revealed seven other lionesses standing around the silver pool, faces hard and without expression. Still there was no sign of Womby. As we descended the rocks the lionesses fell into place around me: two on my right side, two on my left, and three behind. The three guards from the cave took the front and Lena led the way. For about an hour we traveled in silent procession. Not a word passed among the lionesses and none made any conversation with me. Even the night creatures of the forest were quiet—undoubtedly because of us. But at least the fireflies weren't afraid. They floated about like green lanterns, lighting our way through the underbrush with their dreamy light. Having never been this way before I was grateful for the help, though there was little doubt in my mind as to where we were headed. It was a comfort Womby was not with us. I only hoped it was because he had gone to forage in the night and not because he had met one of the lionesses.

At length we came to the base of a steep hill. Lena immediately picked out a narrow but well-worn path up the incline. We had to position ourselves single file to follow her. Giant boulders and twisted trees protruded all around us, but the small trail wound among them and continued to climb. Higher and higher it led us, until we were above the tree line of the forest. For the first time in four days I saw the full glory of the night sky all studded with stars. The moon was also still visible, resting barely above the horizon. The mountain air was clear and sweet to my nostrils; just breathing it in lifted some of the weariness from my body. My mind became sharper.

Looking ahead, I could tell we were nearing the summit of the mountain. In another moment we had cleared the top, and I found myself standing on a large and surprisingly flat area. A clear view of the whole jungle stretched out on every side of the summit with no hindrances to block the grand view. The ground of this impressive overlook was mostly dirt and short grass with a few large rocks scattered about, but at the far end from where we stood grew one lone kapok tree. It was a giant, colossal thing apparently having stood there for a very long time. It towered to such a height its smooth, spindly branches almost looked like arms stretching out to hold the sky, while the great gray roots clung to the earth, making the whole tree look like a mediator between the two. At the base of the tree was a wide, flat rock that seemed to serve as a kind of platform. Or throne. Several lionesses were stationed around it, some standing, some lying, but all were silent and attentive to the one who lay at the base of the tree.

Reclining with his back against the bark and his massive paws stretched out upon the rock lay the "Emperor of the Jungle"—a gargantuan hunk of flesh, fang, and claw known only as Mantos. Similar to Lena in color and likeness, he was at least twice her size (a good deal larger even than me) with a bushy frock of wiry hair around his neck. His two front fangs were a good ten inches long, thick as a man's arm at the top then tapering down to a razor sharp point. The terrible things would not fit inside his mouth but always hung out over his jaw like twin warnings against anyone who would dare challenge him. At the moment they were gnawing on a fresh carcass. Slowly we made our way towards the platform. The other cats stared as we walked past, but Mantos never looked up. Finally we stood before him; yet he still refused to acknowledge our presence. No one said a word; it struck me even Lena remained quiet. When at last every bone had been picked clean Mantos gave some kind of signal to a cat nearby, and she approached cautiously. Only after she had drug off the remains and flung them to a hungry group of lionesses standing nearby did the lion turn his keen black eyes onto us. Or, I should say, "eye" since nothing but a gaping socket remained where his left one should have been. When the other fell on me it narrowed to a slit. He looked back at Lena.

"Speak!" The command boomed.

Lena bowed her head submissively, "Your Majesty, we have brought you the trespasser Sengali, as you demanded."

"Hmm," replied Mantos in a low growl, "let him approach." The three lionesses who had resumed their position in front of me now cleared the way, and Lena stepped back with a smirk on her face. Flight was not an option so I steeled my nerves and walked forward, stopping to bow slightly once I reached the foot of the platform. Then I raised my head and calmly met the Emperor's penetrating gaze. "So this is the mighty Sengali," he began, "the one who threatens my servants and challenges my rule!" His voice was deep and rumbled through the air. "I must say I am disappointed. From the way Lena described you I expected a cat the size of an elephant." He stole a sharp glance sideways at the lioness; her head drooped. "Tell me," he directed my way again, "what brings the 'King of the Mountain' so far from his own domain—and into mine?" All eyes were now on me. I knew I must weigh my words carefully. One false slip of the tongue and there would be no second chances. Telling him of the Dream and the Voice was out of the question, but to give an honest answer was equally important. Mantos had a reputation for knowing when he was being lied to and a way of dealing with it I didn't care to experience.

"I have decided to leave the jungle." Even as the words came out of my mouth my mind was screaming, *What are you saying?!* There was a murmur of astonishment among the lionesses. Now I had to carry through. "Yes, to travel east beyond the tree's end. Your empire is so vast, Mantos, I could not help passing through it on my journey. But I have harmed nothing belonging to you."

The tyrant wore a dry smile. "Nothing except my fish, which you have eaten; my game, which you have killed; and my land, which you have defiled!" he corrected in a low growl.

"The land I cannot help, but as for the fish and the game they are free creatures, with life and breath the same as you and me. You cannot own them any more than I could own you."

Mantos snarled but moved on. "So you say you are leaving the jungle? I assume you mean permanently, for surely Sengali the Great would have never abandoned his mountain kingdom otherwise." I made no reply. This adventure had lasted longer than I originally hoped, but I certainly was not *abandoning* my home. The Emperor mistook my silence and smiled wryly, "That's what I thought. And why I claimed it as my own so quickly."

The hairs on my back bristled.

His quick senses noticed the reaction. "Yes," he continued, "the morning after you left. My spies had been keeping an eye on your mountain for me for quite some time. As you so eloquently stated to Lena when last you met, it was the only property within this jungle not included in my empire. A 'hole' in the kingdom, if you will. Happily, that is no longer the case," his heavy face beamed with a cruel pleasure, "and now I find I have *you* to thank for it. Hardly the turn of events I was expecting!"

His words cut like razors. My heart sank and a surge of blood rushed to my head.

No!

I had lost my home! My mountain—my beautiful, plentiful, glorious mountain—was taken! Stolen by a power-hungry monster! Grief and rage flooded my heart as my eyes locked on the heartless beast before me. The last outpost of peace and safety from his tyrannical reign was gone. He would rip and ravage his way through the green slopes and hillsides till nothing remained but death and fear.

And it is my fault. I should have never left!

But this was no time for revenge. I was in a game of survival and it would do no good to lose control now. "I am surprised you waited so long," I spoke at last with a bitter chuckle, fighting desperately to maintain my cool, "What kept you from moving in the moment after I left?"

"A blunder of one of my lionesses let you slip past unnoticed delaying things. Fortunately for her, she picked up your trail and followed you bringing me word once she was sure you would not return to the mountain. You have her to thank for being invited here." I heard a low growl to the side: it was Lena.

I looked around at the grim company, "Well, now that you have me where you've always wanted me, what do you intend to do?"

Mantos laughed, but a queer gleam came to his single eye. "My dear Sengali, that depends entirely upon you. I could have you torn apart slowly and eaten alive. It might prove amusing. But I am a reasonable ruler merciful to those who prove they are worthy of it—even old enemies. So I have a proposition for you."

A night breeze started to stir, blowing his foul breath in my face, "A 'proposition'?"

He leaned against the tree, full of confident pride, "Swear your allegiance to me and I will let you live. Prove your loyalty and...", he didn't continue, but the strange gleam became stronger. "I have a job that needs doing: a mission worthy of the great Sengali of the mountain. Something requiring your unique—oh, how shall I say it—*talents*. Succeed and I will give you a place of honor in my empire, your own harem of lionesses," he paused for effect, "*and* your mountain back to you!" His eye burned with greed, "I can give you power like you never dreamed of! You can reign like a prince in the jungle, second only to me. That is, *if* you accept my generous offer."

My ears could not believe what they were hearing. The monster was actually trying to bribe me! "And if I refuse?"

The Emperor's face broke into a cold smile, "Then you die."

Undaunted, I held his gaze. "Death comes to all creatures; I do not fear it."

There was silence as a thick tension hung in the air. Mantos slowly nodded his massive head. "I thought you might need some persuasion," he said at last. Then he addressed a lioness standing nearby. "Tell Saphirra to approach!" Without a word the lioness bowed and sprung away over the hillside.

SEVEN

IN A MOMENT she returned with another lioness following closely behind. This one reminded me very much of Lena in form, slightly smaller perhaps but just as sleek and strong. Her white coat glowed like a shaft of moonlight. Every movement she made seemed effortless as her silvery paws met the earth without a sound. With graceful poise she glided so silently if the lioness had been alone I might have thought I was only seeing a phantom. One glance at what she carried in her jaws, however, brought me into hard reality. It was Womby, limp and still, his eyes big and staring into space.

I went cold all over.

As if in slow motion, the white lioness ascended to the throne before Mantos (and from the respect the other cats showed her she must have been of some importance herself). There she bowed low and laid the wombat's body before his terrible claws. She continued to bow and back away till at last she stood on the far end of the platform, a look of cool indifference on her face. Suddenly I wanted to lunge for her smooth throat, to tear that cold gaze clean off her skull! And not just her but to rip into Mantos as well, and Lena, and all the rest of the bloodthirsty, heartless pack! What difference would it make if I died in the process? They had already killed half the jungle and now poor Womby. Eventually they would kill me too. At least this way I could take some of them with me!

But just when I was about to spring a slight movement caught my attention. I paused. Had those glassy eyes just blinked? Holding my breath, I waited to make sure I wasn't imagining things. They blinked again! Womby wasn't dead—just stunned! The black weight of rage lifted off my mind all at once; I almost felt like laughing! The wombat's eyes were clear now, looking around. At last they fixed on me.

"Li!" A squeal of joy erupted from my little friend, making even Mantos jump. Before anyone knew what was happening, Womby had sprung up and scurried to me as fast as his claws could manage on the slick rock. In a moment he was nuzzling his furry head against my two front legs. I could not see him directly under me, but I heard his sigh of relief. Every muscle in the plump body relaxed. In his mind Womby was safe.

Too bad I didn't feel the same way.

You could have heard a pebble drop. The she-cats stared in disbelief; even the white lioness dropped her jaw slightly. Lena rolled her eyes. Mantos was silent, but a look of strange satisfaction spread across his face. "Friend of yours?" He asked sarcastically. Womby was as settled between my front paws as if we were back on the mountain taking an afternoon nap.

"And if he is?"

"Then I would say you have finally found the right company." There was a round of snickering from the females, Lena in particular. The white lioness alone remained quiet and aloof. "How touching," the Emperor continued, "the hunter and the hunted as friends. Predator and prey united at last. 'The strong protecting the weak', and all that sort of thing. Quite an inspiration, Sengali."

I could feel an ultimatum coming.

"It would be a shame for it all to end so soon, eh Lena?"

The lioness licked her chomps, "Shame indeed!"

My claws came out of their sheath. "Touch him, Mantos, and you'll lose your other eye!"

A sudden growl came from the white lioness. "Trespasser!" she broke in, eyes flashing, "You dare threaten the Emperor of the Jungle?"

A CAT'S TALE

"Quiet, Saphirra!" Mantos snapped and the lioness lowered her proud head, "If I need your help I'll ask for it! Join the pack." Reluctantly Saphirra obeyed, withdrawing behind Lena like a scolded kitten. Mantos managed to bring his anger under control. "I suppose you think I want to fight you, Sengali," he said to me, "that I want you dead. But you are wrong. I want you alive. I want your power, your skill: I want you as my ally. But first I need to be assured of your loyalty—which brings us back to my proposition. Call it a 'test'. Pass it and you will roam the jungle as my ambassador while the wombat goes free, unharmed. But fail..." he did not finish, yet his eye flashed a ruthless light as it passed from me to Womby and back to me again. My mind quickly processed my options. None of them were good. I could try and break free myself—but only if I left Womby behind. Then again, if I stayed and fought to give the wombat a chance of escape he still couldn't get far, not with his short legs and Lena's gang on his heels. There was no other way.

"You win, Mantos," I said quietly, "What do you want with me?"

* * *

Sleepy stars peeked through the forest roof, their pale light growing tired as it fought its way to the jungle floor. Only a slight haze remained to brighten the unmarked path beneath my paws as I followed Lena and a small host of other lionesses. For around two hours we had been traveling through brambles and cool, wet plants without arriving at our destination. Around me was the escort that had taken me to Mantos. I glanced behind. Six other females followed—faces grim and without expression—while Womby and Saphirra (silent and proud as ever) brought up the rear. Poor Womby. His pace had grown slower with each mile and now the white lioness was forced to swat him from behind just to keep him going. I could hear him huffing and yipping with every sting of her claws. She wasn't hurting him badly, yet from the way he carried on you would have thought chunks of his skin were being torn out. But it could have been worse. Originally Mantos had not wanted to part with his hostage, since my cooperating with his plans depended entirely on him holding the wombat. "Fine," was my argument, "but if he stays behind we have no deal. Just go ahead and kill us both." After grinding his jaw and twitching his long whiskers the Emperor had finally relented. "Very well," he grumbled, "the wombat will go—but *only* under guard, and any communication between the two of you will result in his immediate termination."

Thus the white lioness had joined our party. But aside from a few rumples in his fur and his pride Womby was none the worse for wear. To be honest, my little friend was not my main concern as we cut our way amidst the ever green, never-ending brush. What did occupy my mind was just exactly where we were going and what our goal was when we got there. Just before we left Mantos, he and Lena had held a private conference to the side. Whatever he said must have pleased her. She smiled like a weasel told it could raid the snake's nest. Until Saphirra joined our group and her smile melted to a sullen scowl. Since then, the lioness had said nothing at all to anyone but basic commands, keeping us moving at a relentless pace. Further and further we plunged into unfamiliar territory. Thick, twisted tree roots and large, glossy leaves were replaced by short blades of grass in rich, dark soil. The trees we walked under were shorter and grew further apart than any I had ever seen, so much so that large patches of night sky were visible in places. The air even smelled new as a strange, earthy breeze played around us, something that never happened in the deep forest. *We must be nearing the jungle's end.* And still Lena remained quiet—not chiding, mocking, or complaining even once. Something was obviously on her mind.

Finally we stopped under a small grouping of tangled trees none of which grew much taller than the top of my head. Lena called for two of the guards and without a word they vanished into the darkness ahead of us. A few of the other lionesses relaxed enough to sit down. A loud "humph" from behind let me know Womby had taken their example. Lena just paced around in agitated circles. Studying the excited tremble of her muscles and the moody shadow over her face, I decided to remain standing. If there was one thing I had learned about the she-cat it was never to relax while she was restless. The forest around us was quiet. Somehow, however, it did not feel like the silence was only on our account.

When the scouts returned, a thin band of pink light was visible between the black forms of the trees. It would not be long till the sun once more took its place far above their branches.

"Well?" Lena demanded impatiently.

"All is ripe, Commander," one of the lionesses replied, "we saw no guards posted and all seems at ease. There is no sign of suspicion."

"Good. What about the traps?"

"Old and abandoned. They should be easy to avoid."

The she-cat smiled grimly. Then she turned to the rest of us.

"From here on we move single file. Total silence. Break either command and you'll wish you never came on this trip!" The cunning eyes fell on me. "Watch your step, Sengali," she murmured. Taking her place at the front of the line, the lioness began to slink along the floor head low and wagging back and forth. Falling into step behind her the whole party was soon immersed in a sea of giant ferns.

We had not travelled long when three sounds came from behind all at once. First was a sharp "Stop!" Then came a havoc of snapping branches and rustling leaves, followed by two screams: one short and shrill, the next tiny and muffled. I spun around to see Saphirra bent with her head to the ground, while Womby—wait, where *was* Womby?

I barely heard Lena hiss, "Stay where you are!" Before my guards even knew it, I was crouching across from the white lioness separated by a hole that had suddenly opened up at her feet. It was deep, dark, and narrow with unnaturally smooth mud walls. I had never seen anything like it. Peering through the blackness my eyes caught movement at the bottom of the pit.

"Womby?"

"Li?!" floated his high strained voice out of the darkness, "Help! Help m,m,me Li! P, p, please help, p, p—OW!" interrupted a cry of pain.

I glanced up at Saphirra. Her blue eyes looked back at mine amidst her pale face like sapphires inside a cloud. Gone was the arrogance, the cold pride I had always seen before. In its place showed an open lack of confidence.

She is young, I realized, *young and vulnerable*. "We must to get him out of there!" I said, half commanding, half pleading. Maybe she had a heart after all?

Or not. Her noble head shot up as the pride returned. *"We?"* she repeated, and though her voice was soft her words stung with an air of superiority. "You forget your place, prisoner! The wombat was entrusted to *my* charge. You are to have no contact with it. Any breach of this command on your part and my orders are to kill it immediately!"

I was about to reply when Lena came bounding from behind. "What happened?" she growled. "Never mind! I knew it was a mistake to bring..." she stopped abruptly but glared at Saphirra with such contempt the lioness pinned her white ears back against her smooth head "...to bring a *wombat* on this mission. And you, Sengali, why can't you *ever* do as you're told? Is it dead?"

"No," the white lioness replied shortly.

"Just stuck in the bottom of a hole no one can get it out of!" The other shouted, "Well done, Saphirra! I hardly think Father will be pleased..."

"You blame *me?*" The cool voice began to boil. "I warned the wombat to stop before it ever laid its paw in the snare! Is it my fault the dumb-witted creature was too slow to respond?"

"It's your fault he got off the path in the first place!" Lena retaliated, "You should have forced him to stay in line, but, *as usual*, you were too soft. Just like when you let him (she shoved her head my way) get off his mountain without a scratch!"

So you're the one who trailed us through the jungle! I studied the white lioness with bitter admiration.

"Then tell me, commander," she snapped back at Lena, "how your prisoner broke through his guards and reached here before you did? You have failed to keep a dangerous prisoner in check, on whom the success of the entire mission depends! If I am guilty for not stopping a half-blind wombat from falling into a hole, where does that leave *you?*" Lena responded with a very unpleasant noise.

"Help!" Womby called from below.

I stepped in, "May I suggest we deal with the problem at hand? There must be some branches around here—a vine—something to pull him out of there with."

Lena turned on me, "And just *how* is he going to grab onto a vine?"

"With his teeth." From the look the two lionesses gave me I gathered they did not know much about Wombats. "Take my word for it, they're strong enough."

After a moment Lena shrugged, "What have we got to lose?"

Saphirra crinkled her nose, "I don't know..."

"Do you have any better ideas?" the other snapped.

The white lioness narrowed her eyes slightly but held her peace and began searching for something to aid Womby's rescue. I wasn't allowed to participate but after a few minutes a long enough vine had been found. With some coaching on my part and some muscle on the part of the guards, Womby's head appeared at last over the brink of the pit, eyes wide and teeth clenched so tight on the green rope it would have snapped had it been any thinner. Once safe on level ground the wombat started to run for me but instantly tumbled over with a cry. "Orders" or no, I leapt over to him. "What is it?" I asked, lowering my nose to support his trembling back.

Womby looked up in pain, "My l,l,leg—it hurts."

Lena broke in, "What do you mean 'it hurts'?" Poor Womby was too shaken up to even look at her.

Ignoring the urge to give the she-cat a good thrashing, I leaned down closer. "You mean it hurts to walk on it?"

The furry head nodded pitifully.

"Well that's just great!" Lena moaned. Then she started mumbling to herself, "As if having a wombat come along wasn't bad enough. Now it's lame!"

Silence prevailed while a general depression spread through the ranks over their commander's mood. For me the stillness was wonderful. It let me think. "How far to our destination?"

Lena temporarily revived from her self-pity, "Without the wombat in tow we would have arrived when the sun stood directly over us. But now..." her voice trailed off and she started staring into space again.

"There is no need for us to even slow down. He can ride on my back." Several gasps burst from the guards standing nearby (which I rather enjoyed) as I continued, "I carried him four days before you found me in the cave. She knows," I nodded at Saphirra, "if she followed us. He's a fine rider and will cause less trouble that way than when he was walking on his own good legs."

"Impossible!" interjected Saphirra, "The prisoner was entrusted to my care and you are to have no contact with it whatsoever; you're fortunate I have not killed it already!"

"Very well," I replied calmly returning her fiery stare without so much as a flinch, "then *you* carry him!"

The lionesses' jaw dropped and her eyes grew large, indignant. Lena's eyes, though, lit up with sudden pleasure.

"You must be joking?" the former huffed.

"You said yourself the wombat was entrusted to your care—so care for him!"

"*In no way* will I permit a wombat to cling to my back like some giant leech!"

"And in no way will I move so much as a claw from this place if the wombat doesn't come with me! Mantos himself agreed for him to accompany this mission. Do you dare place yourself above the orders of your Emperor?"

EIGHT

HORRIFIED AND SPEECHLESS, Saphirra shut her mouth. Lena (now fully recovered from her brief depression) took command. "That settles it then," she said, and I thought I could see the smallest hint of a smirk around her ivory teeth. "You shall carry the wombat, Saphirra. Just make sure it doesn't fall off!" Then she began ordering the other lionesses to resume their previous positions. In the bustle of activity that followed I crouched beside Womby.

"Do you think you can ride on the white lionesses' back?" I whispered.

He crinkled his nose, "Can she reach me with her c,c,claws?"

"Not if you hold on tight."

He heaved a little sigh, "I wish it were y, y, you!"

Gently picking him up by the neck I carried him over and set him on Saphirra's back. I would have broken out in laughter but for fear of making her angry and having her take it out on Womby. Still, the dignified, proud, miserable lioness trying to keep the jolly, awkward, crippled wombat on her back was something to see. Plenty of jeers and snickers were heard, Lena's being loudest. When finally the furry bundle managed to balance on that graceful spine a round of hysterics broke out and Saphirra's humiliation was complete.

"Now," Lena said, once she composed herself, "Once more, single file. No noise. Saphirra, take your place in the middle of the line. Sengali," my ears pricked at the change of tone in her voice, "you're up front with me," and though she quickly turned I saw her smile my way. I glanced back at Womby with a reassuring nod then followed her through the ferns to the head of the column. As soon as I reached her side we started moving again.

"Brilliant!" Lena whispered, breaking her own rule of silence, "I don't know what you're up to, but sticking Saphirra with the wombat was brilliant!"

"What makes you so sure I am 'up to' anything?"

The she-cat stifled a laugh, "*Please*, Sengali! You don't expect me to believe you've left your mountain kingdom forever and gone traipsing through enemy territory with a wombat on your back for some kind of a holiday, do you? We've never seen eye to eye, I know, but I've always considered us equals. Our only differences are I serve my father as commander of an army, while you prefer to maintain your male 'ego' by going it alone. Other than that we're basically the same. Assassins. Best to be had in the jungle." A look of excited hunger flashed across her lean face. "Imagine what we could do if we joined forces?"

I kept my pace steady and controlled. "I'm listening."

Lena stole a nervous glance behind us to make sure no one could overhear. Then she moved even closer and lowered her head towards mine. "Listen," she began earnestly, "Mantos isn't the lion he used to be. Oh, he's still strong enough, and in an out-and-out fight, *shew!*" Her tawny coat shivered at the thought, "Let's just say I wouldn't want to cross him. But he's not aggressive; not the hunter who brought the whole jungle to its knees. He just sits on that boulder throne of his and sends me out to do all of his dirty work for him. I'm getting tired of it." Even the wind ruffling some leaves as we passed could not hide the resentment in her voice.

"But aren't you second-in-command?" I asked, dodging a thorny shrub.

"Hmph!" She grunted bitterly, eyes darting back at Saphirra. "Not for long!" But before I could ask what she meant the green orbs turned on me, "Do you believe in dreams, Sengali?" I tripped on a root and just about fell onto my face; she noticed and

chuckled, "Oh, that's right, I forgot. You were having one when I found you by the waterfall weren't you? Let me guess. Same one you've been having for days? Probably the reason you're here to begin with?"

My astonishment was beyond words!

"Don't look so surprised," she sneered, "my father has them, too. Strange how the two strongest, most powerful males in the jungle could be spooked by a nightmare."

"Mantos? Has had the Dream?" I stammered, finally finding my voice.

"So *he* says. But she'd do anything to take my place," the lioness spat through her fangs, "lying little brat! She's using his weakness, twisting it to her advantage. Just like her mother! But I'll show her. We may both be his daughters, but only one of us can get his throne—and it isn't about to be the dainty, upstart, weakling who should've been drowned at birth!"

I had no idea what she was talking about, but my mind was too busy to care. "What about this Dream? What does it have to do with anything?"

Lena stared my way, keeping her head level while the rest of her loped and bobbed along the ground. "Don't you know? That's what this whole trip is about! Without the Dream Mantos would've just killed you. Believe me, he would have never let you live even just a few weeks ago. But now he's using you instead: forcing you to do a job he's too scared to do himself!"

She shot another hateful glance at Saphirra, "And it's all because of *her!*"

Now we were getting somewhere. "What do you mean 'too scared to do'?"

Hesitation. Clearly Lena wondered if she had overstepped her bounds and said too much. Then she shrugged, "Eh, you're going to find out soon enough; might as well have it now." She looked at me with a queer gleam in her emerald eyes. "Have you ever hunted 'man' before, Sengali?"

Man? All my life I had heard of the creature. According to owl's fables they were strange beings that walked upright like a bear, had skin smoother than a baboon's chest, and wiry fur growing in different colors out of the top of their head. Legend had it they were cunning trappers and hunters living outside of the jungle in giant boxes of iron and marble. Truthfully, I had heard so many stories about the creature that the whole idea seemed like a myth. "Hunt 'man'?" I admitted, "From all I've ever heard they sound more like ghosts than real flesh and blood."

That drew a wily smile, "Oh, believe me, they're flesh and blood just as much as we are." Something about the way her lips smacked as she spoke made me nauseous, though I wasn't sure why. "Mantos found that out a long, long time ago. He used to like man as a delicacy sometimes sneaking down into their camps along the Great River to grab one at night. He was a terror. They even sent out hunting parties to catch him. But nobody could." Her face turned sober, "'Till the Man of the Tree."

My ears perked up. Lena's cocky tone had vanished into a nervous hush. "'Man of the Tree?'"

"It was a long time ago," she rumbled, keeping her voice low, "Mantos was still in his prime. Nothing could stand in his way and live to tell about it—not even man. Or so he thought. But one night he got too greedy. He snuck into one of their camps they call 'towns' to grab a cub for a snack. The flesh of young man is tender and sweet as you could hope for," she paused to wipe a burst of saliva from her gums. "He'd done it lots of times and always gotten away with it. Men don't look after their young much—they're too busy looking after themselves. Anyway," she continued, "sneaking through one of their small forests ('gardens', they call them) he finds an opening into one of their strange caves. Sure enough, lying around a pile of bright, scorching stuff called 'fire', is a young human cub curled up asleep." The she-cat snuffed, "I don't know what happened. Apparently my father just lost his head! He walks right over, calm as can be, and, instead of breaking its neck right then and there, *picks up* the cub in his jaws to carry it off alive! Of course the thing wakes up and starts screaming! The next second Mantos hears a thin, 'twang' kind of sound and a sharp stick flies straight into his left eye! Mad with pain he turns to run and something slams into the side of his head, knocking his prey right out of his teeth! He stumbles and suddenly there's a man standing in his way—between him and the cub and the opening to the outside. A younger man, 'bout half the big one's size, stands behind him holding up two sticks—one long-ways with a string tied to it and the other pulled back against the string, pointed right at Mantos' other eye. This young man grabs the cub and runs off carrying it, but the bigger man holds his ground. He doesn't turn tail like all the other men Mantos encountered. He stands, fearless—a long, straight branch in his hands, pointed and sharp at the end. Mantos lunges for him but the man darts to the side and grabs a piece of the fire. One quick move and it flies into my father's shoulder plunging fire in his side, burning his hide off like a viper sheds its skin. Mantos barely got out of that place alive! Part of him never did. By the next morning his left eye was gone. To this day his shoulder still has burn scars." Light had grown around us as she spoke and now the sunrise became visible through the gaps of green in front of us. "Ever since that night Mantos hasn't dared set a paw within miles of a man town. He turned from the river and went the other way stretching his empire across the jungle (except for a few spots like your mountain)—away from man. But he never stopped hating them, especially the one who took his eye," the lioness stared into the light of the sun, "'The Man of the Tree'."

Something about the way she said the name made me curious, "Why do you call him that?"

She shrugged, "Mantos does. He couldn't really tell what the man looked like—everything happened so fast—but what he did see was something like a tiny tree hanging from the man's neck. It's the only way he can be recognized."

I listened intently to the lionesses' story, though it all sounded rather far-fetched (not to mention irrelevant). "I still fail to see what any of this has to do with me."

She seemed annoyed but went on anyway, "All these years my father has been content to leave man alone. He's let me take a few hunting parties, but that's it. He's stayed out of it. He wouldn't leave the jungle, which meant the river and everything beyond got left to whoever had the guts to take it. And whoever conquered man..." She stopped short, but there was a gleam in her eye.

"...would own both the jungle and the river?" The pieces were beginning to fit. Mantos was old, and (if what Lena said was true) known to fear man. If a strong leader rose who proved he—or she—was *not* afraid, the pride would follow them away from Mantos. They would rule the empire. I looked at the lioness beside me. "So *that's* why you know this terrain so well."

A sneaky smirk appeared. "Welcome to *my* territory, Sengali! For years I've roamed it, scouting it, raiding, hunting. It was mine. Mantos was content to stay out of it. *Until* a few weeks ago," a quick, vicious snarl escaped her mouth, "when this Dream showed up! *Apparently* the jungle is destroyed in it by something horrible—some dark catastrophe. But the kicker is at the end. After everything is over a man shows up. He's highlighted in the darkness by a light from behind, looking huge and completely black—except for a white tree hanging from his neck. Mantos takes it as an evil sign, some kind of prophecy that the Man of the Tree is going to come destroy the empire and take away his power. Ridiculous!" she spat, "but he believes it. Thanks to Saphirra."

"What does she have to do with the Dream?" I looked back at the white lioness struggling to keep Womby on her back. *So they're half-sisters. Both daughters of Mantos. No wonder she's so proud and aloof!* I had also noticed Saphirra did not mingle with the other lionesses.

"She won't let him forget about it! She's using it to control him, manipulate him, stir him up against man and make him head for the river again—into *my* territory—just so she can one day take what's rightfully mine! And now nothing will satisfy Mantos until the head of the Man of the Tree is laid at his claws with the Tree still attached to it." She looked at me and smiled dryly, "Which is where *you* come in."

My eyebrows rose, but instead of answering, the lioness just looked forward and fell silent, her face still plastered with that smile.

That was the end of the conversation. All this time we had been slowly descending; now the hill we walked on leveled to a flat plain. The night sky had turned bright blue through the gaps of the green canopy above, and as we continued to travel there was more and more blue with less and less green. Bushes and vegetation were everywhere, only much shorter: growing dense along the ground but ending abruptly just a few feet above our heads. The grass became tall, taller than any I had ever seen in my life, and very lush. It was wet and silky, and tickled my whiskers like thin, dewy fingers. Now the warmth of the sun broke fully upon my head the likes of which I hadn't felt since I left my mountain. It was wonderful to see the light of heaven catch in the wet tears of the grass as it glistened and bent in the morning breeze. As the glory of the morning washed over me, a new scent came with it. I stopped moving and raised my nose to the breeze. It was an odd smell. A combination of aromas I knew, yet still completely different. Salty and sweet. Strong and fleshy. The scent of a living creature (several, actually) I had never encountered before. I looked at Lena. My curiosity must have been written all over my face because a cruel grin spread across hers. She responded with only one word.

"Man."

NINE

SHE BANKED TO THE RIGHT and I followed, travelling parallel to the jungle's edge caught between its trees on our right and the open fields on our left. I couldn't see much except grass and sky, yet there was a bigness to it all—a sense of clear air and large sweeping spaces that let me know we were on the edge of a lot of open land. Crossing a tiny creek we found ourselves immersed in a small quarry of rocks, every shape and size, all piled together around a dirt floor. This formed a kind of natural fortress. As soon as the whole party was inside the crude fort, two lionesses climbed the boulder walls and positioned themselves for guard duty. One faced the forest while the other stared steadily towards the plain. Womby tumbled off of Saphirra's back with a loud "humph". I smiled while watching him hobble over on his injured leg to rip up a vine from its roots, devouring it without mercy. *Poor little guy is famished.* Aside from that, however, he looked to be feeling much better, which was more than I could say for Saphirra. Soon as the wombat was off her back the lioness fell down in a huff, furiously licking and grooming her matted fur. As everyone settled in Lena stood and addressed the group. Her sandy coat blended into the dust of the floor.

"We'll take turns standing guard. Two at a time. Those not on duty will spend the day sleeping. Can't sleep? Stay quiet. Make any noise and I'll shut you up myself," the echo of this command bounced off the rocks as if to add emphasis. "We have a big night ahead of us, ladies, and *others*," she added, with a sharp glance my way. "Much is at stake. Success of our mission depends on speed and alertness. In the heat of the hunt there won't be time to think or plan. That's what today is for; don't waste it!" And after one more look at me the shrewd cat threw herself in a lonely corner and fell into a fitful sleep.

* * *

Dusk was closing in when the last lioness slipped passed the dark walls of the fortress and into the night beyond. Once again, I was among them; only Saphirra and Womby remained behind. I glanced back for a moment. Though my little friend bravely raised his paw to wave goodbye I knew he was not at all happy about being left alone with the lioness. Yet what else could I do? This was no stroll through the woods we were taking. What had to be done had to be done swiftly and alone, without a wombat in tow. Saphirra watched in silence. Our eyes met, and for a brief moment I thought I saw apprehension, even fear, in her blue depths. But we moved too quickly. Another step and both lioness and wombat were hidden from sight by the rocky border of the cove.

The outside world had changed drastically since the morning. The dusky light seemed to match the grim look on each lioness's face as they floated about me like ghostly masks dancing in the twilight. The blades of grass towered straight and rigid in the still evening air. The black bars of their shadows weaving together formed an ominous web across the ground. Now stiff and dry, they clipped at my whiskers and stung my nose like flat, blunt razors. A warm thickness clung to the air. All around was dreadfully quiet. But while my senses were flooded with new discoveries my mind was consumed by what lay ahead. A challenge loomed over me like the sinking rays of the sun, now dissolving into the horizon like blood in water. Through the course of my talk with Lena and some careful reflection that afternoon my reason for being on this mission had become all too clear. My "job" (as Mantos so casually called it) was to find this dreaded apparition, this "Man of The Tree", and do what no other cat (including Mantos) had ever been able to do before—kill him. Never mind the fact I still wasn't sure man existed at all, or that (if the creature was real) he might possess a power capable of overthrowing Mantos' entire kingdom. I was to find and eliminate this unknown terror. And I was to do it alone. An ultimate test of skill and strength, pitted against a foe I had never faced before, all for the pleasure of a tyrannical beast I despised. That was the price of my freedom and Womby's life. My head shook grimly. It was like standing atop a sheer cliff and being told to either find a way down or get pushed off the edge.

Soon the crackle of thirsty grass and dull plodding of our paws was joined by another sound: running water. Still off in the distance (about two miles, I judged), it did not gurgle and sputter like a forest stream but flowed heavy, deep, and constant. *The Great River*, I concluded. To my left, and much nearer, I heard a cow moan. Then another and another, sniffing and chewing loudly. A whole herd of them must have been grazing not far away. Lena stopped and turned to face the rest of us. All motion instantly ceased. Only vague outlines of the other cats could be seen in the murky light, without so much as a tail flick to give away their position. I had to admit, Lena's soldiers were very well trained. The general stiffly lowered her head—neck rigid, jaw taught, eyes hard and shifty.

"We are nearing the town," She whispered, hoarse and excited. "You each know your orders: don't move or leave your posts until you hear my signal. The prisoner will come with me!" A short nod my way indicated I was to follow, and without a word the party disbanded. "This way," the lioness muttered sharply, "keep your head low!"

I matched her nervous pace stride for stride, "Is man's sense of smell any good?"

She shot a glance my way with a wry smile. "So you finally figured it out? No, it isn't worth much by itself, but," she snorted in disgust, "they keep wolves. Fools! Only a dog would let itself be pushed around by man! But they do have a nasty sense of smell. If you can get past them you won't have much to worry about, as long as you keep to the shadows and don't make any noise. *If* you can get past them."

"I've never met a wolf yet that could get the better of me."

Lena said nothing; we stalked the grass as noiseless as two sharks in the sea closing in on their quarry. An anticipation of blood hung in the air. You could sense it. You could taste it. It burned in the she-cat's eyes as a savage hunger only satisfied by the kill. My own senses were very alert now. I could hear the drum of what felt like a thousand heartbeats. They were very, very near. Presently we came to a large, sprawling tree and stopped. The river lay to our right; I could hear the steady slurp of its waves as they lapped against the shore. Lena bounded up the large trunk and I followed close on her heels. Finding the support of a sturdy branch she looked back at me with grim delight, then stepped back to allow me a better view through a gap in the dark leaves. Sure enough, to the right and towards the south lay the Great River: a wide, silver swath, shimmering under the stars. Almost directly under us grazed the cattle I had heard: a ridiculously large group of fat, pampered creatures. But I barely noticed them. My gaze was fixed on what lay beyond their plump hides, something I would have never believed existed if I had not seen it with my own eyes.

"The Man Town," Lena breathed.

Out of the ground it grew, about five hundred lengths in the distance, spreading out on the grassland like a dark mass under the stars and dotted here and there with spots of yellow light glowing like fireflies stuck in the night haze. The town of men was big and solid, marking a jagged line along the horizon where hundreds of flat roofs met the sky. These almost looked like they were stacked on top of each other, growing gradually taller towards the center of the town, giving the whole thing the appearance of a small mountain rising out of the flatland. All around were cultivated fields and (along with the cattle) pastures of sheep, goats, and myriads of other livestock. No wall surrounded the town because none was needed: the sides of the outer houses were built together, smooth and thick, and their windows were high and out of reach. Actually, it appeared the entire town was basically made up of houses built together with no paths or alleys in between. As far as I could tell there was no way to get in.

"You'll have to get on top," the lioness explained, guessing my thoughts, "man's trails are on his rooftops. Sometimes they have sticks like skinny trees propped on the sides which you can use; if not, well, you're clever; you'll figure it out. Once on top, it's a maze of walls, ledges, and corners. Like a canyon, only with men everywhere. Lots of them sleep at night, but not all, so watch your step."

"And what about the Man of the Tree," I voiced my primary concern, "Any idea as to where he might be found?"

The she-cat snickered, "Nope."

"No clues from the Dream?"

"Not one."

I let out a long, low whistle between my teeth. It was like trying to find a needle in a haystack when you did not know what a needle looked like and you had never seen a haystack before. "This is madness," I muttered.

"Happy hunting," Lena quipped, then fell to the ground without so much as a thud. "Bring back the Tree—*with* a head attached to it. I'll be waiting for you here when the moon stands right over the river to see if you're as good as Mantos thinks you are.

Oh—and so you know—my soldiers are posted all around the Town to guard any possible way of escape, just in case you were to get some wild idea about not meeting me. So don't be late, Sengali; I hate to be kept waiting!" With that the lioness slunk out of sight among the bull-rushes of the river. The next several minutes I sat there in deep thought, tail dangling from the limb like a lazy monkey swinging back and forth. My mind worked furiously to twist together a plan of action. Eventually I dropped to the cool soil and started picking my way through the fields at a tedious pace. Stop and go. Glide past a grazing cow. Stop again. Move, pause, crouch, listen, move— inching ever so slowly towards the border of the sleeping town as the moon inched higher into the sky.

* * *

The first order of business was to find a way onto one of those roofs. Keeping to the shadows along the walls of the town, I skirted around for a while looking for a good option. Finally I came to a house whose window was slightly lower than the others, though still much taller than a man could reach. Here, however, I had the advantage. Scrunching my back legs and springing straight up my claws caught the wide, brick windowsill, and propelled the rest of me over the edge of the roof. Once safely on top, I took a moment to survey the situation. It was like I had jumped into another world. The surface of the roof was smooth and flat, made out of a thick, strong clay, and shaped in the form of a large square. There were plants scattered about growing out of odd, round containers, along with other, stranger articles like decorated rugs and ornate wooden furniture. There were no men in sight, but in the far corner was a doorway jutting up out of the flat rooftop. From within came the same fleshy scent I had smelled earlier, only much stronger.

That opening must be the way inside the dwelling.

Not quite ready to jump in the nest of an unknown foe I decided to keep moving. Behind the door was a sloping partition with a vent built in as a chimney; out of this came a warm, succulent smell (much like duck, only different). Just a few feet opposite the chimney was another short wall—the upper half of the house next to the one where I stood. Cautiously I hopped over this to find myself on another roof. It was smaller and less furnished than the previous one. The rugs were simple and made of animal skins, which were also draped on several wooden racks standing around. There was, however, a door very similar to the first (though more crudely made) with a chimney behind it. This roof was enclosed on two sides. One by another short wall, the other by a taller, with three windows carved in its side. Two of the windows were dark, but out of one a light flickered. And through this one I finally got my first look at man.

It was a solitary male well-groomed and dressed in a simple white tunic. He looked to be somewhere in the prime of life. In his hands he held a strange bowl full of a strong smelling herb. Taking a candle he lit the herbs, and the smoke billowed in a scented cloud. *That must be what Lena called "fire"*, I thought, watching with amazement as he held up the burning plants and slowly walked to the end of the clean, empty room. Well, almost empty. Against the far wall, gleaming gold and sparkling with jewels, stood an image. It looked like a bizarre cross between an eagle and a dragon made with stone wings and a gaping silver mouth. As the man approached he seemed to be mumbling words; what they were I couldn't tell. Standing before the image he bowed his head, the light of the flame in his hand flickering off the golden face. Then the man laid the bowl of incense in the clawed hand of the bizarre, lifeless creature, knelt down, and touched his forehead to the floor at its feet. For some reason I felt a pang of disgust, as if I had just tasted something rotten. I did not know what the man was doing, but something about it felt unnatural, even wrong. Since there was no Tree in sight—around his neck or otherwise—I gladly moved on by leaping onto the man's roof.

More flat spaces, more rugs, more furniture met my gaze. More doors, chimneys, and walls. As I huffed and contemplated which way to turn, a slender, pale streak began to appear in front of me, slowly fattening as it rose over the top edge of the dark wall. It was the moon.

Get a move on, Sengali!

Lena was right: the whole town was like a maze, a man-made canyon of brick, mortar, and stone, suspended between earth and sky. For what must have been two hours I wandered around, stopping and going, staying in the shadows as much as possible, always making my way towards the center. The only break in the endless rooftops were places where they dropped off and left large, walled-in spaces between the houses. These giant holes were usually filled with fountains, flowers, trees, and other plant life like miniature forests dropped down in a wasteland of rock. Some of them were full of people—too busy dancing, laughing, and reveling to notice me watching them from above. But the men walking around or gathered on the rooftops were harder to avoid. Fortunately, though, most of them stayed inside their strange houses. Peeking in windows lined with silk, stalking marble lattices, glancing through cracks in mahogany doors, I got a very clear picture of what kind of creatures these humans were. There were fat men and hefty ladies dressed in shiny clothing, lying on fluffy couches and eating roasted lamb; there were skinny men and frail women dressed in dull rags standing at their feet, waiting to bring them more food. There were solemn musicians chanting and wild musicians banging on instruments. Men boasted about their strength; women boasted about their beauty. Some men bowed down to the women, some women bowed down to the men, and almost all bowed down to those strange golden statues.

These were everywhere. Some looked like things found in the heavens: sun, moon, and stars. Others were forms of things I recognized: birds, bulls—even a winged lion (which made me chuckle as I passed by). Many, however, were far more bizarre, and if they were supposed to be creatures that actually existed I had never seen them before. All over the town these things showed up: on tables in banquet halls, in quiet chambers next to ivory beds, on shelves in huge libraries filled with scrolls. They seemed to be the common thread, the heartbeat of the culture. But they were not the only thing I noticed humans had in common. Rich or poor, young or old, male or female, every single one of them I saw was selfish. Whether being served, or doing the serving, each man was out for himself: despising, manipulating, abusing, flattering, and using other men to whatever end he or she thought was best. It was sickening, and as I pressed on further and further I found myself wanting to find the Man of the Tree if only to get the job over with and escape the awful place. Yet the moon rose higher and higher into the sky and still I had no reason to believe I was any closer to my goal than when I started. The only thing that seemed to be going my way was that I had escaped detection. So far.

As the evening wore on I found myself steadily climbing higher. Since the houses grew on each other it was like picking your way up a mountain slope of flat plateaus. Pausing on one of the wider ones to look back over the sea of rooftops my heart suddenly leapt in my throat. Moving lights were headed towards me! Around the corner of a nearby house-top a group of men and (even worse) dogs appeared, closing in fast! The men were huge, grim-looking brutes, shrouded in turbans and uniforms of black and green, loaded down with weapons: curved swords, spiked clubs, jagged whips. The wolves were no better: shaggy, slobbering beasts, jerking their chains and snapping at each other as they sniffed the ground. A few more steps and they would see me! Frantically my head darted around, searching for a way of escape. Slowly I backed up, keeping my body low and out of the wind. Suddenly I was enveloped in branches! My back paw had nothing to stand on and as I turned I saw I had come to the edge of the roof. A garden lay below, where a great fruit tree had grown so tall that its top limbs stretched out over the housetop. They were like welcoming arms. I sprang into them, grabbing onto their branches with an iron grip. Thankfully the sturdy wood was able to support the force of my weight. Even then I would have been discovered, had not a sudden burst of wind disguised my clamoring through the leaves and blown my scent downwind from the dogs. Breathlessly I dropped to the empty blackness under the tree. A small uproar of sniffing and baying closed in overhead. But then it passed. I was safe—for the time being.

With a shiver of relief I surveyed the refuge I had invaded. It was a quiet grove of melon trees, filled with flowers for beauty and herbs for healing. It reminded me very much of my home in the jungle, only there were no weeds, brambles, or deadly plants in sight. Everything was tame, ordered, and well-tended. For the first time since I had entered the town I started to relax. There was a dry crackle in the air and through some manicured bushes I saw the light of a fire. Oddly enough, however, I sensed no fear. My curiosity began to get the better of me. Beneath the watching eyes of the peaceful trees I slipped forward, my large paws absorbing all sound in their dense pads. When just beyond the halo of firelight I suddenly halted in surprise.

There on a seat in the midst of the garden, illumined by the flickering light of the dancing flames, sat a man. His skin was dark and thin, folding itself into many wrinkles and lines across his quiet face. Frail hands, now weak and worn, rested on the top of a short staff, but the white scars they bore were marks of long forgotten strength. The man's garments were simple but well-made, and a long cloak of deep gray draped over his shoulders. Only his white head remained uncovered, almost appearing to have its own dull glow, like the moon behind a thin cloud. The longer I watched him, the less he moved, and the more he began to resemble the aging trees around him. Minutes passed. I lost track of them but all the while he just sat there: eyes fixed on the fire, chin resting on his hands, no motion whatsoever.

Does Man sleep with his eyes open?

Just then the wind stirred again and it seemed to stir the old man to life with it. Like a tired oak rousing itself from a stupor, the man sighed—a long, heavy sigh—and stretched his trembling fingers. Then slowly he straightened his bent back, revealing his upper chest, which had been hidden from view till now by the knob of his staff. The firelight glistened off of something hanging from his open neck. Suddenly my breath drew in sharply. Every muscle in my body instantly tensed. My eyes narrowed.

The Tree!

TEN

THERE IT LAY on the thin chest: a small ivory amulet, carved in the form of a tree in full bloom. I blinked and looked again to make sure I was not imagining things. This was it? This was the fearsome specter from Mantos' Dream? A tired, worn out old man? I watched in disbelief as the feeble body struggled to stand up, laying much of his weight on the wooden cane. It seemed unthinkable that the infamous "Man of the Tree" and the pitiful creature I saw before me could be one and the same. Yet there was no denying the pendant as it gleamed in the darkness. My job was clear. In the wild my pride would have never stooped to such an indignity as killing an old one. That was left for toothless vultures and tigers who had lost their own strength. But this was different. I had no time for scruples. Old or not, weak and easy prey as the man was, the Tree was the price of my freedom and Womby's life. It was either it or me.

As the old man labored to pull himself up onto his feet, I shifted my weight closer to the ground, balancing upon my claws, ready to spring. My target was locked. As soon as he was upright I would lunge straight for the fragile neck. Once—and only once—was all it would take. Those brittle bones would snap like dead twigs.

"Sengali."

I froze. Was that the wind in the trees? Or had someone just whispered my name?

"Sengali."

My heart stopped. *It can't be!*

"Sengali!"

But it was! *The Voice!* The Voice in the Dream! It was speaking to me! *Out loud*—it was speaking to me! Ever since the night Lena found me in the cave it had been silent. Now it came like an echo in the darkness from nothing, out of nowhere. Only this time I was not dreaming!

"Sengali," it repeated, with a quiet force that turned my legs to stone, *"Do not touch him!"*

My heart started pounding. The man was standing now leaning heavily on his cane. This was the chance I had waited for, yet my limbs refused to move. I felt dazed, stunned like a bird knocked to the ground by an invisible hand. I wanted to argue with the Voice, but my mind had gone dumb. *Why?* was the only question it could form. Then the man himself turned my direction, looking where I crouched along the borders of the firelight. His eyes met mine. I do not know what ran through his mind at that moment, but what went through mine I shall never forget as long as I live. There was no fear in those gray eyes, no terror; they were clear, strong, and intelligent. The age racking his body turned to wisdom in their depths; they were lit from within with a flame burning brighter than the firelight reflecting off of their surface. They pierced into me like daggers; it felt as if *I* was the one being hunted. The man said nothing, his gaze searching deep into my heart. Then, all at once, it softened. I cannot explain why. All I know is that somehow I felt like the man understood me—like he was looking into the face of a servant, turned enemy, whom he would have rather called "friend". It filled me with an odd sensation. For the first time in my life I knew shame, but not the kind of shame that brings resentment. Looking in those grave, kind eyes made me want to make amends. It was almost as if they were calling me to try and make right some terrible wrong. A wrong that had been done long before either of us stood in that garden.

Slowly I raised myself upright. Silently we continued to watch each other, lost in our own thoughts. My tail twitched and his arms trembled, but our eyes never faltered. There are few moments in life where one feels the gravity of them while they are happening, but this was one of them. And in that moment I realized the reason the Voice had stopped me. To kill such a spirit, no matter how old, would have been worse than disgrace. It would have been evil, and would have turned me into the very thing I despised. I would have been no better than Mantos.

The man stood his ground still studying me. I could tell he was waiting for me to decide what I would do. Slowly I bowed my head in respect. Then my eyes rose to meet his steady gaze. It was no longer sober. A smile of pleasure and relief lightened his face and a few of the man's long years seemed to have lifted off of his shoulders. The white head nodded.

All was forgiven.

After one parting look of gratitude and admiration I turned to leave. But no sooner was my back turned than a new sound flicked my ears. A gritty, guttural, breathing sound—like heavy rocks rubbing against each other. Instantly I recognized the deep-throated snarl and spun around.

"LENA—NO!"

But too late! The lioness was already in mid-air, her razor talons stretched for the old man's back! Where she came from or how long she had been there I had no time to think about. Another moment and it would be over: the man would not even have a chance to scream.

I sprung forward with all the power in me! The man was down on the ground now, his feeble body pinned under Lena's—her fangs about to go for his throat! Like a battering ram, I plummeted into her side. The she-cat went sprawling into some nearby bushes, completely taken off guard. But only for a moment. As if in slow motion she pulled herself up, muscle by bulging muscle, rage coursing through every move she made. When the lioness stood erect her tawny neck was stiff, her head poised, and her green eyes smoldered in the light of the fire.

"So *now* we get to it!" She growled low, her sides heaving with anger. "I knew you wouldn't have what it takes! You're *weak*, Sengali!" She spat, "Mantos was a fool to trust you!"

Between her and the man I held my ground. "Try to touch him again, Lena, and I'll show you how weak I am!"

Her voice was cold and ruthless, "I'm not leaving here without that Tree!"

"Then take it," I challenged, digging my claws into the earth, "if you can."

Three eternal seconds passed.

The she-cat lunged in a burst of fury! Bracing myself on my haunches I rose to meet her attack. The impact was terrible! Her fangs met my claws and the smell of first blood met my nostrils. I had no time to tell which one of us it flowed from. She came at me again, talons bare. Dodging the fatal swipe I dove under, thrusting all of my weight against her stomach. She flipped over with a scream but dug her claws into my shoulders on the way, dragging me down. Up she was again, going for the back of my neck! Just before the savage teeth could sink into my skull I spun around and struck the side of her face with my forepaw, leaving red trails on her cheek. For a moment she stumbled and backed away. The green eyes glared as drops of blood fell into them. "You'll...pay...for...that!" She heaved.

I could feel my own blood burning as it left the wounds in my shoulders. "Leave it, Lena," I panted fiercely, and the rumble of my warning shook through the speechless trees, "or Mantos will have to find himself a new heir!"

Her face contorted as she ushered a short, cold laugh. "I told you: he already has! But not once I have the Tree!" Her voice was raspy and wild, "Nothing will stop me then! If Mantos won't listen to me, the rest of them will; the whole jungle will know who killed the Man of the Tree!" The black pupils narrowed to slits. "Nothing, and *no one*, will stop me from getting what I want, Sengali—not even you!" From a dead stand-still she leapt again, reaching for my head. I sprung forward; we collided in mid-air. One quick move and my teeth buried in her tan throat to yank out a mouth full of fur and flesh. *"RAAOW!"* Lena roared in pain. She retaliated in a mad frenzy, and we went crashing into the nearby garden like a ball of fury. One moment I was on top, the next she was—legs, heads, and claws rolling over, diving under, and grasping at each other in a savage dance for survival.

In the midst of our tumult, however, another sound suddenly broke in. Other voices, and lots of them! In the distance I heard frantic cries of "The Old One!" mingled with angry shouts of "Lions!" Even the trees shuddered in panic. Tearing myself away from Lena long enough to glance around I saw dozens of lights gathering around the campfire.

They've found the old man!

Searing pain dug into my left cheek! Lena's razor claws raked across my face like knives furrowing into my skin! A reeling sensation overwhelmed me and I stumbled to the ground. For a moment the whole world looked fuzzy and dark. I recovered only in time to see Lena's hindquarters disappearing above the garden wall. My body trembled from pain as I struggled to get back on my paws; the whole left side of my body felt like it had been sliced into ribbons.

But no sooner was I standing than a new set of jaws dug into my right shoulder! With a loud moan, I jerked my head around and came face to face with a gray wolf. I tried to spin, swiping from every angle I could. It was useless. The thing had latched onto me like a leech on a water buffalo! The harder I pulled away the more it clung, gnawing and snarling through clenched teeth. Never in all my life had I faced such a demon! With remarkable strength and ferocious tenacity it ripped into me like a mother defending her young. It was all I could do just to stay on my feet! The lights were upon me now; the voices and shouts very near. A few more seconds and there would be no escape.

Amid the noise a strong voice sounded out above the rest. "Nathak!" It called, "Nathak—OFF!"

Instantly the wolf pulled away, taking part of my shoulder with it. For one brief moment I was free! I remember seeing the gray beast run to a man who was ahead of the others. He carried a torch in one hand, hair black in the firelight, bare chest firm and brown. I did not wait for a closer look. Desperately I darted for the tree that had so willingly invited me into this death trap. My bleeding claws found its rough trunk and began to frantically climb. But suddenly there was a small jab in my thigh, like the tiny incision of an insect's stinger. The next thing I knew all of my strength seemed to drain from my body. My head got light. The talons of my paws retracted. I felt myself falling, falling, and hitting the ground with a thud. Lying on my side, I looked to see the man with the wolf remove a small object from his lips. Then he turned, running back towards the fire where the old man lay. His back became lost in a mob of angry faces. Blinding lights and deafening shouts surrounded me.

Then everything went black.

A CAT'S TALE

PART TWO

"Nightmares"

ELEVEN

"**G**ET UP, YOU LAZY BEAST!" A cruel voice echoed through the darkness. It sounded vague and far away. A sudden, swift pain followed that seemed much closer: something hard struck my left side.

Where am I? I thought drowsily. My body was as limp as water and, for some reason, my eyes felt like they were stuck together. I could not seem to get them open. Sounds swirled through my head, all of them distant and strange. My senses felt murky and slow. *What happened?*

"Come on!" The voice screeched again, a little nearer, "Get up, I said!" Another painful jab to the ribs, "I've got customers waiting!"

Wha—Who? My brain slurred while the rest of me tried to revive. *Who's waiting for what?*

"Move!" came the shout right into my ear, and this time whatever struck was pointed and horribly sharp. The shock jerked me out of my stupor. My eyes burst open. In a second hundreds of sensations washed over me. All of them were bad. The hot glare of the sun poured from above, revealing a sight that made my head swim. Men were everywhere! Males and females. Old ones, young ones, and in-between. Fat and skinny, tall and short, clean and dirty: they swirled and hustled, shoved, pushed, and shouted all around like a swarm of busy ants. Fear gripped me. I felt like a rock in the rapids, surrounded by a rushing, angry river of humanity! The only thing I could see separating me from the sea of people were some iron bars standing in front of my face.

Wait a second—bars?

My eyes focused on the gray poles gleaming in the sunlight. I glanced upwards: a solid metal roof hovered only inches from my head, blocking all view of the sky. My heart started racing.

What kind of trap have I fallen into?

My neck felt incredibly heavy. In dismay I realized I was wearing an iron collar. A sudden jab to my left brought my head around with a snarl. More bars. And, just barely on the other side of them, a lean face (embellished by gold teeth and a nasty scar on the right jaw) broke into a wicked smile.

"That's more like it," the man cackled, and his breath smelled like rotten fish, "now on your feet!"

With a short spear gripped in his bony hands, he gouged me again. I jumped up, boiling in rage and knocking my head against the low ceiling. Now I could fully observe my situation. It wasn't good. An iron cage held me prisoner: barely tall enough to stand in and not wide enough to turn around. The openings between the bars were very narrow: too small for me to reach through but large enough to expose me to every onlooker and threat passing by. I was a side-show trapped in a narrow, claustrophobic, metal box.

"Move him to the platform!" The lean man shouted and suddenly several other men—all smelly, hulking brutes—gathered around my cage. They managed to lift it up to their shoulders (something I didn't like one bit) and carry me up a flight of wooden steps. We mounted a kind of stage looking to be in the middle of a large public square. There were booths all over the place, where loud salesmen shouted out the daily bargain and hundreds of people pressed in to see what the fuss was about. My ears also detected noises from other animals but I did not have a chance to see where they came from. Without warning the men let go and my cage fell to the stage with a thud that almost knocked me out again. As minutes went by other cages were dropped in around me. These were filled with all kinds of creatures: animals and (to my surprise) even other humans. The latter were treated no better than the rest of us.

Actually, in some ways they were treated worse, and I could not help but wonder what sort of a creature would do such a thing to its own kind. Once all of the cages were gathered onto the stage a trumpet blared, wailing like a sick elephant. Instantly the people who had been browsing around the booths turned towards the stage and crowded around. We in the cages became the object of their attention, and to have so many eyes staring at me without any way of escape or fighting back made me feel more vulnerable than I had ever felt in my life.

The thin man with the golden teeth took to the platform. "Ladies and gentleman," he cried out, "gather round! The Sale has officially commenced! You all know Marsed brings only the best," he made a theatric bow, "and to show you I haven't changed in all my journeys," motioned to a burly man standing nearby, "we're going to start things off with the most radiant jewel of them all!" The burly man opened one of the cages and drug out a young woman. I was hardly a good judge of human females, but from the approval of the crowd she must have been quite a thing to behold. They made her stand on a large wooden block in the center of the platform and then the thin man went to work. "Can Marsed deliver, or can Marsed deliver?" he cried with a gleaming grin, and the people cheered. "Now, for such a beauty as this, what say we start the bidding off at one hundred pieces of silver? Who will give me one hundred and fifty?"

A well-dressed man towards the front lifted his hand. "One hundred and fifty!" he repeated.

"I have one hundred and fifty," the thin man shouted with pleasure, "Who'll give me two hundred?"

"Two hundred," called a fat man with a large turban on his head.

"Well met, friend! I now have two hundred, who'll give me two-fifty?"

The first man piped up again, "Two-fifty!"

"Three-hundred!" broke in the second, before the Salesman had a chance to say anything.

"*That's* what I like to see!" He cackled, "Nothing like a little competition to sweeten the thrill of victory for the lucky winner!"

"And to line Marsed's pockets!" cried someone from the audience, which brought a round of laughter.

"True enough, friend, true enough," the slick Salesman joined along, "but no one could call me ungenerous—letting such a goddess slip through my fingers," he made the girl turn full circle on the block. "Now there's a sight no amount of money is too good for!"

A few whistles and hollers proved the crowds' approval, but the fat man called out with a huff, "You have a bid for three hundred pieces of silver. I move the auction be closed!"

"*You* would!" shouted the well-dressed man angrily.

"Easy gentlemen, easy!" the Salesman cooed, "I don't blame you for getting excited—not one bit—but the day is young and so is the maid. We've got plenty of time! I have a bid for three hundred pieces of silver, who'll make it three-fifty?"

This went back and forth a while, each man raising the other's bid, till at last the well-dressed man shouted, "Eight hundred!" There was a general gasp. The fat man grew red in the face and stormed out of the crowd, apparently unable to match such a price. Everyone laughed; the Salesman grinned.

"I have a bid of eight hundred pieces of silver for this lovely vision. Are there no more bids?" A general quiet prevailed. "Very well: eight hundred going once, eight hundred going twice—"

"One thousand pieces of silver!" called out a voice from the back of the crowd. To my utter confusion it was that of another woman. All the people erupted with cheering. The well-dressed man looked shocked; then he shook his head sullenly.

The Salesman rubbed his hands in glee. "*That's* why I love this city!" he shouted. "*One thousand* pieces of silver is the final bid? One thousand going once, one thousand going twice—SOLD!" and he slapped his hands together, "this beauteous creature to the *lady* in the back!" Everyone laughed and cheered again. The girl was hustled off the platform and into a colorful entourage that came forward, where another woman (much older, but still very fine looking) handed the burly man a bag full of something heavy. I assumed it was the "one-thousand-pieces-of-silver", whatever that was. The older lady looked over her new property, seemed pleased with what she saw, and motioned for her own servants to escort the girl somewhere beyond the square.

This scene was repeated over and over as, one by one, each human in a cage was purchased and taken away by a human in the crowd. Though I did not fully understand what was happening, something about the whole process seemed wrong. Just gazing out over the faces of onlookers made me nauseous. They were greedy, eager, and hollow like a pack of hungry jackals closing in on the kill. When the last of the men were sold the Salesman (now giddy from the mass of silver he had collected), started raffling off the animals. I watched as cage after cage disappeared. By the time they finally drug mine onto the block I was so parched from baking in the afternoon sun I barely noticed when the bidding began. What anyone wanted me for I didn't dare imagine; all I could think of was finally getting off that horrible stage.

I think I remember hearing the Salesman rattle, "That's five-fifty, who'll say six hundred", when a sudden commotion at the back of the crowd interrupted the bidding. Someone started shouting, "Make way! Make way for the Master of the Games! Make way for Hittan, the Mighty!"

People scurried to and fro like they were trying to get away from an elephant stampede. A wide path was cleared where only seconds before the crowd had pressed so tightly together they could barely move. Then everyone bent over and bowed their heads to the ground. On the far end of the newly formed pathway appeared six fully armed men: each large in his own right but looking like mere boys compared to the towering beast in their midst. A true giant of a man, nearly four heads taller than the guards surrounding him. I wondered why anyone of such size would even feel the need for guards. His powerful frame was draped in a robe of black and green, decked with golden fringes that clinked as he walked. His bare arms showed solid muscle while swinging at his side, where a huge, curved sword hung in a jeweled sheath. His dark head bore a golden circlet studded with emeralds and rubies. On his shoulder perched a raven, black as a starless night. With an air of proud confidence, the giant came towards the stage, making the earth tremble slightly under his massive feet. At last he stopped directly in front of the platform. The raven squawked while the salesman made a sweeping bow.

"Your L,l,lordship," he stammered, still looking down, "this is an unexpected honor!"

"Save your flattery," the giant boomed, apparently unimpressed, "I am in haste. What do you have for me this time?" His black eyes fell on me; I pinned my ears back and hissed. A faint but cruel smile flashed across his over-sized face. The hairs of my neck stood on end. Something about his presence made me feel more uneasy than all the men I had seen so far, put together.

The salesman stood upright (giving him just a slight advantage over the giant due to the height of the stage), "Only the best—*Always* the best for the Master of the Games!" He laid a bony hand on my cage, "I found this devil stalking the fair town of Nod. Already killed a man, he has. Throttled him in cold blood—"

"So I've heard," the giant interrupted, "You forget, Slave Master, news travels faster than your caravan—especially when it involves the death of the father of the High Priest of Nod. But I have no use for a cat that kills old men. Give me a beast that will put on a show worth watching, not just fill its stomach." All this time he kept studying me intently, boring with a relentless gaze. I returned it, figuring it would be better to face him head on. I wasn't watching my back. Several jabs of searing pain suddenly cut into my haunches! I lashed out blindly, wild with rage, not realizing what had happened until after it was over: Marsed's henchmen had gouged me with spears. But apparently the display was precisely what the men wanted to see: both Slave Master and giant were smiling with pleasure.

"*That* I can use," Hittan confessed with cool satisfaction.

"I thought your Lordship might be interested," cackled Marsed, rubbing his hands again, "now about the price—"

The giant erupted in a laugh that felt like fists pounding my ear drums. The raven on his shoulder jumped and squawked. "Price?" he bellowed, "Your price, Slave Master, is that I do not confiscate your goods, seize your money, and turn you out a beggar on the streets! You dare mention 'price' to Hittan the Mighty—Master of the Games?" The thin man was so shaken he sank to his knees, pale as a rodent's ear. This seemed to please Hittan. "Fortunately for you," the giant continued, "I am feeling generous. I accept the cat as a gift and graciously allow you to continue your trade in this city—with the provision that, from now on, you come to me *first* Slave Master. To ensure your merchandise is always 'the best', as you claim." The booming voice lowered with menace, "If I find you have done otherwise I will not be so lenient. Am I understood?"

Marsed gulped, "Your Lordship is too generous!"

"Indeed," the giant replied with a cunning smile, "I am certain ours will be a most profitable relationship." His black eyes gleamed as they turned to me, "Have the beast delivered to the Barracks by sundown." He lifted his right hand in the air as a signal to his men it was time to leave. I stared at the huge thing in amazement.

It had six fingers!

TWELVE

"COME ON, YOU DEVIL; let's see what you've got!"

WHISH! A thick strand of rawhide whipped through the air to crack within an inch of my face, singeing my whiskers. I growled in protest. For four days I had been locked up in a small, brick cell. No food, no freedom—the only light from a tiny window in the roof, the only water from a dirty bucket in the corner. Now I stood in an enclosed arena, trapped under a net of barbed wire arching overhead like a thorny, over-turned bowl, listening to threats and insults from a creature even Mantos would have cowered from: Hittan the Mighty. Men called him "Master of the Games"; I called him "The Man-Beast". It suited the monster well. He was twice the cunning, twice the cruelty, and three times the size of every other man I had seen. His arms were hard and bulged with muscles. His legs, like long and powerful tree trunks, shook the ground with every stride. Yet for all that bulk he moved remarkably quick, possessing an almost un-earthly agility. No matter how hard I tried I could not get at him.

"Ha!" The giant taunted, "Is that the best you can do?"

Weak from hunger, I tried to spring again but stumbled with a groan. The giant easily swerved and came at me from behind. A wicked laugh rumbled through the air as the whip lashed my back legs.

"Perhaps I should send you back to Marsed; you may mean more to him as a rug than to me." From above came a "kaw-kaw!" I looked to see Hittan's pet raven perched on top of the barbed roof, twisting its head and watching us through beady eyes.

SWISH! Raw-hide whistled past my left ear.

"Do you think this is some kind of a game, cat?"

WHOOSH! Then the right ear.

"Well, play-time is over!"

CRACK! It descended onto my skull, cutting a groove of blood across my forehead.

"You have a new Master now. To survive my games you'll have to fight harder (SWISH), think faster (WHOOSH), and kill quicker (CRACK) than any of your opponents. Succeed and you'll be lauded as a hero, feared as a monster, worshiped as a god. But fail," suddenly the whip wrapped around my neck and jerked me to the ground. The Man-Beast let out a deep, cruel chuckle and started lashing me without mercy. Again and again my body convulsed in pain as the rawhide slashed my skin. My blood boiled; the giant's laughter was awakening a savage will. Without thought to pain, hunger, or weakness I surged to my feet, sprung with a roar, and sunk my talons into his huge neck. For a brief, desperate time we struggled, wrestling strength against brute strength. But at last he broke free. Quickly the Man-Beast slipped through a door in the barbed wall to stand panting on the opposite side, dripping red sweat from head to foot.

"I may have been mistaken," he gasped, a flame of grim pleasure in his dark eyes. "Perhaps you have possibilities after all!"

* * *

I was not returned to my lonely cell, but found myself hustled down a narrow tunnel, through an open door, and into a new kind of prison. Another, bigger cage, only this time the iron bars were covered with a kind of mesh, made out of small, metal squares. It was the most room I had had since being captured. This new cage was set inside a large, narrow room full of other cages, many of which were filled with other animals. They stared as I entered the room—hopeless, hollow stares that chilled me more than any of Hittan's threats. But then they ignored me, going back to their listless lives. I looked around.

Slats of narrow windows high in the rafters let in some dingy sunlight. That was not the case with any fresh air. Whatever I was breathing was as musty and dead as a tomb. All around the walls of the room were stone doors just like the one I had passed through, each emptying into a different cage. These were all closed, mine included (it had slammed shut behind me as soon as I entered). Only one door was open in the entire room, at its end. Two guards sat by it, playing a game of some kind with cards and rocks.

I watched dully as more men arrived, skinny and dressed in rags. They bowed to the guards, never looking them in the eye; in turn the guards shoved them around a little, laughed, and started demanding supper. A small boy came forward carrying a basket and a jug that one of the guards jerked out of his hand while the other waved the rest of the slaves through the door. They came into the room with buckets and crates full of food: rotten roots, nut shells, grain and hay full of maggots, fruit covered with flies and gnats. As hungry as I was, my appetite vanished when they started flinging it into the cages. But what was worse was how the animals ate it. Chowing down, even fighting over the filthy stuff like it was a gourmet feast! For me the very smell of it was nauseating. Until they brought out the meat. When old bones and flesh carcasses started being thrown my mouth started watering. And as a bucket of fish got closer I realized I had not eaten in almost a week. I stood up excitedly.

My legs trembled from lack of nourishment and my head got so light I was afraid I was going to pass out. The slave carrying the bucket saw me and his eyes widened with fear. His own legs started trembling but he walked over, lifting the bucket to empty it into my feeding trough. Hunger crushed my sides together.

"Hey! You!" one of the guards shouted. The slave jumped and dropped the bucket, spilling all the fish on the ground. "Yeah, you!" He bellowed with a mouthful of bread, "No food for the cat! Hittan's orders!"

No! My mind cried. The rotten fish were sprawled over the floor not two feet away, yet I could not reach even one because of the cage bars. I wanted to scream in despair. Instead I just collapsed into a heap, finally overwhelmed with hunger.

"Clean that mess up, you clumsy fool!" barked the other guard, sloshing his drink out of the jug. The rattled slave cursed under his breath and knelt to pick up the bucket. I watched weakly as he reached for a flounder near my head.

Death by starvation, I thought grimly.

Suddenly a rapid "chit-chit-chittering" broke out overhead. A furry, reddish-brown body dropped in front of my eyes. A second later it was gone—along with the flounder! All I saw was the face of the shocked slave. He stared blankly a moment or two then reached for a salmon nearby.

"Oo-a-a-a!"

Before the man knew it a fuzzy tail had swiped the fish right out from under his nose! Again the slave swore, glancing behind him to see if the guards were watching, but neither he nor the guards saw the creature that snuck from the side and carried off two more fish. My head raised slightly.

A monkey!

This time I had gotten a clear view: a small guy with thin, nimble arms, quick, limber legs, and a long tail curling and twisting like a snake. He was covered all over with short brown hair except for the undersides of his feet, hands, and rubbery little face. The latter was bright and full of expression. Large, almond eyes looked almost oversized as they darted back and forth, the monkey constantly checking his surroundings. He took the salmon in his hands, slung it into an empty, over-turned barrel, and jumped right in after it. The slave turned around, scratched his head, and started throwing the rest of the fish in the bucket as fast as he could. The monkey's small head poked out of the barrel, watching the man fumble with the slippery food. Then he opened his mouth (showing a row of sharp, tiny white teeth) and let out an "Ee-oo-a-a-a!" The slave spun to his feet and tore into the barrel, while the monkey slipped out a hole in the other end, dragging his fish behind him. The man was crashing away, waist deep in wood, as the little thief threw the stolen goods behind a crate and ran back to the scene of the crime. Quickly, he gathered up what was left of the biggest fish. Coming back for the last one the monkey looked my way. He stopped. Standing up on his hind legs, he held out a cod in his hands as big as he was—almost as if he were offering it to me. Then he grinned and cackled.

"Thief!" The slave cried, realizing he had been taken for a fool. Instantly the monkey darted off.

By now the guards saw what was happening. "Give it up little man!" they roared with laughter, "You'll never catch that trickster!" The slave stumbled out of the mess he had created like a clumsy buffalo. By the time he stood up the monkey was already almost in the rafters. Reaching the very top cage he stopped and looked down. The man raised his fist in the air and hurled up every insult he could think of; the monkey just chattered and hurled them right back. One of the guards grew tired of the noise. "Alright, that's enough!" Marching over he smacked the slave on the ear, "Get back to work!" The beaten man stooped low and shuffled off, carrying his empty bucket with him.

"Wua-wua-a-a-a!" The victorious monkey howled, struck a snappy salute, and went swinging off through the rafters.

THIRTEEN

I THINK I MUST HAVE passed out after that point. My eyes were still closed when something wet and smelly hit my head.

"Hey—Stripes!" a voice whispered. Something oily smacked my nose. "Wake up!"

My eyes barely opened; it was dark.

"Wakey, wakey!"

WHACK! An oozy, slimy mass dropped right into my ear! I jolted up with a moan.

"Suppertime!"

Two objects fell from the sky: one on my right paw and the other on my left. I blinked in amazement. It was raining fish! I looked up. A little bit of moonlight through the windows outlined a furry silhouette on the top of my cage. Even in the darkness I saw the monkey's white smile.

"Evening!" He chittered, "Name's Eddie! Looks like you could use a friend! But fish first," he reached into a pile of salmon chunks right beside him and squeezed one through the square bars. As it showered on top of my head he cackled, "Eat hardy; got lots more!" And off he scrambled. I didn't argue. Never in my life had anything tasted so good! In seconds every bite was gone and I was licking the floor for left-overs. True to his word, the monkey returned in no time with three more fish. Down they came, bit by bit; me swallowing them whole while the monkey laughed. He was careful, though, to not be too loud. The guards were still snoring in chairs by the door.

"You full yet?" he asked as the last bite was gulped.

I could feel my strength coming back. "You out of food?"

"Oo-oo-ee!" he cackled, climbing down the outside of the cage, "The day Eddie runs out of food you can eat him!" Reaching eye level he stopped and pointed his finger at me, grinning mischievously, "That's just a figure of speech, by the way." Then he leapt off and half-walked, half-loped over to the crate where the stolen fish were stashed. Out came three more, including the huge cod. "*Ugh*, this is heavy!" He grunted. With a perplexed look the monkey sat down on the cod and scratched his hip, glancing from the fish to the top of the cage. The almond eyes studied me. "You wouldn't bite the hand that feeds you, would you?"

"Not if it keeps feeding me."

"Hmm," the monkey thought, pushing out his lips, "Guess I'll risk it." Ripping the fish apart he hopped over in front of my face, "Bite me and I'll never steal for you again!" As the fish squeezed through the bars, I snapped my jaws just close enough to Eddie's fingers to make him jump. "You did that on purpose!" he cried.

"You dropped salmon in my ear," I smiled through a mouthful of cod.

Eddie huffed. "Fine, Smartie-Cat!" as he shoved another piece through, "Just don't expect a present on your birthday!" I chuckled but took it gratefully: not knowing the monkey well I didn't want to push him too far. At last, my stomach no longer felt like a hollow drum! When the final bite was gone, the monkey jumped onto the wall of my cage, perching there with his hands and tail wrapped around the bars. "Hear you bested Hittan in the ring today? Impressive! Last time that happened was Razor Claw. How'd you do it?"

I shrugged, not caring to relive the moment, "He made me angry, I suppose."

"Shew!" the monkey whistled and rubbed his head, "Remind me not to make you angry! Where you from Stripes? What brings you to Khanok?"

"Khanok?"

The monkey laughed with a snort; then he realized I was serious. "Wait. You mean you don't know? Really?"

"Know what?"

"Khanok! Where we *are* right now! Capitol of Nod? Biggest city in the world?" I looked at him blankly. "Home of a Thousand Temples, Door to the Great Sea, Center of the Games..." he paused for breath, clearly puzzled. "You from out of town or something? Don't you know where the Barracks are?"

"What are those."

"Oh brother!" he exclaimed, doing a sideways flip and landing right back in the same position, "You *are* from out of town! *These*," swinging wide with his arm, "are the Barracks: where everything and everybody lives that has anything to do with the Games. And don't tell me you don't know what those are!" The emptiness on my face made Eddie drop to the ground and sit there, scratching his head. "Where *do* you come from, Stripes?"

"The jungle." Just saying the word brought a pang of desire to see the thick canopy of leaves over my head again, "And my name is Sengali."

The monkey waved his hand, "That's o.k.—won't hold it against you. The name, I mean," he added, "but the jungle—that's different. Tell me," he asked eagerly, climbing over my head, "is it really like they say? Nothing but green everywhere far as you can see?"

The pang turned into real pain as I thought of the view from my mountain. "Yes, in some places."

The monkey shuddered, "Sounds scary!"

Now it was my turn to be surprised, "You mean you've never seen the jungle before?"

"No way, man! City-dweller. Born and raised. Only thing I've ever seen as far as I could see is stone and marble. And gold. And steel, and bronze, and...well, like I said, biggest city in the world! Once I went three days in one direction just for the fun of it. Never got out. Not that I really wanted to." He hung upside down over the side, "Now if I was human that'd be different: I'd either scat out through the sewers under the city or get rich like Hittan. Probably choose the sewers. Not much fun being a giant jerk. But I'm not human, so I'll never leave. *Way* too many pockets to pick! And people to feed," he added, twisting his head to smile down at me.

I was too distracted to smile back. *A city as big as the jungle? Nothing to see for miles but stone and metal and men—and I'm trapped in the middle of it all!* I felt like suffocating.

The monkey noticed. "Aw, don't worry, Stripes," he reassured, landing on his feet in front of me, "Stick with Eddie: he'll take care of you! Eddie always takes care of his friends!" And with another snappy salute he went bounding off into the shadows.

* * *

I looked all night for the monkey's return, but he never showed. As the light of dawn began to grow through the windows, choked by the dust of the rafters, my stomach started to growl again. Back and forth I paced in my cage. Back and forth. Forth and back. Mostly trying to keep my mind off my growing hunger.

Where is he?

I was beginning to fear the monkey had a short-term memory when some activity at the main door caught my eye. A middle-aged man dressed in green and purple was talking with the guards. I could not hear what they said, but the new man pointed at me and the guards smiled.

I didn't like it.

FOURTEEN

THEY GRABBED LONG TOOLS with spikes on the end and came towards me. I hissed, backing up against the solid stone door. One guard walked to the side, grabbed a rope hanging from some pulleys, and started to pull. Instantly there was a heavy rumble; the stone I was leaning on suddenly vanished, leaving a black hole in its place! Half of me fell into the dark, narrow tunnel. The guards started shouting, jabbing at my other half with their sharp poles, trying to herd me through the hole. I hesitated, but soon the noise and jabs became too much. I sprang into the hole for some relief.

What I got was torture. The tunnel had been turned into a tube of barbed wire, running like an underground river in a corridor of stone. But this river had angry men standing on both sides of it: yelling, goading me on, gouging at my flanks with spears and pikes. I ran ahead as my coat snagged against the barbed walls. It was like running a gauntlet; my only thought was escape. The tunnel turned a sharp corner. My eyes winced. Up ahead was sunlight—real sunlight! It gleamed from a shaft at the end of the tunnel. My heart jumped as I realized I was headed straight for it towards open sky, into fresh air! I rushed forward.

CLANK! An immense weight fell on my neck! My weakened frame reeled at the shock. With horror I recovered only to see a massive chain hanging from under my chin! Somehow an iron collar had been slapped on me; now link after iron link draped about my paws like the coils of some monstrous snake. I couldn't see where the other end disappeared to. The men seemed pleased. One who looked like a hawk without feathers screeched out, "Release the cat!" All at once the shaft of sunlight became a flood as a trap door over my head flew up. My eyes focused on a flight of stone steps. The men started shouting and jabbing again, but it was unnecessary. I lunged up eagerly: climbing towards the sun, dragging the clanking chains up the staircase behind me, bursting through to open air.

Instantly a deafening roar erupted. As my eyes adjusted to the brightness of the sun I found myself standing in an arena. The floor was hard with burning sand, encircled by a marble wall several feet high. Above this wall rose an army of marble bleachers, filled to the brim with humans. They cheered and yelled, all the while pointing down at me and laughing with each other. I got the feeling they were discussing my attributes. The way their faces leered reminded me of vultures watching a fight knowing they are going to get a carcass no matter who wins or loses. It wasn't comforting. But I didn't have long to think about it.

From the far end of the arena another gate swung open. A waft of musty air flew into my nostrils, thick with a greasy, dirty smell. A deep, heavy snort rumbled out of the dark cave. My claws dug into the sand. Senses poised, I listened and waited—tense and rigid. Before the paw had even smacked the arena floor—black and massive in the afternoon sun—I had already guessed what I was up against. The strong odor and lumbering movement was unmistakable. Pulling bit by bit against its own chain, looming from the dim hole like a monstrous, moving shadow, emerged a great black bear. Its matted fur was littered with scars; its eyes fierce and furious as they wandered around the arena. As the beast came into view the crowd gave a standing ovation. Then they started shouting. "Bulk! Bulk! Bulk!" The bear didn't notice them; its head had turned my way. The large, wet nose twisted about tasting my scent in the air. Then the eyes locked onto me. They turned deadly. The bear roared in sudden rage, its mouth gaping wide to reveal the broken, jagged teeth of a seasoned fighter.

Now you're in for it!

With nowhere to run and no way of escape, I braced myself against the ground, waiting for the beast to make the first move. It didn't take long. In a moment the bear charged: huffing, snarling, pounding into the ground with its fists. I did my best to swerve out of the way but the chain around my neck slowed me down giving the bear time to adjust its course. It was a nasty collision. The huge body rammed into mine with terrible impact knocking my wits loose for a moment. When I came to, its long nails were clawing into my rib cage. The crowd was on their feet. But the awful pain was awakening my own rage. Roaring as well, I reached up and sunk my teeth into my attacker's throat. There was a cheer from the audience as the bear reeled back stunned by the quick defense. Rising up on its hind legs it poised to strike a crushing blow to my head. But I was mad now; a savage instinct for survival had taken over my mind. With all the force in me I plunged right into the bear's belly knocking it backwards in a cloud of dust. As it rolled over to regain its feet I leapt onto the wide back clawing and biting—refusing to let go. Like a leech, I hung on no matter which way the animal squirmed pulling its flesh off like one peels a banana. I never gave the beast a chance; had it not been for the chain around my neck the bear would have been mutilated. But a severe yank tore me off, dragging me back towards the tunnel. I fought back in mad fury. But in the end iron proved stronger than rage. Wild-eyed and breathless I finally stood still and allowed my eyes to focus. The bear lay motionless on the bloody sand.

At first there was no sound. No laughter. No shouting. Nothing but an eerie quiet, as if the heartless crowd was actually speechless with horror. Then wild applause. Men started slapping hands, paying off wagers, and sloshing out barrels of wine in sloppy toasts—all the while pointing at me. Watching them my mind slowly returned; the full weight of what had just happened sunk in. I started feeling sick all over.

So this is "the Games". I gazed in disbelief at the celebrating crowd around me. I gazed in disbelief at what I had done. All my dignity, all my honor, all my ideals, was strewn over the red sand like ashes. And for what? Entertainment? An afternoon amusement? A life and death struggle that left a bear mangled and me as its butcher had been nothing more than a *show* for these people? With horror I searched the celebrating crowd looking for any sign of pity. All I saw was indifference plastered on their faces. And now, with their thirst for blood satisfied, the men began to leave. A swift jerk on my chain snapped my head around. Too weak to fight back and too broken to care, I finally just gave in—sucked like a limp insect back into the depths of the tunnel.

* * *

When the monkey returned that evening I was still limp, laid out on the floor of my cage. All that afternoon the horrible scene had replayed in my mind: the bear, the crowd, the red sand. I tried to tell myself it had been self-defense, that I was just a victim of circumstances. Yet somehow I knew it wasn't true. I could have pulled off of the bear when it went down, could have shown some kind of pity. But I hadn't. I let my anger blaze out of control and played right into the men's hands. Now an animal was dead because of it. Not from self-defense, or even self-provision. Just selfishness, through and through.

So I'm no better than Lena or Mantos, after all.

It was in the middle of this despair that Eddie appeared hopping along the cages with a bag swinging behind him. He landed overhead with a thump. "Hey Stripes! Brought you supper; hope you like lamb-chops. They weren't easy to get; let me tell you! That cook's got the biggest knife you ever saw! Good thing he's got a bigger belly; slows him down. Otherwise you'd be going hung—" he stopped short, finally getting a good look at me. "Whoa! What happened to you?"

I was too upset to respond; too ashamed of myself to even speak.

Leaving his bag up top, Eddie climbed down the cage bars like a ladder, "Guess you fought you're first game today. How'd it go?"

Still nothing came out.

"That bad, huh?" The monkey landed where he could look me in the eye. "Did'ya win?" He smiled, trying to cheer me up.

Finally, I brought myself to speak but the words came slow and painfully, "If you can call slaughtering a bear without mercy 'winning'."

All at once the smile vanished; for the first time since I had met him the monkey actually frowned. "A bear?" he asked anxiously, "What kind of bear?"

Dull from shame I replied, "Does it matter?"

"Wasn't black—was he? Big and black?"

Something in the monkey's voice made me raise my head. "Yes," I answered, surprised to see the worry on his face.

Eddie's hands were wringing together. "Scars everywhere?"

"Yes."

Now he was trembling. The monkey gripped the bars between us, pressing his face as close to my cage as he could. "And did..." his voice cracked, "did they shout *'Bulk, Bulk'*?"

The awful chant still rang in my ears. I said nothing, but my silence spoke louder than words. The monkey's eyes widened with sorrow and his lips started to quiver. He sat down on the floor, covered his head with his arms, and fell silent. After a few moments he spoke in a shaky voice, "That was his name: 'Bulk'. He was—my best friend."

I stared back. *Best friend? The only creature to show me kindness in this horrible place—and I just killed his best friend?* The thought was too much. It might have broken me, but a sudden clanking sound grabbed both of our attentions. Looking over to the cage on my left we saw the trap door had raised. The dark tunnel beyond echoed with heavy huffing and grunting. A familiar smell brought my head up. Eddie sat erect. Out of the darkness appeared a long, brown snout with a great black nose at the end of it.

FIFTEEN

"BULK!" THE MONKEY CRIED and sprang over to the cage. I rose to my feet in astonishment. Sure enough, the bear emerged out of the tunnel into the dim evening light, alive and on his own four paws! His steps were painfully slow and he groaned with each one, but, still, he was alive!

Eddie was beside himself with happiness; he kept jumping around, saying his friend's name over and over, along with things like, "You're alive! We thought you were a goner! What *happened*? Where were ya, anyway? Looked for days but couldn't find out where they'd took you—where *did* they anyway? Boy, you big galoot!" The bear tried to smile, but his face was drawn with pain. He limped to the side of his cage nearest mine and fell to the floor in a heap of black fur. I grimaced. All along his back were trenches of dried up blood. My claw marks.

"Easy there, Big Guy," the monkey climbed right next to his friend's head and stretched his skinny arm through the cage bars, "just take it easy—Eddie's here for ya." He stroked his friend's large forehead with his tiny hand, "How you feelin'?"

Bulk shifted with a moan. "Sore," he mumbled so weakly I could hardly make it out.

"You look..." Eddie hesitated. "Uh, you look—pretty good." There was a rumble as the bear tried to laugh, but then he groaned and shivered, his dirty coat shaking from head to foot. The monkey moved to the side to better inspect his friend's wounds.

"Bad?" The bear wheezed.

"Naw—just gives you character! Besides, all the ladies love a scar or two. Think they make you look buff," but though he sounded cheerful the monkey's face clouded with worry. He looked at me as if to say, *"You weren't playing around, were you?"*

A sniffing noise broke our concentration. Bulk's black nose was twisting around, tasting the air. He had caught my scent. "Who's that?"

The monkey stared at me. "Oh, um," he fumbled around, "just a new neighbor." I knew, however, the bear's sense of smell was far too good to have forgotten me that quickly.

Taking a deep breath I cleared my throat. "We met earlier today—in the arena."

Bulk shifted his head my way. His small eyes narrowed and expanded as he tried to make out my form in the dusky light. Then they closed. "Thought so," he huffed quietly. I wasn't sure what to say. *"Please forgive me"* stuck in my throat like bitter fruit. The words just seemed so empty. But then something incredible happened. With eyes still closed the bear smiled. In spite of his pain, Bulk actually chuckled and said, "You got a mean slash!"

I was stunned. Eddie burst out the breath he'd been holding and wiped his shaggy brow whistling in relief. "Aw, he just got you on an off day," the monkey laughed, ruffling the fur behind his friend's ear. "Just wait till you're back on your game; we'll see whose slash is meaner!" He looked at me, "Believe me, Stripes, Big Guy here could beat you any day of the week with paws tied together! They yell 'Bulk' for good reason: one of the greats! You just got him on the down beat."

I smiled, just relieved the bear was alive, "I believe it."

But Bulk grew somber. "Eddie," he groaned, "they starved me."

The monkey's smile vanished. "You mean—*on purpose?*"

The bear nodded his head as best he could. Eddie's body slumped and he hung limply from the bars. His brow knotted together again.

"What does that mean?" I asked, "After all, they starved me too."

"Yeah, but you're a rookie," the monkey explained, "They always starve rookies. But not Champs. Champs get treated like gods—fame, food, the works! They *never* starve Champs! Never! Not until—" he stopped short, obviously not wanting to go on.

"Til they're through," the bear finished.

"You're *not* through, Bulk!" His friend insisted, "You're just gettin' started! It was a mistake. That's it! Just a mistake. You'll see! Eddie'll fix it; he'll fix it if he has to go straight to Hittan..."

Before the words were out of his mouth the door of our prison flew open. The guards scurried to bow their heads to the floor, and in marched the Man-Beast, flanked by attendants. Eddie jumped behind a nearby crate as the other animals in the room shuffled in fear. Bulk and I were the only ones who didn't move. The giant approached, passed my cage, and stopped at Bulk's. For a while he scowled in silence, studying the wounded champion, towering like a dark tree over everyone and everything else around him. His attendants shuffled nervously while the same black raven squawked from his huge shoulder. "Silence, Crow!" He rumbled, waving the bird away. Then Hittan looked from Bulk to me. I pinned my ears back and a wicked smile spread across his face. "The bear is finished," he said at last, speaking to the men around him, "Have it moved to my tanner before sunset. But do not slaughter him until after the ceremony! All must be present for the sacrifices."

The what? I wondered.

His attendants bowed and the giant turned to leave. But as he passed by he glanced my way and murmured, "Let the Games begin!"

When the humans had gone I turned to Bulk still lying on his side, eyes staring blankly ahead, listless and empty. Hittan's sentence of death seemed to ring in the air.

"Forgive me, Bulk," the words felt small and dry in my mouth. The wave of guilt rushed back and I sank to the floor under its weight. "This is all my fault!"

"No it isn't—not really," Eddie's voice was bitter as he came out from behind the crate. "It's *theirs!* They do this on purpose—play everything, everyone, their way. That's why they call them 'games'. If they want you to lose, you lose; they want you to win, you win. Only no one ever really wins. No one—but *them*. It's how they keep control," his almond eyes flashed with anger and grief as they fell on his doomed friend, "and humans got'ta have control—*always!*"

For a while we sat in silence lost in our own thoughts. The dreariness around did not help matters. Outside the sky must have been overcast; very little light found its way through the narrow windows. The other animals were lifeless as ever. It was as if nothing in the world existed but that dim, hopeless room. At some point, however, a change began to occur, so slowly and subtle at first I didn't notice it. Yet it grew, and kept growing. At last I realized what it was.

Sunlight.

The clouds had parted enough to let it through. Even from those tiny windows the effect was strong warming the whole room with a soft, yellow glow. I felt its warmth. It brought strength to my legs. Standing up I shook off the dust of my cell. My eyes searched the crowded hall. "There *must* be a way out of here!"

Eddie shivered like he'd been awakened from a bad dream, "What?"

"Is there a way out of here? You know this city backwards and forwards; you told me so yourself. There *must* be a way out!"

"You mean—like escape?" The monkey's mouth dropped open.

"That's exactly what I mean!"

He started scratching his head and fidgeting nervously, "I don't know. No one's ever tried before—escape, I mean—at least not that I've heard. That is, no one's ever tried and made it. I'm not sure you even could..." he trailed off, muttering and chittering as only a monkey can. But then I remembered something he had said the day before.

"What about the sewers?"

"Huh?"

"The sewers. You mentioned something before about getting out of the city through the sewers."

"Oh, well, yeah—maybe—I mean, I guess it's possible. That was just an idea, though. You know—not really something I've tried before."

I became more determined. "But it is possible?"

"Maybe—could be—If you get to them. That's not super easy."

"But it *is* possible?"

He threw his hands in the air, "Sure it's *possible*. But *possible* don't mean *probable!* You can't just say 'I'm a huge striped lion and I want to sneak out of the biggest city in the world with a wounded bear and a blabbering monkey' and expect to do it no sweat! Besides," he added, "you got to *want* to escape first! And, like I said, I'm not leavin' Khanok. Humans are no great shakes, but they sure beat starving to death out there in a jungle somewhere—*or worse*—getting eaten myself (not all of us have claws the size of meathooks, you know)! No sir!" The shaggy arms crossed, "Eddie's a city-dweller, and in the city he's gon'na stay!"

I almost said something desperate when a groan broke in. Bulk began to stir. "Eddie," he said weakly, "the Dream!"

My head snapped around.
The Dream?

Every day I had been in the Barracks the Dream had continued to haunt me—sometimes in a black wave, sometimes in a sea of death—robbing me of whatever sleep I could have had. Womby had had a similar one. Even Mantos. Now the bear?

The monkey deflated in a second. "Oh no, Bulk!" He said quietly, "Not that!"

Bulk raised his heavy head off the floor, wincing in pain, "The Dream, Eddie."

His friend jumped to his side, "Easy, Big Guy. It can't be. It, it doesn't mean anything!"

"It does," Bulk argued, beginning to shake with excitement. "It does, Eddie. The Voice said so!"

The Voice! My heart started drumming. "What did it tell you?" I broke in eagerly. Eddie saw my face and his own filled with questions.

"You mean you've heard it, *too*?" He asked, wide-eyed.

I could barely breathe. "The Voice is why I'm here."

The maimed bear tried to rise to his feet, "I *told* you, Eddie—told you he'd come!" But his right paw was still too injured to hold his weight. With a moan he tumbled onto the floor.

"Take it easy, Bulk, will you!" the monkey pleaded, filled with concern for his friend.

But the bear would not relent. "Tell him, Eddie!" Wheezing and exhausted he looked up at the monkey, "*Please.*"

Eddie was distraught now, huffing and chattering, climbing and darting all around. But finally he wound up back on top of my cage. "For several nights," he began, "Bulk's been having this Dream. The same Dream..."

"And you," the bear added.

"Yeah, me too, but mine's a lot scarier. Don't wan'na talk about it. Anyway, in Bulk's Dream he's in this dark, noisy place. Then up ahead he sees a light. He goes towards it (or it comes to him, not sure which). The light gets bigger, till finally he sees something standing in the middle of it. Bulk says it's a big cat; he can't see any details though 'cause its back is turned to him. He stops a second. But then, out of nowhere, this—I don't know—*Voice* starts speaking. *'Bulk'*, it says, *'follow the cat.'* So Bulk does and the cat leads him through the light to a field full of green grass under a blue sky without any houses or buildings anywhere in sight (sounds awful to me, but not to him). Then he wakes up. And now he's sure some cat's gon'na come along and lead him to that bright, green place: 'the safe place', he calls it."

"But you're not?" I asked.

"What do I need a 'safe place' for? Khanok's 'bout as safe as you can get if you're quick with your hands and fast on the get-away. Long as this city's here I'm safe as I wan'na be." The monkey sounded confident but his face wrinkled with doubt.

"Your Dream, Eddie," Bulk reminded him. "The city. It falls..."

"Don't wan'na talk about it!" The monkey snapped, "Dreams don't mean anything, I tell ya. Just too many bananas before bed!"

The bear fell silent. Immediately Eddie regretted his words. "Sorry, Bulk," he dropped to the ground next to his friend, "but this place is my life. It's all I've ever known. Next to you, I guess you could say it's the only real friend I've ever had. I can't just leave it, you know. It'd be like—well—like dying, I guess."

I had said nothing during all this, listening and observing. But now I had to. "And what do you think will happen to Bulk, Eddie, if he stays here?" The monkey bit his lower lip. He looked at his friend lying stretched out in the cage. I kept my voice low. "We can't do this without you." Fear came into the almond eyes. Fear of what might happen to him if he left the city. Fear of what *would* happen to his friend if he stayed. Deep down Eddie knew I was right. Bulk and I could never make it out of Khanok without his help. But still he hesitated, unsure. Unwilling to let go of the only world he had ever known.

He didn't hear the guards coming from behind. Spears in hand, they closed in around Bulk's cage before any of us hardly knew what was happening. They started shouting and prodding demanding the bear get up on his feet. Bulk moaned in agony barely able to move. The jabs kept coming. The men were determined to drive him to his doom. I became furious, pacing back and forth, wanting to do something yet held back by my own cage bars. But not Eddie. As soon as he realized what was going on the monkey went wild. "NO!" he shouted, then flew onto one of the guards: biting, spitting, and pulling out any hair his hands could grab. "Leave him alone!" Eddie spat, "Stay away!" while doing everything and anything he could think of to try and draw them off his friend.

"Get off of me, you imp!" The guard fumed, grabbing at his attacker. At first Eddie was too quick for him, but then the gloved hand found its target. WHACK! The monkey went sailing off into a nearby pile of wood.

"Eddie!" Bulk groaned. But there was no answer. Eddie was out cold. The men kept shouting and jabbing. Finally the bear struggled to his feet. His left paw bent under him as he fought to step forward. The guards didn't even give him a chance to catch his breath.

"Go on! Get moving!" Head down, the bear limped forward. The stone slab in the cage wall lifted and he turned towards it. Back to the black tunnel; forced to march to his own death.

"Bulk!" I called out, feeling utterly helpless. The bear paused in front of the doorway and looked at me. He smiled sadly—a smile that made my insides ache. Then he shuffled out of sight. Eddie woke up just as the last of his friend's black fur was swallowed in shadow.

"NO! Bulk!" But his cry was lost in slamming stone as the doorway closed shut. All that remained was a cold, gray wall. Their job being done, the guards walked away kicking Eddie as they swaggered by. I don't think he even felt it. The monkey stood with his brown back facing me, shoulders slumped, arms drooping, staring at the empty cage of his friend. I sat down, heavy and miserable. All at once, Eddie spun around. His nostrils were flared. His rubbery jaw was set and his eyes flashed like he was about to give a speech. "Just remembered something," he said, "I don't like living in Khanok! Wan'na move—*right now!*"

SIXTEEN

TURNS OUT I WAS RIGHT about Eddie knowing an escape route. Once he made up his mind to leave, the monkey informed me he knew almost every inch of the Barracks and Game Arenas by heart, along with the rest of the city. He said the men had taken Bulk to a section called "The Tanner"—a grisly place where animals were butchered and skinned for Hittan's profit. As I listened I began to fear we would be too late to save the bear even if we could come up with a plan.

"Uh-uh," Eddie shook his head, "if this was any other night, maybe, but not tonight. You heard the giant. Tonight's the offerings—the opening ceremonies. No one dares miss the opening ceremonies for the Spectacle." He went on to explain "The Spectacle" was the highpoint of the Games, the championship, when once a year the land of Nod gathered to watch the best of the best compete. "What you've seen so far is nothin' compared to the Spectacle. Man's glory at its best. And worst. That's how come nobody will do anything to Bulk till after the ceremonies are over. No one misses the offerings—it's law." I was about to ask what an "offering" was but he moved on too quickly. "That'll be the time to jump. Nobody'll be in the tannery. I'll sneak in, set Bulk free, and find our way to the sewer before anybody knows we're gone," he gulped, "I hope!"

Sounded good enough, but I still had one question, "What about me?"

Eddie held his forefinger to his chin a moment and scrunched his face, thinking. Then he started rubbing his hands together. "Might work," he chattered to himself, "Complicated, tricky—really long shot. But it just might work!"

The afternoon sped away as we discussed our plans. The yellow light overhead became more intense and the shadows began to deepen. We decided on a scheme that was desperate to say the least. But it was a chance. And that was enough for me. We were right in the middle of finalizing details when, all at once, a horn blasted through the air making such a horrible sound shivers ran down my spine. Eddie leapt away and nimbly climbed up whatever he could get his hands on to one of the skylights overhead. The russet glow of a setting sun lit his flat face as he peered out of the window. "It's started," he called down. "The Spectacle."

Another horrible blast rang out. The monkey covered his ears and I groaned out loud. "What is that?" I exclaimed. The jarring, mournful sound seemed to cut right through me.

Eddie's brows furrowed together as he replied, "The call to the opening ceremonies."

My nostrils caught the scent of fire like a thousand torches being lit. Then a hum of noise outside gradually started to swell, growing till it was a virtual storm of voices. A huge crowd must have been gathering just outside the Barrack walls.

"What is happening out there?" I called up, both curious and unnerved by the torrent of sound.

The monkey looked at me, clearly troubled, but turned his gaze back out the window. "You don't wan'na know."

A deep rumble shook the floor I stood on—the rumble of a giant gong. For a moment everything went deathly quiet. Then a singular voice began floating down through the skylights. I couldn't make out words because of how it echoed off the stone walls, but it seemed to be saying something of great importance. There was a thunderous response as the whole crowd shouted "So be it!" Then the voice started up again.

"Who's speaking?" I wanted to know, "What are they saying?"

"Hittan," Eddie replied, never taking his eyes off the sight beyond the window. Something evil was happening; I could feel it under my skin. An eerie presence seemed to dominate the very atmosphere. I started holding my breath as if waiting for some invisible dam to break, hoping it would not sweep me away with it when it did.

A scream split the air. Solitary, desperate, pierced with terror. One long, helpless shriek followed by—nothing. It chilled me from head to tail. Then the silence was broken by a mighty cheer. Fearing the worst, I looked up at Eddie. His eyes met mine then dropped to the ground. "The offerings," he mumbled.

Another scream and eruption of applause. My stomach began to turn as I started to realize what was happening. The crowd was actually applauding the death of their own kind!

Eddie turned from the window, disgust written all over his face. "I hate this part!" He moaned, "Maybe even if they were full-grown it wouldn't be so bad. But they're so young..." a pitiful cry broke in, so high-pitched it must have come from something very small. More mad cheering. Hittan's awful voice started chanting and the crowd joined in like the droning of a million bees. I shuddered. More screams, more cheers. The monkey glanced out the window one last time. "Every Spectacle they do this." Shaking his head sadly Eddie dropped to the floor, "Ironic. The whole country comes together to celebrate the best of the best, but if you ask me they kill off the best of them before they're old enough to even have a chance! Just makes no sense!"

My mind was filled with horror. "*Why?*" I asked breathlessly, finding it hard to believe even humans could do such a thing, "What would make them kill their own young?" I remembered how hard my mother and father had fought to keep me alive as a cub. Even then I had still been the only one of three siblings to survive to adulthood. How could any creature deliberately *kill* their own offspring? It was beyond comprehension!

Eddie pointed upward where the rafters were burning with the glow of sunset. "The sun," he said simply.

"What?"

"They think the sun wants them to. That's why they do it. I know it's crazy, but humans worship the sun like a god. And the moon and stars. Plus the ocean, rivers, trees, birds, animals—well, basically everything. They're obsessed. But especially the sun. So at sunset they kill things: animals, people, whatever. They call them 'sacrifices'. And since the Spectacle is such a huge thing they make a big deal of it—throw parties, have feasts—then bring some of the best and the brightest of their young together to the opening ceremonies and..." the monkey hung his head. "Craziest part is they think it's a good thing. They say the sun takes the sacrifices to heaven and blesses the land. That's why they cheer; they think they're doing their kids a favor." As if on cue another massive applause shook the walls, making the cage bars ring.

My mind was filled with horror. Yet one thing still puzzled me, "But if the sun is God, who made the sun?"

Eddie shrugged, "Ask the humans. They're the ones who claim to know everything." Then he snapped his fingers, "Got'ta move—before they finish and come for Bulk!" The monkey took off, calling over his shoulder, "Remember, Stripes: all you got'ta do is win!"

In a blink he was gone, leaving me alone to listen to the carnage outside. I found myself getting angry. We were slaves of creatures who murdered their own young! What might they do to us? Somehow, someway, we had to get out of there; I could not live within the same walls as such monsters!

Little did I know how quickly I would have a chance at turning that resolve to reality. Soon the door at the end of the room burst open and in charged those same guards, armed with those same wretched poles. But this time I knew what to expect. Leaping up I waited impatiently for the door behind me to rise. As soon as the gap between it and the floor was large enough I darted inside. The same black emptiness engulfed me, the same violent men goaded me on, but this time I was ready for them. A sharp anticipation pulsed in my veins. This time it was purpose, not fear, that met the darkness. This time I would not fight to survive.

I would fight to be free.

SEVENTEEN

THE TUNNEL TWISTED a different direction than when I had been in it before (a wall must have been raised to turn me a different way). I felt myself going uphill. These new walls were smooth and very close, blocking any chance of turning around. Smells flew into my nose: trace odors of bears, lizards, other cats, and every kind of strange beast. I was not the first victim herded through the tiny space. I would probably not be the last. But every step fueled my determination that—no matter what—I would never pass that way again myself! Pretty soon another sensation hit me, one that wiped out all others in a moment: the clamor of a hundred thousand voices ricocheting from up ahead. It was the crowd, that infamous crowd. The Great Arena—largest of all arenas for the Games—was close.

A sharp grating sound fell in behind me. I couldn't turn, but as it drew closer and closer I realized what it was: one of the walls of this underground maze was speeding my way, closing in fast!

They're pushing me from the rear!

Now there really was nowhere to go but forward. I jumped ahead and ran towards the roar, towards the unknown. Fear and hope collided within and I felt the impact charge every stride. *Kill it!* I told myself over and over. *Whatever it is, just kill it! That's all you have to do.* Once again, freedom hung on the skill of my claws. All else was a blur till I finally faced the iron gate barring me from entering the arena. The rushing wall stopped just before it clipped my tail—locking me between it and the gate. The sound outside was unbelievably loud! Time seemed to freeze as I held my breath, waiting.

The gate sprung up and the wall shoved from behind thrusting me through to the outside! I felt the cool night breeze, smelled the open air. It was full of the aroma of men, but all I could see were the glare of torches overhead and more walls, only these walls were not made of rock but of leaves, growing as towering green hedges all around. Above them arched the black night sky. The sight and scent of something so organic and alive shocked me. I hesitated. A sharp object flew down from somewhere overhead, sailing over top of the green walls. It stung my hindquarters.

Then another and another; people were hurling glasses and bottles! I couldn't see them for the leafy walls, but there must have been hundreds of thousands filling the marble stands of the Great Arena; as soon as I moved they started cheering in a sheer ocean of sound. Quickly I followed the path between the hedges. It led like a maze, swerving back and forth—always curving inward. As I followed it deeper and deeper, my apprehension grew. Every corner I turned gave me a greater feeling something was lurking just on the other side; every empty path I met just increased it. One thing was for sure: I hadn't been forced in there for a pleasure stroll. Sooner or later I would meet up with whatever else was in that maze, and it would try to kill me. The further I went the quieter the crowd became; they were also waiting for something. What's more, I was sure they *saw* something, something I could not. The expectation in the atmosphere grew so strong you could taste it.

Slowly rounding a final green hedge, I entered an open circle surrounded completely by green walls except for another opening about thirty feet across from where I stood. The circle was empty, but through the opening I could see the end of another maze.

Perfectly scripted, I thought. *They are leading us right to each other.*

I glanced around the pit of green walls and sand. The glaring light of the mounted torches flickered against the trimmed, glossy leaves. Their effect made me nervous; every moving shadow turned into an enemy.

"Where are you?" I challenged under my breath. Two things answered at once. A scent, warm and near. And the slight snap of a branch above and behind me.

The wall! My senses screamed. *Look up!*

But before I had the chance a crushing weight fell onto my back! The impact of the force pinned me to the ground. I tasted sand. Sharp incisions sank into the back of my neck. An explosion of pain surged through me almost hurling me into a total black-out. The crowd erupted. Rolling over I twisted to break free from the killer gripped onto my spine. It hung on tight. I couldn't see it, but I felt the hot breath and growl of a lion rumble against my back. Thrashing and tumbling, I was locked in a death crawl. The pressure of those jaws around my neck kept drawing in tighter and tighter. Having used the same tactic, I knew I had to break free or my neck would snap in seconds! With a desperate lash I reached behind making a blind swipe for the cat's head. A yowl of pain pierced my ears; the fierce grip loosened. It was all I needed. Instantly I shook free and spun to face my opponent: fangs bared, claws out, ready to buy my freedom with their life!

Then I stopped cold.

There before me, panting and wild-eyed, crouched a lioness; her white fur stained dark from the oozing wound on her face. My wrath turned to shock and I stumbled back a step or two. At the same moment her own snarl vanished. We both stared.

"Saphirra!"

"Sengali!"

What are you doing here? I thought in dismay. Her body trembled with adrenaline and I could tell by her open mouth the lioness was thinking the same thing. *Where's Womby? How did you even get here? Never mind—now what do I do?* all raced through my head in seconds. Our escape plan was falling apart right in front of me. I had come prepared to kill, to mutilate, to do whatever it took to buy a chance of escaping from this nightmare. But now?

Kill Saphirra?

A thought hit my head. *Maybe Lena was right. Maybe she is just a lying manipulator! She could be manipulating me even now!*

But kill Saphirra?

Gazing at the lioness I saw the same look in her eyes I had seen when Womby fell into the trap. The same uncertainty, the same vulnerability. Under that deadly exterior was something young and fragile. Whatever she was, she was not like her father or sister. I could see honor in her. Even now, when the lioness could have used my shock to her advantage, she refused to move, staring back at me with eyes showing the same dilemma mine did. In that moment, neither of us wanted to move. In that moment, without a word, we realized we respected each other. And in that moment, I was faced with a terrible decision.

The crowd grew impatient, their cheers turning to shouts. We were ruining their show. Fear sprang into Saphirra's blue eyes, fear and desperation. She might still kill me if she had to. My desire for survival surged back as well. *So what if I know the lioness? Freedom, Sengali! Just one fight and it's over: no more slavery, no more slaughter. Just one victim to please the masses, and then no more: not ever again. I'll be free! It's her life or mine!*

But kill Saphirra?

Our eyes locked again, and my resolve stumbled. It was unfair: an impossibly unfair situation we had been forced into. The options made me sick to the core. But I *did* still have an option. I had a choice. It was the one freedom no man or beast could ever take from me.

"Saphirra," I managed over the booing and shouting, "I don't know how you got here—there's no time to find out—but what I need to know is: if you had a way to escape, would you take it?" Her look of shock returned but I could not wait, "Would you?"

"Yes," she replied quickly, her voice shaky but strong enough to be heard.

My choice was made. "Alright, listen to me carefully. Somewhere under this arena is a tunnel—the Victor's Tunnel—and somewhere inside that tunnel is a drain. Uh, like a large hole in the floor," I explained, using the same words Eddie had used with me earlier. "Under the drain is a sewer of water that empties outside the walls of the city. I have friends, a bear and a monkey, who are (hopefully) waiting there to escape with me where the sewer meets the daylight." I swallowed hard, "You go. Take my place. It may be your only chance!"

The roar of the angry mob swirled like a cyclone around us but Saphirra was wide-eyed and still. "How do I know I can trust you?" She finally asked, a wary look in her pale face.

"Because I have to trust you." I did not mince words, "To get to the Victor's Tunnel you have to *be* a victor. You have to win. And the only way for you to do that is to pretend to kill me," my mouth felt dry, "I would say that evens the risk for both of us!"

The young lioness didn't answer, but as the reality of what I was saying sunk in, a remarkable change took place. All traces of fear shed from her face like clouds vanishing before the moon. Her features became soft, even humble. "You would do this? For me?"

In the midst of the turbulence, on the verge of forever losing everything I had ever hoped for, a new feeling suddenly gripped me: terribly painful, yet incredibly sweet. The sight of the lovely creature before me, so full of hope and gratitude, cut straight to my heart. Never in my life had I seen anything more beautiful, and I knew I would never see it again. "We need to move," I pressed, trying to shake off the sensation, "quick..."

"But how do I find your friends? And what if they don't believe me? They are waiting for you!"

"'Follow the water; it'll lead you to daylight'," I said, quoting the instructions Eddie had given me. Then I paused. "Take care of them for me, especially the bear." A lump formed in my throat, "Tell them Sengali said to follow the Voice—for his sake." A spark of wonder lit the clear eyes and pity washed over her white face. It was too much for me. "Now go! Hurry!"

Without another word Saphirra charged, reared on her hind legs, and lowered a blow to my face that might have killed me had she not retracted her claws. When I recovered from seeing stars I was on my side in the dust. The fickle crowd had changed moods again, cheering thunderously, pleased by the sudden attack. I glimpsed the lionesses' white form headed for the open path she had come out of. Yet before she reached it she stopped and glanced back at me. A faint, grateful smile graced her mouth. Then she disappeared behind the green wall.

Slowly I closed my eyes. My throbbing head hit the sandy floor. Despair flooded over me like the black wave in my Dream. I had given up my chance of escaping the nightmare.

My only hope of freedom was gone.

EIGHTEEN

BOOM!
All at once the ground shivered.
Boom-BOOM!
Something was happening underneath my body. My ears caught the sound of gears grinding together.

Suddenly the green walls started rushing straight down sinking into the sand! One second they were there, the next they had disappeared under the floor! I struggled to my feet as the face of the arena changed before my eyes. Instead of a green maze was now a long dusty wasteland, encircled by a marble wall twice as wide and three times as high as any I had seen so far. It was like standing in the middle of a desert enclosed by sheer cliffs. I turned to my right to see Saphirra on the far end like a small white statue, staring around the same way I was. We both were thinking the same thing.

Now what?

The crowd was deafening. Then, on the opposite end of the arena, to my left, part of the wall started to rise. Even from where I stood I could see something moving under the crack it left: something huge, brown, and scaly.

Oh no!

The wall flew up and my worst fears were realized as a hideous, gigantic, reptilian head emerged into view! Jagged teeth, a crown of pointed horns, eyes like a dark morning, an armor of iron plates for skin—a dragon, the likes of which I had never seen before. Slowly the monster pulled itself into the arena, walking erect on its two massive hind legs. Its long tongue licked the air. The black eyes found me and the monster let loose a roar that felt like it would split my ears wide open. The humans screamed with delight, *"Razor-Claw! Razor-Claw!"* I looked at Saphirra on the other end; she stared back in fear. It was then I realized I was the only thing standing between her and the dragon. No other doors had opened. The walls could not be scaled. There was no way out.

Except to fight.

"Saphirra!" I shouted, "Don't move!" The dragon started towards me: slow and easy at first, marching back and forth, stalking its prey. I stood my ground and waited. The ugly claws started picking up their pace as the tree-like tail whipped from side to side.

Another piercing shriek and the monster came right for me, barreling down the arena at terrible speed! Bracing myself against the floor I felt the earth shake under its weight. The short arms disappeared from view as the dragon lowered its fore-body to attack position. The great jaws gaped open, dripping saliva, ready to swallow me up! I sprang to the right and the huge mouth dug into the ground where I had just been. Twisting around as fast as my legs could turn I ducked under the monster's tail. It spun in anger, hacking sand. I kept under that tail. For a few moments we just turned in circles: it slashing around with its claws and me trying to keep out of their way. Then suddenly the thing jumped! Not very high, but enough to throw me out in the open. The dragon came down with fangs barred and I darted out of the way. Now it was behind me! Running was my only option. I sprinted down the arena towards the gate the monster had come from. Just as I reached the wall, it slammed shut. I spun around poised for another attack. But to my horror I saw the dragon was not there. It had turned during the chase and was now headed the other way—towards Saphirra! My heart stopped as I watched the lioness press herself against the opposite wall with nowhere to run. A few more seconds and the monster would have her in its jaws!

I ran towards the center of the arena with everything I had. Filling my lungs with all the air they could hold I let loose a roar echoing like thunder in

A CAT'S TALE

the marble coliseum. It did the trick. The dragon stopped, looking around. My roar bounced off the walls in every direction, made even more maddening by the noise of the crowd. I didn't wait for it to find me. Charging forward I leapt onto the dragon's back. It was slick with scales and incredibly thick. The beast screamed more from anger than pain, like a warthog stung by a bee. Saphirra dodged to the side out of harm's way. "Run!" I called to her, "Find a way out of here!" She hesitated. "Go!" The dragon slammed itself into the wall trying to shake me lose. It felt like everything inside my body was knocked out of place. *Ooomph!* Again I was rammed against solid stone! And again, and again. My senses started to black out.

Suddenly, I realized we had pulled away from the wall. The giant lizard was scratching with its claws at the ground turning and ducking to try and get at something under its belly. Then I heard a hiss between its legs.

Saphirra!

She was underneath the monster! The entire coliseum was on their feet now in excitement. Razor-Claw swerved and jumped to try and see the lioness, but the quick female kept right underneath slashing at the feet as she could. Now was the time for me to move. Hanging on for dear life, I pulled myself up the dragon's back. The infuriated beast roared but kept its attention on trying to get at Saphirra. I reached the huge neck. Wrapping my back legs around its shoulder blades and planting my front claws right behind the holes of the dragon's ears, I braced myself—then sunk my jaws into its spine. For the first time the dragon screamed in real pain. It jerked almost straight up. Still I clung. If my teeth found the spinal cord we might have a chance! The raging beast took off in a dead sprint down the arena. I clamped down tighter, digging my canines deeper. It darted, spun, twisted, swerved, pounded into walls. By all rights I should have never been able to hang on. Yet somehow I did. I knew when my incisors found the nerves wrapped around the massive bones.

And I felt it when they snapped.

A mind-numbing shriek escaped the dragon. It whipped its head violently and I flew off, landing with a thud on the ground near a curve in the wall. Saphirra was by my side in a second, helping me up.

"Are you alright?" She asked. I leaned against her to stand on shaky legs and watched as the dragon thrashed around, still on its feet. It couldn't last much longer. "What do we do know?"

"Wait," I replied breathlessly.

All at once a piece in the wall right next to us opened up! A small, hidden door. A gray wolf appeared out of the darkness, standing just beyond the light of the arena, hidden from sight of the crowd.

"Quick!" it barked. "In here!"

I didn't know who it was or why it was there but for once I was glad to see a dog! "Go!" I urged

Saphirra. She took off and in no time her tail disappeared into the safety of the tunnel. I followed behind. My front paw had just stepped into shadow when a pain beyond description suddenly gripped my sides! Dozens of jagged objects wrapped around my ribcage like knives, digging into my flesh like meat-hooks. I felt myself drug along the sand then lifted into the air. One moment of suspension, caught between earth and sky, and a view passed of a hundred thousand human faces, lit by ghostly lanterns, leering with awe and delight.

I heard Saphirra scream, "Sengali!"

Then my body was flung from side to side like a rag doll. When the awful grip finally loosened I felt myself fly free through the air, crash against a wall, and tumble limp to the sandy floor. It was like being in a dream. All sound stopped; I heard nothing. Everything moved in slow motion. I watched as the dragon tottered, having used its last strength on me. It was dead even before the massive body crashed to the ground. Then my vision went; everything blurred. My breath became labored as blood leaked out of the wounds in my sides.

In moments my entire life seemed to flash before my eyes. The place where I was born: a den of thick vines twisted together like a bower overhead. The quiet pool where I spent hours learning to fish with my Mother. Homeless as a young adult, driven away to make my own place in the world. And then—

seeing my mountain for the first time. In vivid color it all came back: emerald green, azure blue, golden yellow. Glorious sunrises, perfect sunsets. The clear, babbling stream. Pure, fresh air, delicious with a thousand different smells. I was there again: standing on my cliff, gazing out over the sea of green treetops, a soft breeze blowing from the east. Peace overwhelmed me. I was home. I was safe.

But, like a thing too good to be true, the vision disappeared. In its place came darkness: thick and heavy and final. I knew I was dying. And then it all faded.

NINETEEN

A SOUND BROUGHT ME OUT of the blackness, one I hardly recognized at first because it had been so long since I heard it. Birds singing. Then trees sighing in the wind. Slowly I found I could open my eyes. Sunlight rushed in and for a moment I was blinded.

Am I dreaming again?

My eyes adjusted. The first things they made out were bars standing in front of my face.

More bars.

Yet these were different somehow: they were flat and wooden and smelled like fresh cedar. Then my eyes focused on what was beyond them. I gasped in so sharply it hurt. Blinking, I looked again to make sure I wasn't imagining things. But no. It was still there.

Green!

The color green was everywhere! Green ferns, green bushes, and short, green grass all sprawled out over a sandy, shaded landscape. There were tree trunks, too: shaggy pillars, topped with palm branches waving in the morning breeze, sheltering the oases below. Another sound met my ears: gurgling water. I tried raising my head to have a look around. Amazingly, it not only raised, but the fiery pain was gone! I was exhausted and horribly sore, but that was all!

"I must be dreaming!" I mumbled out loud.

"Not unless you talk in your sleep."

My head spun round and I found myself face to face with the keenest pair of blue eyes I had ever seen. Their icy depths flashed with a powerful intelligence set in a chiseled silver and white face that neither smiled nor frowned. It was stoic, confident, and wary: the face of a male wolf. His muscles were firm and wiry under his full, silky coat, a mark of endurance as well as strength; and his long legs were supported by large, great paws. Though he sat on the other side of the cage I judged the wolf to be a little smaller than I was, about the size of Lena. But what he lacked in stature he made up for in presence, and at the moment all of it was directed towards me.

"Who are you?" I huffed, not used to having to talk again, "What do you want with me?" The wolf didn't answer, yet in a moment his gray fur triggered my memory. "Wait—*You?* I just saw you—in the Arena!"

The wolf nodded gravely, "Among other places."

I tried standing up, but my head reeled. When my ears finally stopped ringing I suddenly remembered Saphirra. "The lioness?" I asked anxiously, "What happened to her?"

"She left," the wolf explained, and his voice was as deep as you would expect a male wolf's voice to be, "Got out through the sewers."

So Saphirra had escaped after all! I was surprised at how relieved I felt. But it did not linger; my curiosity turned to the wolf. Somehow I had the feeling I had seen him even before the arena. "Who are you?" I asked again, "Why were you helping us?"

The wolf's expression never changed. "I do my Master's bidding."

There was a sudden, high whistle from behind. The wolf's large ears perked forward and he bolted past me. I turned to see a small, colorful tent pitched next to a running brook flowing into a calm pool of water. The tent's doorway was covered by an ornate, textured flap; this rose from the inside and out stepped a man. He was younger than most I had seen, not nearly as large as Hittan or even the guards I had encountered. But he was strong. Firm muscles shone under his simple tunic, and his rolled up sleeves revealed arms used to hard work. His skin was smooth and deep brown. His eyes were dark and his hair was darker, but his face brightened with a wide smile as the wolf approached.

"Good morning, Nathak!" He greeted as the wolf yipped happily, fairly colliding with his legs, "How are you boy?"

'Nathak'? I wondered. *Why does that sound familiar?* The man's voice also seemed to trigger a vague memory. Actually, everything about him made me feel like I had seen him before, but I could not recall where. Now the man was rubbing the wolf all over. Nathak wagged his tail and playfully nipped at his Master's hand. I stared, dumbfounded. Not once in all my encounters with man had I seen them on even pleasant terms with an animal. These two, however, were positively friendly!

"And how is our patient this morning?" The man looked my way and his black eyebrows rose, "So, you awake at last!" I started to bristle, but then something checked me. His glance seemed different than other humans I had seen. Bold, but not threatening. The wolf fell into step at the man's side and they approached my cage. I drew back. When just beyond reach of my claws, the man crouched down bringing himself to my level. I was struck by the depth of emotion in his eyes. There was memory. And grief. As if the sight of me brought something—or someone—else to his mind. Then a slight movement at his neck distracted me. As the man stooped, a small object, dangling on a leather string, shook loose from behind the folds of his tunic. An ivory amulet, carved in the form of a tree in full bloom.

If the thing had been carved of brick and swung right into my face it could not have hit me any harder.

The Tree!

He was wearing the Tree! I had not seen it since the fateful night in the garden with the old man when the Voice had spoken out loud. In a flash it all came back: fighting with Lena, men shouting, glaring torches, the demon wolf. That's when it dawned on me.

The wolf!

With a sharp glance I looked at the dog standing nearby. *The wolf in the garden!* My mind sped back to that night: Lena disappearing over the rock wall, the angry mob moving in, a pair of razor teeth grabbing my right shoulder. Then someone shouting, "Nathak! Nathak, off!"

"Nathak"! I glared into the man's eyes. *That's what you just called the wolf!* Finally I recognized him: the young man in the garden, the one who had drawn off the wolf—and probably the one who had struck me with some kind of sleeping dart, because the next thing I had known was falling out of a tree and waking up on a slave block! My defenses flew up. My eyes went from the Tree, to the wolf, to the man, and back to the Tree. A growl rumbled from within.

What do they want with me now?

"No need for that." The man spoke firmly, though not necessarily cruelly, "You are in no danger here. Let us just have a look at your wounds," and he slowly stretched out his hand towards my back. With a hiss I swiped at him through the bars. The wolf instantly flashed his teeth and charged at me. "No Nathak!" The man shouted, grabbing his fur and pulling him backwards, "No!" He gripped the wolf's large head and forced him to look into his eyes, "Would you have me break my promise! *Stay!*" Nathak dropped his ears and sank to the ground. The man turned to me again. "Perhaps I deserved that," he admitted, rubbing a new scratch on his left hand, "if not for me you might not even be here. For that I am truly sorry. Then something strange happened. Wetness came to the brown eyes. His voice actually trembled. "You gave me a chance to say goodbye." Quickly the young man's calloused fingers ran over his face, like he was trying to wipe something away, "At least let me thank you for that." I watched in wonder as he rose and quickly disappeared into the tent.

It was the first time I had seen a human cry.

Soon he re-emerged, carrying two dead pheasants by their necks. "I imagine you might enjoy these," he said and threw the birds (from a safe distance) at my feet. Their aroma was sweet, wild, and fresh enough to drive me mad with hunger had I not been so distracted watching the man. Nathak did the same, following his Master's every move, while never budging from where he had been told to "stay". The human stooped by the stream, filled a small clay bowl with clear water, and carried it to the creek bank. There a large, curious rug was spread on the ground, covered from corner to corner with neatly stacked piles of dried herbs, flowers, and other fauna. Carefully choosing a small, star-shaped leaf the man crushed it in his strong hand. Then adding some delicate, white petals he dropped the mixture into the bowl. Still carrying it, the man slowly re-approached my cage. His eyes never left mine. "You need not fear this," he whispered, bravely reaching through my bars to set the bowl in front of me, "it will help the pain." I saw the wolf tense up ready to spring at the slightest movement on my part. His worries were unnecessary; the smell of water so close drove every other thought from my head. My tongue soaked up each drop, and, though there was not much of it, the sweet water was amazingly refreshing. With my thirst quenched, my hunger took over and I tore into the pheasants. They were superb! The delicious meat seemed to go into every inch of me. When finally the last tiny bone had been picked clean a heavy drowsiness set in. Batting my eyes I looked around. The man and wolf were nowhere to be seen, though I heard them at a distance. Long shadows crept from the palm trees as the sun shifted towards the west. The oases grew sleepy and still. An evening bird perched on some nearby bushes and started twittering a lullaby. For the first time in more days than I cared to count, I felt at peace. Sleep overtook me: wonderful, restful sleep. And, remarkably, something happened that had not happened since the night I rescued Womby.

There was no Dream.

TWENTY

WHEN I AWOKE the shadows of the trees had changed directions. The lone bird had been replaced by a chorus of morning songs and the sun had moved to the eastern sky. It is an odd feeling as a cat to realize you slept the whole night through, but this once I didn't mind. The soreness in my sides was all but gone, and my whole body felt like it had slept a hundred nights. I stood to my paws, relishing the feeling of strength in my legs. My lungs drank in the fragrance of morning as my eyes took in the clean, fresh light. There in the beauty of earth re-awakened I could almost believe the misery of the past few weeks had just been a nightmare and dawn had come at last.

But I was still surrounded by bars.

As I stood listening another song joined in with the music of the birds. It was light and weighty at the same time, coming from behind me. I turned to see the young man kneeling by the stream. His muscular arms held a large water skin under the clear flow while his mouth sang words I had never heard before. I could not understand what they meant, but the very sound of them felt like a clean, mountain breeze blowing through my heart. I stared at him intently. Who was he? Where had he come from? And why was he being kind to me? After all the cruelty I had seen of mankind in general, this noble, frank, honorable human did not even seem to belong to the same race. He had fed me, healed me. But why? What did any human stand to gain by helping a half-dead wild beast? As the man turned to reach for another water skin I caught a glimpse of the Tree. It flashed in the sunlight much like it had gleamed by firelight that night in the garden. Then it had rested on the frail chest of an old man; now it hung from the sinewy neck of youth. What was it? What did it mean? All I really knew about the Tree was that Mantos hated it, which was one thing in its favor. But what did it stand for? And why did my destiny seem so interwoven with it?

All these thoughts were running through my mind when my ears caught the soft fall of footsteps behind me. The wolf emerged from some underbrush growing around the oasis, his coat shimmering in the morning haze, fir wet with dew.

He loped over, sat down next to my cage—and completely ignored me.

Typical canine, I mused, *no manners whatsoever.* "Uh," I stammered, trying to be polite, "I don't believe we have actually introduced ourselves. My name is Senga—"

"He saved your life, you know," the wolf interrupted, gaze following his Master, "the least you could do is show some respect!"

"Is that supposed to be an introduction?"

The glacial blue eyes locked on mine. "I have no wish to be friends, *cat*," Nathak growled, making sure to emphasize that last word. "This was not my idea. But he deserves better than you have given him; he deserves better than you could ever give him."

I watched as the man carried the dripping water skins into the tent. "Who is he, anyway?"

"A Man of the Tree," Nathak replied quietly, almost with awe, "and a better one never lived. From a pup he raised me. He is the best of Masters and of men." The wolf directed all his intensity towards me, "And I will never allow any harm to come to him; not while I live!"

Despite being the brunt of this threat I had to admire the dog's loyalty (*perhaps* the only thing dogs do better than cats). But it still didn't answer the questions rolling around in my head. "Why do you say he saved my life?"

"Because he did. If not for my Master you would be dead by now; probably a rug for Hittan to wipe his boots on." He studied me intently, "You don't remember?"

"Am I supposed to?"

The wolf paused like he had not thought of that before. "No," he huffed reluctantly, "I suppose you couldn't have. Not after the dragon got through with you. My Master bought you from Hittan."

"'Bought' me?" I echoed in surprise. "Why?" Recalling the bleeding, dying condition I had been in after the games, the idea anyone would have wanted me for anything, let alone pay money for me, was unbelievable.

"Because of a promise." Nathak looked up; a golden dawn was melting to blue beyond the green palm branches. "Several nights ago you attacked an old man in a garden—"

"I did not attack him!"

The wolf ignored me, "That man was my Master's Great-Grandfather. My Master shot you with a sleeping dart and left you with the other men. If he had not been so concerned for the Great-Father he would have killed you on the spot. But as the Old One lay dying, he told my Master you had actually saved his life. He made my Master promise to make certain no harm came to you. 'Be it judgment or mercy,' he said, 'His justice is for all creatures.'" The wolf had a far-off look in his eye as he added, "They were the last words the Great-Father spoke. Since then my Master has not ceased looking for you, tracing you to Khanok at the risk of his own life. He heard of Hittan's new champion that had mastered the bear," the wolf noticed me cringe but continued, "and when my Master learned of your upcoming duel with the lioness and dragon he formed a plan of escape for you both, if you would take it."

"The tunnels," I nodded. "But how did you get access to them?"

"Men without principles are easily bribed," he shrugged, "and arena guards are especially short on principles. But after the rescue failed, my Master's only hope was to buy you from Hittan before you were skinned. It was dangerous and costly. The giant has no love for my Master or his family and he'd lost a great deal in wagers on account of you. Apparently *you* killing the dragon wasn't part of his plan. But my Master made him an offer he couldn't resist. It cost him every coin he had." The wolf's eyes softened as he watched his Master only to harden again when they turned on me. "Now he's spent four days in this place: four days of very precious time (which he doesn't have) to heal you, when other things of far greater importance weigh on his mind."

I sat down. My own eyes followed the man now carefully loading the dried vegetation on the rug into earthen containers. "You mean he actually came looking for me?" I asked softly.

The wolf nodded, "My Master never breaks a promise."

I could see it now: a resemblance so strong I wondered how I had not noticed it before. Looking at him was like looking at a mirror of the old man, only much younger. His features were darker, of course, smoother and more robust on the outside; but inwardly they were made of the same mettle. The same depth of wisdom, the same strength of spirit shone from this man's eyes as it had shown from his Great-Grandfather's. It left no doubt in my mind Nathak's story was true. It did not, however, make it any easier to believe. *Why?* I marveled. After all of the cruelty I had seen, all the violence and selfishness— why would these men be any different? How *could* they be? "I did not know such men existed."

"None do," Nathak explained, "except those of the Tree."

'Those'? That word caught my attention, "You mean there are more?"

"And how is the patient this morning?" The man broke in. A warm smile lit his face as he neared my cage. "Well, I must say, you look much better!" Leaning down to observe my wounds through the bars he added, "Another day and you should be as good as new. But you, Nathak," he addressed the wolf playfully, "you should not torture our patient with freedom he cannot have. Not yet, anyway." That last part the man meant for me, and from the glow in his brown eyes I gathered he meant something good. But he called for the wolf to follow him, and off they trotted never bothering to explain just what that something was.

* * *

It was well into the afternoon before their attention returned to me. For hours I watched the man gather, organize, and pack up all manner of herbs, shrubs, and leaves. Some he gathered from the oasis and the rest, I assume, had been brought from somewhere else. It was fascinating to watch a human who actually seemed to enjoy things that grew from the ground and brought life. All I had seen was a fascination with whatever brought pain and death. But this man was different than any other I had known. The longer I watched him the clearer that became. He was genuinely happy and not at the expense of someone else's suffering. At the same time there was a weightiness in everything he did that was hard to describe. It was like his heart was full of joy and his body full of urgency. With every passing hour he grew more agitated, working faster. The tempo of his songs increased. Even before he started dismantling the tent, I knew the man was anxious to be somewhere else.

When at last the final pole had been removed and the last container was loaded into the cart, he paused for a moment to wipe his sweaty brow. The heat was intense, but a welcome breeze stirred under the shade of the trees. Nathak stood panting at his side also glad to take a break. I don't think the wolf had sat down since our conversation that morning. All day he had followed the man around wagging his tail while staying alert to any possible threat. Even now, as the man descended to the creek for one last drink of water, the wolf fell right into step behind him only stooping to take a drink himself after his Master had finished. I shook my head.

Loyalty must be exhausting.

As the man stood up his eyes scanned the peaceful oasis. Suddenly his breath caught sharply, like the sight was painful to him. He looked up at the heavens. Then down to me. Something about his gaze made my skin tingle. He started towards my cage and I stood to my paws. There was a weight in the air. As Nathak came up beside him I wanted to ask the wolf what was about to happen. But I could not speak; I could not take my eyes off the face of the young man. It was a mixture of agony and peace. He knelt before me lowering his eyes on level with mine. I saw respect, worry, grief, and hope wash over them like waves on a lake shore. At last the man spoke, but only one word.

"Godspeed," he whispered.

What does that mean? I wondered.

Then the man straightened. "Nathak, cart!" The wolf looked wary but his Master reassured him, "Go on." One last glance my direction (whether in parting or as a warning I couldn't tell) and the wolf loped away, jumping into the passenger seat of the cart. The man moved to the right side of my cage. He laid his hand on a lever jutting from the wooden roof, looked at me for a moment, and sighed. Then with a great heave he pulled the lever, sliding with it down the entire side of the cage, front to back. And as he did so the unthinkable happened.

The bars in front of me began to lift, flying right up through the roof! Suddenly there was nothing between me and the world beyond! The shaggy palm trees, the sandy ground, the grassy prairie off in the distance: the whole dazzling picture was complete without a bar in sight! The change was so quick and so dramatic it caught me off guard. Joy and doubt surged in my heart at once. Afraid to believe what seemed too wonderful to be true I looked at the man now behind me.

Does this mean what I think it means?

"Yes!" He laughed a hearty, joyful laugh, "You are free!" His eyes were gleaming. "You are *free!*"

Free?

After all the fear, all the fighting, all the slavery: in one moment—just like that...

I am free?

My whole body froze. A seizure of emotions turned my limbs to stone. I hesitated. The freedom I had given up on was now waiting right in front of me, and I couldn't move. I even felt frightened, frightened to leave the bondage that had become so familiar.

"Go on!" The man urged, "You are no longer a slave!" The power of his voice did more to move me than any stick or spear ever could. It filled me with courage. I laid a trembling paw on the ground beyond the cage floor. The feel of pebbles and dirt and short, stubby grass shot between my claws, spreading through my body like new life. The bars of my wooden cage melted away. In their place was clean, open air. One paw followed another, till the last one lifted from the cage floor to fall on soft sand. My tail cleared the gateway—and I was free! No bars, no roof, no chains; just trees and earth and sky. It took a few feet, but as soon as I stepped beyond the shade of the oasis and into full sunlight the reality finally sunk in.

I was free.

Warm rays washed over me, dissolving every shred of doubt. This was no dream, no mirage in a dark prison. This was real. This was true.

I am free!

I felt like roaring! I wanted to run and leap! But instead I looked back. The man still stood by the now empty cage, the ivory Tree gleaming on his chest. Nathak watched intently from the wagon. The man raised his hand to the sky, palm towards me. A gratitude I never thought possible welled up inside. Sitting on my haunches I rose up and swiped my right paw in the air. The man smiled, nodding his head. Without a word, we understood each other.

The debt had been settled.

TWENTY-ONE

THE FIRST THING I DID when Nathak and his Master were out of sight was plop down on the soft prairie grass and have a good roll. It was glorious! To be bathed once more in the dew of heaven, to smell the purity of rich soil, to wash all the filth and stink of captivity from my fur with the clean brush of nature; even the soreness of my body as it pressed against the ground was a sweet pain. I was *free*—never again to wear the yoke of slavery! Never again to be trapped in a cage! I rolled and rolled and rolled, unable to get enough of the good earth. The sky was bright and clear overhead, the sun shining from its blue canvas as if it were watching with a smile from above. I closed my eyes and inhaled. Every lovely scent seemed to pour into me, and I drank in every drop. But a more substantial thirst finally kicked in and I set out to find some water. In very little time I had struck on the same stream that watered the oasis and, without a thought, dove right in: splashing into the cool flow like a duck. It was wet and cold, covering only my paws, but if it had been a river it would not have mattered. At that moment everything was wonderful. I found myself thinking it would have been hard to be angry even if Mantos himself had suddenly appeared. The thought brought a laugh and, oh, how good it felt! Then, lowering my head into the stream, I drank and drank until my stomach could hold no more.

The remainder of the afternoon I wandered around the solitary field as if in a beautiful dream: sometimes resting, sometimes frolicking—always relishing the feeling of being alive. As evening fell I climbed a small green hill, crowned on top with one lonely cedar tree that was quickly becoming a dark silhouette against the amber sky. The setting sun blazed on my left as I relished the view. Other hills rolled on gently for miles, spaced comfortably apart by open fields much like the one where I had spent the day. Beyond them, to the north, lay a deep purple horizon caused perhaps by a great forest or a wide range of mountains. I sat under the cedar, watching as the fields began to blush pink from the last kisses of the sun. A slight breeze cooled the clear air, stirring the quiet branches above me and creating a rippling effect in the tall grasses like waves in a sleepy sea. All alone in this peaceful world I finally began to think.

What do I do now?

Beyond all hope I had been given a second chance, passed from death to life. It was a gift I had not earned or felt like I even deserved, yet here I stood: free, healed, and with a chance to begin again.

But now what?

Where did I go from here? Nothing remained of my old life to return to. My mountain was gone and everything I once knew had been taken from me forever. I did not even have Womby to protect. No Mantos, no Lena, no other foes to fight. Eddie and Bulk were (hopefully) far away enjoying their own freedom. And Saphirra—the reality I would probably never see the white lioness again brought a quick stab of regret. I brushed it off. It was just me on that hill in the middle of nowhere. Whatever decision would be made, whatever course would be taken, it would have to be mine; no one else could make it for me or take my place. My destiny was my own. The only problem was I had no idea what it should be. Looking up I saw the first faint whispers of a star glimmer in the east. The flawless light pierced my soul. Only a few hours before I lay dying in a dungeon; now I was watching the stars come out. Surely there was a purpose behind it all. For some reason I had been rescued.

But how do I find it?

Just then my ears pricked forward. A faint sound stirred from the distance, carried like an echo on the breeze; familiar but very vague. "Probably just the wind," I murmured. But then a chill swept through me and I was on my feet.

There it is again!

I held my breath. The wind blew in that empty country from every direction howling like a jackal looking for a home. But that was not the sound I listened for; what I thought I had heard came from only one direction. Every fiber in me leaned towards the north. Once more it came and this time there was no mistaking it.

"Sengali."

Deep and quiet, barely audible above the wind that bore it floated the Voice! I do believe for a few seconds my heart stopped beating.

"Sengali."

From the north-east it grew, so gentle and powerful that I felt my legs weakening. Just like in the garden, I saw no one but heard it as clearly as if someone was standing right in front of me. The call leapt over the hills rushing near from somewhere far off in the distance. A desire seized me so intense I had to force myself to stand in one place, a desire to follow the Voice. My breath drew in sharply. *But can I trust it?* When I followed it the first time I went from being King of my mountain to Mantos' prisoner. Then I listened to it in the garden and wound up as a slave on an auction block. What if it only led to more trouble? *Of course*, I remembered, *I'm also free because of it. If I hadn't listened to the Voice and spared the "Great-*

Father", Nathak's Master would have never rescued me. My heart wrestled for an answer. Was the Voice friend or foe? Had it doomed me to slavery or caused my salvation?

Or both?

"Sengali!"

Violently I shook my head. This was no time for doubts! The sun was sinking lower and lower; somehow I knew if I hesitated till it was gone I would never hear the Voice again. Either I followed it now, or would live without it—suffering whatever consequences that might bring. There would be no second chances.

Once more it came, this time as a whisper.

"Sengali."

I ran. I ran until my lungs felt like they would burst. Through the fields of flax and flowers, across little streams and wide rivers, over hills and under wooded groves I charged: ever always headed northeast. The stars glowed from their courses and the moon rose like a celestial lantern to light my path. The Voice did not call again because it did not have to. My decision was made. Determination fueled me like fire. Every step hitting the ground surged my legs with new energy till it felt like I was flying across the earth. I would find out where this mysterious Voice came from and why it wanted me to follow it if it took the rest of my life!

And still I ran.

TWENTY-TWO

NOT UNTIL THE EARLY morning hours pulled a thick mist up from the ground, choking the light of the setting moon, did I slow down. I am not sure how much territory I had covered throughout the night but it must have been substantial; the terrain I now picked my way through was far different than the open field where I had started. It was a pristine forest of massive gofer trees; just avoiding their huge trunks in the darkness proved challenging. The land was level enough, full of ferns and sticky cones that had fallen from the branches far above. The whole place had a distinct, spicy scent that was new to me. All around was extremely still except for a few insects and a bird call every now and then. The heavy mist only increased the solitude. Unable to see very much, my best guide became my other senses; more than once I was grateful for whiskers that could feel in the dark before I rammed my skull up against a hidden stump. It struck me how many of these there were, and yet I had not come across a single fallen tree. It didn't bother me too much, however; after running all night I was feeling rather tired and hungry and more interested in finding breakfast or a place to bed down for the day.

It was in this frame of mind my nose caught a new smell. It did not snap with the fragrance of twig and leaf; it tingled with the pulse of blood under flesh. Instantly I was on alert. Dewdrops soaked my paws as I crept through the fauna of the forest floor. The scent in the air led like an invisible path in the mist. Tracking swift and silently, head low and locked in place, I neared my target. The growl of my stomach grew louder and louder, until I was almost afraid it might scare off my quarry. But then another sound came to my ears.

"*Please*," a deep, muffled voice floated out of the darkness ahead, "Please help me to be faithful! Keep me from falling!" My curiosity perked. Cautiously, I moved forward and the new voice continued, the words almost seeming to pour out, "I ask for strength. Strength to hold fast in this wicked generation. To not deny You or Your ways. To bear the shame of the Tree with honor!"

I stopped in my tracks.
The Tree?

There was a heavy sigh and the pulsing of the heart I was hunting sped up. Apparently I had found my prey. Yet, for a moment, I hesitated. Somewhere ahead was a man who knew of the Tree. Slowly I snuck forward, careful to not disturb even the slightest leaf on the ground. Crouching amidst a carpet of thick ferns, I came to the edge of a small clearing under the trees. There, only partially visible in the low light, knelt a man. His body was bent over double against the ground and his back was turned towards me. It shook with the force of silent weeping. I watched as the morning around us steadily awoke, turning the black fog to gray. At last the man's tears seemed to subside. He raised his torso, revealing an uncovered head of rich, silver hair entangled with brown. But he did not stand. He remained seated on his knees for so long the cool mist swirling about him almost made his form look like just another stump of the forest. When he finally spoke again, the stillness of his voice made me tremble, though I didn't know why.

"Great God of my Fathers," he breathed, "Maker of heaven and earth—so good and great in mercy—help me, I ask You. I *beg* You, help *us*—to never doubt Your word or Your promise. No matter what they say. Or do." There was a mournful sigh. "They hate us. You know how much—and why. Yet if they would just listen, if they would just turn..." his voice choked with emotion. "Oh, *why?*" Suddenly his fist beat the ground, "*Why* must man be so stiff-necked? Why must we always, *always* insist on destruction? On death? *We* chose this! *We* chose death over life. Yet we spit on Your mercy, spurn Your kindness—then shamelessly blame *You* for not blessing *us*. Oh, *why* does the world hate You so? Hate Your good ways? Hate each other?" There was a heavy pause as the man struggled to compose himself. "But help me not lose faith—no matter what may come. This task," the deep voice wavered, "this task is far too great for me! Doubt crouches at the door; help me believe! Help me wait faithfully—help *us* to wait. And to prepare. Strengthen our hands," the man lifted his arms in the air and I saw wiry muscles and scars from years given to labor. "I pray I have not erred—for *their* sakes! If so may the consequences fall on me alone." Humbly he bowed to the earth again. There was a short silence. "If only I could be *sure*," he murmured. "To know I had done what was pleasing. To know I had not strayed. It has been *so* long. Please," he pleaded, face to the ground, "show me what else I can do if there is anything I have left undone! I ask You, in Your kindness and grace, please let me know I still have Your favor." He sighed deeply, "I ask for a sign..."

Just then there was a sharp CRACK; I must have leaned on a twig too heavily! The man jumped to his feet and spun around. "Who goes there?" He demanded, "Show yourself!"

I stared. The figure I had seen bent against the ground hardly prepared me for the tower now standing just a few feet away. Older than Nathak's Master but younger than the "Great-Father", this man appeared to be only slightly past the prime of his life. He had just enough wrinkles to give the impression of wisdom, aided all the more by a trimmed beard of white and brown falling from his chin. His clothing was simple: rich enough, but obviously durable. A coat of deep brown and blue flowed to his sandaled ankles to guard against the morning chill. Tall and stately, head held high, his gray eyes flashed with a bold fire. "If you be a man," he boomed again, "show yourself!"

That would have been an ideal time to stay put. Yet, for a reason I cannot explain, I stepped forward. The man froze; seeing a tiger emerge from the shadows was probably not the answer he had expected (the fact I was crouched low and on guard did not help matters). In a breath he glanced over to the side, where a grim-looking spear lay propped against a tree trunk. Following his gaze I bristled. *Don't try it*, I warned internally, which came out as a menacing growl. The man's eyes steeled over and he flexed his hands. I flexed my talons. We were at a stand-off; one quick move by either of us would turn it into a blood bath. Yet even as I poised to strike I felt a check inside. Something was telling me not to harm this man. *Don't be a fool!* My mind screamed, *He'll skewer you the second your guard is dropped!* But another impulse, much stronger and much deeper, came from my heart.

Trust him.

Maybe it was my own curiosity, or the peacefulness of the woods, or the way the man's eyes reminded me of the Great-Father and Nathak's Master: the only men who had ever shown me any kindness. Maybe the Voice was speaking to my heart. I don't know, but for whatever reason I relaxed my stance. My body softened and my ears came up from my head. The man, however, did not move.

Trust him.

A ridiculous, terrifying idea came to my mind. But I went with it. Slowly—careful not to move in any way that would seem aggressive—I laid down. Then, in one chilling act of surrender, I rolled over on my back, let my paws dangle, and looked up with the friendliest expression I could manage. The man's fierceness melted to shock. His mouth dropped open. An extremely awkward few moments passed. But soon his shock melted to something else: something I can only describe as courage and faith welded together. Calm confidence rose in his eyes and they shone on me with the kindest, most compassionate gaze I had ever seen. Then he moved, but not towards the spear; instead, he inched my way.

My heart pounded. Desire fought inside me: desire to get up and run, get up and fight, or stay down and see what happened. Fear flushed my mind. Memories flashed by of the Slave Driver and Hittan, the brutes who tortured me and the crowds of the Arena. I flinched. The man stopped and stood still. He was far too close for comfort. I fidgeted as my instinct for survival started to kick in. But then he knelt down. Sitting on the wet grass, the man quietly laid his hands on his legs, where I could see them. He did not move any closer. My heart slowed down. Rolling over on my side I looked at him anxiously. He took a deep breath then let it out—slow and deliberately. I caught his meaning. My own breath returned to normal. A few moments passed. His right hand twitched, lifted, and quickly lowered back to his leg: as if unsure of itself. Our eyes met and it felt like he was asking my permission for something.

Trust him.

I lowered my head to the ground. He stretched out his hand again, reaching towards my neck. My heart jumped. *He is wanting to touch me!* I yearned to bolt, yet somehow I stayed. One second the heat of the man's skin stood a few inches from my fur and then the full weight of his hand rested upon my neck.

I wish I could explain in words what happened in that instant. The closest I can manage is it was like I came home. All the fear and distrust faded away, replaced by an overwhelming sense of peace. Instantly I knew I was safe. The man must have felt the change as well; he began moving his palm from the back of my ears to the blades of my shoulders, gently stroking my fur. It was mesmerizing: as if that one rough hand was wiping away all of the abuse I had suffered at the touch of so many others. A deep contentedness welled up inside of me. Before I even knew it, something began happening that had not happened for what felt like a lifetime.

    I started to purr.

A CAT'S TALE

PART THREE

"Friends"

TWENTY-THREE

WE RESTED TOGETHER for what must have been an hour and watched as the light of morning gradually chased away all traces of night. Neither of us stirred, unwilling to break the stillness. It must have been quite a sight: the man and cat sitting together in that pristine grove. It was more profound to experience. Such a feeling of peace flooded me while lying next to this strange human; I never wanted to move. I could have stayed there for hours more, but finally the man stood to his feet.

"Come," he said and began walking away—leaving the spear where it lay against the tree. Without hesitation I sprang up and fell into step a few paces behind him. Despite his silver hair, the man was quite swift (for a human) and moved with a smooth dignity. As we travelled the sunlight grew, falling through the branches overhead to illuminate both tall, towering tree trunks and blunt, stubby stumps. The stumps always appeared in groups and created little clearings in the forest, bathed in golden sunbeams pouring from the window of open sky above. This happened more and more, till up ahead I could see where the tall gofer trees vanished all together and everything turned to sunlight and stumps. At the edge of the forest the man stopped briefly to see if I was still following, smiled, and then plunged into the open beyond.

The sun greeted us with a warm embrace as the dark roof of the woods gave way to a shining blue heaven. We stepped out onto a large, open plain; a grassy flatland that looked like it had also once been part of the forest, but was cleared out long before. Almost completely encircled by those same giant trees (except towards the south), the flat, airy field seemed a little out of place. But that was nothing compared to the marvel standing in the very center of it.

What in the world?

In the middle of the field stood a massive structure, supported all around by great bronze beams as if it grew from them out of the ground. It was made of dark, rich, brown wood—like the forest of gofer trees we had just left. *So that's where the stumps came from*, I concluded. In shape the gargantuan thing resembled very much a long, square log, only tapered underneath and at the ends. There it changed somewhat: with one end jutting out at the bottom (similar to the lower curve of a fish's tail) and the other jutting up at the top like a wide, flat horn (reminding me very much of a blunt rhinoceros). As we approached it, I felt increasingly smaller. The man walked right into the structure's enormous shadow, but I couldn't help hesitating. It looked to be longer than twenty-five large elephants standing end to end. In awe I stared up at the great wooden side. It was at least as tall as three full-grown long-necks, rising higher and higher into the sky until it blotted out the sun.

Meanwhile the man was rounding the end closest to us and vanishing beyond sight. Hurrying my pace while still keeping an eye on the towering thing, I followed him into the sun on the other side. He was walking towards a small house only a short distance away. Beyond this house seemed to be others as well (I counted three at a distance), along with several sheds and a large barn. In between ran open pastures, large gardens, and an abundance of fruit trees. But the only creature I saw was a wolf sleeping near the doorway of the first house. It stood up when it heard the man approach, bouncing and wagging its tail. That is, until it saw me. Instantly the wolf's brown and black hair stood straight on end, and it broke into a vicious bark.

The man held up his hand. "Peace, Rhia!" He called, "He is a friend!"

Several things happened at once. First, Rhia stopped barking (much to the relief of my ears), and cocked her head. Next, a young woman emerged from the doorway of the house: small, vibrant, her petite frame wrapped in a white dress bound by a purple sash and her jet black hair falling in waves over her shoulders. At sight of me a cloud of terror darkened her olive face. She started pointing my way, like she was trying to warn the man.

"I know, I know," he called kindly, "Everything is fine; Do not be—"

Suddenly an axe split the earth right in front of my paws! Spinning to the right I turned just in time to duck another blade flying at my head! With an awful shout a man emerged from under one of the great beams supporting the ship: teeth clenched and eyes blazing, two other axes gripped in his large hands! He ran at me with terrific speed. From reflex I snarled and crouched, ready to strike the first blow.

"No!" Cried the older man, "Kawm, stop!" Jumping between me and my attacker he grabbed the other man's arms in mid-swing.

"Let go, Father!" The other man boomed, struggling to break free, "Get out of the way!" His outburst triggered the wolf and she lunged forward.

"Chenna, hold her!" The first man called over his shoulder. The young woman instantly threw her arms around Rhia's neck, fighting to keep the dog from breaking loose. The barking resumed even louder. I almost ran away right then and there.

The younger man fought against his father. "Are you *mad?*" he cried.

"Hold her, Chenna! Keep her still!"

The girl tried as best she could to soothe the raging wolf. Meanwhile the older man tried to soothe his son, "No, Kawm, this is not what you think! The cat came with me of his own will. He is no threat!"

The man known as Kawm ceased struggling but still clung to his axes. "What!" He snapped, and doubt knit his stormy brow, "What do you mean he 'came' with you?"

"He found me in the woods this morning. He came to me *freely*—without any prompting. I did not catch him, Kawm; he *came*. Lay down your weapons."

The younger's eyes flashed and his brown skin flushed with emotion.

"Trust me, son," his father whispered, each word deliberate, *"lay them down."*

Looking at his father Kawm's anger began to subside. But then he glanced back at me. His nostrils flared and his jaw clenched under his short, curly beard. Just then three other women came running up: a lean, charcoal-skinned beauty with a bow and arrow in her hand, a lighter one with a long, golden-brown braid and a basket of fruit on her head, and an older, stately lady with silver hair pinned back. The latter came from the house where the wolf had been and was the first to speak.

"What happened, Noak?" She panted, "What is..." then she gasped, seeing me. The fair girl froze as well while the dark one put an arrow to the bowstring. Kawm's grip around the axes tightened. Things did not look good. But thankfully, Noak saw it. Quickly he grasped the deadly tools out of his son's hands and threw them to the side.

"Peace, everyone!" He spoke firm but calmly, "All is well!" He looked in his son's dark eyes and laid a reassuring hand on his shoulder. Then he turned to me, "Do not fear. No hurt will come to you in this place. You are safe now."

Safe? I wondered while staring at the axe still stuck in the ground at my feet.

"Noak, what do you mean?" The woman asked again, "What is happening? I looked at her. She tensed, but there was a fearless poise in her face I had to admire. The older man also looked her way, his thoughts in his eyes. For a moment words failed him. When he finally did speak there was a tremendous weight to his voice:

"The gathering has begun."

You could have cut the air with a knife. Each person stared: at me, at the ground, at each other. None said a word or hardly even breathed. It was like a massive bell had tolled and the reverberations were rumbling through the humans, shaking them to their core. Even the wolf stood as still as a statue—until a sudden a commotion broke up the mood. From behind the women a furry blur came streaking past their feet, straight towards me. It slammed into my front legs like a small boulder, nearly knocking me down. A little, hairy head was rubbing against my chest almost before I could believe my eyes.

"Li!" it squealed in delight, "You're here! You m,m,made it!"

That stutter was unmistakable! "Womby?!" My surprise was beyond words, "How? What?"

The wombat just laughed and rubbed all over my legs, "I knew y,y,you'd make it!"

A dark cloud lifted from my heart. Throwing all questions to the wind I dug my face into the wombat's scratchy hair. It smelled like good, wholesome dirt. I started laughing myself and it felt like a spring of joy that had been dammed up inside of me finally broke loose. We romped and wrestled and laughed for a long while barely noticing the amazed humans standing around. When at last we did look up there were tears and smiles, though some of the tears looked bitter sweet. But Noak's eyes shone brightest; somehow I felt he, more than any other, understood what we were feeling. A desire came over me to tell him the whole story and for the first time I wished I could speak the language of man. But the man spoke instead.

"Come, we must make ready."

He held out his hand to the silver-haired lady; she grasped it and together they walked alongside the huge structure, towards a long plank walkway. Supported by heavy stilts, this walkway ran from the ground to a very large opening high up in the wooden wall on the far end: a great doorway. Around this door other humans were huddled together—probably hired workers, judging by the tools in their hands and the way they murmured to each other as the man and woman approached. The dark girl and light girl stood still a moment, staring at me and exchanging looks. Then they followed Noak and the woman. Chenna lingered a little longer, glancing back and forth: from Womby, to me, to the wolf in her arms. Finally she made a firm gesture with her hands to tell the wolf to stay and ran to catch up with the others. Only Kawm remained, still smoldering with distrust. At last he pulled away, but not before picking up the axes tossed by his father and tucking them into his leather belt. I watched the man's broad shoulders as he climbed the plank (glancing back at me a few times along the way) until he was finally swallowed up by the great doorway with the rest of the men.

My attention now turned to the wolf. She sat silent, staring at me intently. Womby followed my gaze. "Rhia, Rhia!" he called out excitedly, "He came! I told you he w,w,would!" Again my little friend rubbed his head against my leg. "I told you he would c,c,come!" he sighed blissfully. Looking down at him I smiled. Deep happiness swelled my heart. So much had happened since I first saw that funny little face staring down Lena's pack. How much water had flowed downstream! Yet here we were (wherever "here" was), back together again. Somehow it made the misery of the past few weeks seem a little less futile. As the wolf quietly watched the wombat her golden eyes softened. Finally she relaxed into a smile.

"Well," she spoke at last, "if Noak and Womby trust you, that's good enough for me." Striding forward, she bowed good-naturedly, "My name is Rhia—you probably caught that by now—and on behalf of the Masters I bid you welcome!"

TWENTY-FOUR

I BOWED IN RETURN (no point in letting a dog out-do a cat in manners), "I am called Sengali, and with gratitude I hail you as my gracious host."

She cocked her head and a twinkle came to her eye. "Just 'thank you' works fine. Well, Sengali, since it looks like you'll be sticking around with us you might as well have the whole tour." She picked up her long legs and set off at a lope towards the houses, calling out, "Come on, cat; keep up!" over her shoulder. I gained the wolf's side with ease, matching her stride for stride. Womby's short legs took a little longer. "You've already seen the main attraction," Rhia spoke, nodding to the wooden structure, "without it none of the rest of this matters. But that doesn't mean it's not all important." We rounded the side of the house: a simple structure of rich timber and polished brick.

"This is Noak and Marriet's home (she was the silver-haired lady you saw), though the rest of the family is in and out of it all the time." Around the house were flowers planted in beds on the ground, pots beside doorways, and boxes on windowsills. Behind was a large stone patio, where a great wooden table sat surrounded by nine ornately carved chairs. "This is where the Masters eat together," the she-wolf explained, "and if you're very good and stand around long enough you just might get something tossed your way. Doesn't always work, but it's worth a try: But if you're going to beg, go for the women, especially Chenna or Nina, the golden-haired girl (she bakes the best bread you've ever tasted). Atani is a little harder to manipulate. She's the dark one you saw with the bow and arrow. Don't let that fool you, though; under her serious face is a sweet gem. She just stays cool-headed to balance out her husband."

"That's Kawm," Womby added, huffing alongside.

"Hmm," I rumbled, "we met."

"He's not always that way, though he could show his father more respect: after all, without Noak none of this could be possible. But at least his brothers try to make up for it," as she spoke the wolf led us on a path winding its way by herb gardens full of aloe, ginger, peppermint, and all kinds of spices. We passed fields of wheat, corn, and every grain you could imagine. There were also several large pastures, surrounded and divided into sections by rows of stone fences; these were mostly empty except for a few cows, sheep, and goats. When I asked Rhia why they were empty she just looked at me strangely and said, "Maybe they won't be much longer." From there we wound our way around the three other houses belonging to the sons and their wives: Yeffeth and Nina, Shem and Chenna, and Kawm and Atani. Yeffeth and Shem were away—something about being "on mission". I was going to ask what she meant but there was no time: being a typical dog, Rhia did not like staying in one place very long. We moved on to the great barn in the midst of the pastures, where (to Womby's relief) we stopped to drink at a well that had been channeled into a series of irrigation drains, which ran all through the valley like man-made veins of water. The barn's large doors were closed and when I asked the wolf about it she said it was for storage. "Animals aren't allowed inside," she explained. I wondered why; she just shrugged her brown shoulders and said, "The Masters have their reasons. There is one place, though, that is never off limits. My favorite." She winked, "This way."

Following her to the eastern end of the barn we rounded its side to find a grassy lane open up before us. This led under the largest, loveliest, most luscious grove of fruit trees I had ever seen. Apples, peaches, mangoes, pears—all hung from low, graceful branches intertwined with each other like the arms of very old friends. The air was filled with their sweetness. Everywhere you looked, full, delicate blossoms and thick, glossy leaves filtered the sun's rays into patches of dreamy light. I stopped and breathed in deeply. Rhia turned. "It *is* nice, isn't it?" she asked, pleased I seemed to notice. "This is a very special place. Many times the Masters will come here to rest, or think, or talk with the Creator. They always let us come. When Noak goes into the forest, though, it's usually alone." The wolf sat down on the soft grass, "Sometimes he stays there for hours, under the great gopher trees. Trees are very important to the Masters," she explained, a far-off look in her eye, "I think it is because they remind them of the Tree in the garden."

By this point I had also sat down. Now I leaned forward, "The 'Tree'?"

If she noticed my eagerness the wolf did not let on. "Yes, the Tree that gave life. It grew in a garden—the perfect garden—at the beginning when the Creator made the world and everything was good. Before there was evil; when the first man walked with the Creator."

"That was a l,l,long time ago," Womby added, plopping down beside me. "He failed."

"The first man," Rhia clarified, noticing the confusion on my face. "There were many trees in that garden (a lot like this one, I guess), but two were very special: one was the Tree that gave life forever, the other had fruit that brought death. The Creator told the first man he could eat from any tree in the garden except the tree that brought death." Her dark ears dropped and sadness came into her voice, "But the first man failed: he and his wife both chose to eat from the Death Tree..."

"On purpose?" I asked with horror; the wolf and wombat nodded. "But why?"

"They thought it would make them wise, like the Creator. They did not want to walk *with* Him; they wanted to *be* Him—to control everything themselves."

"So they ate the fruit," Womby said.

"And evil came to the world. That's why terrible things happen, why most men are so wicked." The she-wolf dropped her head, "They chose the wrong tree."

It was an awful thought, but in my heart I knew she was telling the truth. "What happened to the Life Tree?" I asked.

"The Creator blocked it off with a sword of fire, so the first man could not eat its fruit and live forever in evil." Her golden eyes sparked with hope, "But later on some of his sons remembered it. They talked about it with their sons, who told it to their sons, until the Life Tree became a symbol. They even carved it into ivory pendants and wore them around their neck as a reminder of what had once been, and a hope for what might one day be again: man able to walk with the Creator in a perfect world. That's why the Masters come to this place, why Noak goes into the woods to be alone." Her voice lowered to a hush, "They walk with God."

In the stillness of that hallowed place, answers were finally piecing together in my mind. "The Men of the Tree," I whispered.

The wolf's sharp ears caught the words. They pricked forward. "You know about the Men of the Tree? How?"

Womby gazed up with the same expression. I shook my head at them both, "It's a long story."

The she-wolf lay down, stretching her black paws out in front of her body. "We have all day."

I hesitated, unsure whether or not I wanted to go into it right then. But one glance at Womby's smiling face took me back to the first time I saw him—the same day I first had the Dream and my journey began. Before I knew it I was telling the whole story. The day wore on, I was tired and hungry, yet words kept coming, pouring out of me like a waterfall I could not stop. At some point I lost the wombat to a nap on a nearby bed of clovers. But not Rhia: the dog was glued to every word I said. When I mentioned "the Man of the Tree" she looked especially interested but said nothing, letting me go into detail about the old man and the fight with Lena. She winced once or twice and her bright eyes clouded over but she did not interrupt me. She even waited quietly as I struggled to talk about being a slave; the pain and fear were still so recent. But I could not leave out Eddie and Bulk. When I got to Saphirra with the dragon and the wolf in the arena Rhia sat up excitedly. As I told her the wolf's name was Nathak her golden eyes glowed, and when I explained how he and his Master rescued me, healed me, and set me free her face was positively beaming. It made me curious, but I decided to go on, continuing right up through meeting Noak in the forest and the moment when she had seen us walking towards the house. I fell silent, worn out from talking yet also strangely relieved; somehow it felt good just to get it all off my chest. We listened to the birds and insects carry on their afternoon business in the fruit trees.

"This 'Voice'," Rhia finally whispered, "what does it sound like?"

I was not prepared for that one. The Voice was the part of the story I almost left out, knowing how crazy it would sound. Once I *had* decided to mention it I expected the wolf to laugh or sneer. But she had done neither. Actually, her face looked dead serious. "Deep," I said after a pause, "very deep—and strong. But light, too; it floats on the wind like a whisper. Gentle, quiet, uh, yet powerful and frightening: kind and severe at the same time. I don't know—it's difficult to describe—but somehow whenever I have heard the Voice it has made me want to both run towards it and cower under it, all at the same time." I huffed, frustrated at the weakness of my own explanation. "Forgive me. I imagine that doesn't make much sense."

"It makes more sense than you realize!" I looked at the wolf, surprised at the wonder in her face. Her sharp eyes were filled with compassion, knowing, and even a kind of fear as she quietly added, "*No one comes to the Ark by accident.*"

TWENTY-FIVE

"THE 'ARK'?" I wondered, "What is tha—" but the sound of laughter cut me off. Looking back I saw the three young women coming up the path. This time Nina held the bow and arrow while the other two had baskets in their arms. They set about picking fruit at the far end of the grove. As we watched them I noticed Nina and Atani talked, sang, and carried on conversation, but the smaller one, who had run out of the house to grab Rhia, never made a sound.

"That one," I asked, nodding towards the woman, "does she ever speak?"

"She used to, a long time ago; but before any of us ever knew her." The wolf moved closer, "Her name is Chenna, Shem's wife. Actually, your stories are much alike: she was a slave once, too. Her parents were poor and sold her as a child to a wicked man. She was beaten, abused, starved for no reason. One day she saw another child slave, even younger than she was, being whipped just because they'd not done a job fast enough; it was too much for Chenna's tender heart. She tried to stop her master, saying he was an evil, cruel man and if he did not stop being so God would certainly see and punish him for it." Rhia shook her head, "So he cut out her tongue. Afterward the poor girl was seen as less than worthless and forced to suffer and do things I won't even repeat. Finally she wound up on the slave block, caged and helpless just like you. But Noak was passing by; he saw her and had pity, spending every coin in his purse and even the robe off his back to buy her. He and Marriet took her in like a daughter: caring for her, loving her, teaching her the ways of the Creator. That was years ago. It took a while, but Chenna finally healed—inside and out (except for her tongue). Eventually she and Shem fell in love and were married, to everyone's joy." The wolf smiled softly as she watched the quiet girl, "This place just wouldn't be the same without Chenna." I looked at the small form with new admiration. Knowing all too well the cruelty of men, I didn't doubt Rhia's story was true. But it was hard to believe such a peaceful creature could have gone through such horror and come out the other side of it, happy and whole. She gave me hope.

As we sat there the young women slowly made their way closer, working through the rows of trees.

Chenna was ahead of the other two. A gentle breeze stirred through the still grove and the girl stopped to look around. The sun glistened off her jet black hair against the white blossoms and danced on her olive skin as it seeped through the branches overhead. I was not a man and therefore not a good judge on women, but if I had been I imagine I would have been hard pressed to have found a lovelier one. Standing there with the basket dangling from her small hands, her graceful form reminded me very much of a gazelle. She took a deep breath and glanced wistfully around the grove. Then her eyes fell on me. Startled, the girl drew back a moment. But she relaxed when she saw Rhia wagging her tail and Womby sleeping nearby. Curiosity replaced the fear in her face. Her bare feet started tip-toeing towards us. My body tensed as I went on alert. She stopped again and held her breath.

"Relax," whispered Rhia, "you'll scare the poor girl."

I tried to take her advice but sometimes it's just hard for a big cat to not look threatening. Never mind the fact my stomach kept growling from hunger. At first the girl did not move, but when she did it was to cock her head and place her hands on her hips. She seemed to be thinking intently. Then Chenna turned and darted back up the trail, stopping to hand her basket of fruit to Atani before disappearing from sight.

"Now what is she up to?" I wondered out loud.

"You never know," Rhia said, but the smile on her face made me question if that was really true. If the wolf did know something, however, she was not going to tell me; instead she lay down on the grass and closed her eyes. But I was too hungry to sleep. After a while the two other women left, leaving me alone and awake in the quiet place. I was just about to go in search of some food when the patter of soft footsteps stopped me. Chenna reappeared on the path between the trees, but this time she held a wooden platter in her hands piled high with three fresh pheasants. I stood up excitedly. The girl slowed down, becoming more cautious the closer she came. My tail flicked as my nose twitched at the spicy smell of the birds. About five feet from me Chenna stopped, laid the platter on the ground, and walked away—standing at what she thought was a safe distance. We both watched each other and waited; silent in the stillness of the afternoon. I took a step forward. The girl did nothing, so I took another one. Chenna held her breath as I inched towards the platter, always keeping my eyes on her. She never moved; her own eyes fixed on me like large violets, wet with dew. As my nose reached the pheasants I sniffed around them. Nothing seemed suspicious so I nibbled on a small piece. Chenna relaxed. A look of profound peace came to her eyes: so profound it made me pause and stare at her. Incredibly gentle yet full of strength, the kind of strength that only comes through great pain. It almost felt like the girl was looking straight into me, reading me, understanding more than I could have explained with words. A tear ran down her smooth cheek and a compassionate smile overtook her face. I was captivated—until Rhia's good-natured voice broke in.

"If you're not going to eat that, Sengali, I will!"

Typical dog, I thought, *no tact whatsoever!* But it did not keep me from digging into the birds. As Chenna turned to go she gave me a parting smile; after that I was blissfully unaware of anyone. And when at last my hunger was satisfied, it gave way to a deep, wonderful, dreamless sleep.

* * *

I was awakened by Rhia barking. The warm light of late afternoon streamed all around, giving the quiet grove a golden glow. The shadows had moved. There was no sign of the wolf or the wombat, but her shrill noise came from not too far away, towards the southwest. Reluctantly I pulled myself up from the velvet grass to investigate. It was a pleasant evening: cool, clear, and breezy. Grasshoppers leapt around my paws and tiny bugs floated like specks of gold in the air. Following the sound of Rhia's bark, I found myself between the back of Shem and Kawm's houses on my right and the edge of a thin forest on my left. The latter's tree line grew farther and farther apart, till finally it disappeared completely, revealing a wide open plain. All you could see for miles was flat grassland, open sky, and two roads. One ran parallel with the tree line, headed east to west, while the other branched off of it to run straight south. At the end of this southerly one a gray mass rose on the horizon looking like a city; besides that the only other civilization I could see were a few lonesome dwellings scattered here and there along the plain and some straggling travelers on the roads. Then something else caught my eye: an iron cart rumbling northward on a small dirt lane, towards the little settlement. Rhia's barking turned hysterical but not angry. It was high-pitched and playful.

Rounding the corner of Yeffeth's house I got another clear view of the mysterious structure, its great wooden outline gilded by the light of the setting sun behind it. It seemed to loom even larger than in the morning. Under the end looking like a fish's tail, Rhia was jumping with excitement. Beside her stood Marriet, her dignified face beaming with a smile and hands waving in the air. Noak and Kawm came from inside the structure's great door, took one look at the road, and ran down the long boardwalk, tools still in hand. The younger reached the ground first and burst into a sprint, but the elder held his own for his age. They came to a stop beside Marriet, who hugged Noak while Kawm yelled excitedly. I decided to join them—at a safe distance. Together we watched the cart slowly approach, pulled by two young dragons (about the size of small oxen): huffing, snorting, and sending up small clouds of dust as they trudged along with their heavy, clubbed feet. Their thick skin ran like armor all over their bodies; one was green, the other gray. A hard frill of bone grew to protect their dense skulls, aided by two sharp horns protruding from their foreheads and one short one sticking up from their hooked snouts. Around these wrapped an elaborate harness of thongs and leather reins, held at the other end by the strong hands of a young, dark-haired man in the driver seat. When I saw him my mouth dropped open.

The man who rescued me!

There was no doubt about it: by his side sat a great gray wolf, so straight and proud it could only be Nathak. I shook my head in wonder. But things were finally beginning to come together in my mind. *This place is home to all Men of the Tree.* I gazed at the massive structure, dark and towering against the glowing western sky. Rhia's words came back to my mind, "No one comes to the Ark by accident." *The Ark. That must be what they call it—whatever it is.* I didn't know what it was for, but as I stared up at the imposing thing a strange feeling came over me: like hope mixed with fear.

Meanwhile the man was standing in the driver's seat and waving back at the happy crowd. They cheered in return. Noak called Rhia. "Bring Chenna, girl," he said. "Go find Chenna!" The wolf danced on her paws and then took off as fast as she could towards the main house. Nathak yipped loudly. Before the wagon even came to a full stop both he and the young man leapt down and were instantly clasped in the arms of Noak and Kawm. A chorus erupted of "Shem! How is everything? It's good to see you safe! Did you have any trouble? Thank God you're back!" till I couldn't tell who was asking what. During all this Nathak pranced around the three men, enjoying some hearty rubs in the process. But all made way for Marriet as, with tears in her eyes, she grasped the broad shoulders of her son and started weeping.

"There, there Mother, all is well," the young man soothed, kissing her cheek, "I told you it would be!" Over her head, however, he gave Noak a look that made the older man's smile fade.

Just then Nina and Atani ran up. "Shem! Shem!" they cried, "Welcome home!" and smothered the young man with sisterly hugs.

Marriet looked at the cart. "Where is Great-Father?" she asked, but before Shem could reply a shrill bark split the air. Rhia came bounding up while Nathak yelped for joy. The two wolves fairly collided: tumbling, snuggling, and nipping at each other as only dogs in love can. I nodded to myself. *So they're a pair; that explains some things!* They fit so perfectly together I wondered how I could have missed it before. Yet just when I was thinking this little reunion could not get any happier Chenna arrived: her olive face all aglow and a bunch of white lilies in her raven hair. Shem saw his wife and broke away from the others as she flew into his arms. In one move he had lifted her into the air and spun her around with a hearty laugh. Then he placed a long kiss on her lips. "My Lily," he whispered in her ear, "How is my Lily?" and Chenna positively beamed at him through those big, dreamy eyes. The gladness was contagious and as I observed the whole scene I realized I was smiling. In the midst of it all only one thing seemed to be missing.

The Tree was nowhere in sight.

"Shem," Marriet repeated, "where is Great—"

"There will be plenty of time for questions later," Noak broke in gently, "Right now, first things first. Marriet, you and the ladies finish preparing supper while we unload the wagon; I am sure our son would rather talk on a full stomach." They exchanged glances and the wise woman nodded. Then she gathered the younger women back to the house (after Shem stole one more kiss from Chenna).

"Has Yeffeth returned yet?" He asked, watching his young wife walk away.

"No." A shadow passed over Noak's face, "We have had no news from him for weeks."

Shem touched his shoulder as they turned back to the cart, "Don't worry, Father: the Almighty kept me. He will guard him as well."

"And Yeffeth can handle himself," added Kawm while straining against one of the dragon's sides to get them moving again. "Up, you lazy beasts!" he groaned, pulling with all his might on their harness and growing more frustrated by the second. "*Ugh!* Shem, *do* something!"

But his brother had already jumped back up to the driver's seat. "Hup! Hup!" He shouted, gripping the reins, "Hup!" The two lizards lurched and the iron wheels started rolling. Nathak and Rhia scurried to get out of the way as the giants lumbered past. Shem leapt back to the ground and Kawm took over, leading them towards the ramp of the Ark.

"Father," Shem said in a low voice, hanging back behind the cart as it rumbled away. Noak's gray brows knit together as he turned and saw the trouble in his son's face. For a moment Shem struggled to speak. Then slowly he reached into a small leather pouch strapped onto his belt; even before his hand opened I knew what it held.

Noak's clear eyes fell on the Tree and clouded with grief. "He has passed, then?" he whispered. Shem nodded gravely. His father swallowed hard, but a tear still slipped down the weathered cheek. "He was a good man," he managed to say, "a true man who fought his fight well!" He looked towards the golden heavens, "May the Almighty raise up others in his stead!"

"He already has," replied his son. "Great-Father spoke of you before he died: of you and Grandfather's prophecy. He bade me tell you, 'Be strong and courageous. Fear no man—only God!' He did not fight death, Father; he welcomed it."

Noak stared at the ground, lost in a stream of thoughts. "What else did he say?"

"That 'deliverance had come early' for him, but the journey remained for us," and as he spoke the son held out the Tree to his father.

Noak gazed at the tiny ivory shape and sighed deeply, "So be it!" Yet he closed Shem's hand back over the amulet with a brief, proud smile. "You keep the Tree. Great-Father did nothing by accident, Shem; he gave it to you for a reason." Noak's lips quivered, "How I shall miss him! But grief must wait. Time is growing short and we must work while we can." Then he looked from his son to me, "The Gathering has begun." Shem followed his gaze. The bold, dark eyes found me and his strong jaw dropped like a weight. By this time Nathak was also staring, standing speechless at his master's side. The expression on his face was absolutely priceless.

Noak noticed their reactions. "You've seen the cat before?" he asked in surprise.

Shem just gawked, unable to tear his eyes from me. "It's *you!*" He whispered. I looked back steadily.

Now it was the father's turn to touch his son's shoulder, "Come—explain as we unload." Shem looked from him to me and back again, gradually allowing his father to lead him away. They headed towards the bottom of the Ark's long boardwalk, where Kawm was already unloading the cart. Nathak, on the other hand, never budged; his blue eyes were glued onto me like sap on a tree. I wondered which of us would speak first, but Rhia took care of that.

"I believe you two know each other," she said sweetly, hiding a little grin, "though you've probably not been introduced. Sengali, this is Nathak, my mate. Nathak, this is Sengali: he's going to be living with us for a while." The male wolf looked aggravated but said nothing, making instead a loud noise sounding like something between a choke and a growl. "That's what he does when he loses his voice," Rhia explained.

Nathak glanced at her sharply then back at me. "I never thought I'd see *you* again!" he rumbled.

The she-wolf smiled apologetically, "And that's what he does when he finds it."

TWENTY-SIX

AFTER THAT THE WOLF and I basically avoided each other until Chenna rang her loud little hand bell for supper. The men gathered eagerly to the back of the main house, where the large wooden table was covered with food and neatly set dishes. There were baskets of steaming rolls, large bowls filled with vegetables, little bowls piled with nuts, plates of hot potatoes, and pitchers of cold water. Bright flowers and candles lit up the feast while the song of crickets and frogs played in the background. But the sound that most struck me was the laughter: the house and little patio were filled with it as the women brought out basins of water for the men to wash their hands and face with. More than a little water got playfully splashed around; I guess it was the excitement of Shem's arrival. Only Chenna was silent, but her glowing eyes showed she was clearly the happiest of all. Rhia jumped and barked between the laughing humans while Nathak took up a stoic guard near the doorway of the house. Needless to say, I found a comfortable spot on the *opposite* side, on the top of an old stone wall. As the people settled down to supper I heard a shuffling noise come up beside me. It was Womby. He looked up with a smile to say "hi" and waddled right onto the patio. Shem saw him coming.

"Now who is this?" He asked.

Nina giggled, "Right on time!" and started scratching behind the wombat's tiny ears.

"He showed up a few days ago and now we *cannot* get rid of him," Atani explained, but the white smile in her dark face showed the girl did not mind.

Nina scooped Womby up in her arms, "Isn't he sweet? We have not given him a name yet..."

"I have," cut in Kawm, "'Trouble'! The nuisance eats more than any creature I've ever seen—especially my crops!"

"I've been thinking about that," Noak spoke as he took his place at the head of the table. "We need to strengthen the walls around the food supply fields. More will be coming and they will want to take whatever they can find, not knowing it is their livelihood. We will have to keep them from it if there is to be enough for them to survive—and for us." The mood turned quiet as the others joined him around the table. Nina lowered Womby to the floor and sat down; he stayed expectantly by her chair.

"I wonder how much will be enough," Kawm muttered as he took his seat.

"As much as we can grow," Shem said from the other side of the table.

"And whatever the Creator provides," their father added, "though we may have to tighten our belts before all is done. We must remember He never promised this journey would be comfortable or easy. It will be dangerous and difficult—of that I am certain. But, whatever happens, He will not abandon us; God cannot break His word. He will care for His own."

"He always has," Marriet spoke from behind him, emerging from the house with a platter of steaming mushrooms and onions. She set it before Noak and took her place by his side, "Now how about we eat what He has provided for us tonight before it gets cold?" Her husband smiled at her from under his gray beard. Then he stood to his feet. The others bowed their heads as the man lifted his hands to the dark heavens and began to speak:

"Blessed are You, Almighty God, Creator of heaven and earth: Who brings up food from the ground and causes the rivers to flow. We bless and thank You for this abundance, as well as for Your mercy and goodness towards us, Your Servants. May we always be faithful. So be it!"

"So be it!" The others repeated. I can't explain why, but for some reason the hair on the back of my neck stood up, not necessarily in a bad way. The family then began to eat and talk and laugh, simply enjoying the gift of being together. In this happy scene I only noticed two things out of place: there were two empty chairs at the table. One was beside Nina. The other stood at the end opposite from Noak; over its back was draped a small, white object. The Tree.

* * *

The meal that followed was enjoyable to watch as Womby made his way from chair to chair begging for food. Kawm shooed him away and Marriet managed to ignore him pretty well, but the young women more than made up for it. Even Noak may have snuck something under the table; it was hard to tell from where I sat. Suffice to say, Womby wasn't going hungry that night. Rhia watched with a smile and Nathak with a scowl as my friend systematically made his way around the table till he finally reached Shem. Yet, just when he started begging, the human's conversation turned serious. The intense young man totally focused on what his father was saying, and, try as he might, poor Womby could not distract him. I chuckled to myself—until their words grabbed my attention.

"The time is near," Noak was saying. "It *must* be; the Ark is completed according to the exact specifications He gave." The man's rugged, calloused fingers tapped the wooden table as he reviewed out loud, "Three hundred cubits long, fifty cubits wide, thirty cubits high. Completely gopherwood. Nest-like rooms inside; covered with pitch both inside and out. Lower, second, and third..."

"And the door," added Marriet.

"Yes, of course, the door."

His wife's face looked troubled, "I still do not know how you are going to shut it: it is so large!"

He gave her hand a squeeze, "I'm certain God did not leave out that detail by mistake. He has His reasons and does not always explain them to us. But my heart tells me as long as He continues to extend mercy towards men the door to the Ark will stay open."

"And when it shuts?" Shem asked slowly. There was a heavy silence around the table.

"I pray as many are inside as can fit," Noak replied.

Everyone was quiet. I realized I was holding my breath. Though not sure what all the words meant there was a weight to them that was impossible to shake off, as if they were building to something. All day long I had felt it growing: an inescapable feeling that this strange place, these strange people were part of the answer I had been searching for. I sat up and leaned forward; for some reason my heart was pounding. Nathak saw the movement and took it for aggression. Positioning himself between Shem and myself, he stood like an unblinking gargoyle staring me down. I barely noticed; all my attention was directed towards Noak. He knew something—this grave, kind, mysterious man—much more than he was saying: something that I felt somehow was what I had been searching to know for weeks. The next few moments seemed to drag on forever, but when the silence finally broke it was like a dam bursting open. And it came from Shem.

"'The end of all flesh'," he murmured. It sounded in my ears like a cry from heaven.

The end of all flesh?

"Those were the Creator's words so long ago," his father answered. "*'The end of all flesh has come before Me, for the earth is filled with violence through them; and behold, I will destroy them with the earth'.*"

Suddenly the images from the Dream jumped into my mind. Falling trees and churning earth. Ear-ripping screams. The black wave. No escape.

Noak continued, "God said the floodwaters would destroy from under heaven all flesh in which is the breath of life." My heart nearly stopped.

Floodwaters?

A sound behind me made me jump and spin around, almost expecting to see the terrible dark wave rising into the sky. It was just the wind in the trees.

Still my veins pounded. My whole body started trembling, inside and out. It was Noak's voice, solemn and powerful, that caused me to slowly turn back around.

"'Everything that is on the earth—*shall die*.'" His eyes met mine with awful clarity. My mouth went dry; I wanted to look away but couldn't.

Everything...that...is...on...the...earth...shall...die!

The words buzzed in my head, driving in like a fatal hammer.

The Dream is true! The end of all things is coming!

My worst fears were realized. Right then and there, in a moment too horrible to explain, I felt myself lost: sucked into the black wave of death, beyond rescue and without hope. Dread seized my mind and I almost passed out.

Yet just then a change came to the man's face. It softened. Compassion filled the grave eyes and his voice lifted. "*'But I will establish my covenant with you; and you shall go into the Ark',*" gazing at each of his family, he continued the words of God, "*'you, your sons, your wife, and your son's wives with you'.*" Then he looked back at me, "*'And of every living thing of all flesh you shall bring two of every sort into the Ark, to keep them alive with you... two of every kind will come to you to keep them alive'.*" A glimmer of light broke through the darkness in my mind.

Two of every kind will come...to keep them alive.

The words "to keep them alive" felt like a hand reaching down to pull me out of a bottomless pit. My lungs started breathing again.

Does that mean there is hope after all?

Suddenly I realized everyone was looking at me. Even Womby had apparently forgotten about food long enough to listen to what was being said; his eyes were as big as little saucers. I wasn't sure why the humans stared, but as the wombat and I looked at each other we each knew exactly what the other was thinking.

The Dream is true!

It was a heavy moment—full of fear, wonder, and significance. And, of course, it was broken up by a growl from Nathak.

"Get off the wall," he rumbled, "You're making them nervous!"

"Peace, Nathak! It's alright," Shem corrected, while Chenna let go of her beloved husband's arm long enough to give the wolf a rub. But I took his advice anyway. Too many thoughts and feelings were coursing through me to sit still any longer. Besides, I needed solitude. Dropping into the shadow on the other side of the wall, the glow of the patio was suddenly blocked, making way for the glow of the stars overhead.

For hours I wandered by their light through the woods going nowhere in particular, giving little heed to what passed around me. There were birds enough, a badger or two, a fox and jackal, along with the usual company of bugs. They held little interest for me. My mind was consumed with bigger things: things I knew, if true, would change the course of my life—and every other creature's. I must have walked for miles, mostly in circles, trying to mentally unravel everything I had seen and heard that day. Over and over I replayed the words of Noak. Memories, both dreaming and waking, seemed to flash before my eyes in the dark. *"Floodwaters"*—the black wave. *"The end of all flesh"*—the screams in my Dream. Death. Despair. Judgment. But then, "Two of every kind will come to you to keep them alive". What did *that* mean? Why did it fill me with such hope and dread all at once?

Round and round the questions flew while I tried to grab them and piece together some kind of answer. On and on my legs churned, as if the movement might help my brain.

* * *

I don't know if it was by chance or not, but eventually I found myself standing at the bottom of the long boardwalk to the massive structure in the midst of the quiet, moonlit field. One thing I had determined by now was this monstrous wooden thing was indeed what the others had called "the Ark". It loomed silent and daunting against the starry sky, blue and ghostly in the pale light. The boardwalk looked like a vague, dreamy highway leading up into the misty heavens; at the far end of it, halfway up the side of the Ark, stood the infamous doorway, looking small and dark. I found myself creeping up the smooth planks. Higher and higher I rose into the air: like climbing a narrow, gently sloping hillside made of flat wood. The air was very still and the night had grown so late there was almost no noise at all, except for my own breath. As the ground fell away beneath the boardwalk the whole valley opened up in an aerial view. There were the four houses and giant barn, now dark and lifeless, then the fields and groves of trees laid out in an orderly pattern. Beyond these lay the forest, stretching in a wide circumference as far as the eye could see, and overall arched the ancient sky, cold and awesome in its silent grandeur.

It felt like I was the only creature awake in the whole world as I slowly, quietly, and cautiously made my way up the hull of the giant thing. The door grew closer and larger. When I finally reached the top I stopped. The view from the scaffold platform must have been something to behold, but I could not take my eyes away from the door. Or perhaps I should say doorway, since the door itself was swung back against the Ark's wall: a gigantic, square-shaped thing that looked as immovable as the side of a mountain. *No wonder Marriet wonders how they'll shut it!* I observed.

But it was the gaping black hole the door was supposed to cover that captivated me. The doorway. Wider than three elephants side by side, tall as a young long-neck, it stood open and blank: dark and mysterious within, outlined in silver moonlight. Curiosity filled me as I gazed into the black shadows. What lay inside? There was fear also, but not the kind that makes you hate whatever caused it; more like how you feel on the edge of a cliff, beholding a wilderness you've never seen before. The sheer size of the doorway seemed like an invitation in itself. I stretched out my right paw past the thick wooden doorposts, into the darkness of the Ark. Then my left. I was halfway inside. Looking up I saw my head had passed under the doorway: under a roof built by men. Suddenly memories of another man-made roof flooded my mind: the roof of my slave cage. As if burned, I quickly backed out of the doorway, and sat down on the platform.

For a long while I sat there just staring into the shadows, twitching my tail and thinking—uneasy yet unable to turn away. I lost all track of time, but eventually the shadows began to lighten and the inside of the Ark started to glow with an amber hue. The silver lining of the doorposts became golden. I turned around to face eastward: the horizon above the forest was coming alive with color. Some movement far on the ground to the left attracted my attention: one solitary figure leaving the nearest house. It was Noak, spear in hand, headed towards the same glade of gopher trees I had found him in only the morning before. As he shrank in the distance I shook my head. How much had happened since that moment! And then, as if to gild the thought, a warm light washed over me. I looked up.

The sun had risen.

TWENTY-SEVEN

THE NEXT FEW DAYS passed rather quietly: a very welcome change. Life at the Ark may not have been the most glamorous in the world, but it was peaceful and well-ordered, something the rest of the world knew nothing about. The men worked from sun-up to sun-down (and sometimes afterwards) strengthening fences, working in the fields, and gathering all kinds of food and materials either into the great barn or up into the Ark. The women helped them all they could, picking in the fields or tending the gardens and fruit groves, while continuing to run their houses and feed their men. It was a busy time for everyone on two legs, though not so much for those of us with four. There were a few oxen, a couple of camels, and a pair of elephants who did their part; but the real workers were the green dragons from Shem's cart. Their names were Huff and Grunt and they were great fun to mess with, so long as you didn't get them angry enough to actually fight back. It took me a little while to remember how to play, but eventually my mischievousness returned. One of my favorite games became stalking the two lumbering lizards, sneaking up just out of reach of their horns, and giving them a light swat. The tricky part was dodging out of the way before they could lash back. It didn't really hurt them; truthfully, I think most of the time they enjoyed trying to get me as much as I enjoyed avoiding it. Still, you had to be pretty fast on your legs to keep from getting nicked by one of those long spikes. It was a great challenge, especially when Womby decided to play along: getting them all stirred up by running under their big bellies and in and out of their stumpy feet. Then Rhia would jump in, darting in between and around the lizards, barking like she was herding a flock of sheep. All around, I think it was a great romp for everyone—except Nathak, of course. He just scowled from a distance. Always. The wolf had not smiled since he and Shem first returned, and whenever his glance fell on me it turned especially cold. I tried avoiding it as much as possible, but that proved easier said than done. The wolf watched me like a hawk no matter where I went.

But what Nathak lacked in liveliness Womby made up for with droves of mishaps and adventures. I had no idea wombats could get into so much trouble!

In his defense, though, it generally came from being nearsighted and clumsy. He had a tendency of running into things. Most things, actually. First there was the water barrel behind Shem's house. Then the pole holding up Nina's washing. After that was the pile of fencing material, the stack of clay pots, and the trek through an open door to leave muddy paw prints all over Marriet's clean kitchen floor (for which he was violently chased with a broom). Finally it reached the point when anyone saw the wombat coming they would quickly move whatever obstacle might be in his way or block off anything he might damage. And when his eyesight wasn't getting him into trouble, his appetite was. Womby had as much of a knack for finding food as any animal I had ever seen: whether out of Kawm's wheat fields, Chenna's berry patch, or Nina's "thief-proof" bird feeders. But the wombat met his match the day he tried to steal food from Grunt's private feed trough; I can still hear him squealing in panic as the thundering lizard chased him all the way down the pasture. It is a good thing the men had just reinforced the fence or the wombat might not have made it. Even so he only managed to scoot under the lowest slat just in time. I laughed and shook my head at the sight: for everything he was, Womby would never be a master thief. Not like Eddie, anyway.

As the days passed, I found myself thinking more and more about the monkey, and Bulk the bear, wondering what had happened to them—and

Saphirra. Every time I thought about the lioness the image of her looking at me in the arena, eyes blue as the cloudless sky and full of pity, would come back. With it came a strange, sharp feeling—pleasant but painful, all at once. I would shake it off with a shudder, reminding myself that, whatever happened, I would probably never see her or Eddie or Bulk again. Not exactly a comforting thought either, but I tried to stick to it (not always successfully). After all, it could have been worse: I could have been Nina, waiting for Yeffeth to arrive. The delayed arrival of Noak and Marriet's eldest son had not caused too much concern at first; he and Shem had left at the same time on similar missions and apparently he was equally as capable of fending for himself, being an expert with the bow and arrow. But as the moon changed from skinny, to plump, to invisible, you could feel the anxiety begin to grow among the family. No one said much about it, but they looked more and more towards the southern road, and their prayers often turned to the oldest son's welfare.

And their concerns were not unfounded. The longer I stayed at the Ark the more I realized just how different these Men of the Tree were from the rest of humanity (in a good way)—and just how much the rest of humanity hated them for it. Being so close to a city and main road, it was a common event for bands of people to gather at a distance and mock Noak and his family, always focusing the brunt of their attacks on the Ark. That wouldn't have been so bad (aside from being obnoxious), but sometimes their words turned to actions. Usually it was attempted vandalism, either to the boat itself or some other property. At least there I could help; I started patrolling the perimeter of the valley. Most of the time just showing up did the trick. One look at me approaching and any would-be troublemakers took off in a dead run.

But other threats were more serious. All I saw were angry looks, but from what Rhia told me there had been some scrapes in the past. Men had just laughed at the Ark first being built—until Noak told them what it was for. Then they got angry. Most humans didn't like being accountable to anybody for their actions—let alone an all-wise, all-good, all-powerful God who rewarded obedience but punished rebellion. Noak warned them over and over, pleading with them to turn from their evil and come to the Ark to be saved. But instead of heeding the message the rebels turned on the messenger. More than once they had attacked the Men of the Tree, physically and with words. Noak and his sons bore it as best they could, showing mercy and patience. But when their wives and homes started being attacked the Men of the Tree took up arms: not to strike first, but to defend what the Creator had entrusted to them. That was why they carried weapons, even the women. Because of this there had been no real confrontations for many years. But tensions remained high. The Men of the Tree were outnumbered and out-muscled. God would have to be their shield, and they knew it—because they also knew it was only a matter of time before the mocking and the threats turned into something else. Something deadly.

Which was why when a troop of men on camels were seen approaching one cloudy day that Shem and Kawm grabbed their swords and Noak came out of the house spear in hand. Marriet peered over his shoulder. "Stay inside," he said calmly yet with an authority that made his wife obey without hesitation, shutting the door behind him. Nathak and Rhia were both barking angrily as the cloud of dust drew closer. Chenna, Nina, and Atani ran in from the fields to see what was happening.

"Go in with Mother," Shem called, adding as he looked at Atani, "keep the bow handy." He gave Chenna a reassuring smile then turned to face the oncomers. The girls disappeared inside the house, Noak making sure they were safe within before he moved from the door. Then he joined his sons. Tall and grim, the three stood side by side, weapons in hand: the father in the middle with a son on each side. I had taken a position under one of the supporting beams of the Ark hidden in its shadow and not too far from where the men stood. The wolves greeted the camel troop first: snapping and growling at their heels. Still the lanky beasts pounded closer. Noak held up his spear and pointed it at the man on the lead camel.

"That is far enough!" He bellowed, the thunder of his voice making my ears wince, "Come no further!" The animals jerked to a stop, moaning and huffing. As the dust settled I counted seven of them: all shaggy and outfitted with what once must have been very colorful gear, caked over with mud and dirt, as if they had been travelling a very long ways. On their backs rode men almost as dirty as the camels, bare chested and broad, their bottom half wrapped in faded rags and their heads topped with soiled turbans: the only thing bright or shiny about them were the long, curved swords at each of their sides. This description fit all but one: a skinny, well-dressed man, emerging from their midst on a black, winded beast. As the others made way for him he flicked the camel's rump with a sharp whip; the worn out creature folded to the ground. After brushing off his robe of green and black silk and readjusting his own, spotless turban (which looked far too big for his long, narrow head), the man approached Noak and bowed low.

"Hail, Lord of the Ark," he cried in a high, crackly voice. "I see you have *finally* finished your masterpiece! Tell me, when will it be ready to sail?" The man's mouth broke into an oily smile, showing a row of golden and jagged teeth. From the second I saw him on the camel my ears had pinned straight back on my head, thinking I recognized him (though I wasn't so sure under all that fine clothing). Now there was no doubt.

Marsed, the slave trader!

A sudden impulse came over me to jump on the evil little man and shred him to ribbons! But I held back, more out of curiosity than mercy. I wanted to know what he was up to. "And how are the famous 'Arkians' these days," he whined, "still preparing for the end of the world? Or—oh no! Did it come already and I missed it?" His grin reminded me of a weasel.

Noak held his composure and his head high. "It's been a long time, Marsed," he replied calmly. ("Not long enough!" I heard Shem whisper) "To what do we owe this sudden visit?" The older man's words were gracious but he kept his spear ready.

Marsed sighed like a wheezing tree, "Business—always business!" He waved his bony hand, "A man in my position cannot be expected to take the time for mere social calls, not now that I've been promoted to official Supplier of the Games by the Master himself!" The proud man adjusted his green robes, "But that doesn't mean we cannot mix business with a little pleasure." With a sharp clap two of his slaves came scrambling up: one carrying a richly embroidered rug and the other holding a good-sized chest made of oak. "May I?" Marsed asked slyly and, after a nod from Noak, signaled for the man with the carpet to spread it on the ground. As soon as the deed was done, he sank down on it cross-legged and snapped his fingers. The same servant pulled a long pipe and small pouch out of the belt at his waist. Marsed took it roughly, waved the servant away, then motioned for Noak to join him. The regal man sat directly across from the skinny villain; never before had I seen such a vivid contrast of character. Shem and Kawm remained standing on either side of their father, as did the two servants behind Marsed, the one still holding the oak chest. There was a span of silence as the Slave Trader lit up his pipe, offered it to Noak (who refused), and started to smoke. Only after a few puffs did Marsed speak again. "It *has* been a long time, hasn't it? Not since the mute girl." He laughed, "Now *that* was a day to remember! I have to say, you did impress me, Noak; a shrewd move it was, offering your cloak like that. Good thing for me you have good taste: pure silk. What a pretty price it sold for! Yes, sir: you made me a very happy man!"

"You drove a hard bargain," Noak said with a dry smile of his own.

I found myself smirking. *The Slave Trader has met his match!*

Marsed's eyes took a cutting gleam, "Like I said: you have good taste. I'm sure she's more than paid off her weight in gold." Shem's face grew hot as he continued, "Handsome maid, she was, too—powerful attractive—and unable to talk back. The perfect woman, one could say!" He looked at Shem with a wicked grin, "Many times I've wished I had kept her myself!"

Noak wisely intervened before his son could retaliate, "I see you have not lost your flair with words, or your lust for trouble. But you will find none here unless you bring it with you."

The beady eyes turned from Shem to his father and the grin grew wider. "That all depends on what you call 'trouble'."

Noak's face remained cool and relaxed, but I saw a spark jump in his eyes as he replied, "Go on."

Instead, Marsed leaned back and took a few more long puffs. "Are you still interested in shrewd bargains, Noak?"

"Why do you ask?"

(Puff) "I may have one for you (puff)—a deal you cannot afford to miss."

Noak didn't flinch. "I don't make deals with slave traders, Marsed, you know that. What do you want from me?"

TWENTY-EIGHT

MARSED LOOKED AROUND: a crowd of people was beginning to gather. Seeing a troop of camels approach the Ark had perked their curiosity. There was a dry cackle as the greasy man gleefully popped his knuckles, always happy to draw a crowd. "You might want to hear what my deal is first, Noak, before you jump to conclusions. You *may* find it irresistible."

"Get to the point!" broke in Kawm. Noak held his hand up to calm his son, but Marsed nodded with approval.

"Quite right, quite right," he wheezed, throwing billows of smoke around in the air as he waved his hand. "Time is money and talk is cheap! Bring forward the merchandise!" The brute with the oak chest stepped forward and laid it beside Marsed. The Slave Trader reached into his robe and drew out a ring of heavy keys. One by one he went through them, taking far longer than was necessary to finally find that which would fit the chest. As the lid jarred open he smiled at Noak from the corner of his mouth. "I thought you might be interested in this," and as he spoke he reached into the chest, pulled out something long, and threw it on the rug between him and Noak. It was a bow: smooth, slender white wood, perfectly curved. The old man's face went pale and his two sons stared in dismay. Their reaction must have pleased Marsed; grinning larger than ever, he also pulled out of the chest a fine leather quiver, full of perfectly fletched, white arrows. "I believe these also go with it," he remarked and dropped them on top of the bow with a clatter.

"Yeffeth!" Shem breathed, eyes wide and jaw clenched. Kawm looked shocked and furious. Noak slowly raised his eyes from the bow to meet the Slave Trader's. Something was in them I had not seen before.

Fear.

"So I see you *do* recognize them," said Marsed, "Good! Now perhaps we can get down to business."

"Where is he?" Noak asked, voice low and strained.

"Not so fast; we haven't discussed pricing yet—"

"*Where is he?*" his voice was louder now and (though I was probably the only one who noticed) the strong hands tightened their grip on the spear.

Marsed's skinny shoulders shrugged, "He's safe—for now. Though I can't say how long he'll stay that way once the Master gets a hold of him. Have you ever seen Hittan break a creature? He certainly has a way about him; it really is something to watch." Full of arrogance the vile man leaned forward and lowered his voice so the crowd could not hear, "And I can promise you, they *will* come to watch. 'Yeffeth, son of Noak, builder of the infamous Ark'—in the Games! What a crowd-pleaser that would be!" He leaned back and took another smoke, "But I wouldn't worry: with your son's skill as an archer he should last for some time in the arenas. At least a week or two!"

His words hit their mark: Shem and Kawm both surged forward and the servants drew their swords. The men on the camels stirred in their saddles. Noak threw up his hand again to hold back his sons. Everything froze. The father looked from his two boys, to the servants, to the Slave Trader. Then at the white bow and arrows. The fierce light in his gray eyes melted. At last Noak let out a heavy sigh and his shoulders slumped; for the first time since I had met him the good man appeared old and tired.

His voice was weak, "How much do you want, Marsed?"

The Slave Trader smiled wickedly, but I didn't hear what he said in response; a sudden commotion in the crowd distracted me.

"My purse!" yelled a fat man, "My purse is gone!"

A lady just a few feet from him grew wild-eyed. "So are my rings!" she cried.

"Where's my satchel?" I heard someone else say, while another shrieked, "Someone stole my money-bag!" In a matter of seconds almost everyone in the crowd was calling out something expensive that had suddenly gone missing. The panic quickly turned to anger as fingers started pointing.

"It was him!"

"No, I saw her take it!"

"*Me?* What about *you?*"

"Thief! I saw you the other day—ogling over my jewels! Where are they?"

But while the humans were busy turning on each other, I caught glimpse of a long, furry tail swish behind the legs of Marsed's camel. On the ground in its wake lay a shiny, green stone: an emerald. Then a brown arm stretched from behind the black camel's leg and a leathery hand snatched up the jewel. I perked up.

I think I know that hand!

Moving towards the camel, I had to pass by the angry crowd. That broke things up rather quickly; one look at me and the humans went screeching away, forgetting all about their stolen goods. The men on the camels got a little nervous, too (to say nothing of the camels), but they kept in place pretty well. As I rounded behind Marsed's black beast there was nothing on the ground, but the long, furry tail was disappearing into a box strapped to the saddle on the camel's back. There were holes in the box: big enough for air to get through, but not for anything to fall out of. It shook a little as whatever was inside moved around. A scent wafted down that was unmistakable.

"Eddie?" I called out. There was a rattling and the box's lid opened up a few inches, revealing a pair of big, almond eyes peering out of the dark. As soon as they saw me they almost popped out of the furry brown head.

"*Stripes?* No way!" The monkey flew out of the box, clambered onto the camel's back, and sat down scratching his head in shock. "Stripes? Is it really you?" Then he let out a piercing *oo-oo-ee* and jumped onto my back. "I don't believe it! You're dead!" He chattered giddily and climbed onto my head, "You *were* dead right? What happened?" His face dropped in front of mine, upside down. "Why aren't you dead anymore? Don't look like yourself—kinda fat and healthy—not like yourself at all!"

"Good to see you, too, Eddie!" I chuckled.

"No, really!" The monkey hopped down to my feet and waved his arms around, "But what happened, anyway? Why didn't you show—waited for I don't know how long—and *why on earth* did you send *her* instead? What're you doing here? Where is 'here', anyway?"

"What are *you* doing here?" I countered, deciding to get to the other questions later. "I thought you'd be hundreds of miles away by now, sitting on a velvet pillow somewhere. Where is Bulk?" Immediately the monkey's face darkened and his arms dropped to his side. For a moment I feared the worst.

"Back behind bars," he said, "thanks to your lady friend."

"Saphirra?" I asked, pulse quickening, "What about her? Is she alright?"

"Oh *sure!*" the monkey threw up his hands, "As 'alright' as anyone can be in one of Marsed's jails! Not that I feel sorry for her—it's her own fault—just guess I'd feel sorry for anyone trapped in one of those clapboard, portable prisons, except for Marsed, that is. *O-o-ee!*" he cackled, "Now *that* would be pretty!"

I shook my head, "Focus, Eddie! Try and tell me what happened, from the beginning. And as fast as you can," the camels were starting to get restless and I wasn't sure how much longer it would be before the men decided to do something about it.

The monkey drew in a breath so deep I feared his lungs might explode. "I got Bulk out of the tanneries, wasn't easy, we waited and waited and waited for you in the sewers till finally this lioness shows up saying you sent her, wasn't so sure about that till she mentioned the dreams, then I figured she was telling the truth so we took up with her and headed out, and everything was going pretty good, Bulk wasn't feeling great, and had to go *sooo* slow but kept moving anyway, covered lots of miles, was even starting to like her till one night Saphirra gets all excited 'cause she thinks she smells something on the wind, something familiar, try holding her back but it's no use, stubborn female takes off, then Bulk right after her goin' *way* too fast for his leg, I go off after both of them..." Eddie ran his hand over his eyes, "Why did I *ever* get mixed up with athletes?" He moaned, "What was I thinking..."

"Keep going. What happened?"

"We wind up sneaking into what looks like a travelling circus with wagons and cages all over the place, a jack-rabbit could've seen where that was leading but Saphirra—oh *no*—she just *knew* that smell, so in she barges, right smack dab in the middle of everything, gets herself nice and captured by a bunch of thugs and then, *oooo*," Eddie shook his head, "Bulk charges in to rescue her. Poor big guy didn't have of a chance! Outnumbered and crippled..."

"You mean they captured him?"

"SMACK!" The monkey clapped his hands together, "Like a bug in a fly trap! Now they're both locked away, ready to be shipped right back to Khanok and slaughtered in the games while I got'ta be Marsed's Pick-Pocket, livin' on nothin' but peanuts, just to keep an eye on them!" Completely out of breath the monkey collapsed on the ground. "*Shew!*" He wheezed, "Fast enough for ya?"

No sooner were the words out of his mouth than the men began to move. Apparently the conference between Marsed and Noak had ended and now the Slave Trader was headed back to his black camel, a smirk on his scarred face. The sight of the man made my blood boil; I had plenty of reasons to hate him already, but knowing Saphirra and Bulk were in his clutches made me want to tear his throat out right there. Almost without thinking I planted myself between him and his pathetic camel. I didn't growl. I didn't hiss. I just stood there, ears pinned back. The smirk vanished and the wicked man's face turned white as a cloud. Like a weed in the wind he started trembling; I expected his knocking knees to give way at any moment. The slaves behind him cowered backwards, while the men on camels shifted nervously: torn between risking their own necks to save their master or staying put. My eyes never left the slimy man's throat.

"Let him pass!" a voice bellowed. It was Nathak, coming up at an agitated lope. "I said let him pass!" he growled again and took up a position beside the slave trader's wobbling legs. I scowled at the wolf, annoyed by his interference—until the look on his face made me hesitate. It was a marked combination of worry and anger: not one I had seen before. Reluctantly I backed away. The Slave Trader mustered enough courage to get to his camel. As he clambered on the dark hump I saw Eddie scramble up the rear. With a squeaky "hut-hut!" and a crack of Marsed's whip the camel came to life and the whole caravan started to move. I watched as Eddie lifted the lid and climbed into his small box. Then suddenly I looked at the Ark.

"Eddie!" I shouted, "Eddie!" The lid opened and his furry head popped out of the box, swaying around with the jog of the camel. I ran to catch up and the camel started to panic.

"Get away!" Marsed screeched, cracking his whip at me, "Get back, you monster!"

"What're you doin'?" Eddie called, clutching the box sides to keep from falling out.

"Eddie, stay here!" I shouted, dodging the Slave Master's whip, "The dreams! The dreams are true! All of them! This place," swerving to miss an angry camel's kick, "it's the only way to be saved!"

Through all the chaos I saw the monkey's eyes grow large. I saw him stare at the Ark and knew he believed me. But then his head shook, "Someone's got'ta take care of the Big Guy!"

Nathak charged in among the camels, all bristled. "Leave them alone!" he shouted, "That's an order!" But it wasn't necessary; I had already come to a standstill within the swirling dust. Away the animals thundered, wild with fear, barely giving me a last glimpse of Eddie's flat face before they were nothing more than a speck of movement on the southern horizon. "What were you *thinking?*" the wolf barked angrily, "Are you trying to get us all killed?" I glared at him and he stared back, eyes full of fire. For a moment I thought he would charge. Instead he snuffed and took off back towards the houses. I watched until the last sign of the caravan had disappeared beyond sight. My heart felt like a lead weight.

Saphirra. Eddie. Bulk. All of them prisoners. Again.

Minutes turned to hours as I stayed there, eyes locked on the southern road.

TWENTY-NINE

THE WIND HAD STARTED to pick up when I made my way through the brushy hillside. The sun was gone, having set an hour or two before, and the sky was black and inky with clouds. There was no moon or stars to light the way, but I had my sense of smell, which worked even better on nights like this. Judging from which way the wind blew and what smells were on it I could narrow down a mouse to a radius of a few feet and a family of mice to a few inches. But I wasn't hunting mice. As Marsed's troop had vanished into the south east my mind had formulated a daring plan, and as soon as it had grown dark I slipped out of the valley and into the tree line of the southern forest. The camel scent was still strong that way and easy to follow. The trick was not following it too closely lest they caught wind of me, too. So I took my time, gathering my thoughts as I went. My plan would take strategy, and lots of it, if it was to succeed—especially with no one but me to implement it.

Yet, just as I was pondering how to get past a troop of armed guards alone without being detected, my own ears detected something moving in the shadows behind me. I stopped. Still it came on, steady and quiet, but definitely drawing closer. The wind was blowing at my back masking the scent of whatever it was. I strained my eyes into the darkness of the blowing bushes. They creaked and slashed at each other in a war of shadowy branches, but eventually another form appeared among them: hunched but graceful, with four long legs sailing along the ground and two large ears pointing through the leaves. One whiff as the wind changed directions and I immediately knew my stalker's identity.

"Nathak!" I growled even before the wolf was in plain sight. Another moment and we were face to face in the darkness, almost nose to nose. "Why do you keep following me?"

The wolf snuffed. "Don't flatter yourself, cat!" he said gruffly as his gray mane blew about in the wind, "My business isn't with you tonight. Move out of the way!"

"And what business, besides following me, would bring Nathak the loyal so far from home?" For some reason the dog always brought out my impertinent side.

"I said *move!*"

A slight smile curled my mouth, "You may not have noticed, wolf, but I was here first."

For a moment our eyes deadlocked, each waiting for the other to budge and neither of us moving a muscle. At length the wolf's ears pinned back, "I don't have time for this!"

"Neither do I—"

"Then get out of the way!"

"Oh no," shaking my head, "Not until you explain why; I have no desire to be ambushed up ahead."

Now it was the wolf's turn to smile, "If I wanted to kill you, *cat*, I wouldn't need an ambush," his icy eyes flashed in the dark, "but right now I have more important things to do."

"Such as?"

"Such as freeing my Master's brother!" He must have sensed my surprise because he let out a snort and sat down impatiently, "You saw the bow and arrows. You heard the Slave Trader. He has Yeffeth ready to sell to the Man-Beast as his slave in the games." The wolf's look was keen, "You of all creatures should know what that means. Unless the masters pay Marsed what he's asked for by sunset tomorrow they have no hope of ever seeing Yeffeth alive; and even then I don't trust the Slave Trader. He has an evil smell."

I had to nod; much as I hated to admit it, the wolf was right on that point. "So what do you intend to do?"

Nathak stood up again, aggravated by what he considered an obvious question, "Find the Slave Trader's camp and rescue Yeffeth."

"Alone?"

He huffed, "Do you see anyone with me?"

I didn't answer. I was too busy thinking. My brain had started churning in a direction I did not care for. The wolf took my hesitation as resistance.

"I'll tell you just once more. *Get out of my way!*"

A deep breath was required for me to keep my cool. But I had to. A new plan was forming in my head: one I hoped would make restraint worth it. All I had to do was convince the bristling dog in front of me we both might have more chance at success if we worked together: as allies. Nathak growled and I bit my tongue.

This isn't going to be easy!

* * *

The wind was still kicking things around as I peered through a thick holly bush to the clearing beyond. The dirt under my claws was grainy with pebbles and sand due to the inky black river flowing about half a mile away. Sprawled out on the shore in between, like a dismembered monster, lay Marsed's caravan. At least twenty-five wagons, either piled high with cages or acting as cages themselves, were scattered in no particular order along the wide, stony beach, and in between them were campfires. There were guards, too, all over the place; just a few feet from the holly bush stood a pack of eight, each burly and grim. Most likely they were some of the same lot who had paid the Ark a visit, especially since the herd of shaggy camels was tied up right behind them. As I observed the whole situation a low whistle escaped through my teeth. It was a little more of a challenge than I had hoped to find.

In the midst of the shifting leaves and creaking branches there was a "huff" at my side. "Not quite what you were expecting?" I turned to see the wolf crouching in the darkness, scowling even more than usual. His gray ears were up, his black nose out, his glacial eyes sharp but not towards me: they were pointed at the camp, making their own observations.

I couldn't help but smile a little, "You came after all?"

Nathak gave me an icy stare. "This isn't for you, cat." Turning again to the men and wagons he rumbled, "Are you sure about this plan of yours?"

"No," I whispered honestly, "but it's the only one I've got. I don't suppose you have any suggestions?" The dark scowl remained but Nathak just grunted and shrugged.

"Let's get this over with!"

I nodded, "You know what to do?"

Wrong question. Slowly the wolf's face turned around as if to say, "I *always* know what to do!" With some effort I kept from smacking it, "I mean: you remember what we discussed..."

"I know my job," he snapped, "just make sure you do yours."

This is for Saphirra and Eddie and Bulk, I reminded myself hastily, *just think about them!* "Fine," I said out loud, "get over beside those camels and stay out of sight." The wolf took off instantly and was almost beyond earshot before I could add, "Remember, wait for my signal!" Then he was gone.

I shook my head in frustration and went back to assessing what would be the best course for me to take. *Under the wagons?* Of course, that would put me on the ground, closer to the men, but I would have the shadows. *On top of them?* Could be riskier, but the height might be an advantage: humans did not look up much. *But getting from one wagon to another could be tricky, they're spaced so unevenly.* Minutes went by as I weighed my options. There was also the problem of not knowing exactly where Marsed was. I had my hunches, but could not be sure. It would take a lot of stealth and strategy to find him, a lot of careful deliberation. *One wrong move and—*

Suddenly a piercing, lonely howl broke out on my right! I jerked out of my thoughts with a jump. The camel heads all shot up in panic. The guards were shaken, too, though they tried not to show it till another vicious wail, this time even closer, set them all shivering. My surprise turned to anger.

He didn't wait for my signal!

A third howl echoed under a grove of blowing trees right next to where the camels were tied; they started bellowing and pulling against their ropes. Seeing them, one of the guards rallied the others to grab their weapons and follow him to take a look around. Reluctantly, they scattered into the bushes and undergrowth. I watched with growing frustration as two of them started to head my way.

Well, so much for strategy!

Darting to the side, I left an empty holly bush for them to find, and circled around to the edge of the clearing. For the moment it was empty, with nothing but a lonely campfire and several yards of sandy dirt between me and the nearest wagon. As I darted across the open space I decided my plan of action.

Under.

Slipping beneath the wagon, I paused in the shade of its under-belly to look back. The men's torches they had grabbed from the fire were zigzagging through the woods, while Nathak's howls seemed to come from all directions. Angry as I was with him, the speed at which he got around without being detected *was* rather impressive—for a dog. The wind also helped, carrying the wolf's terrible moan through every leaf and twig, making it much harder to tell where it originally came from. Satisfied the camel guards would be busy for a while, I turned my attention to the rest of the camp and struck out under the shadows.

THIRTY

IT TOOK SOME MANEUVERING and a lot of following my nose, but I finally found my objective: a flamboyant, brightly colored wagon directly in the midst of all the others. Marsed's. Two guards stoically stood by the steps of the front door, but they never saw me sneak around to the rear. One good push of the back legs and I was on the roof; it rocked slightly, but a stiff gust of wind easily took the blame for it. I looked around and saw what I was hoping to find: a large vent in the middle, swung open wide.

So far, so good.

Creeping over I peeked through the wide hole into the wagon below. No lights were burning and there was a terrific snore from further in: the Slave Trader was obviously sleeping. Searching the dark with my eyes I caught sight of a small little box in a cluttered corner, poked through with tiny holes. As lightly as possible I dropped through the vent into the dim wagon. Once my paws met the rug floor I held my breath, waiting to see if anyone had heard. Nothing but snoring came from the far end, and now I could see Marsed stretched out on a small, plush bed. Silently I tip-toed to the box, stepping over and in between more junk than any one person should ever own.

"Eddie," I whispered when I reached the box, "Eddie, wake up!" There was a little shuffling and sniffing inside and two eyes appeared through the holes.

"Stripes!" He gasped, "Wha...how?"

"Shhh! There's no time! Can you get out of there?"

"With the key."

"Where is it?"

"Over there with Sunshine," his skinny arm poked out of a hole and pointed to Marsed's bed. With dismay I looked and saw a heavy ring of keys dangling from the Slave Trader's hand. Thankfully, they were dangling very loosely; a little wiggling with my teeth and they slipped off without detection. Eddie thrust his hands through the holes in the side of the box, grabbed the keys, and unlocked the lid in a matter of seconds. The monkey jumped out like a spring. "You're a treasure! A jem!" he exclaimed, bouncing to my head and furiously rubbing the fur between my ears.

"Enough of that," I hissed, "Grab those keys!" He obeyed, a smile stretched all over his leather face.

"Bulk?" He chattered excitedly.

"First things first," I said, watching to make sure Marsed was still sleeping, "Can you tie a knot?"

* * *

When the Slave Trader awoke he found himself face to face with me. I straddled the bed, my front paws on his wiry chest, holding him down, while my agile friend wrapped him tightly with a handy length of rope. I lowered my nose within inches of his pointy one and snarled. The horror in Marsed's eyes was short lived: another second and he had passed out.

"There!" Eddie exclaimed, tightening the last knot, "I'd like to see him get out of that—or not!"

"Good work." I stared at the wicked, greedy man, now helplessly bound and unconscious beneath me. *I could snuff him out like a candle right now!* But then I remembered the Men of the Tree. They did not like revenge. I jumped to the floor. "Gag him!" I commanded Eddie, "Then see what you can do with the guards." Both tasks were done quickly. After sneaking out the vent, the monkey found some way to distract the guards and opened the front door once they were gone.

"You know, I'm startin' to think *you* can't get along without me either!" He cackled with a twinkle in his eye.

"Where are Bulk and Saphirra?" I asked as he closed the door, locking it tight with the heavy keys.

"This way!" He waved, bouncing around the corner of the wagon—only to come screeching back the next second and dive under my legs. Simultaneously, Nathak's lanky shadow came into view.

"What took so long!" he said, "I've been waiting half an hour for that door to open!"

I had my own bone to pick with the wolf. "Why didn't you wait for my signal?"

"There wasn't time."

"You mean you got impatient!"

"If I *had* waited, cat, we'd both still be in the bushes!"

I was about to retaliate when Eddie jumped in between us. "Wait—hold up! You two know each other?" The wolf and I glared, but had to shrug reluctantly. "So he doesn't wan'na eat me?" the monkey asked, pointing a long thumb at Nathak.

"No," I answered.

"Are you mad?" the wolf added.

"Great!" Eddie exclaimed, "Come on, then!" Bounding back around the corner, he rattled the keys and called out, "Hurry up!" Nathak and I stared at each other; then the wolf rolled his eyes and followed the monkey, forcing me to bring up the rear. I snuffed.

Someday, Wolf!

* * *

The monkey led us on a twisting, turning path between wagons, which worked out pretty well so long as he remembered we couldn't swing on things or squeeze into spaces the size of a twig. We passed by several campfires, round which were huddled groups of men sleeping on mats, playing games and gambling, or loudly talking and jesting with each other; between their own noise and that of the wind and river they never saw us. I couldn't tell about the creatures in the wagons themselves, but if they knew we were there they kept quiet (captivity will do that to you). There certainly were many of them; almost every cart and vehicle we passed was loaded to the brim with cages, boxes, and containers filled with living things—bird, beast, and human. The smells brought back memories. Terrible memories. But just when I was beginning to wonder how much more of this I could take, the monkey stopped and clambered up the iron wheel of a wagon. On the wagon's flatbed was a large wooden box (surrounded by smaller ones) with narrow slats near the top; Eddie jumped on the box and looked upside down through the slats.

"Bulk!" He whispered hoarsely, "Bulk, can you hear me?" There was a tense silence. Then a deep moan.

"Time for breakfast?" the bear yawned.

Eddie cackled, "Not yet, Big Guy, time to get you out of there!" Up came the keys and Bulk's heavy cage door fell open. The big, black creature blinked sleepily as he looked around, still not quite awake. His forepaw was swollen and bent underneath him. The monkey jumped in the cage, pushing and shoving his friend, "Come *on* Bulk! Got'ta get up, got'ta *move!*" but the drowsy bear would not budge.

"Allow me," Nathak mumbled and disappeared into the shadows. He returned shortly, a large piece of bread in his mouth, drenched with honey.

"Where did you get that?" I asked in surprise.

"You'll never know," he replied through his teeth, waving the bread in the air. The bear's big nose started wiggling and his eyes brightened; with a struggle he pulled up and half-lumbered, half-fell off the wagon. He limped severely on his wounded paw, but Nathak still just barely had time to toss the bait before the bear stole it right out of his mouth.

I nodded to the monkey as he hopped down beside his friend, "Now, Saphirra..."

"Wait a second," the wolf broke in. "I'm looking for a man," he said to Eddie. "His name is Yeffeth: tall, slim, reddish-brown hair—"

"Yeah, I know him: Marsed's golden boy," the monkey waved his hand to the side, "Way over there on the other end—lots of guards. But what about Bulk? He can't sneak around like you two!"

"Which is why we need Saphirra," I insisted, "now where is she?"

Three wagons away we found her: crammed in a cage of iron not big enough for her to stand in. She lay unconscious, her fine coat matted with mud and her white head resting listlessly on her paws. At sight of her my heart gave a jump, quickly followed by a wave of pity. I had never approved of her pride, but it was still gut-wrenching to see so fine a creature brought so low. "Saphirra," I said quietly. The sound of my voice made her stir. The blue eyes came to life. When they saw me they grew wide.

"Sengali?" She breathed, "No...it...it *can't* be!" The white head shook in disbelief, "I thought you were dead!"

I smiled softly, "So did I. Are you alright?"

Her eyes were like sapphire pools reflecting the starlight. They filled with tears and a grateful smile lifted the edges of her mouth as she answered, "Yes, fine."

I was just realizing I had never seen her smile before when Nathak gruffly added, "Which is more than I can say for the rest of us if we don't keep moving. Hurry it up, monkey!"

"Yes, your Lordship!" Eddie made a sweeping bow, somersaulted onto the bars of the cage and applied the keys, riding the door as it swung wide near my ears. "Next time," he whispered, "let's leave Grumpy at home!" I was too busy watching Saphirra to reply. She leapt to the ground with fluid grace, and, in spite being a little haggard, was still beautiful enough to be a distraction. The monkey turned on her. "Girl, did *you* make a mess!" he chattered, "If you even *think* of ever running off like that again—"

"Don't worry, Eddie," the lioness spoke, voice weak and broken. "Thank you for coming back for me."

"It wasn't for you," the monkey spat.

"Enough," I broke in, "Nathak is right—we need to keep moving." The wolf glanced in surprise: apparently amazed we agreed on something (which kind of surprised me, too). "How are you doing, Bulk?"

The bear grunted as he licked his festering paw. "Can't complain," he rumbled, though clearly that was not entirely true.

"Saphirra, I need you to stay with Bulk; see he gets safely into the western woods. If all goes well we will join you there before daybreak. If not, keep heading west and north until you find a place called the Ark—and stay there. Do you understand?"

"Yes," the lioness nodded and I knew she could be trusted.

Eddie pointed his long finger in her face, "And don't you leave him, not for a second! Don't you hurt him, either, or you'll have *Eddie* to deal with!"

* * *

Once sure the bear and lioness were safely on their way, Nathak, Eddie, and I turned inward again, heading for the other side of the camp. Getting there without being seen took longer than I hoped it would, especially when there was always the possibility Marsed might be discovered any minute, tied up on his bed. But eventually we wound up in the shadows around an opening in the wagons. In the center was another box, much like Bulk's only made out of iron, and in between it and us was a small host of guards. Fifteen, to be exact.

"That's him," Eddie whispered, "the golden boy." Nathak growled in anger. I just shook my head.

That's a lot of guards!

"We need a distraction," the wolf said, and for the first time he sounded a little out of control, "a big one!"

Eddie waved his hand in protest, "Don't look at me: fourteen men is my limit."

I glanced around. We were surrounded by wagons filled with cages just like the rest of the camp. Some had locks on them while others were closed with wooden latches. Many had bars I could see through, but some were completely enclosed. All held some kind of prisoner. Ape, ostrich, rhinoceros, lizard, elephant, turtle, snake, man—all packed in like so much meat for the marketplace. I knew how that felt; I had tasted the bitterness of slavery. Now I stood on the other side of the bars—by a miracle given a second chance. *But what about them?* My mind asked. The answer came out of my mouth almost before I knew it.

"Set them free."

That got the other's attentions.

"What?" the wolf barked quietly.

"We set them free!" I repeated, the idea turning to conviction, "Open the doors, break down the cages. Cause so much chaos the guards never see us coming!" Eddie was in shock, but what struck me more was the look on Nathak's face: a subtle smile of approval.

"Are you *crazy?*" the monkey cried, his long arms dangling.

"We need a diversion; they need their freedom."

The almond eyes scanned the myriad of wagons and locks. "*All* of them?"

"All of them!"

As I turned to get to work I heard the monkey mutter, "Good thing I didn't have plans for tonight!"

THIRTY-ONE

WE STARTED with the small things—ferrets, squirrels, badgers, chameleons—hardly enough to create a disturbance. Until they started pouring out in droves. But before the men had a chance to respond, out came the bigger creatures: buffalo, hyenas, crocodiles, giant monkeys. By the time we got to a pair of young longnecks there was widespread pandemonium. Men were running everywhere, shouting or screaming, trying to either catch something or keep from being caught. Eddie handled anything requiring a key, while Nathak and I got to use a more direct approach: with fang, claw, and brute strength we busted latches, broke doors, smashed crates open, and lifted up roofs. It was a beautiful mess—one big circus of chaos—and I loved every minute of it! Predator and prey ran side by side to freedom in an unspoken truce. I even enjoyed setting the birds free. "Eddie," I called, while watching a pair of white doves fly off like two small clouds into the night sky, "this way!" The monkey jumped on my back and we ran towards a group of wagons I had not seen yet—the only section still locked up. Jumping over some splintered wood and dodging a sprinting kangaroo, we prepared to quickly open the last three wagons and go free Yeffeth.

Till I looked up. Staring down at me from a cage in the corner of the nearest wagon stood a lioness: green eyes big and shaggy jaw dropped beneath her long fangs.

Lena!

I froze. Everything around us swirled, but the lioness and I did not move. The last time I had seen her she was jumping over the wall of a garden, leaving me and the Great-Father to die by wounds she had given to us. One of us had. Now she was staring at me from behind bars, a look of horrified shock plastered on her smug face. Eddie bounded off my back and started unlocking her cage.

"Wait!" I growled. The monkey looked at me in surprise. My eyes narrowed. *So the tables have turned!* Lena lowered her head and pinned her ears back but her whole body trembled. Her life was in my power and she knew it. Hate and fear poured out of her eyes. This was my chance. All I had to do was walk away and revenge was mine. The lioness would finally pay for all the pain and suffering she had caused. But then

I remembered the Dream: the coming flood. She knew nothing of it. I did. There was no time to warn her; if I left her chained in captivity with no way of escape—*knowing* she would die, *wanting* her to die...

I'll be a murderer, too.

Nathak came up behind. "We need to move," he panted, nodding towards the growing number of men now running around with weapons in their hands. Still my mind wrestled with justice and vengeance.

But she deserves it!

The lioness's eyes narrowed to hateful slits. "Go ahead, Sengali!" She spat bitterly, "You've won! Take off!"

Suddenly a voice came to my mind, a memory. *"Be it judgment or mercy, His justice is for all creatures"*. The Old One had spoken those words to Shem just before he died; they were the words that caused the young man to search for me and spend his last coin to redeem my life. Those words had set me free to find the Ark. I had been shown mercy. Could I now withhold it? Eddie waited, keys in hand. Nathak glanced back and forth from me to the lioness. Lena glared. I took a deep breath.

"Eddie, set her free!"

The lionesses' mouth dropped wide open. In no time at all the lock had sprung and her cage door flew up. Still she hesitated: too stunned to move.

"Get the rest of them!"

With a salute the monkey swung down to the other wagons. Nathak stayed with me, his body tense and focused on Lena.

The lioness finally found her voice. "What's the catch?" she asked warily.

"There is none," I responded. "It all depends on whether or not you want to live." Suddenly Nathak bristled and spun to the right; a host of lionesses were leaping out of the remaining wagons! The men started running in all directions, their angry shouts turning to cries of panic.

Lena grinned, "Thanks, Sengali: you just rescued Mantos' whole pride!" and with one powerful leap jumped to the ground. In a moment Eddie returned.

"That's the last of them," he exhaled, wiping his hand over his face. "Shew! What a madhouse!"

"Come on!" Nathak called impatiently and took off at a sprint, while Eddie leapt to his back and held on tight.

"You're with me," I said to Lena, deciding I wanted her where I could keep an eye on her.

"Says who?" She sneered. But the way I lowered my ears and glared made the lioness shrink. Thanks to Hittan's Games, I was not the same cat she had faced only a few weeks before.

"Let's go." I didn't have to say it twice; Lena lowered her head and shuffled in front while I drove from the rear.

The scene around Yeffeth's cage was a very different one than a few minutes before: no guards were in sight, except those running around in a frenzy—far too preoccupied to notice the furry monkey shuffling through keys in front of the iron door. As the heavy thing swung open Nathak rushed inside, tail wagging anxiously. But his fears were unfounded. In a few moments a man emerged with him: tall and thinner than he probably should have been (thanks to Marsed's hospitality) but still wiry and muscular. His brown hair and beard were tinted with red, framing a face both frank and intelligent. Two sharp hazel eyes darted about, assessing the situation, while he held his left arm as though it was injured. He leaned down to the dog.

"You lead, old friend," he spoke low and calmly, "I'll follow." On cue, the wolf started off at a lope, though careful to go slow enough for Yeffeth to keep up. The young man was stiff from captivity and stumbled a few times, but his strength grew as we kept moving. Steadily we made our way through the chaos back towards the western woods: Nathak leading with Eddie on his back, followed by Yeffeth, while Lena and I brought up the rear from a distance so as not to frighten the young man. We were just about to reach the tree line where the herd of camels was tied when there was a screech behind us.

"There they are! Stop them!" Looking back I saw Marsed cowering between two guards, frazzled and hysterical, thrusting his bony fingers our way. More guards came up beside him.

"Run!" Nathak shouted.

"The camels!" I called back, "Into the camels!"

In we rushed, sending the beasts into hysterics. Lost in their havoc, the guards lost us—though not for long except for some quick thinking by Yeffeth. Grabbing an ax that lay nearby he cut several of the animals' ropes as we passed through, setting them lose and creating even more confusion. Soon the guards were far too busy chasing camels to pursue us, and we slipped beyond their reach into the safety of the forest just as daylight began to break.

* * *

It did not take long to find Bulk and Saphirra (more like they found us) and soon we were all on our way, headed back through the same woods Nathak and I had met in the night before. At first Yeffeth seemed a little concerned by his new travelling companions, but the wolf's calmness helped assure him all was well. Actually, it impressed me how quickly the man adapted to our presence as if we were as normal to him as the dog. The latter still led the way, though his long legs were forced to go much slower than he would have liked, thanks to Yeffeth's injury and Bulk's wounded paw. Eventually the man had to rest: collapsing onto a fallen log while the bear fell in a heap on the ground. The wolf checked on his Master, then approached Eddie, who had taken turns riding on different backs and now sat rubbing Bulk's.

"He's hungry," the wolf said, nodding towards Yeffeth. "Go find some food he can eat, monkey."

Eddie looked up. "Ever think about using people's names?" The wolf just scowled. "Alright! Alright!" He got up with a groan, but then rumpled the bear's fur. "I'll get somethin' for you, too, Big Guy," and scampered off into some berry bushes.

It took a few trips before the man had had enough berries to renew his strength (Bulk never had enough), but he did revive. His attention turned to a gash in his left arm: a nasty looking thing that must have been neglected for several days. With effort the man managed to gather some herbs and, mixing them with the amber sap of a tree, applied the salve to the wound. He winced at first then relaxed as the soothing medicine took effect. When his eyes opened again they were clearer. They fell on the bear. Moving slowly, Yeffeth approached Bulk—now furiously licking his swollen paw. The bear caught wind of him and tensed; the man stopped but began speaking softly. He pulled out a branch loaded with berries and held it forward. Instantly Bulk's long snout started twisting. As Yeffeth handed the berries over he started rubbing the healing salve gently into Bulk's paw. The bear shifted a little, but he was too pre-occupied wit heating to do much more. Once out of salve, the man placed some leaves over the wound of his own arm and fell asleep against the fallen log.

I stood peering into the woods around us. Ever since we escaped the camp I had felt wary, my ears and nose detecting things that made me look behind more than once. Saphirra and Lena seemed to notice it, too, though they said nothing. But as soon as the man was asleep Nathak walked up.

"We're being followed," he mumbled.

"I know," I replied in an equally low tone. A minute passed where we both stared into the surrounding forest, poised for any sign of pursuit. All was quiet. Too quiet. "Stay with them," I said at last, "I'll see what I can find."

Overhearing, Saphirra came up. "I'm going with you," she said. I shook my head, but she insisted, "You can't go alone."

I was about to ask her why when Lena cut in, "And what about me? Where do I go?" Something in the lionesses' voice made me think I might not want to be left alone with her.

"Where I say." Then I nodded to Sapphirra, "Alright. Let's move." As the half-sisters turned back into the woods I whispered to Nathak, "Don't wait for us."

The way he said "I won't," left me in no doubt the wolf would keep his word.

THIRTY-TWO

WHEN WE HAD GONE a few minutes through the thick underbrush I stopped, convinced we were out of earshot of Nathak. "What've we stopped for?" Lena said impatiently. Gazing around, I observed we were in the bottom of a dip in the forest, almost like a natural bowl. I looked straight at the she-cat.

"Call them."

Saphirra glanced from me to Lena. The latter just grunted, "Huh?"

"Call them!"

"What are you talking about?"

My eyes narrowed, "Your soldiers, Lena—the ones Eddie set free—they've been following us all morning."

She rolled her eyes and guffawed, "You're imaging things, Sengali!" but Saphirra stood as still as a stone.

I wasn't in the mood for nonsense, "*I said*—call them!" The grin vanished. The proud lioness dipped her head; she knew she had been found out. With a very unpleasant expression she stared at me then opened her mouth in a deep throated moan. Several times she made the horrible sound, and as she did there was a rustling up above us. One by one, lionesses appeared, standing on the circular ridge around us, their tan and speckled forms blending in amidst the green foliage. I counted twenty-seven.

"What you were hoping for?" Lena asked, beaming with contempt and pleasure, confident the game had turned her way. But I wasn't satisfied. One person was missing whose distinct, repulsive smell had troubled me all night long. At first I blamed it on the plethora of men and animals in the caravan. Until I had seen Lena. Then when the other lionesses had jumped out of their cages, my hunch became even stronger. Now, after smelling it for a few hours— always lingering behind but never far away—there was no longer any doubt in my mind.

"Where is he?"

Saphirra's face was on full alert, while Lena pretended ignorance. "*He?*"

"You know who I mean," I said dryly. "Where is Mantos?" The older lioness just looked around, avoiding the question, so I turned to her younger sister, "He was in the caravan, wasn't he? A prisoner?"

The blue orbs were big and transparent. "Yes," she answered honestly.

"And that's why you left Eddie and Bulk—to try and rescue him? To rescue all of them?" The white head lowered and her ears drooped; feeling the stares of her peers she could only nod. "Well," I repeated to Lena, "where is he?"

She shrugged, "How should I know? Mantos goes where he pleas—"

"Mantos!" I called out, "Show yourself! I have something to tell you—something about your Dream—but only face to face!" I could smell his foul scent; it was close. "I know you can hear me! Come out in the open if you dare!"

"You don't have to shout." Slowly he appeared to the left, one gargantuan piece at a time, looming up over the rim of the hill like a monster rising out of the earth. "So, we meet again Sengali," he rumbled, his one eye gleaming down at me, "in different—yet similar—circumstances. You still seem to be outnumbered and I still have the upper-hand."

"You have nothing, Mantos, except a warrant of death hanging over your head. Listen to me all of you!" I addressed the whole gathering, "The Dream—your Emperor's Dream—is real! Judgment is coming, sent by the Creator to punish the evil of men: a great flood of water, mighty enough to sweep away rocks and forests and mountains. Everything—*everything*—alive on the earth is going to die!" There were some gasps and low murmurs through the ranks of lionesses. "There will be no escaping it!" I looked straight at the lion, "You were right, Mantos: the Dream *is* an omen, but not just of the end of your empire—of the end of all things!" There was a stir among the she-cats: some seemed angry, others confused, a few even acted frightened. Lena and Saphirra stood behind so I could not see their reactions. But the smug look on Mantos' face showed he was unimpressed.

"And the Man of the Tree?" he asked casually, though not without a slight tremor in his voice.

"Him you were wrong about: he was a sign of hope, not evil. A sign of mercy."

While I spoke the lion's face had turned nasty. Now he erupted, "Mercy! Is *this* what you call '*mercy*'?" He tossed his head to emphasize the hole in his left eye socket, "I suppose next you'll be telling me I should be grateful to the two-legged butcher for leaving me half-blind!" The bitter beast turned his contempt on me, "You are a *fool*, Sengali! You and your gloomy prophecy. A weak-minded, feeble fool—or a desperate liar. Which is it?"

I held my ground, keeping my voice as genuine as I could. "Everything I have said is the truth, Mantos, whether you believe it or not. But for those who do believe me there is hope." I made sure all could hear,

"There is a place called the Ark: a safe place—built as a way to escape the horrible flood. But it is the only way..."

"Who told you all this?" Mantos mocked, "Your furry wombat friend?"

But I was not about to tell the murderer about Noak and his family. "It makes no difference who told me. And it makes no difference who believes me, either, Mantos. What I have said is true!"

That caused a greater stir, this time mostly in anger. "Who does he think he is?" the she-cats spat, "How dare he talk to the Emperor in such a way?" "Let's just kill him now!" Like music to his ears, the sound of his loyal subjects brought a smile to the lion's jagged mouth. Only two voices didn't join in: Lena's, because she was silent, and Saphirra's, because she spoke out in protest.

"Father," the lioness pleaded, "Maybe we should listen to him!" I turned to see her glowing in the morning light, face turned upwards, eyes full of agony. "*Please*, Father!" But it was no use; Mantos had no heart to appeal to.

"Silence, Saphirra!"

"But the Dream..."

"You know nothing! Neither does this spineless dog!" He nodded at me. "And if *I* did not know better I would say you had joined him," the single eye became a slit, " joined him *against* me." Her face fell and her head dropped low. "As for *you*, Sengali," the lion's voice was slow and deadly, "I have decided I have let you live too long."

I looked at the host of drooling, snarling females, ready to rush down on me at any second.

Mantos smiled cruelly, "You may be right about the Dream, but, unfortunately, you'll never live to find out!" He gave a signal and the lionesses started moving.

During all this Lena had slipped into one of her sullen moods: obviously thinking, but just what about was anybody's guess. Now suddenly she came to life. "Stop!" she cried, much to everyone's surprise (including mine). "Don't touch him! Respectfully, of course," she bowed to her father. He glared at her, but the shrewd female continued, "He isn't worth the blood he'd cost us. Besides he *did* just save our lives. Maybe we should call it even and go our own ways?"

"Have you lost your mind, daughter?" Mantos growled.

Lena glanced at me, "Not yet." I stared back with suspicion.

Now what is she up to?

Mantos looked at her furiously, then seemed to change his mind. He signaled for the she-cats to back off. "Very well," he rumbled, "We shall call it a draw. But if our paths ever cross again, Sengali," Mantos drew himself to full height, "you will not be so fortunate!" The lion roared out and the lionesses clambered to join him. Lena also bounded up by his side (after shooting me a parting smile).

Saphirra started after her—then stopped, mid-stride. She looked back at me, eyes filled with questions. "*Saphirra*," her father boomed, "Come!" But the white lioness was frozen. I could see the turmoil inside of her playing out on her face. She looked back at her family, her pride—everything she had ever known or longed to be a part of. They stood on the crest of the hill, a visual reminder of the only life she had known: the life she had always been told demanded all her loyalty. Yet now she hesitated. Back towards me the blue eyes came, as if searching for an answer she had not asked for but desperately needed. My mouth could find no words but my mind cried out, *Stay!* The fair face softened, but her agony remained.

"Saphirra!" Mantos called again. The other lionesses flicked their tails, waiting. Lena watched, silent and keen. There was a long moment of tension.

Then something switched in Saphirra's eyes. The white head rose. Slowly, she turned to face her pride. "No," she spoke at last, firm and clearly, "I am not coming." Her companions on the hillside looked shocked. Lena seemed pleased.

Mantos lowered his intimidating gaze fully on her, "What did you say?"

His daughter didn't back down, "I am going with Sengali. I am sorry Father...I do not mean to dishonor you...but you are wrong about the Dream! He is right. It means something, but not what you think it does. I *have* to find out what—I must follow it," her voice shook, "even if I follow it alone!"

The lion growled: a spiteful, hateful rumble. "Then go! Get out of my sight, you ungrateful little fool! You are no longer my daughter! And if I ever see you again I will deal with you the same as I will him: as an enemy!"

I came up beside Saphirra and saw the tremble of her muscles. "Come on," I spoke softly. Without a word she turned and walked back towards the way we had come—away from her family—as if to have said anything else would have broken down what courage she had left. I followed her, but only after staring down the lions on the hilltop. Mantos glared, Lena looked away, the others started to cower. Finally they all turned—disappearing beyond sight one by one. When sure they were gone for good I caught up with Saphirra. We travelled in silence: her heart heavy with the separation she had just gone through—unaware of the admiration growing for her in the heart walking by her side.

When we caught up with the others Yeffeth had improved a great deal and taken the lead with Nathak running as scout. Bulk's paw was also much better, allowing Eddie to ride on his back without causing pain. No one asked us where we had been or what had happened to Lena and we did not offer any explanations. We just fell into step behind them and followed the man.

THIRTY-THREE

THE SHADOWS HAD GROWN long and the warm air was cooling when we returned to the Ark, the great ship standing dark and still against the glare of the sun as it lowered in the western sky. The fields were quiet and peaceful filled with crickets jumping for joy in the afternoon light. As we cleared the forest I heard Yeffeth draw in a deep breath. Then he stopped breathing completely. Following his gaze to the nearest house, I noticed some movement on the front steps. It was Nina, her golden-brown braid glowing in the sunlight, her arms full of folded cloths, pottery, and as many items as they could hold. She was in a hurry and didn't see us on the edge of the field, but as her back turned Nathak started barking. She stopped and spun around, looking to see what the fuss was about. When her eyes found Yeffeth she froze; the items she was holding fell to the ground. Nathak kept barking: a very happy (*very loud*) sound. Other forms appeared at a distance as the rest of the family heard his commotion. Just like Nina, they all stopped when they saw us. But not for long. Yeffeth took one step forward and suddenly everyone started running towards him, Nina first of all. As she drew closer, bounding like a doe through the fields, her exhausted husband quickened his steps—as if her nearness brought him strength. In moments they were in each other's arms: her two fair ones wrapped around his brown neck, while his good right one pressed her to himself as hard as it could. Soon they were both enveloped in hugs, tears, and laughter as the whole family embraced. Questions flew around—no one really caring whether or not they were answered—while the tears flowed freely, especially from Nina and Marriet. Noak clasped his son and I heard his strong voice crack as he whispered, "Thank You, God!" The brothers just shook their heads, grinning and grabbing each other affectionately as only brothers can do. It was a joyous reunion—and not just for the humans. Rhia came bounding up, her brown wolf face positively glowing.

"I knew that's where you had gone!" she laughed, jumping on Nathak.

Close on her heels ran Womby, colliding into my legs. "You're b,b,back! Rhia said y,y,you would be!" I played with him a few moments, rolling around and pawing while the wolves did their happy dance and the humans rejoiced. But then the wombat stopped. "Who are y,y,you?" he asked, looking over my head. I turned to see Bulk with Eddie on his back, both staring at us all like we had lost our minds.

"Womby, I would like you to meet some friends of mine. This is Eddie and Bulk. They are the ones who helped me in Khanok."

"Hi!" the wombat waved. Bulk grunted while Eddie hopped down to the ground.

At first the monkey stroked his chin. Then he cackled, "Any friend of Stripes!" and grabbed the wombat's right paw, shaking it like humans shake hands. My good-natured little friend just laughed and went right along with it. Rhia introduced herself as well and soon the whole party was talking and swapping stories: wolves, monkey, wombat, and bear.

All except Saphirra.

The closer we had gotten to the open field the more she had hung back. Now the lioness stood watching from the shadows of the forest—silent, unsure—like an eaglet looking out of the nest for the first time.

I went back to her, asking as I stepped under the trees, "Would you like to join us?"

The blue eyes brimmed with distrust, "You did not mention there were other men!"

"They are not like other men, Saphirra," I explained, hoping the calmness of my voice would soothe her, "you will be safe here."

"You should have said something!" she insisted, an undeniable fear on her face.

"Would it have changed your mind?" The lionesses' eyes dropped; then they went from me to the happy crowd. "Come on," I encouraged softly. She took a shaky breath, but slowly the white paws began to move. Without a word she came up beside me and together we walked out into the open. By now Yeffeth was being escorted back to the houses by all except Noak and Shem who remained behind to make acquaintances with Eddie and Bulk. When they saw us coming, the men looked at each other with even more amazement on their faces. Saphirra drew close to my side (which, I must admit, didn't bother me). Noak stepped forward and the lioness stopped in her tracks. Then the good man knelt to the ground, holding out his right hand. I could hear Saphirra's heart racing. "It's alright," I whispered to her, "you can trust him." She glanced at me, trembling slightly. But finally she inched forward. One cautious step at a time, the graceful creature forced herself closer, stopping within inches of the long, scarred fingers. Noak waited, not reaching out any further. We all watched breathlessly and for a while no one moved. Then Saphirra placed her muzzle in the palm of his hand. Noak smiled and gradually began stroking the velvet fur between her fine, white ears. Shem and I looked at each other and the young man nodded; a grin of approval spread across his rugged brown face.

"Welcome home," the older man said gently. At his voice all the lioness' defenses seemed to melt; she even started rubbing against him like a cub with its long lost mother. Then a smooth sound started to come from her body. I smiled.

It was purring.

* * *

That was a happy night. The Men of the Tree stayed on the great patio far into the evening: eating, talking, singing, praying and laughing. Several times Yeffeth drifted off to sleep, stretched out on a long bed they had moved outside, but that did not seem to bother anyone, including him. They were all full of gratitude to be a family—together and safe—and thanksgiving to the Creator was a common theme throughout the whole evening. The rest of us gathered around the stone edges of the patio: resting and enjoying the overflow of food and affection. Eddie and Bulk especially liked the food. Once the monkey had stuffed enough fruit and sweet things in his mouth to feed a small army he started chattering; then there was no stopping him from telling Rhia and Womby the whole story of their rescue. Of course, he wound up being the main hero and the number of guards we outran doubled, but the wolf and wombat seemed to enjoy every detail. More than once I saw Nathak shake his head and grumble, but even the wolf could not be disagreeable for long that night. He wagged his tail and played with his masters, finding total satisfaction in their happiness. I watched with pleasure, just glad to be at peace again. Yet from time to time my eyes wandered sideways to where Saphirra sat at a short distance. The lioness said very little, but her clear eyes observed everything. Eventually, however, I noticed her slip away: vanishing like a wisp of clouds beneath the stars. A few minutes later I followed.

In the grove of fruit trees I found her draped across a thick, low-lying limb, her white coat glowing almost with its own light amidst the pale new blossoms. I approached slowly, not wanting to disturb her. When within just a few feet of the tree I sat down at the base of another one. She had to have known I was there, but she never looked at me. I did not press her, sitting silently as crickets sang around us and a slight breeze murmured through the trees. I had just closed my eyes to drink in their sweet fragrance when Saphirra spoke quietly.

"Thank you."

"For what?" I asked, looking up.

"For being silent and not saying anything," she still looked ahead, but the softness in her voice let me know my presence was welcome. "You have been kind to me—much kinder than I deserve."

I smiled at this newfound humility. "I wouldn't say that. Besides, kindness is not earned; it is given."

Her head turned and the blue eyes fixed on me. "You're a strange cat, Sengali," she said after a moment. "You have the power and intelligence to be an Emperor yourself, yet you live here, in a world built by men, submitting to them and calling weaker animals your friends. Why? What made you leave your mountain?"

Now it was my turn to look ahead. "The Dream."

Her body shifted so she could look down at me easier, "Tell me about it—your Dream." At first I hesitated, not sure I wanted to darken the beautiful moment. But the way she added "please" made me go into the whole thing from beginning to end, even the Voice.

"But strangely," I closed, "ever since coming here—to the Ark—the Dream has left me; vanishing as abruptly as it came. And it hasn't returned."

"The Ark," she repeated, her voice hushed. Though we could not see the boat because of the trees her face pointed in its direction, "You mentioned that word in the forest. You called it 'a safe place'." She drew in a deep sigh filled with longing, "Perhaps it will take away mine as well." The curiosity in my face prompted her to add, "My Dream."

I stared at her. "*Your* Dream?"

She nodded timidly, "My Father claimed it as his own to control the pride. He wanted them to believe it was his idea so they would not know he had listened to me. He succeeded except for Lena. She thought I invented it to manipulate our father's fear of the Man of the Tree. But I did not invent anything," her voice quivered a little. "He was real—as real as we are sitting here now! He always came at the end of the Dream, after the fear and the death, silhouetted against a dying sun: Tree glowing on his chest like a star. At first I was afraid to tell anyone about it; then I was afraid not to—it came *so* many times! I hoped if I shared the Sream with my father he might notice..." she faltered a moment. "I just wanted to help him. But I was never convinced—not like he was—that the Man of the Tree was a sign of evil. The darkness, the chaos, yes. But not the Man. Which was strange. I have never trusted men, but feared and hated them. Ever since..." Saphirra's voice broke and she did not continue.

"Go on," I urged gently.

Her eyes glistened, "Ever since they killed my mother. It was a hunting party. I was still very young, but I remember. I remember her—and the loss when she was gone. Since her death I have never been loved. Not really. Never belonged: not with the pride, not with my sister, not with my father. He never wanted or needed me. Until recently. Until the Dream." Saphirra's wounded heart unfolded like a flower, "Lena has always disliked me, but now it has turned to hatred because she thinks I am trying to replace her: to steal our father's throne. But it isn't that; it never has been. All I've ever wanted was to feel like I belonged with them. That's why I told him the Dream. I just wanted to be..." she stopped in mid-sentence, unable to go on.

"...accepted?" I finished for her. The white head turned away, as if the lioness was ashamed to show any kind of weakness. The grove was quiet. "Well, now you are." Slowly her face came back into view: soft and fair. She said nothing; she didn't have to. Her eyes shone like portals into the night sky itself. It was awhile before I realized I was holding my breath. Neither of us moved. I'm not sure how long this would have lasted if Womby's voice had not broken in.

"Li!" He called from up the trail, "Li! Where are y,y,you?"

I shuddered a little: trying to shake off the weak feeling that had overtaken me. "I'm sorry," I mumbled, making my legs stand up and walk away. Yet even as I did I felt the lioness watching me from behind. I also found myself hoping she was smiling. But I didn't have the courage to turn around and find out.

* * *

Everyone woke up late next morning. It was one of those clear, perfect days you wish you could live in forever: azure blue sky, no humidity, and golden sunshine bringing out every shade of grass, leaf, and flower as vivid as could be. Even the Ark looked glorious: its giant, gopherwood sides gleaming a rich, deep brown in the bright sun. After shaking off the pile of hay I had napped in and giving myself a tongue-bath, I went searching for some breakfast. Turning the corner of the barn I saw Shem and Yeffeth standing by the well in deep conversation. The elder brother certainly looked better: his reddish beard had been trimmed and the rest of him already seemed to have fattened up a little. Aside from the sling holding his left arm one might have never known he had been a captive two days before. At that moment his right hand was turning over something small and white.

"I spoke with Father," Shem was saying. "He agreed with me that you should have it. You are the eldest." For a while his brother said nothing, gazing at the little Tree in silence. Yeffeth was not a man to speak quickly, especially about a thing of such importance.

"No," he said at last, his voice deep and resolute. "The Great-Father commanded you to bear it, and so it should be," he placed the string over his younger brother's head, " 'with honor and with fear'." As the Tree slipped around Shem's neck, Yeffeth laid his right hand on his shoulder. Then the older brother's serious face brightened. He smiled, "You always were his favorite!"

Shem laughed, "Oh certainly: which is why when we were children he gave *you* the bow instead of me!"

"No," his brother teased, a twinkle in his hazel eyes, "he gave me the bow because I was a better shot."

"Only because you were bigger."

Suddenly the big brother caught the younger in a headlock with his good arm, ruffling the thick, black hair. "Still am!" A playful tussle followed that ended with both men laughing and walking off together towards the Ark. After rounding up a rogue chicken I followed them, joining my friends where they rested under the shadow of the great boat. By now Eddie and Bulk had made themselves quite at home, thanks to Rhia's hospitality, while Womby did his part by giving Saphirra a tour of the valley. At first I was surprised the wombat trusted the lioness so much (considering her treatment of him on the trail when we were prisoners), until I found out that she had actually helped him escape during the chaos following my fight with Lena in the garden. Womby showed his gratitude by never letting the lioness out of his sight (which wasn't very far), but Saphirra bore it gracefully—as she seemed to bear almost everything. Nathak fell right back into routine, guarding and accompanying his masters as they went about their business of the day. Thankfully, however, he no longer spied on me; instead I watched him lope back and forth for hours—always at a man or woman's side as they carried, loaded, and gathered things into the Ark. The humans seemed to enjoy their work more than usual, the joy of Yeffeth's return still lifting their spirits. Altogether, it was as pleasant and peaceful a day as you could hope for.

I should have known something was about to happen.

A CAT'S TALE

PART FOUR

"Enemies"

THIRTY-FOUR

IT WAS MID-AFTERNOON; the sun had shifted westward, though a good deal of daylight still remained. Suddenly an alarm rang out: rapid, clanging! It was so abrupt it made my heart jump (and the rest of me jump with it). At first I was annoyed—until I caught sight of Chenna running through the fields as fast as she could. My muscles tensed.

Something's wrong!

She and Rhia had gone looking for nuts and mushrooms in the southern woods; now the wolf sprinted in front of her towards the Ark as if pursued by lions. The triangular instrument usually strapped to Chenna's belt was in the girl's hands, ringing violently as the girl beat it while she ran. The horrible noise got everyone's attention. Marriet and Atani came from inside the house, Nina and Noak from the barn, while the three brothers came running down the gangplank of the Ark. Shem leapt off the edge and got to her before anyone else did, followed by Nathak. The girl collapsed in his arms, exhausted; the rest of us gathered around Rhia.

"What happened?" Nathak asked, supporting his mate as she caught her breath.

"What is it?" I echoed, followed by a chorus of "What's going on?" "What's wrong?" "Something b,b,bad?" "Tell us!" till the poor girl couldn't have said anything if she tried.

"Be quiet!" Nathak barked, "Give her a chance!"

After a moment Rhia revived. "Men," she finally managed to pant, "lots of them...hundreds...thousands! On the southern road...headed this way!"

There was a general gasp.

"How far are they?" I asked.

"Not far—two, three miles!"

By this time Chenna had recovered; using signs, she managed to tell the family the same thing. Noak fell to one knee with Marriet at his side; without a word his sons and their wives followed. The rest of us watched in wonder as they bowed their heads (some all the way to the ground) and Noak began praying out loud.

"Almighty God, Creator and Sustainer of Life, Merciful Judge—You see us! Here we kneel, in the dust You have created and created man out of. You see how we have sought to be faithful, to walk obediently and keep Your ways. And You see how we are hated for it! Now this mob has risen, surely to destroy not only us, but the Ark You have commanded us to build—and for no other reason than we have trusted in You. Deliver us from this evil! Remember Your promise to establish Your covenant! We are *Your* servants...save us, *oh God*, we pray! Pluck us from the mouths of these lions! You *alone* can deliver!" His arms wrapped around Marriet as tightly as they could as he ended, "Yet we are in Your hands. Your will be done!"

"So be it," some added, while others fought back tears.

A brief kiss to Marriet's forehead and Noak was on his feet. "Take the girls into the Ark," he told her. "Do not leave the doorway. Stay on alert! And pray." She grasped his hand as if unwilling to let go. Yet she had to.

"Come girls," the lady said quickly, gently drawing them away from their own husbands. The partings were tender and quick; soon the women were climbing the long walk to the Ark's great door. Chenna looked back and Shem saw it, waving cheerfully. But I watched his smile fade when she turned around.

"Go with them," Nathak spoke to Rhia; fear came to her face as she looked at him, but she obeyed, loping up after the women. "You should all go," the wolf said to the rest of us. "You'll only be in danger down here."

But Eddie protested, "Uh-uh! No way I'm going inside that wooden box with no way out—not with a mob coming!"

Bulk just shook his head "No".

"Womby, follow Rhia," I urged. "Help her guard the women."

The wombat seemed perplexed, hesitating and looking up at Saphirra. "Are you g,g,going?" The white lioness looked at me, her eyes asking what I thought she should do. I glanced from her to Womby.

"Yes," she answered, understanding my meaning, and together they went after the she-wolf.

Meanwhile the men had scattered around the valley opening pasture gates, bird coops, and stall doors: giving the other animals a way of escape. It was a risky move, but Noak said if they were meant to return they would. Anything of personal value that could be grabbed in a hurry was rushed up to the women, who took it inside the Ark. But it was not long before a black rim appeared along the southern horizon: moving, boiling, and getting bigger every second.

"They're coming!" Kawm yelled out.

"Arm yourselves!" Noak commanded, "But do not fight unless for defense. Trust in God and stand your ground!" The older man seized his spear and thrust a knife in his belt; Kawm secured his pair of axes. Shem had just strapped on a long sword and was running to join his father when a voice called out behind him.

"Shem!"

The young man spun around. It was Yeffeth. In his right hand he held out the white bow and arrows.

"You take them. They're of no use to me now!" Shem hesitated but Yeffeth shoved them into his hands and grasped his brother's shoulder, "You're a much better shot than I am, anyway." Shem's dark eyes filled with honor; in no time he removed the sword from his own waist and strapped it around Yeffeth's.

"Show them what the right arm of a Man of the Tree is made of!" He said proudly, adding with a wink, "Just try not to hurt yourself."

"And you just try not to break my bow!" Yeffeth retaliated with a dry smile. Together they took off to join the others.

I stood still as all this activity swirled around me. My claws could feel the ground shaking under them. My ears heard the roar of a multitude—an *angry* multitude. My eyes saw the black line grow like a stormy cloud into the blue sky stretching to swallow everything in its path.

* * *

Soon we were surrounded by an army of men at least ten thousand strong. Some were actual soldiers, fierce and deadly looking in bronze armor. Many were angry citizens—no less fierce and no less deadly. Noak took his place standing between the Ark and the massive mob with his spear planted in the ground beside him, tip down, and his right hand holding its shaft. Kawm was a little ways to his right, Shem to his left, and Yeffeth stood near the entrance of the gangplank, guarding the way into the Ark. Each of them held their weapons down, but ready: the white shaft of Yeffeth's arrow notched to the bowstring by Shem's hand. Atani also held her bow where she stood with the rest of the women, watching from above in the shadow of the great door. Rhia, Womby, and Saphirra stood by their feet, while Nathak, Eddie, Bulk, and myself took up positions under the great beams which supported the Ark.

But we were grossly outnumbered. Like a swarm of killer ants the crowd of men encircled the front of the ship, spreading out until the whole valley was teeming with them. And at their head marched the giant himself: Hittan, the Man-Beast, Master of the Games. Adorned in golden armor from booted foot to towering head, crowned with a helmet and flowing plume of black and green, the monster gleamed in the sunlight like some creature from another realm. There were others as well who stood head and shoulders above the tallest men: equally massive as Hittan though not so grandly dressed—a wicked looking bunch. Drawing up in a line behind him, they stood side by side to form a literal wall of giants. In this way they advanced until the Man-Beast came within a few yards of Noak; then the six-fingered hand rose in the air. All motion stopped. The mob fell silent, waiting for their leader to speak. But it was Noak who took that privilege.

"What is the meaning of this, Hittan?" he asked, calm and bold. Instead of replying, the giant crossed his muscled arms and stared down at him. After a few moments a crafty smile spread across his over-sized face.

"Noak, son of Lehmek, son of Methooshelak," he bellowed, his evil voice echoing through the valley, "you and your family have been tried as traitors to the land of Nod—tried and found *guilty*. All your goods are hereby confiscated by the city of Khanok: including your wives, lands, and all valuables. You and your sons, however," the black eyes gleamed, "face a more severe fate!"

The good man seemed unaffected, "On what charge?"

"I do not need one!" The giant laughed viciously, "The Master of the Games condemns who he wishes! But so you know the reason for which you die..." he gave a signal. Out from the side came Marsed, looking much more like himself than the last time we had seen him. Unfortunately.

"That's him, your Worship!" he squealed, pointing his bone-skinny finger towards Yeffeth, "*That's* the man I saw!"

Noak motioned for his oldest son to join him while Kawm took his place guarding the boardwalk.

"Thought you could get away with it, didn't you?" the slave trader spat, "Well *now* we'll see *who* gets away with *what!*"

"Read them the sentence," Hittan commanded.

With great flair Marsed pulled a document from inside his robe, proceeding to read in his best auctioneer voice: "For wholesale thievery and destruction of property belonging to the Master of the Games, for damage and injury caused to his servants and vehicles, for assault of a *violent* and *vicious nature* on one of his Lordship's *particularly* favored officials (emphasizing those words by rubbing his wiry neck), and for general trouble-making and peace-breaking in the form of maniacal prophesizing of a most disturbing nature..." the excitement of the crowd was building and the Slave Trader was loving every second of it "...the traitor Noak and his sons are hereby sentenced to," he paused, "*death!*" The roar of the multitude nearly drowned his finishing words, "To be carried out immediately!"

"This is madness!" Yeffeth cried, "I never even touched you!" But to no avail: his pleas were lost in the tumult of the crowd. One wave of Hittan's hand, however, and they instantly hushed.

"Let us hear their arguments." He seemed to be enjoying himself.

The young man tried reasoning with his accusers, "You must first own something for it to be stolen; I was taken by force and held against my will. To escape such a fate was my right before God! I have stolen nothing belonging to the Master of the Games."

Hittan's black eyes narrowed, "*Everything* belongs to me!" He snapped his fingers. "Take them!" The wall of giants started to move.

"Stand back!" Noak warned, grabbing the spear out of the earth; there was a power in his words that made the giants hesitate. Standing tall, he looked fearlessly at Hittan, "You have no jurisdiction here, Giant! This is dangerous ground for you. Leave while you still can!"

Another hideous laugh, though this time with a malicious ring. "You *dare* threaten *me*, little man? 'No jurisdiction'? I could have you crushed in an instant. I could do it myself!"

"It is *you* who will be crushed," and Noak pointed the head of the spear directly at his giant face, "you and all who follow you, if you do not turn from your wickedness! You defy the living God, corrupt His justice, mock His mercy—and now you dare threaten His servants with death! I say it again to all of you," his voice seemed to travel for miles, "*repent!* While there is yet time! Come to the Ark and be saved! Otherwise you shall all surely perish—*every last one of you*," and the steel gray eyes locked onto the giant's. The giant's smug smile was gone, replaced by a look of rage.

"So, you believe *I* will perish? You think your God can destroy *me?* Well, I will show you who is god on this earth!" Turning to the multitude he shouted, "Plunder the houses!" The people went wild: ransacking, vandalizing, ripping into everything. Nathak and I were on our feet, waiting for a sign from the Masters to do something. But it never came; they just stood their ground and watched silently as their homes were gutted out right before their eyes. The wolf started forward but Shem saw him.

"Nathak, stay!" he called out, though his voice choked at the words. Reluctantly the dog obeyed. Soon there was nothing left but empty husks of buildings where only minutes before had stood beautiful houses. It was agonizing: doing nothing while the greedy scavengers devoured everything in their path. My heart surged with anger. Yet it was not my call.

The Man-Beast set his evil gaze on Noak. "Burn the houses to the ground!" Torches were lit and within seconds the homes were blazing infernos. Their smoke rose black and thick against the perfectly blue sky, creating a haze that blocked out the sun. An unnatural darkness covered the valley as the smoke above reflected the flames below. Through all this the Men of the Tree still did nothing, holding their positions before the Ark. I looked up at the women. Nina was weeping in Marriet's arms, Atani stared in horror, bow limp in her hands, and Chenna clung to Rhia and Womby. Saphirra stood motionless. I looked back at the blazing ruin as it reflected off a sea of angry faces—all pointed towards us. For the first time, I felt truly afraid.

We're surrounded!

They had destroyed everything except the great barn and the Ark. They would be coming for us next. Glancing from side to side a panic started to set in.

We're completely trapped! There's no way out!

As the flames rose behind him like a backdrop of death the Man-Beast broke into a jagged, wicked grin. His face waved in the heat of the fire and his eyes burned from within like a demon. "Where is your God *now*, old man?" he breathed.

The other giants started advancing towards the Ark. Shem drew back the arrow, Yeffeth held up his sword, Noak and Kawm stood poised with their weapons...but what could they do against such monstrous flesh? They would be dead in minutes. And with them would die the hope of the Ark. The roar of humanity was deafening, the blackness growing by the second, death hovered in the air. All my strength drained away like water; fear was swallowing me whole.

SENGALI

"Sengali!"

Suddenly my head flew up.

The Voice!

In the midst of the chaos it came again, loud and clear.

"Sengali—stand between them!"

The giants were nearing Noak: their feet shaking the earth, their six-fingered hands filled with massive, grim-looking weapons.

"Sengali! GO!"

There was no refusing it. Throwing my front legs before me I bounded out of the shadow of the Ark. My claws ate up the earth. Darting in front of Noak, I dug them into the ground, taking my stand between him and the giants. Then my ears pinned back and I let loose the loudest roar of my life! They stopped: I don't know if I frightened them or if they were just surprised, but, for whatever reason, they stopped. Out of the corner of my eye I saw Nathak and Bulk join me: the wolf growling before Shem and the bear standing on his haunches to shield Yeffeth (Eddie hanging onto his back for dear life). Saphirra and Rhia bounded down the boardwalk, leaping in front of Kawm. Even Womby hissed and sputtered at the great door, guarding the women.

Hittan and I locked gazes and the Man-Beast's eyes grew wide. He recognized me. I stood before Noak and hissed so that each and every one of my teeth showed.

Touch him, I warned the giant, *and it will be over my dead body!*

There was a stand-off. Then the giant changed his plan of attack.

"Destroy the barn!" He barked to his followers.

"Father!" Shem cried. He looked at Noak and for the first time I saw worry on his brave face. He was thinking what the rest of us were thinking. The barn! It was full of food—the work of months, even years—gathered and set-aside to sustain those saved by the Ark. Now it was going to burn to the ground!

"No!" I heard Marriet cry.

The men were helpless to do anything. Nathak, Bulk, and I looked at each other, completely at a loss. We could try and stop them but would never make it in time—if we made it at all. Already the men were lining up to throw their torches into the large building; with so much hay and fodder inside it was sure to catch like kindle!

Suddenly Noak's voice rose above the tumult and his hands rose to heaven.

"Lord God, help us!"

THIRTY-FIVE

SUDDENLY THERE was a scream: a piercing, thundering, mighty shriek! Out of the smoking sky overhead, cutting like a golden comet through the darkness, dropped an eagle, its great wings flat against its body. It sped straight towards the men gathered round the barn. With another shriek the bird's wings flipped out and its sharp talons grabbed a torch right out of a man's hand, wheeling around to drop it on his head as he took off running and screaming. Close on the eagle's path came another, darker one, followed by a string of falcons, vultures, ospreys, and owls. They descended on the arsons: ripping torches away, zooming in among them, clawing with beak and talon. The men fled in panic. Almost instantly a host of flying creatures rushed out of the treetops surrounding the valley: bats, flying reptiles, birds of every size and shape. With a maddening clamor they fell upon the huge mob, wreaking havoc. Here the giants' size became a disadvantage: their heads and shoulders sticking above the rest became easy targets. Hittan himself was soon swarmed by flying insects: hornets, dragonflies, wasps, bees. But it was the pair of eagles who really gave him trouble. Like meathooks their massive claws tore into the Man-Beast, ripping both armor and flesh. And as if this aerial assault was not enough, suddenly a host of screams began growing from the outskirts of the mob. I couldn't see what was happening, but what my senses were picking up on was overwhelming.

The ground shivered under the force of thousands of feet: some crawling, some creeping, some stomping, some leaping. My ears rang with roars, hoots, trumpets, hisses, bugles—cries of every kind. Never before had such smells come all at once: fur, skin, antler, hair, scales, all in mind-blowing excess. Those of us around the Ark watched amazed as the crowd—that massive, boiling, threatening crowd, only moments before about to kill us—started to scatter like so many sheep pursued by a pack of wolves. It was terrible. People ran everywhere—over, around, and through each other—rushing to escape some terror pressing in from the outside. Yet none of them ran to the Ark. The boat was avoided like a plague (along with the men who stood by it) as if an invisible fence was surrounding us. It almost felt like we were watching everything unfold from another world.

But then I saw Marsed slinking through the crowd. Thinking no one was watching, the sneaky man grabbed a bow and arrow someone had dropped on the ground. He straightened up and pulled back on the string, eyes full of revenge: fixed on Yeffeth. The young man didn't see him. No one saw him—except me. In a flash I charged into the frenzy, streaking towards the Slave Trader. He never even saw me coming. One quick move and it was done. In a moment all the man's selfish gain—all his greed and all his lust—was gone forever. Nathak charged in after me and together we joined in the fight. Chasing whatever men crossed our path we soon encountered the giants, now on the run from the flying creatures. Hittan had held his position longer than the rest, but even he had finally been forced to flee cursing the God of Noak every step of the way. The wolf and I focused on him. Soon the Man-Beast was stumbling south as fast as his bleeding legs could take him—flooding back the way he had come along with rest of his followers.

And as the sea of people began to thin out we finally saw why.

Animals were everywhere! Big ones, small ones, creeping ones, flying ones, plant-eaters, meat-eaters, predator, prey—they had completely taken over the valley! Elephants and apes, crocodiles and buffalo, rhinoceros and hippopotamus. A small army of spiders, snakes, and scorpions. Squirrels, mice, rabbits, and beavers. A literal host of living creatures (mostly in pairs) were running, scampering, and wandering all over the place. Nathak and I stared in shock totally astounded.

"Where did they all come from?" I breathed.

After a moment the wolf replied in a voice full of wonder, "The same place you did." My head turned towards him; he nodded, eyes full and penetrating. Then, without another word between us, we headed back to the Ark.

The burning houses had reduced to ashes, their flames dying with them. A breeze began blowing chasing away the dark clouds of smoke to reveal the blue sky beyond. As we made our way among the mob of creatures, the sun broke through showing even more what a strange gathering it truly was. Every kind of bird, beast, or insect I had ever seen (and many I had not seen) were represented by at least two: male and female. No wonder the humans had been terrified! The sheer number of them would have been enough to overwhelm anybody, but some were quite dangerous. And when I saw the giant lizards I knew why the men had run. They were young ones—many still very small—but that did not make them any less deadly: two-legged flesh-eaters like Razor-Claw, quick, cunning egg-stealers, lumbering spike-backs, nimble whip-tails, some with tall fins growing out of their spines and others with large heads looking like hammers. When I saw the two long-necks I started in surprise.

The ones I released from Marsed's caravan!

In fact, I recognized many faces as we passed by. Some were from the caravan—including the pair of white doves I had watched fly away into the night sky. Others were more familiar, like Huff and Grunt and the other livestock Noak and his sons had released. Most, however, were completely new to me. But strange or familiar, neighbor or newcomer, they were all here now—at the Ark.

As Nathak and I neared the giant boat we found we were not alone: thousands of feet were gathering with us, moving towards Noak and his family (the women having joined their husbands on the ground). The humans stood, solemn and amazed, as we approached. Within a few feet of them the wolf and I stopped; the host of animals did the same. Saphirra, Rhia, Womby, Bulk, and Eddie were standing behind the men, looking as surprised as the rest of us were. Then they silently walked forward to join Nathak and myself. As one multitude, we stood before the eight people and the Ark. Even the winged creatures flew to the ground. A few moments passed under the clear sky, the wind blowing in the tops of the trees and through the tall valley grass. Then, one by one, we started to bow—first me, then the wolves, wombat, lioness, monkey and bear, followed by the eagles, owls, apes, and elephants, until every bird, insect, reptile, and beast was kneeling in submission to the Men of the Tree.

* * *

When the incredible moment passed a question took its place: *what happens now?* The houses were nothing more than a pile of embers. The barn remained, so did a few of the pasture fences, but there was no way they could hold the thousands of animals now scattered through the valley (many of which were too small or too winged to be held by a fence, anyway). There was the Ark, but it was more or less restricted, set-apart for the proper time. Besides that there was nowhere else to go. Yet none of us considered leaving; we knew we had been brought together for a purpose. It quickly became common knowledge that each animal had experienced a Dream of their own: always similar, though individually different. I found it interesting how not all had heard the Voice (though some had), but all knew, to one degree or another, we were not drawn to the Ark by chance.

Yet, what happens now?

As evening settled, that was the question on everybody's mind, but none more than Noak. For a while he helped his sons clear the valley, including burying Marsed and others like him so the animals could not get at them. During this grim job Marriet and the women rummaged through what was left of their houses, seeing if anything of value might have survived. But at some point Noak drew away, disappearing into the Ark. The shadow of the great door swallowed his tall form.

Stars appeared and still there was no sign of him. You could feel anticipation building—an expectation, though we weren't exactly sure what of. But when the man finally did come out again the word was clear:

"'Come into the Ark, you and all your household, because I have seen you righteous before Me in this generation... For after seven more days I will cause it to rain on the earth forty days and forty nights, and I will destroy from the face of the earth all living things that I have made.'"

"Seven...more...days!" The Creator's words to Noak spread through the ranks like wildfire.

Seven more days!

Seven days to feel the sunlight, smell the sweet breeze, roam the firm earth—and then the doom in our dreams that had driven us all to this place would be reality. The only world we had ever known was about to end.

And we had seven days to prepare.

* * *

A CAT'S TALE

That was an interesting night. The humans slept in the barn, taking turns standing guard along with the wolves (though there wasn't much chance of the mob returning). Those of us who were more nocturnal scavenged around, doing whatever instinct demanded and leaving the day-dwellers alone (mostly). It was quite a sight: thousands of creatures scattered all through the valley—on the ground, under the ground, in the trees—like an animal refugee camp. What amazed me was how well everyone got along. But we knew we were there for a common purpose—survival—and that has a way of uniting even the bitterest rivals.

As I strolled through the fields of scales, feathers, and flesh all pressed in together, musing over the events of the day and the days ahead, a pair of round, furry objects headed my way.

"Li! Li!" the closest one shouted (waking up a sleeping warthog nearby). It was Womby, charging full speed towards me. "She c,c,came, she's here, she's safe!" he cried, in one over-joyed breath. Behind him waddled another wombat, slightly smaller and more brownish in color. He stopped, all smiles, to let her catch up and then they both approached, side by side. "She c,c,came!" my friend laughed again, tears of happiness rolling out of his button eyes. The shy female cuddled to her mate until she saw the smile on my face; then her own softened to a picture of perfect sweetness. I could see why Womby was in love with her.

"Sengali, at your service," I bowed.

Her voice was tiny and gentle as she replied, "I'm Glori."

"She had it, Li!" her mate stuttered joyfully, "the Dream! She had it, t,t,too! Now she believes m,m,me—believes her Womby. She's safe!" and the two furry heads nuzzled. My own heart filled with gladness for my little friend: for them both. When the little female looked at me again her eyes held both fear and hope. I nodded kindly.

"Welcome to the Ark, Glori!"

THIRTY-SIX

SEVEN DAYS MAY SEEM like a long time, but that week went by faster than any week ever should. From before sun-up, to sun down, and through the night the humans worked. First they concentrated on moving all the food stored in the barn into the Ark. Carts and wagons loaded with hay, grain, seeds, nuts, dried meat, dried fruit, and various plants and herbs made their way from the large building to the much larger boat. Everything else that was not perishable had already been stored inside of the Ark, so when the barn was finally empty the men turned their attention to the only thing remaining to be loaded: us.

But that was quite a job. Herding even a few animals can be a challenge; herding several thousands (many of whom do not usually like being together) would have been utterly impossible under normal circumstances. However, these were not normal circumstances, and the strange power that had drawn the animals to the Ark seemed to draw them into it as well. Starting with the bigger ones like giraffes, elephants, giant lizards, and rhinos, they began going into the ship. Two by two, male and female, up the great boardwalk they lumbered in orderly fashion, with Yeffeth, Shem, and Kawm simply having to help direct them into the great door. The only exceptions were Bulk and a handsome brown she-bear he had become fond of. They remained with the rest of us. Ever since the terrible mob, we who had stood with the Men of the Tree had been treated almost like we were part of their family. So we stayed with them, outside the Ark. Womby and Glori did what they could by helping to keep spirits high, and Eddie and his new mate (a slim, golden, lively little thing) attached themselves to the humans' shoulders to cheer or prod on those being loaded. Eddie especially enjoyed bossing everyone around.

"Alright hurry up! Get moving! Shake a leg!" he would chatter, jumping over, under, and around creatures as they climbed the long walk, "Don't have all day—pick up those feet!" The larger animals humored him; the smaller ones not so much. Camels, cattle, ant-eaters, deer, tapirs, and armadillos, shrank down to weasels, rabbits, porcupines, sloths, mongoose, and lemurs—and the monkey's endless badgering started bringing a few kicks, stomps, and

A CAT'S TALE

swats. But he kept dodging and they kept moving so no harm was done (not worth mentioning, anyway). The turtles were more frustrating. No matter how much he insulted them the pokey things would not change their pace. But it was the frogs, toads, crickets, and locusts who proved to be Eddie's greatest challenge; he had finally met his match at making noise.

The whole lot of them was gathered in a marshy section of the valley and no matter how loud the monkey shouted he could not get them to listen. Their chirps, croaks, and hums made such a racket his voice was drowned out. But Eddie was not easily beaten. Enlisting my help, the monkey stood on my head and yelled "QUIET!" at the top of his lungs. That got their attention—and the roar I let loose at the same moment. Instant silence followed.

"*Al-right*," Eddie swaggered, strutting on my head like a rooster, "that's more like it! Now get in step there! Straighten that line! Move those webbed feet!" and up the gangplank went the whole group, him jumping around them, as neat and quiet a bunch as was ever seen.

I shook my head and chuckled.

There will be no living with him after this.

Then my eyes wandered towards the great door. The smile faded. Creature after creature was going into the Ark, passing through the gaping shadow into the boat beyond—surrounded by wooden walls. Under a wooden roof.

A roof built by men.

For some reason a cold feeling came over me. It was a feeling that had been growing ever since the loading process began. Ever since the word about *"seven more days"*. I shuddered. Initially I had ignored it, but as the hours and days went by that had become more and more difficult to do. First I found myself avoiding the boardwalk as much as possible. Then the Ark itself. Being near it only made the feeling grow worse. I spoke to no one about it, and, thankfully, no one seemed to notice my behavior. Yet gradually the feeling grew. I didn't want to face it. But I knew what it was.

Fear.

A fear of being trapped. Aside from those brief minutes in Marsed's wagon, I had not stepped under a roof built by man since Khanok. Not felt the closeness of walls or touch of any floor except dirt, grass, or stone. Now I was about to be shut up in a man-made structure built of nothing but wood for who-knew-how-long...perhaps even until I died. And what made this even worse was when Eddie informed us the animals in the Ark were being placed inside cages locked with bars and latches.

Cages!

I cringed. The very thought of ever being trapped in another cage was almost more than I could stand. It wasn't a sensation I wanted; I fought it as hard as I could. Yet the harder I fought, the stronger it became—and with it came dark memories. Memories of iron bars and starvation, hate and death, grew in my mind until a kind of panic would set in and I had to get out of there—away from people and walls. And so I took to roaming the fields and forest more and more, and staying near the Ark less and less. Enjoying freedom while it was mine and trying not to think about what was coming on the seventh day.

* * *

Nevertheless, the days wore on. First and second day: gathering the food and making final preparations within the Ark. Third day: larger animals boarding. Fourth day: smaller ones. Fifth day: tiny reptiles, snakes, and creeping things, two by two. Sixth day: every bird of every sort flew or walked through the door—ostrich, chicken, owl, eagle, woodpecker, parrot, raven, dove—male and female, they all came. Some of them were in groups of seven instead of two, as had also been the case with different cattle, sheep, and other split-hoofed animals. This was because they were something the Men of the Tree called "clean" (not that they were actually cleaner than the rest of us, but they symbolized something sacred). The Creator had told Noak to take *"seven each of every clean animal, a male and his female, two each of animals that are unclean, a male and his female"*, and also, *"seven each of birds of the air, male and female, to keep the species alive on the face of all the earth"*. And so they entered in flurried droves: a virtual parade of wings, feathers, and stork legs. As the last sparrow and chickadee fluttered into the shelter of the Ark, the sun was setting gold and splendid against the horizon.

The few of us who still remained outside of the Ark paused to watch the glowing orb's descent. There was a stillness to the atmosphere as the last light faded: a stillness that was not unnatural except for the pounding of our hearts. I looked around at those of us left. Noak and Marriet, standing hand in hand before the great door with Rhia at their feet. Kawm and Atani, with Eddie and his mate on their shoulders, side by side on the boardwalk. Nina, Chenna, and Saphirra near the foot of the ship with Womby and Glori nuzzling nearby. Shem and Nathak before the ashes of the main house. Bulk and the she-bear by the well, where Yeffeth also stood, still holding his healing arm. No one spoke. No one had to.

Sunset of the sixth day!

As darkness fell the women went into the Ark and the she-wolf, monkeys, and wombats disappeared with them. Saphirra followed. But just as she reached the top, the white lioness turned and looked at me. Even from so great a distance her sapphire eyes shone clear and piercing, probing into mine. Then she vanished into the great door. Meanwhile the men were meeting one last time in front of the great ship. Not really wanting to hear what they said, I joined Nathak where he sat nearby, next to one of the huge supporting beams. We both scanned the valley and surrounding woods in silence: taking in the sounds and smells of the night, along with all of those stuffed behind us inside of the Ark. It was like standing between two worlds.

Finally Nathak shifted. "No one's going to sleep tonight," he rumbled. When I did not respond the wolf glanced over. "You've been quiet lately," he said, "and absent." The icy blue eyes locked onto me. I deliberately looked away, pretending to be enthralled with the southern woods. "Something wrong?" he asked and despite his gruffness I could tell it was a genuine question.

For a brief moment I actually found myself wanting to be honest with the wolf. Tell him everything. But then my pride kicked in.

"No," I replied flatly.

It was a deliberate lie and I knew it. What's worse, so did Nathak. He didn't say anything, but his keen gaze studied me like a book. He sighed, shook his head, and turned his attention to the men. They were disbanding: Kawm heading towards the Ark while Yeffeth, Shem, and Noak went different ways through the fields. Noak headed to his favorite sanctuary: the wooded glade where I first saw him. Yeffeth walked slowly towards the grove of fruit trees, Bulk lumbering behind him. Shem made for the eastern woods. Nathak rose to follow while I continued looking away trying to ignore my guilty conscience.

"Sengali..."

I turned in surprise. The wolf had actually spoken my name! He was looking back at me, long legs paused in mid-stride. His silver face glowed in the dark with a kindness I hadn't seen before—not directed towards me, anyway.

"...just remember what brought you here."

Something almost like a smile appeared on the edges of his mouth and then the wolf took off after his master. Reaching the edge of the trees, Shem paused to let Nathak catch up. As he looked back at the Ark the ivory Tree gleamed like a white star on his chest. Then he and the wolf turned together and faded into the shadow of the forest.

THIRTY-SEVEN

I SAT THERE AWHILE, ALONE. The stars overhead were brilliant: their white light looking cold and distant. Nathak's words played over in my head.

"Just remember what brought you here."

I looked behind me, where the giant boat loomed, dark and mysterious. All at once the uneasy feeling returned. My paws started to itch; almost before I knew it, they were carrying me through the southern forest. Prowling, wandering, hunting for nothing in particular, I made my way through bush and bramble, uphill and under hill. Turning west, north, and back again I circled in the ancient forest trying to run off the nervousness in my heart. Or outrun it.

As the night wore on I found myself wandering towards the rocky terrain of the eastern woods. Here the flat ground rose in steep, random inclines, or fell away in sudden drop-offs with a small stream usually winding several feet (sometimes a hundred or so) at the bottom of a ravine. It was a land of twists, turns, and surprises: a rocky labyrinth under a canopy of lofty, heavy tree limbs. The perfect place for getting lost—or to go when you already felt that way. Often things were not what they seemed: sight, scent, or sound. But one thing even that place could not conceal was the feeling I was being followed. It was hardly more than a feeling yet every now and then I thought I caught the soft padding of footfalls behind me. When I stopped to listen they would cease. If there was something back there it knew I was aware of it. At first I moved carefully, but as the stalker persisted I tried a different approach. Taking off in a sprint (which was dangerous in such broken country) I ran to what I thought was a safe distance and leapt up a twisted oak tree. Concealing myself on a lower branch I waited, barely breathing hoping the sudden move had thrown my pursuer off long enough for them to not know where I was hidden.

It wasn't long before footsteps approached beating quickly but still surprisingly light in my path. They stopped suddenly before they got to the tree. Apparently whatever it was realized something was amiss. But now I got a good whiff of it. My eyes widened—then narrowed. I pressed my body closer to the branch. In a minute or so it appeared, stalking slow: its long, tan form advancing inch by hesitant inch. When it was directly beneath me, I rose to a seated position.

"Up here, Lena."

The lioness jumped a little and looked into the tree. "You're a hard cat to sneak up on!" she huffed.

"Then stop trying," I replied, adding with a growl, "Why are you following me?"

Her head was twisted at an awkward angle to see me, "Are you coming down here or staying perched up there like a bat?"

"Just answer the question."

I expected a smart remark; instead the she-cat sat down with an earnest look on her face, "I wanted to talk with you." She saw my raised eyebrows and added, "Don't look at me that way! I...I need your help." Her voice was not like I had ever heard it before. It actually sounded vulnerable.

But I wasn't about to trust her. "Since when has Lena, the daughter of Mantos, Emperor of the Jungle, ever needed anyone's help?"

A strange look came over her. The rounded ears drooped and the shaggy chin lowered. Even her green eyes clouded.

"Mantos is dead."

That caught me off guard. *Mantos?* It took me a moment to fully grasp her words. "Dead?" I repeated finally. From the way her shoulders fell I gathered that, for once, she was not lying. I dropped to the ground, "How did it happen?"

Lena shivered. "Hunting party; we were on our way back to the jungle and ran across them. I suggested we steer clear, but my father wouldn't listen—as usual." She sounded weak and tired. "They butchered him like an old buffalo. I barely escaped with my skin."

"What happened to the other lionesses?"

"Scattered: ran like the cowards they are! I was left alone to try and save him, but..." her voice trailed off. For the first time in my life I actually felt pity for the lioness. Her father had always been a monster and till now she had seemed just like him, but I had never seen her like this before.

"I'm sorry," I said quietly.

"Don't be," Lena shook her head. "It was my own fault. You were right that day in the woods. I never should have followed him. That's why I came back," the green eyes turned on me with a soft light, "to find you."

Somehow I felt like she meant more than she was saying. "Find me?"

"I told you; I need your help." Her voice was sincere, "My father leaves a vast empire behind him: an empire that falls to me as his heir. But it's too much for me alone. I know that now. I need a king beside me—someone wise and powerful—even stronger than me." The lioness moved closer as she continued, "Someone not afraid to speak his mind, but smart enough to know when to keep his mouth

A CAT'S TALE

shut. Cunning, but not reckless, who won't risk his servants' lives for his own greed. Someone brave and fearless: even more than I am." She was right beside me—close enough to feel her purr. "Someone who could reign with me on a mountain: a mountain of green and gold under a blue sky. *His* mountain!"

Up to this point I had just listened, somewhat suspicious. But now my heart skipped a beat.

My mountain!

In one crystal clear vision it came back to me: lush and beautiful and unchanged. No bars, no cages, no roofs, no walls: just freedom without boundaries, rising like a beacon in the midst of an endless jungle, stretching on as far as the eye could see. The lioness saw my excitement.

"It's still there," she said softly, "Mantos never had time to touch it before we were captured. We could live there—the two of us—ruling together as an unstoppable force. *Think* of it, Sengali! The whole jungle for an empire, and you and me on your mountain: the jeweled throne in the middle of it all!"

But the mention of jewels brought another image to mind: two blue sapphires set against a white face. "What about Saphirra?" I asked, remembering the hatred between them.

Yet instead of getting angry the lioness shrugged with a laugh, "Let her come with us. Why not? She can't replace me now. We'll even make her our general, if you like. Whatever pleases you. I would obey the voice of my king," she bowed, "as long as he didn't cross me too much."

My head was swimming. *My mountain!* Hours before I was a refugee destined for life in a cage. Now the lioness was offering me an empire. It would mean turning my back on the Ark and the Men of the Tree. It would mean becoming Lena's mate.

But freedom!

The very word made my mouth water. To never feel wooden walls or see bars again! *What about the Dream?* part of me cried out. But it was quickly overpowered by another instinct: the instinct for control. For the first time since I left my mountain I had the chance to be my own master again completely independent of anyone else. *I could be King of the Mountain once more!*

Yet something was still puzzling. "Why are you offering me all this?"

She looked at me tenderly, eyes shining like emeralds. Lena was not beautiful like Saphirra, but there was something about her I suddenly found very appealing. "Don't you know?" she whispered and started rubbing up against me.

Now I really was astounded! But I didn't balk or pull away. I just stood there—actually enchanted by the lionesses' charms. All of my arguments were falling to the dust and I had just about decided to go with her when a sudden, still sound floated on the air.

"Sengali."

Immediately my body tensed; Lena felt it and nuzzled me with her cheek. "Something wrong?" she purred.

She didn't hear it, I realized, looking at the lioness.

"Sengali," the Voice came again, deep and quiet, *"Do not listen to her."* Suddenly my head felt a little clearer. I shook it hard, forcing myself to think straight.

What am I doing?

"You don't belong here," her smooth voice continued, "not in this place, not with *these* people. You belong on your mountain with the open sky and free wind blowing in your face. Not cooped up in a wooden dungeon filled with fools!" My mind clouded again as the lionesses' words poured on like oil, "You deserve better!"

"Sengali," the Voice called, a little louder this time, *"she is lying!"*

Her long tail brushed my whiskers, "You belong with me!"

And then they came: Nathak's words, ringing like Chenna's little bell, echoing in my heart.

"Remember what brought you here!"

Instantly everything cleared. I yanked away from the lioness. "No, Lena!" I said firmly, "That choice has already been made. My place is with the Ark—and the Men of the Tree!"

At that moment a sound cut the night around us, echoing from behind! I turned in alarm. It was a howl: piercing, loud, and short. A howl of distress.

Nathak!

"Then die with them!"

I spun around just in time to see Lena's claws reaching for my face! Ducking to the side, they flew over my head but then swerved and grabbed my back. I dropped to the ground and rolled, ripping them loose. In a second the she-cat was on top of me, livid and spitting, going for my throat! I opened my mouth and caught her foreleg, then pushed her off with my paws. She went flying to the side. There was barely time to get to my feet before she came at me again. Her strength was incredible, fueled by her hatred. It was all I could do just to hold her off!

But suddenly a white blur rammed into the lionesses' side, knocking her against a tree trunk! That took the wind out of Lena long enough for Saphirra to turn to me and shout, "Sengali—*GO!*"

I didn't wait. Nathak's howl still rang in my ears as I sped through the maze-like forest. Jumping over logs, ducking under limbs, skirting along crevices, leaping over short canyons, I ran in the direction his signal had come from—listening even as my paws pounded the ground. But no other sound came. I wasn't sure if I was still headed the right way when all at once the wolf's scent filled my nostrils. I cringed. There was blood mixed with it. I followed the bitterly sweet smell through a thicket of laurel bushes, bursting out into a small clearing.

My heart sunk.

There on the ground lay Nathak, covered in blood.

His sides were still heaving, but his silver fur was matted and dark. I walked forward slowly, legs trembling. His keen eyes were shut tight in pain, his strong body shaking like a frightened pup. As I got closer my horror grew. The wolf was slashed in ribbons! With sudden, terrible clarity I realized what he meant to me. What a friend he had become. The wolf must have felt my presence because the blue eyes opened; they fixed on me, big and glassy. My heart tightened. I felt sick. For a few moments he lay there, just looking at me, jerking and gasping for breath—dying yet so full of courage. I never felt so helpless. Then, with whimpers he could not stop, Nathak raised his head. Heart in his eyes, the wolf stared at me, his life's blood pouring out of his sides. I couldn't speak, couldn't say anything. So the wolf spoke for both us. Just one word.

"Shem!"

That was it: all he could manage before Nathak's noble head fell to the ground.

Lifeless.

My heart burst.

"*NO!*"

I roared into the blackness, screaming at the night. My body fell in the clotted dust. Gasping with grief I started to weep—until my eyes saw the huge tracks printed all over the clearing, stained in the blood of the wolf. The tracks of a monstrous cat: headed south-west. My breath sucked in sharply. My teeth clenched. My head pounded with rage.

Mantos!

THIRTY-EIGHT

HE WAS AFTER THE TREE! Kicking over all the power in me I shot through the forest, racing over the bloody trail. *Shem! He's wearing the Tree! That was what Nathak meant.*

The monster is after Shem!

My claws barely touched the ground; fast as it could, my body flew between the giant trees. My breath came in deep, rapid chugs, fueling my muscles. Mantos' trail was painfully distinct; his scent wafted between my teeth like a bad taste, growing stronger with every leap. I was close—but was I in time? The ground rose in a steep hill; my legs charged up it. As I neared the crest my mind was exploding with scenarios, trying to apprehend my enemy's moves. Where was he? How fast could he move? How would he go after—

SMACK!

A huge claw hit my face! My eyes blacked out. My legs tumbled in darkness. I rolled down the other side of the hill, head throbbing. The ground leveled and I hit it with a thud. Before my senses could recover a searing vice grabbed my shoulders, picked me up, and flung me through the air!

Ooomph!

Thick dirt crammed into my mouth. I lay on my side, pain shooting through me like fire! Muscles trembling, I struggled to stand, still enveloped in blackness. But another massive claw descended on my neck, pressing me down.

"So Lena's plan failed," a hideous voice rumbled through the darkness behind my head, breathing in my ears. "Good. Now I can finish you myself! Although I should actually thank you, Sengali," Mantos said, "without your help I never would have found the Man of the Tree." There was a cruel chuckle. "You said I was wrong about him. Called him a 'sign of hope', even 'mercy'." The claw cut into my throat, crushing my windpipe. "Well, can you see your hope now?"

My vision started to return: blurry at first, then clearer. My face was against the dirt and the world looked sideways. Through the darkness I saw another form lying on the ground, not far away.

Shem!

He was alive but groaning, his right leg cut open with claw-marks. I still could not see the monster pressing down on me, but his breath was like death itself.

"Did you think the Tree would save you?" Mantos spat in my ear. "Did you think *he* would save you?"

Suddenly the lion raked my shoulder and hip with his talons! I cried out in pain and the young man's head turned towards me. We looked at each other—bleeding and broken.

The lion laughed. "He cannot even save himself!"

Shem's eyes were wracked with pain. But then they steeled; desperately the man started pulling himself along the ground, trying to reach the sword that had fallen from his sheath. In an instant Mantos' tremendous weight lifted off me. As I gasped for breath the massive beast came into view leaping over my body and bounding towards Shem. He pounced on the man like he was a mouse, pinning him down. Shem groaned, trapped under the lion's weight. Mantos' tail twitched like a snake and his huge muscles bulged. He looked down, placed his terrible paw against Shem's neck, and closed his claws around the Tree. The shaggy head turned my way: eye-socket gaping, fangs dripping saliva.

"You trusted in him, didn't you, Sengali?" He spoke slowly, every word full of menace, "Trusted in the Man of the Tree?" His one eye gleamed in the dark. A devilish smile spread across the Emperor's hideous face.

"Well, I trust in myself!"

Mantos' horrible mouth opened wide in a roar. He went for Shem's throat.

"NO!" With a surge of power I didn't know I had, my body lunged up! Leaping for the murderer, my claws dug into his tawny back, wrapping around him like the coils of a python. The lion roared again—this time from pain—as I pulled him off Shem's chest. Into a thicket of thorns we tumbled, heads over tails; my claws still stuck inside his back. When we stopped, the lion lurched from underneath me, slinging me off into a tree trunk. Dropping into a patch of brambles, I rolled just in time to miss him leaping on my head! With my teeth I grabbed a branch loaded with nail-like thorns, bent it back, and let it go hitting Mantos directly in the face. As he bellowed I slipped out of the bushes, running to a clear hillside.

Turning, I called out, "Is that the best you can do, Mantos?"

The proud lion angrily jerked the last of the thorns from his head, then roared and came after me. I sprinted, leading him up the hillside—away from where Shem lay. The climb was gradual, but steep enough. My lead was an advantage, but the wounds Mantos had given me dangerously slowed me down. Whenever I looked back, the lion was gaining—that evil smirk plastered over his face. Still I pushed on. My lungs felt like exploding, my legs felt like collapsing, my head felt like falling off, but still I climbed, as hard and as fast as my battered body could manage. I could hear the lion's breath closing in like the beat of a dragon's wings.

Finally hitting level ground I burst into a full run—then stopped cold, barely skidding to a stop before tumbling headlong over a hundred-foot drop! I heaved on the edge of the cliff, looking out over a carpet of black tree-tops under a moonless sky. A deep gurgle from behind let me know Mantos had gained the summit. His laugh sounded like a rotting tree creaking in the wind.

"A dead end, Sengali!" he panted, spitting through his long tusks, "For you and your Dream!"

"Don't be a fool, Mantos!" I countered, "The Dream won't end here! You can't stop it. Kill us all and it will still come!" My own blood tasted like sweat as it dripped in my mouth, "The Dream is bigger than all of us!"

But the monster just chuffed, "Well-spoken, as always; but too boldly—for last words!"

Rising on his haunches like a bear, descending like a wave of rage, Mantos brought all his massive weight right down on top of me. I met him full on. Our chests crashed with numbing power! Our jaws locked (mine just barely above his awful tusks), and our heads welded together. Biting, grinding, snarling, the Emperor of the Jungle and I held on: caught in a death grip neither of us would break. When finally we did part of our faces tore away with the other. We swerved and came again full force! Paws boxing, claws out, fangs barred, ears back. Over and over we clashed—flesh pounding flesh—tearing, ripping, searing. I dodged, swerved, lunged every angle I could, but the monstrous, old cat was unbelievably quick! Whereas my own power kept draining, Mantos' seemed to grow with every hit. Mercilessly he dove into me, wearing me down: opening old wounds and creating new ones. His attacks were furious; he knew my strength was fading.

But just as the monster was sure of victory, I saw it: an opening for his throat. I darted in, sinking my fangs in his mane. He screamed and fell back—a stream of dark blood staining his yellow fur. His eye turned red.

"I've played with you long enough!"

Before my exhausted body could respond his iron paw struck my head. I fell to the dust almost senseless. Mantos loomed over me like a ghoulish beast, heaving and panting: a pale, bleeding, hulk of a figure in the early morning darkness.

"You *fool!*" he spat again, "What did you think you would gain? Leaving everything—your mountain, your freedom—to follow *him?* You could have had anything...power beyond your wildest dreams!" The lion's voice gargled, "But you chose your fate! You followed the Man of the Tree." His face contorted to a deadly snarl, "Now *he* will follow you—*to death!*"

A CAT'S TALE

The lion reared one more time, roared, and rushed down: going for my head. But my strength was spent. Gone.

I closed my eyes.

Suddenly there was a piercing howl! My eyes opened.

It was Mantos. He was reeling, stumbling, roaring in agony. The right side of his face was wet and dark—his one good eye pierced through with a white arrow. I looked back at the woods. Standing erect under the trees, face grim and resolute behind the still trembling string of the white bow, was Yeffeth—his left arm extended, recovered enough to hold the smooth shaft steady. Faster than thought, the man flipped an arrow from his right hand, notched it, and sent it flying at the Emperor.

This time it pierced the evil heart. Mantos stumbled back, closer and closer to the edge of the cliff. Yeffeth pulled another arrow. But the final blow was the lion's own; his paws slipped over the precipice. The next second he was gone—his terrible roar ending abruptly at the bottom of the ravine.

I lay motionless: stunned and exhausted, breathing hard. Yeffeth hurried to my side and knelt down, the bow draped around his wiry shoulders by its fine string. He pulled a vial from a pouch at his waist and started applying it to the worst of my wounds. The man's touch was soothing. Eventually I began noticing things besides the throbbing pain:

frogs croaking, bugs clamoring, birds beginning to sing. After a long while I decided to try and stand. Groaning and shaky, and with Yeffeth's help, I managed to my feet.

"Thank God," he breathed, still kneeling beside me. My eyes met his hazel ones and we looked at each other, face to face. Then I bowed my head, knowing no better way to thank the man for saving my life. His long, archer fingers stroked between my ears and when I looked up again there was a single tear falling down the brown, angled cheek. As the clear drop of water slid into the left side of his reddish beard it glistened. Glistened with light.

Morning light.

The man and I looked away from each other, our gaze drawn to the east. Yeffeth stood slowly. I turned to face the same way. We held our breaths and it felt like the rest of the world was holding with us. The air was still. On the eastern horizon, over the tops of the trees, a warm glow was growing—building like a fire to light the dark sky. Silently we watched it appear under a ceiling of low clouds, washing the landscape brilliant amber with one stroke of its burning fingers. The rising sun.

Dawn of the seventh day!

THIRTY-NINE

WE HURRIED BACK to the Ark as fast as my injured legs would allow. Passing the thicket I noticed Shem was gone; no sign of him remained except the smell of his wounds. As his brother and I reached the open field we saw that ours had not been the only fight that morning. Here and there lay the dead bodies of other lionesses. Apparently Mantos' attack had been a full blown assault. But by the look of things his followers had fared no better than he had. That hope grew as I saw a white form standing at the southern end of the great ship, gleaming like a pearl in the sunlight: Saphirra. Even from this distance I could see her relief as we came into view. The lioness bounded towards us.

"Are you alright?" she asked, voice full of concern when she noticed my limp.

"Nothing that won't mend," I replied, just glad to see her safe and unharmed. She helped brace my steps. "What happened with Lena?"

"She escaped," the lioness said reluctantly, "though not un-injured."

"And Shem—where is Shem?" I asked as we rounded the Ark. Bulk and the she-bear were sitting under the boardwalk, licking some very minor wounds. Nina and Atani were standing up by the great door, bows in hand, with Eddie on the dark girl's shoulder and his mate on the other's. They waved happily when they saw us.

"Safe," Saphirra answered, "They are bandaging his leg right now in the orchard. He should be fine. But Nathak," her fair face clouded over, "I don't know...I've never seen such wounds!"

Hope shot through my heart so suddenly it hurt. "Nathak!" I stopped in my tracks, "He's alive?"

The lioness nodded, but her look was solemn, "For now. Though I don't know how long he can stay that way."

I picked up my pace, wincing every step, trying to get to the fruit grove as fast as possible. The lovely branches were still and quiet, their blossoms hanging limp as if aware something was suffering beneath them. The soft glade between their roots had been turned into a temporary infirmary. Shem lay with his back against the trunk of an apricot tree while Chenna and Marriet tended to his leg, wrapping it in clean bandages. Womby and Glori sat nestled on either side of him, giving what comfort they could. The man's face was pale but alert as ever; one look at him told me he would recover. Kawm also wore a bandage on his left hand, though it still held an ax as he stood guard near the edge of the orchard. Noak's left arm was bound with linen. Thankfully, however, no one's wounds looked lethal and would probably cause them no more trouble than leaving a few scars.

All, that is, except one.

At sight of Nathak's broken body stretched out underneath a drooping peach tree I stopped—overwhelmed. "I thought he was dead."

"He basically was when Noak found him," Saphirra whispered back. "The humans have a wondrous ability to heal; they have kept him alive—barely. But I'm afraid..." her voice trailed off, unwilling to finish. As we approached the wolf I grimaced. The bleeding had stopped and his many wounds had been dressed, but still the wolf barely breathed. Rhia was lying beside him, her back against his and her head turned to touch her mate's. Her kind, usually sunny face was filled with deep, quiet sorrow. She looked up as I came near.

"Sengali! Thank the Creator you are safe," but though the she-wolf tried she could not keep her voice from trembling. "Shem says you saved his life."

I just shook my head, my eyes on the gray form between us, "I never would have known without

Nathak." There was a groan and we both looked at the wolf; in a moment his blue eyes opened. They were weak but clear and as they found me they almost seemed to smile. I leaned forward, sensing he wanted to speak. Though his breath was incredibly shallow, he finally managed to say two words.

"Thanks, cat."

I smiled even as my throat started to close with tears. The look on the keen face I don't think I will ever forget: respect, gratitude, and friendship all rolled into one. But it faded as the wolf's eyes closed and he sank back to unconsciousness. All this time Noak was standing close by; now he gently touched the wolf's neck. The man said nothing but his silver brow furrowed. It was Yeffeth I heard instead, leaning beside Shem.

"Is it still burning?" he asked, inspecting his brother's wounds.

Shem winced but shook his head, "Not anymore."

"I have applied the poultice several times," their mother explained. "He should be able to stand soon, providing he doesn't place much weight on it."

Yeffeth grabbed his brother's shoulder, "You can get into more trouble!" But despite his jest the relief on the older brother's face was clear to see.

Shem's dark eyes probed him. "It *was* the same beast wasn't it?" he shook from exhaustion but his voice was steady, "The one that came after me as a child around the fire? The lion you shot in the eye and Great-Father drove off?"

Yeffeth looked at him then sighed. "It does not seem possible," he nodded in amazement, "but no two creatures could be so alike and not be the same. Yet how any cat could live so long—"

Suddenly Nathak yipped in pain. Noak laid his hand on the thick fur collar and Yeffeth came over. Shem struggled in vain to get up, helpless to comfort his pet. Chenna wrapped her arms around him trying to comfort her husband. At Noak's touch the wolf's moans died away but his body was jerking with spasms. The two men looked at each other, eyes full of concern.

"Do you think he can make it?" Yeffeth asked, voice low. Slowly, reluctantly the father shook his head.

"We have no time to find out."

His son's brow wrinkled together. "But Father, if Nathak dies..." he looked at the two wolves and said no more. But I knew what he was thinking.

If Nathak dies what will become of the wolves?

Noak studied Rhia but said nothing. She was pressed close as possible to her mate, nuzzling him, trying to give him strength. Of all the animals that had come to the Ark there had been no others like them, no other dogs. Nathak and Rhia were the only two. Without him the line would die.

"How is he?" Shem asked. Noak said nothing but the look he gave his son was clear enough. Shem's face contorted with pain; he groaned and turned his head away. Chenna placed her delicate hands on his rough cheeks and drew him close. A solemn grief overtook the orchard. Saphirra crept up and nestled by my side like she was looking to me to protect her from the sorrow. But I could not stop my own.

Not Nathak! Not now!

Kawm approached quickly. He spoke low but urgently, "The sun is well above the trees!" Noak nodded, his weathered hand still stroking Nathak's fur. He took a deep breath.

"It is time," he said. His eyes went from the dying wolf to his wounded son. "Shem," the father spoke quietly, "Nathak is yours; it is your decision." The young man looked at him, face twisted in agony. Then his gaze fell on the wolves. The choice was unthinkable; yet it had to be made. I watched the gray sides quiver as Nathak whimpered again. Shem's jaw clenched even as tears rolled out of his eyes.

"He should not suffer," the young man finally managed, "not Nathak."

My heart hit the ground. Rhia dug her face into the male wolf's mane; Saphirra hid hers in my shoulder. Womby and Glori nuzzled against Shem. The humans were no less grief stricken. But there was nothing to be done. After a moment Noak looked at Yeffeth.

A CAT'S TALE

"Lead them into the Ark. I will follow you." His eldest son bowed his head, laid a trembling hand on Nathak's, and moved to gather the family. The tears flowed freely as one by one they said farewell to the wolf. But none so freely as Shem. As he bent down to speak one last time into the sharp ears, Nathak's eyes opened again. The big nose touched his beloved master's cheek and the man started to weep.

"Forgive me, my friend," he murmured, "forgive me!" The wolf groaned and licked his chin. Through his tears, Shem tried to smile. "Good boy," he said, lip quivering, "Godspeed!" Yeffeth and Chenna helped him to his feet. After one final look, Shem turned and they slowly left the orchard. All that remained were Noak and the six of us: the wolves, the wombats, Saphirra, and me. The man looked around, eyes full of pity.

"Go with them," he said gently.

Saphirra obeyed and the wombats followed—but I couldn't move. My eyes were fixed on the wolf. It was like my feet were planted in the ground. I just could not bring myself to say goodbye. Nathak's head swiveled around so he could see me. Then he leaned into Rhia.

"Go with Sengali."

"No," the she-wolf cried, "I'm not leaving you!"

"You have to," he wheezed. "You have no choice." With painful effort he stretched to touch her muzzle,

"You carry more than yourself now." Rhia crumbled; her brown head buried in Nathak's gray neck.

His icy blue eyes looked up into mine, "Take care of them for me."

I drew in a sharp breath as I realized what the wolf was saying.

She's with young!

Rhia was going to have pups! In awe I looked back at him—feeling more admiration than I ever dreamed possible to have for anyone, let alone a dog. Somehow I managed to nod my head.

"I promise!"

* * *

With heavy steps the she-wolf and I left the orchard, stepping out of the lacy shadows into the light of a full sun. Overhead the sky was clear except for a couple of low-lying clouds on the southern horizon. It seemed like an ordinary morning in early summer: warm, sunny, and full of life. But for us it felt like night had fallen: cold and starless. Quietly we walked towards the Ark, our sorrow too strong for words. As the great ship drew closer we saw the others standing near the giant door. I reached the bottom of the long gangplank and hesitated. My paws hadn't touched it since the morning when I sat before the door and watched the sun rise. A shiver ran through me. I knew there would be no going back.

The pads of my feet fell on the rough wood. As we climbed the walkway they never faltered. Every step sealed my resolve. This was where my journey had led me—where the Voice had led me—and here I would stay. Whatever happened, whatever came: *this* was where I belonged. As we neared the door a breeze began to blow whistling through the doorway and into my face almost as if it was welcoming me inside. I breathed deeply, peace settling into my heavy heart.

The Ark was now my home.

We reached the flat platform and Chenna rushed forward, embracing Rhia. Shem stood nearby leaning on an old, gnarly staff—looking old and broken. I went up to him. Slowly he crouched down and his free hand grasped the fur around my neck. His rich brown eyes searched mine for a moment; we saw each other's pain. Then, without a word, he leaned his forehead into mine.

Yeffeth stood before the door—his sharp eyes searching the valley, the forest, the sky. Without a word he looked at his family gathered around, then signaled with a solemn nod. Into the shadow of the doorway he stepped, holding out one arm to Nina and the other to Marriet. Bulk and the she-bear followed then Kawm and Atani with Eddie's mate on her shoulder. Eddie remained; the monkey was hanging from the rail-posts, trying to get as much sun as he could. I looked out over the green and yellow fields, the great barn and pastures, the forest filled with ancient trees, the bright blue heavens. I let the light kiss my face once more. Then I turned to Shem. He stood up and took Chenna's hand; Rhia and the wombats were by their side. But Saphirra stood alone. Her eyes met mine, filled with tenderness. I smiled gently. As soft as a breath she came and stood beside me. Our heads rubbed together and the feel of her smooth fur was like velvet. Together we faced the man and his wife. Shem motioned with his arm and the movement made the Tree glimmer.

"Come," he said.

Only one little word, but it had tremendous power. The couple turned to enter the great doorway, and Saphirra and I fell into step behind them. I realized I was holding my breath.

"Wait!" came a cry behind us. It was Eddie. "Wait, wait, wait! Look!"

We all spun around. The monkey was dancing on the rails, pointing down at the ground, chattering like mad, *"Look, look, look, look, look!"* When we did there was a simultaneous gasp.

And then the tears started flowing again.

Noak was walking towards the Ark with Nathak in his arms—*alive!*

FORTY

"NATHAK!" RHIA SHOUTED. In a flash the she-wolf was down the boardwalk sprinting towards them. I started laughing and crying all at once.

He was alive! Nathak was still alive!

We watched as Noak bent forward so the wolves could touch noses. Then he started carrying Nathak up the gangplank while Rhia barked and leaped in happy circles. The rest of us rushed down to meet them. Noak smiled sheepishly.

"I couldn't do it," he said, clutching the silver body close. "Normally it would have been the merciful thing..." he paused as Shem hobbled up, his face a mixture of relief and confusion. "But," Noak continued, "He said 'two of every kind', and 'two of every kind' it will be. The results are in God's hands."

Shem said nothing yet his dark eyes beamed with gratitude. He ran his hands through Nathak's mane and the wolf licked his Master's arm. It was as if the touch gave new strength to them both. Shem leaned less heavily on his cane and Nathak actually looked around. The wolf was still in terrible shape, but his alertness seemed to be returning.

Eddie cackled. "Aww, *nuts!*" he winked, "I thought we'd finally got rid of you!" The wolf managed a weak smile.

"Sorry."

Laughing, each of us once again fell into place and headed back up the boardwalk, this time with Noak leading the way. He and Marriet passed through the door, with Rhia by their side and Nathak in his arms; Yeffeth and Nina came next, Bulk and his mate behind them; then Kawm and Atani, with Eddie on board; Shem and Chenna with Womby and Glori; and, last of all, Saphirra and me.

Passing under the shadow of the great door was like entering another world. As the familiar outside fell away and the thick walls of the Ark enclosed around us, I was met by thousands of different smells—mostly animal. My eyes adjusted to the change of light. We were in a long, clean hallway, lined on either side with shelves and cages built into the walls. Unlike the Barracks of Khanok, however, these cages were made of fine wood that smelled rich and earthy. The animals within were peaceful and content on beds of soft hay. An even, yellow light filtered from above where a catwalk on the Ark's roof had been designed to double as both a ventilation and light source. Far away to the right, near the Ark's furthest end, there appeared to be an opening in the floor that led to a ramp—most likely descending to the decks underneath us. On the left end, much closer, were some doors and rooms that looked like living quarters for the humans.

The air around us was warm and comforting, giving the whole place the feeling of a large, cozy den made out of gopherwood—a far cry from the dungeon I had been so afraid of only hours before. As I gazed around at the small band of people, rejoicing and embracing each other, I wondered how I could have ever let myself be so deceived. The warm air filled my nostrils. I exhaled. Right then and there I decided that, were every mountain in the world offered to me, I would not take them if it meant leaving the Ark.

Suddenly I froze. Every hair on my body stood straight up! I saw nothing abnormal; heard nothing strange.

But I *felt* something.

Something was behind me: a presence so giant, so powerful, it chilled every drop of blood in my veins! Saphirra felt it too and turned around: eyes big. Gazing past me, they widened in fear.

"The...the *door!*" she stammered.

By now the others were staring at what she saw: totally speechless. I forced myself to look behind. My jaw dropped. The doorway was narrowing—inch by inch—cutting out all view of the outside world. Like something out of a dream, the fields, the forest, the sky, all disappeared from sight replaced by a dark, solid square. Soon they were gone completely. A teeth-rattling BANG shook the whole Ark.

The door—that great, massive, immovable door—had shut: *by itself!*

The silence was deafening; a terrifying awe charged the atmosphere. I'm not sure how long before any of us moved, but when they did, it was Noak. He looked at his sons and spoke just three words.

"Get them secure!"

We didn't argue. Yeffeth quickly escorted Saphirra and me to a roomy cage on the left near the humans' living quarters. As I stepped through the wooden bars my heart was racing—but not from a fear of being trapped. The snug little apartment was swept clean and padded on one side with a wide bed of hay. We could easily stand up inside and move around without restrictions. Nina brought a ceramic jug and poured water into a round cylinder attached to the outside of the bars, which trickled down into a square tray within our reach. Then Yeffeth closed the cage door, securing it with a solid, wooden latch that barely made a sound as it shut behind us. To my amazement, the fear subsided a little. The small, guarded space actually brought a sense of security.

Somewhat.

The men and women scattered through the Ark making final preparations. Yeffeth, Kawm, and their wives disappeared down the ramp to the lower levels, taking the bears, wombats, and monkeys with them. Noak and Chenna went through the top deck, double-checking latches, securing food bins—doing whatever they could as fast as they could to make sure all was ready (though for what, exactly, none of us knew). Marriet and Shem, hobbling on his staff, secured Nathak and Rhia in a cage just opposite from us, taking every measure to ensure the wounded wolf's safety. The wolf groaned and trembled, but Nathak was a fighter. He never whined. As Shem closed the door on the wolves he turned to us. Leaning down on his staff the young man looked me in the eye.

"Godspeed!" he whispered.

The others returned and together all the humans passed into the rooms on the end, closing the small doors behind them.

* * *

My heart was pounding. I could not sit down: something deep, deep within was telling me to stay alert. I stood, motionless, barely breathing, with Saphirra by my side. And we weren't the only ones.

Rhia was poised against the bars, nose up, while Nathak's ears swiveled. The animals near us were quiet and subdued. It felt like we were all waiting for something—something all of us had experienced but none of us wanted to put into words.

Then Saphirra and I both looked down at our paws.

"Do you feel that?" she asked anxiously.

"Yes." Listening through my legs I felt a rumble—almost like a war had started far, far, *far* under the ground. It was subtle and I could tell many of the others did not detect it. But it was definitely there. I crouched to the floor.

BOOM!

From somewhere below—through the Ark, into the ground, out of the very depths of the earth—came a deep, hardly audible, terrible sound! It shook the wood beneath my paws, shooting up my legs and into my chest like a shock! I jumped back; Saphirra pressed against me. The boom sounded only once, but it was enough to cause serious stir among the cages. They were all thinking the same thing we were.

The Dream! The sound from the Dream!

Now every inch of my body strained forward: listening, waiting. Minutes passed. The rumble below continued, but that was all. As nothing happened some of the simpler animals started to quiet down, thinking the worst was over. But I never moved. My eyes and ears were pointed to the light vents overhead.

All at once the light disappeared! Saphirra gasped and some of the animals began to cry in fear as the Ark rapidly grew dark. I could hear birds outside flying over in droves, calling out in panic. Then a noise unlike anything I'd ever heard came from overhead: a growling, cracking, ear-numbing roll of sound. It was as if the very heavens were angry! Again and again it pounded, echoing all around, rattling the gopher-walls. Then, through the darkness, flashes of white light started breaking—hot, blinding streaks that pierced one second and vanished the next. Black, then white, then black again. Over and over—flashing, breaking, slicing—and always echoed by that pounding, rolling, explosion of sound! Rhia darted around, tail tucked between her legs; Saphirra's ears pinned back as she nervously glanced about. Birds were screeching, Elephants bellowing, lizards hissing.

That's when it started.

Tap!

I turned to the wall.

Ratta-tat!

Saphirra looked as well.

Ratta-tat-tap!

From all over came sharp, rapid pattering, as if hundreds of small rocks were being flung against the sides of the Ark.

Tap! Tat! Ratta-tat-tap!

Cautiously I brought my face within inches of the wooden beams.

"What is it?" The lioness wondered. But it was Rhia who answered: her big, wolf nose held against the opposite wall.

"Water," she said, voice filled with awe.

Almost instantly the pattering became lashing, then beating. Water was pouring from the sky! I looked up at the light vents, expecting to see it gushing down inside the Ark. Yet not one drop appeared; the men must have engineered the vents so nothing but light and air could get in. And it was a good thing, because from the torrential sound it made against the boat the water must have been falling in tremendous sheets! It sounded like we were standing under a huge waterfall! But soon another noise broke through, ten times more chilling.

Voices.

There were people outside the Ark: screaming, pleading, shrieking to get inside. We could hear their hands as they beat against the outside clawing to find a way in. But the door was shut. Listening to their cries, I could only imagine what Noak and his family must have been feeling. All those years—decades and decades—they had warned them it was coming. Year after year, they had pleaded—begged—with both stranger and neighbor to repent. But they had refused. Now it was too late. The great door had closed by a hand bigger than any man's and no man could open it—whether outside or in.

As their screams reached their peak another sensation washed over me. Terrifyingly familiar. I stared at the eastern wall.

It began as a tremble. Then it grew to a distant moan. The others felt it too; we all looked at each other, eyes large in fear. Quickly it rose to a shout: a massive, distant whirlwind of noise, closing in fast— from the east. My heart almost stopped; I knew what was happening. My mind jumped back to the Dream: the black wave climbing into the air, swallowing everything in its path! Many of the animals inside started to panic as the people outside became hysterical. With growing horror I listened to the vents overhead. What had been a distant shout turned to a roar: rushing and growling like a mountain of water speeding towards us! Rapidly it increased, churning closer by the second! The noise was deafening.

"Brace yourselves!" I shouted.

Seconds later everything lurched! Saphirra shrieked as we both smacked against the floor and slid towards the wall. The whole Ark was tipping on its side! The roar had crashed into it! Further and further the ship leaned until Saphirra and I were practically standing on the wall; Nathak and Rhia were lying on the bars of their cage. But just when I was afraid we would capsize completely the Ark suddenly surged upward, righting itself and throwing us to the floor!

Just as quickly we rocked the other way, though not as far. Bobbing, tossing, rolling—I could not get my legs under me as the great boat moved around like a bucking horse.

We're floating!

Overhead the water from the sky still pounded mercilessly while the crashing sound and streaks of light rolled. It felt like we were rushing around at incredible speed, like a stick tossed about in a furious ocean. I found myself getting sick and more than one animal lost their lunch.

Eventually the worst of the rocking seemed to subside—but then we started to whirl. Spinning round and round, the only thing to be done was flatten ourselves to the floor, hang on, and try to keep our heads from falling off. I really don't know how long this lasted, but it was some time before I felt like standing up. When I did finally managed to, it was like all of my insides had been re-arranged. But eventually either the Ark began to stabilize or I grew accustomed to its movement, because I started regaining my faculties. Looking about in the darkness I saw that—amazingly—the boat was intact, the cages had held, and everyone was still alive! Saphirra was fine (aside from a few bumps and bruises) and the wolves seemed unharmed (Nathak looked a little worse for wear but, thankfully, not too much). Outside the Ark the storm raged on, but inside we began to breathe again.

We survived!

The ship still tossed abruptly and violently, but not like at first. We had weathered the beginning of the Flood and lived to tell about it! From somewhere below I heard Eddie's voice start laughing like crazy. Then he shouted at the top of his lungs:

"Let's do it again!"

* * *

The storm continued forty days and forty nights. Not that I could tell one from the other much, thanks to the prevailing darkness, but Noak and his family kept track of the time in other ways. After the initial upheaval they had come out from their quarters surprisingly unscathed and set about checking on the rest of us. A few minor injuries and the mess from our sea-sickness had to be dealt with, but the humans seemed pleased things were not worse. All of their hard work and preparation had not been in vain. The men and women fell into different duties: caring for the animals, collecting water funneled from the rain, sanitation, cleaning clothing, etc. Undoubtedly, however, looking after the several thousands of us was their greatest task. They divided the works by sections: Yeffeth and Nina took the lowest deck, Kawm and Atani took the middle, and Shem and Chenna took the top where we were. Noak and Marriet went between all three, helping as needed.

For the first couple of weeks that was mostly on the upper deck, due to Shem's leg.

Since he couldn't move around very well himself (especially in all the tossing and pitching) Shem spent that time focusing his attention on nursing Nathak back to health. The wolf made slow progress; there were moments when we feared he still might not make it. But gradually he began to improve, and when Shem was finally able to stand and walk without his staff, Nathak was also able to hold himself up and eat without any help. Saphirra and I watched all this from the comfort of our cage, settling into a quiet routine of feedings, sleep, and resting. After the excitement of the past few months it was a welcome change. Even the rolling of the ship and the sound of water beating its wooden sides became so familiar it almost felt normal: as if the dark, floating world had always been our home.

But sometimes there were stark reminders of the outer world as well.

With the first, horrible wave that had started the Flood almost all sounds of life outside the Ark had ceased: bird, beast, or human. But not completely. Every now and then we still heard voices. Some were distant and vague, others closer, yet they all sounded alike. Desperate. Hopeless. Animal or human, it was always the same. I finally determined we were circling the tops of mountains not yet covered in water, hearing the cries of those who had escaped the initial wave. But no one could escape for long. The sounds came and went, like echoes from a nightmare; there were times I wondered if they were even real. One instance, however, was terribly clear. It was the last time I heard anything but water outside.

The Ark had just jerked and pulled as if circling some invisible object when a particular voice caught my ears. Loud and angry. Full of hate. I recognized him immediately.

Hittan.

The Man-Beast, the giant—the one men had bowed down to and worshiped as "Master of the Games"—was screaming like a raving lunatic, hoarse and raspy but still strong enough to shout. With every kind of vile word he cursed Noak and his sons, cursed the Ark and everything in it, cursed the God of heaven. I watched Chenna bury her face in Shem's chest as he placed his hands over her small ears. Yet even the crashing rumbles of the sky couldn't drown him out.

Then suddenly another sound met my ears, also familiar. A loud, guttural growl. One moment the giant was cursing; the next screaming in pain.

That was the last we ever heard of Hittan.

The vicious growls of his attacker faded into one long, lone moan: the moan of a lioness.

Lena.

The boat surged, water rushed all around—and then there was nothing. Nothing but the sound of the storm.

Lena had finished the giant. And the Flood had finished her.

Saphirra and I looked at each other too overwhelmed to speak. Her blue eyes glistened with emotion; then the white head nuzzled against my chest, nestling under the protection of my chin. Our hearts filled with a solemn gratitude.

We were safe.

FORTY-ONE

THOSE WERE THE DAYS of healing. The endless storms and constant turmoil made it too dangerous for any of us to venture out of our cages, so we spent the time resting. But I didn't complain. After all the excitement of the past few months it was a welcome change of pace to not have to do anything. Not that there wasn't any excitement. The world outside still ripped itself apart while we tossed around like a twig under a waterfall. The Ark was continually rocking: tilting so violently at times we weren't sure we would make it after all. But the ship held firm. Always it stood between us and the storm, and as the days and weeks passed we learned to trust in it. The Ark became our refuge. Our bodies and hearts started mending. My scars faded, the humans' wounds completely healed, and Nathak recovered beyond anyone's wildest hopes. The wolf slowly grew in strength until he was able to stand. Then he began to walk. By the time he started loping around inside of his cage I was convinced the wolf could do anything. Not that I let him know it (needing to retain some kind of pride), but our mutual respect had grown so much I didn't have to. And that respect was rewarded: when the sky water finally stopped falling the wolf and I were allowed to accompany Shem and Yeffeth on their rounds through the Ark.

The bobbing of the ship took some getting used to; though the raging storm had ended, a strong wind had taken its place, causing the Ark to turn and jump sideways. Keeping a straight line down the long, rolling aisles between cages was quite a challenge. The men laughed at us, saying we should use our "sea legs" (whatever *that* was supposed to mean), but eventually we caught on. It was fascinating to wander down the wooden hallways of each deck. The bright, lively upper one (where we lived with the humans, birds, and smaller animals) was now flooded with light from the vents overhead. Below it, the warmer mid-deck—with its high-ceiling, earthy glow, and thousands of mid-sized creatures—felt like the largest of the three. As we made our way to the far end of this deck, where much of the food was stored, Kawm and Atani came into sight, cleaning monkey cages. Eddie was sitting on the girl's shoulder. He started jumping and waving like mad when he saw us.

A CAT'S TALE

"Hey! *Oo-oo-ee!* You're alive!" he called, leather face stretched in a grin. When close enough he jumped onto Nathak's head. "Even Grumpy looks back to normal!" He pulled the wolf's ears playfully. "Too bad. Wrote you a *bea-u-ti-ful* eulogy. All kinds of nice things to say. Took me forever to come up with them, but—"

"Good to see you too, Monkey," Nathak rumbled and shook his head.

The scoundrel hopped onto my back. "You seen Bulk?"

"Not yet," I chuckled.

"Well come *on*—shake a leg! Can't stay here all day!" He tugged at my neck, "Places to see, stuff to do—"

"People to annoy," cut in the wolf.

Eddie cackled, right in my ear, "Yep. He's back to normal!"

I caught the wolf's wink as we turned back down the aisle. Shem and Yeffeth joined us and we headed to the section of ramps connected to the lowest deck.

It was dark and quiet in the hull of the great ship, lit only by slow-burning oil lamps flickering sleepily from wooden posts. These posts ran the whole length of the deck on either side, like the bones of a great skeleton; in between each were large holding pins. These were home to the biggest creatures—the longnecks, the elephants, the rhinoceros—and here we found Bulk. He was sprawled out on the floor of a cozy den, snuggled up against his mate, sound asleep. I wasn't sure which was louder: the creaking of the Ark as it rocked from side to side or the bear's snoring.

"Hey Bulk! Wake up, Big Guy!" Eddie shouted, "*Oo-oo-ee—*"

"Shh!" Yeffeth grabbed him. "Let the bear hibernate," the man whispered sharply, "unless *you* want to be responsible for feeding him when he wakes up!" Eddie clapped his hands over his mouth and even Yeffeth had to laugh. "Very well, you rascal! But I'll hold you to your word!"

Come to find out, Bulk wasn't the only hibernating creature. Many of the animals were in this strange sleep, or at least some form of suspended rest. Those that did not actually hibernate were unusually sluggish in the darkness of that lowest deck. I was glad to head upwards again.

Once more on mid-deck a light laugh met our ears. It was Nina with Chenna by her side playing with Womby and Glori through the bars of a snug little cage. The girls looked up as their husbands approached.

"What are you two beauties plotting?" Shem asked when he saw the sparkle of their eyes. They smiled mischievously, glanced back at Kawm where he fed some gazelles not far away, and then turned towards the wombats.

"They've been stuck in there so long," Nina said, her clear voice filled with pity. "Couldn't we let them out—just for a short while?"

But before either husband could respond Kawm bellowed, "Absolutely not!" The girls couldn't help but giggle; the hot-headed young man never had forgiven Womby for eating his crops. Shem hid a quick smile of his own while Yeffeth stood calm as ever, arms crossed.

"There's your answer," Yeffeth said.

Nina appealed, "But Kawm—"

"No 'buts' about it!" the youngest brother insisted, "Let the nuisance out and he'll devour everything in sight!" Womby chuffed and rubbed his head against Nina's fair hand. She looked at Yeffeth pleadingly.

"The mid-deck is Kawm's responsibility," her husband replied trying to ignore the blueness of her eyes.

Nina thought for a moment. "Perhaps we could take them to the upper-deck?" At that suggestion Chenna turned to Shem excitedly. But the man cocked his head.

"I don't know," he said, rubbing his dark chin. "The wombat *does* have a way of running into everything." Womby saw his chances dwindling and nuzzled against Nina's hand even harder. Nathak and I glanced at each other in amusement.

But Nina was not easily discouraged, "Then we could carry them!" She looked at Yeffeth, "Couldn't we?"

"The upper deck is Shem's responsibility." This time a faint smile lifted his chiseled face. Obviously Yeffeth was enjoying staying *out* of this conversation.

"*Please*, Shem?" the fair girl asked.

The middle brother still hesitated. "Eh, I'm not so sure..."

Chenna jumped up and laid her small hands on her husband's muscular arms. Then she gazed into his face with those big, violet eyes and smiled sweetly. Shem's head went back with a moan as Yeffeth laughed out loud, slapping him on the shoulder.

"Say 'no' to *that*, little brother!"

And so (after Noak gave his approval) Womby and Glori joined our party on the upper deck: first only occasionally in the two girl's arms, then soon enough on their own four feet, and eventually moving in permanently—occupying a comfortable little cage that had been left empty during boarding. After that Kawm did not seem to mind them so much (so long as they stayed off of his deck and out of his way) and Womby made sure he stayed on best behavior. Eddie also spent a good deal of his time with us by attaching himself to Atani's shoulder. Thus the upper deck became a rather lively place. Soon our numbers grew even more as one particularly gusty day Rhia gave birth to a litter of five healthy pups:

three males and two females. Nathak was beside himself with pride. Noak and his family were also thrilled, taking their birth as a good sign: a sign of hope that God had not forgotten us.

The weeks wore on and the kennel across the aisle became a place of constant excitement as the blind, whimpering, tiny creatures grew into strong, curious young wolves. Thankfully they were contained, yet Rhia still had her paws full keeping them in line. But they were a good lot, overall (though a little loud at times). Saphirra and I grew rather fond of them. It may seem strange for a wolf pup to call a cat "uncle", but on the Ark anything seemed possible. Glori the wombat also began carrying a little one of her own, much to Womby's delight; it was a good five days before the wombat could get out one sentence all put together. Eddie laughed and poked fun at him until the monkey was informed by his own mate he was about to become a father as well. Then the wombat and monkey walked around together like happy dummies—speechless—huge grins plastered all over their faces. That was probably the quietest week of the whole Flood.

* * *

So the days passed, turning into months. As the sixth one came and went the Ark had begun to fill with all kinds of new life, either already born or in the process. But by far the greatest moment for me was when Saphirra whispered in my own ear. Then it was my turn to walk around with a silly grin on my face! Predator and prey both laughed at me; I just laughed with them. By that time life on the great boat had become second nature and we were used to enemies living at peace: jesting and kidding each other but never really threatening harm. We knew the Men of the Tree would take care of us and they knew God would take care of them. This faith was what kept all of us going: learning to trust in each other—and in the only One Who could deliver all of us.

I had known vaguely of the Creator before; we animals are born with a kind of instinctive knowledge of Him. But to learn what the men knew was truly incredible. Every evening, as the golden sun through the vents faded to the silver white of moonlight, Noak gathered his family together in the main room of their living quarters. It was a comfortable place of colorful rugs and pillows draped over simple benches. A low table stood in the middle, nailed to the floor, and along the sides of the room were small ovens (also nailed to the floor) and other cooking utensils. Oil lamps decorated the walls and hung from the ceiling so even at night there could be an abundance of light. Usually, though, only a few of these were left burning as the humans gathered: filling the place with a dull, warm glow. It smelled like cedar and gopherwood (along with whatever spices had been used in the cooking that day) when Noak would sit down and begin to lead his family in worshiping God. They would sing and pray and talk together of His ways—in nature, in history, in everything. Nothing seemed too small or too great for them to speak of and link back to the One Who had made all things. Many times the wolves, Saphirra, and I were allowed to sit in on these meetings. It was always fascinating to listen as Noak told the stories of the past, the stories of the Men of the Tree down through time. Just the sound of his voice was enough to captivate me. But the words he spoke gripped my heart.

He told how the whole world was created in six days, and of the first man and woman who walked with God. He told of the two trees in the garden and their choice to eat from the wrong one. Then there were two sons—one evil, one good. I bristled when Noak said the evil one killed his good brother just because he had brought a better sacrifice to God. But I smiled when the first man and woman were given another son in place of the good one who had been murdered. As Noak recounted the history of his family I saw more and more the goodness and mercy of God towards all men—even those who hated Him—but especially to those few who walked with Him.

There was Lehmek (Noak's father), and his father Methooshelak, better known as "the Great-Father". Just the mention of his name and I could see the old man again in my mind: wrinkled face bent over the fire, weathered hands resting on his staff, eyes piercing through my soul. It was hard to believe anyone so ancient and wise had not always existed, but, as it turned out, even the Great-Father had a father of his own. And that man's name was Khanoke. Khanoke particularly fascinated me—mostly because he had never died! He was such a good man, Noak said, walking so closely with God, that after three hundred and sixty-five years he "was not, for God took him" (that took a little while for me to wrap my head around, but after everything I had seen I believed it). But before he disappeared, Khanoke had been a prophet, seeing visions of things that would happen in the future. He had shared these with his son Methooshelak, who had told them to his son Lehmek, who had told them to Noak. Now, inside the small room of the great Ark—riding out the greatest catastrophe in the history of the world—Noak recited the visions to his sons.

"'Behold'," the father said, "'the Lord comes with ten thousands of His saints, to execute judgment on all'." Noak's voice was deep and weighty as he repeated the words of his great-grandfather, "'To convict all who are ungodly among them of all their ungodly deeds which they have committed in an ungodly way, and of all the harsh things which ungodly sinners have spoken against Him'."

The room was quiet as he finished, except for the constant groaning of the Ark we had all learned to ignore. Each of us pondered in our own minds what the strange words could mean. But Shem broke the silence from where he sat, leaning forward intensely.

"*Another* judgment..."

As if on cue the great boat rocked violently. Then there was a horrible creaking, screeching, and moaning. The whole ship shook with a sudden lurch! We all hung on to whatever we could; Marriet would have been flung to the floor if Atani had not caught her. Then—with a great, crashing THUD—it stopped as abruptly as it came. We each held our breath. Suddenly I realized something.

We aren't moving!

The Ark was completely still!

FORTY-TWO

"WE'VE HIT SOMETHING!" Kawm breathed. Noak was on his feet in an instant.

"Check for leaks!" he said rapidly, "Yeffeth—you and I will take the low-deck. Kawm and Shem, mid-deck." The sons had already grabbed torches, lighting them from the oil lamps. "Marriet, you and the daughters search up here," he gave his wife a quick squeeze to the hand then took a torch from Yeffeth. "Be thorough! Leave no beam un-examined!" As the men ran down the dark aisle to make for the lower levels Nathak and I took off after them.

"Stay up here!" I called back to Saphirra.

* * *

We searched most of the night—back and forth, up and down, over every inch and cranny of the massive boat—but nothing seemed damaged. Some of the others had felt the disturbance worse than we did, especially on the low-deck; even Bulk was awake, looking around with dull, sleepy eyes. But all else appeared ordinary.

Still, the Ark never moved an inch.

Daylight had begun filtering in as a soft gray mist by the time we all gathered again on the upper-deck. The birds would have started their morning songs but the doors of their cages were still covered by dark cloths; no one removed them because they were too busy discussing what had just happened. Several opinions bounced around until Atani voiced the most obvious one that had somehow escaped the rest of us during all the excitement: what if the Ark had finally come to rest? What if the journey was over? No one quite knew what to make of that; we all longed for it yet it seemed too good to be true. And I could still hear the flow of water washing along the outsides.

"We will have to wait," Noak concluded.

And wait we did—for almost three more months. Life continued much the same, with a few changes thrown in: the animals that had been in hibernation began to wake up, we had to get used to walking on a still surface again, and the den that had become home to Saphirra and me got significantly more crowded—in the best of ways. It was on a sunny, peaceful afternoon when my beautiful mate gave birth to the grandest set of twin cubs ever seen (of course, I may have been prejudiced). Being the strong and independent lioness that she was Saphirra did it all herself, though the women were close by just in case. I would have tried to help, but Shem made the wise choice to remove me to another cage. Nathak, Eddie, and Womby kept me company, trying to calm my anxious nerves; I'm afraid it did not help much. Let's just say I was beyond relieved when the man returned with a huge smile on his brown face. He let me out and I bounded to our cage to see two tiny, blind, mouse-like creatures—one black as night, one brownish-gray with little spots—nursing at Saphirra's side.

A daughter and a son!

It was arguably the greatest moment of my life! After a few days their eyes and ears opened and we gave them their names: Tetiana to the little black she-cat and Khan to the spotted, feisty male. They were both curious and full of life—and I wouldn't have had it any other way. Watching them, feeding them, and teaching them became our whole lives. The weeks went by incredibly quickly.

* * *

It was the first day of the tenth month since the flood had started. The Ark was still stationary (same as it had been for weeks) and I was busily teaching my son how to leap from one end of the cage to the other when suddenly Shem started shouting at the top of his lungs,

"Mountains! I can see mountains!"

I strained at the bars to see him perched overhead, on the suspended walkway the men had built to easily reach the light-vents. The young man stood with his head inside the raised cat-walk, peering out the narrow slats of the open vents, bouncing excitedly. As the others came running he kept calling down, "Mountain peaks—they are everywhere! Jutting up from the sea like spear-heads! The Flood is receding!" Quick as they could the other men scurried up a ladder built into the wall with the girls not far behind. As they joined him on the walkway their faces filled with joy; their laughter sounded like music floating down from heaven. Marriet stood by our cages, her stately face pointed upwards as tears glistened down the soft, wrinkled cheeks. The lady's hands grasped together as her lips mouthed three words:

"Thank You, God!"

* * *

After this discovery it was decided the Ark had indeed come to rest somewhere on a high range of mountains. At first hope swelled: if the tops of the mountains were visible, then the water had to be going down. Perhaps soon we would finally feel the ground beneath our feet!

Yet the days wore on and nothing else was seen except a few more jagged cliffs. Hope began to wane. We had been in the Ark for almost *eleven* months! Through them all we had been miraculously protected and sustained. But now a problem loomed on the horizon that was impossible to ignore: our food supply was starting to get low. With the awakening of the hibernating beasts and the new little additions running around the men would soon face a serious problem in keeping all of us fed. If the waters did not dry soon...

Yet, as in all things, Noak and his family prayed, did what they could by rationing food (including their own), and trusted in God to deliver. After forty days the older man also decided to do something else. With Shem's help he raised a hatch in the center of the Ark's roof. The morning sunlight streamed from above in one wide, glorious beam down to the floor of the deck. I stood in its warmth and felt it soak all the way through me. Then Noak took a glossy black raven, held it up to the open sky, and let it go. The black wings of the bird glinted as it flew into the bright blue heavens. I watched silently, wondering if it would ever return, and, if it did, what kind of word would it bring?

"Chenna," Noak called below, "bring the dove as well." Turning, I saw the young woman draw from its cage one of the white birds I had rescued from Marsed's caravan. The gentle creature looked very natural in the woman's hands: its ivory wings glowing against the dark waves of Chenna's hair. Nimbly the quiet girl climbed the ladder and handed her father-in-law the dove. He spoke a brief blessing over it then released the cooing bird into the air. Like a soul taking flight the dove rose out of the Ark, quickly fluttering out of view. They stood watching it a moment. Then the older man put one arm around Chenna's shoulders and one arm around Shem's.

"God-willing, we will know soon," he said.

It did not take long. That afternoon the dove returned and Noak held out his hand to draw her back into the Ark. She had not found land; the earth was still covered with water. My heart sunk a little. I looked at Saphirra and the cubs.

How much longer can we last?

* * *

Six days went by. The raven never returned, but that didn't mean much: it could probably feed on floating carcasses for weeks without having to come back to the Ark. More of the mountains were seen, but they were still bare and rugged. There was no way of knowing what the rest of the world looked like.

Tensions were beginning to mount; word was getting around about the food supply growing thin. The men didn't say much, but I could tell they were beginning to get concerned: they prayed more often and talked in low tones when discussing provisions. It was clear things were close. The portion of dried meat we had been eating kept shrinking; I started going hungry to make sure Saphirra and the cubs had enough. All our hope was in finding dry land.

So on the morning of the seventh day Noak released the dove again. You could feel the expectation, the hope, the fear of those of us watching as she flew away into the clouded sky. Something had to change—and *soon*. But we were helpless to do it ourselves. We had to trust in the One that had brought us here: trust that He would see us through.

And He did.

That evening, as Shem and Chenna lit the oil lamps along the aisles, Nathak and I were discussing the urgency of our situation. The wolf had just mentioned how the men were considering breeding rabbits and other rodents for emergency food when all at once Noak's voice broke out from above.

"Marriet! Marriet!"

I had never heard the man sound so excited! We all joined his wife as she came running. Noak was leaping from the walkway above, shouting Marriet's name over and over, clambering down the ladders with amazing speed. Before we could reach the wall he was already sprinting towards us. I noticed a white flutter overhead; the dove was descending from the hatch. My heart leapt in my throat.

"Noak!" his wife called, "What in the world—"

"Look! Look!" he interrupted, eager and beaming. A small object was thrust into her hand as the rest of us gathered around. "*Look* at it!" His voice was hoarse, his gray eyes shining. With her hands surrounded by her husband's, Marriet looked down—and there in her palm, green and fresh as a spring wind, was a leaf. Perfectly shaped. Long and slender. *Brand new.* Her breath caught in her chest. We stared, mouths open.

"It's an olive leaf," Noak laughed, cupping his wife's chin as she began to weep. "It's an olive leaf! The waters have receded. There is dry land!" She fell into his arms as he repeated, *"Praise God—there is dry land!"*

At that point we all broke into hysterics: laughing, crying, dancing, leaping, roaring, howling.

The waters have receded! There is dry land out there!

* * *

The difference between the next seven days and the previous ones was like daylight and dark. We still lived on minimal rations but the olive leaf filled all of us with such hope that the hunger was almost pleasant: it reminded us the best was yet to come. At the end of the week Noak sent out the dove one more time to confirm the earth was indeed dry. This time she did not return. Now there could be no doubt. The Great Flood was over!

The Creator had kept His promise!

FORTY-THREE

"SHEM, THROW ME THAT HAMMER!" Yeffeth called out.

His brother sent one flying. "Heads up!" The Ark echoed with the sounds of saws cutting, nails popping, and wood cracking as the Men of the Tree removed the ship's large covering. Sunlight—real, actual sunlight—flooded into the upper deck, washing everything in a wonderful, golden heat as, board by board, Noak and his sons took off the roof.

It had been almost one year since we boarded the Ark. One year since the black wave had destroyed everything and lifted us above the world. One year since the Flood began. Now the sky opened up over our heads, as clear and blue as ever I saw it, and the fresh, clean air swept into our weary lungs. It was almost as if the old world had been no more than a dream. I looked up at the heavens and yearned to climb into them, to fly right up like the dove and see the new world for myself. But at least I was light on my feet. The ladders to the roof were a little narrow, but it didn't take too much effort to climb up and find myself standing on the small part of roof that remained. It was surreal—after a year of being enclosed by walls to feel them fall away, replaced by nothing but open air.

Mountain air.

I breathed it in so deeply my chest hurt. My eyes gazed all around. The men were all working steadily to chip away at the Ark's covering, while beyond—oh, beyond! It was the world. Nature. Real dirt and real rocks and real moss! We were nestled in a rocky cradle, surrounded by stone-faced cliffs. They were gray and grim looking.

But they were *dry!*

Carefully I walked to the edge of the boat and peered down: almost afraid there would still be water. Instead I saw brown, sandy ground.

Dry ground!

The mountain peaks were too close to observe the world beyond, but from the smell of things I could tell green plants were growing not far below us: young, wet, and plentiful. I leaned farther over the edge to get a better whiff.

"Careful there, Methooshelak!" It was Shem; he had taken to calling me that during the voyage, naming me after the Great-Father. I considered it an honor.

"Watch your step," Yeffeth added. "Fall off and we won't let you back in!" His warning sounded serious but by now I knew the man well enough to catch his wit. Sauntering over I started rubbing up against him, nuzzling, purring—all the while pushing him closer towards the edge. Finally he threw his hands up. "Alright, alright," he chuckled, "I surrender!" I sat down triumphantly, letting my tail dangle over the end of the roof.

Shem and Kawm just laughed while Noak looked at me and smiled.

"You certainly have a mind of your own!" he said.

* * *

That night was one to remember: seeing the stars for the first time in a year was remarkable enough, but watching them come out with Khan and Tetiana—who had never seen them before at all—was something that could not be put into words. Their eyes grew bigger with every star that appeared. They must have asked a hundred questions: "How many stars are there, anyhow?" "Why do they burn out during the day and light up again at night?" "Do they have pretty names?" "Can I catch one?" "Can I *eat* one?" Most of the questions were beyond my skill to answer, but I loved trying to anyway. Nathak and

Rhia were pelted with the same curiosity from the pups (fast becoming young wolves), while Womby and Glori's little son gazed up at the sky, mouth open wide. Eddie's twin daughters were also beside themselves with excitement, one attached to his back and the other to his mate's. The men and their wives reclined against the floor of the deck, enjoying the beauty as only humans can. A brilliant shooting star sailed across our view and we all (human and animal alike) gasped in wonder. When it faded we cheered. There was no way to be sure, but in that moment I wondered if God was smiling down on us: happy to see His creatures safe and at peace together—just enjoying each other and His handiwork.

* * *

One month and twenty-seven days more: it was the final test of patience, of fortitude, of trust. For most of us, though, the weeks were filled with peace, even as our supplies got leaner and leaner. God had not forgotten us; all would be well. It was just a matter of time. And, on the twenty-seventh day, the time finally came:

"Go out of the Ark, you and your wife, and your sons and your son's wives with you. Bring out with you every living thing of all flesh that is with you: birds and cattle and every creeping thing that creeps on the earth, so that they

may abound on the earth, and be fruitful and multiply on the earth."

It was a brilliantly beautiful day. The sun gleamed unhindered out of an intensely blue, cloudless sky. The breeze was soft and fragrant with spicy, tingling scents: fresh vegetation, running water, blooming flowers. Pounding and hammering had prevailed all morning, ever since the moment Noak announced God had spoken to him at last. After a round of cheering, he and his sons had immediately set about loosening the massive door. Somehow, after over a year of being sealed tighter than the bark on a pine tree, it cracked. A couple of hours later the whole thing swung open wide, pulling back like a huge, dark curtain to reveal the new world beyond. As the gopherwood fell away and the mountain cliffs appeared a charge ran down my spine.

It's open!

The great, giant door was finally open! After almost thirteen months of peril and doubt, wondering and waiting, the way had opened at last. We were leaving the Ark!

But not just yet. While the men built a simple ramp from the doorway to the ground (using the lumber taken from the ship's roof) the women escorted Saphirra, myself, and the wolves back to our cages. Soon the parade began. First came the insects: mantis, spider, centipede, ant, were all carried out in containers, while dragonflies, moths, and butterflies were released to the wind. Then, in a glorious flurry of feathers, the birds were set free: singing and taking to the sky in an aerial dance. Cage door after cage door the humans flung open, faces beaming, while the beating of the birds' wings sounded like a hurricane mounting to heaven. They whirled in a kaleidoscope of color: flashing around, sailing overhead, and scattering as they found open sky. Those that could not fly waddled, strutted, and clucked their way down to the great door. The ostrich caused a little bit of trouble but the penguins made up for it, marching out in such a straight line—little ones as well as parents—that the humans just stood by and watched (Chenna clapping her hands in delight). By the time all the birds were emptied it was after noon and Nathak and I were both pacing. Shem noticed and paused to give each of us a quick rub through our bars.

"Not much longer," he encouraged, the ivory Tree on his chest glinting in the sunlight.

Yet still we had to wait, for next came the prey animals. By the hundreds they poured out of the Ark, this time in more than just twos: families of deer, turtles, kangaroos, elephants, giraffes, skunks, badgers, squirrels, and a host of other creatures were herded from each deck, through the aisles, and to their freedom. I have to admit, watching them all eventually made my stomach start growling—and I realized why we predators had been kept in our cages.

But as Womby and Glori came in sight my hunger faded; I watched in surprise as my friend and his family turned from the door and waddled back to us. Womby's dark eyes were gleaming as he looked up at me through the bars.

"We'll wait for y,y,you," he said decidedly. Nina came to herd them back, but when she saw the contentment of the wombats standing by our cages she just giggled, shook her head, and left them alone. Once Womby's mind was made up it was pointless to try and change it. So we all waited together—wolves, wombats, and cats—until the last of the prey animals had finally passed and the great door stood empty and clear. My blood started pounding.

This is it! my mind cried. *The moment we have waited so long for!*

I turned to look one last time around the cage that had become our home. How much had happened; how much had changed! Saphirra's eyes met mine and I knew she was thinking the same thing I was while Kahn and Tetiana played at our paws.

"Are you ready?" Noak's calm voice broke in and we looked to see the wise, good man kneeling outside the bars. I turned my face towards his and for a moment we were eye to eye. His gray depths shone with joy. Then he placed a hand on Womby's furry head and chuckled. "So be it," he whispered and undid the lock on our cages.

The door slid open.

As we stepped beyond the bars Shem released Nathak, Rhia, and their pups. "Come," Noak said with a smile and we all followed him past the walls of empty cages. We stepped into the light of the great door. All at once there was a huffing, shuffling sound to my left. I smiled; it was Bulk. Completely recovered (except for a slight limp that would never go away), the bear walked steadily behind Yeffeth with his brown mate at his side. True to form, Eddie rode on his friend's back, all grins (I think if the monkey had been any prouder he would have busted something). The she-monkey and twins sat on the back of Bulk's mate and together they came up behind us. From the sounds below I could tell a host of other animals were also ready to taste their freedom. Noak and Marriet stood in the doorway. Nathak and his family lined up behind them. Saphirra and I let Womby, Glori, and their little one go in front of us. Then I looked back at Bulk. The bear nodded his heavy head.

"You first," he rumbled, dark eyes shining.

I bowed my head respectfully while Eddie's shook in amazement. We were all remembering Bulk's Dream. It seemed like another lifetime since the three of us had shared our stories in the Barracks of Khanok, when Eddie had told me of the bear's Dream: how in it he had followed a lion out of darkness into the light of a green, "safe place".

Now here we stood.

I looked forward; the brightness beyond was almost blinding. Noak waited until a good number of the predator animals had gathered behind us. Then the strong, scarred hand lifted triumphantly in the air.

"Come!" He called.

And so we left the Ark. Following the man and his wife, stepping into the full light of the late afternoon sun, we passed out of the familiar and into the new. I paused for a second as my paws came to the last board of the ramp, right before they fell on rocky soil.

The last piece of gopherwood.

I looked back at the giant ship, now still against a backdrop of gray mountain peaks, its weathered sides settled permanently in a cradle of stone. I felt a lump form in my throat. A lump of gratitude. The Ark had been my salvation. Without it I would have been lost. We *all* would have been lost. Now, wherever the path led, a part of the Ark would always go with me. I sighed, heart too full for words.

And then I stepped onto solid ground.

"What is it?" Tetiana's sweet voice was puzzled as she lowered her delicate nose to the earth; it was the first time she had ever felt anything underneath her besides wood and straw.

Saphirra nudged her gently, "It is dirt." The kitten gingerly lowered her black paw, then picked it up and shook it with a sour look on her face.

"Euww," she squeaked. "It's squishy!"

Kahn crouched on the ramp, waited, and pounced onto the rocky soil. "Yeah!" he cried, "It's great!" then pounced on his little sister.

"Alright—that's enough." Picking him up by the nape of the neck I set my excited son to the side. Truthfully, though, I was just as excited as he was. "Why don't you pounce on someone your own size?"

He caught my hint; with a mischievous cackle the young lion sprung for my throat and we fell backwards—rolling, tumbling, and laughing all the way. For the first time in my life I actually enjoyed getting dirty! It was wonderful to feel the earth again: to smell it as we played, to taste it as we wrestled. Down the narrow trail I romped with my son, the trail that descended through the mountain peaks. The parade of predators followed behind while Noak (more or less) led the way. Nathak and the pups joined in the fun, making for a pretty lively trip. That is, until we turned a sharp corner. The sides of the mountains suddenly fell away; the trail still rambled down a cliff to the right but we didn't follow it. All play stopped. Nathak and I stood still while the young ones settled by our legs. All we could do was stare. In a minute the rest of our families joined us, along with Womby, Bulk, and Eddie. The monkey whistled but no one spoke a word: we were all speechless, looking the same direction.

We were standing on the edge of a precipice, overlooking the greenest mountain meadow any of us had ever seen. Tall, shimmering grass blew in the cool breeze like ripples across water. A small, perfectly round lake lay in the midst of the meadow, turquoise and brilliant—its mirror image reflecting the golden sky above. Two small, crystal streams connected on either end of the lake: one flowing into it, fed by a towering waterfall gushing from the stony peaks, and the other flowing down and away, over rolling mountain slopes. In the distance far below, a wide, emerald plain ran on for miles, dotted with the blushing growth of young trees; beyond this rose another range of mountains, painted orange and fuchsia by the rays of the setting sun behind us. The atmosphere was perfectly clear, making every shadow and highlight radiate against each other. Many of the birds who had left the Ark darted about like flying jewels (including the happily reunited pair of white doves), and the meadow was teeming with other fellow refugees. It was so intense—the color, the beauty, the aliveness of it all—that words truly failed. I think Eddie finally summed it up best.

"Wow!"

FORTY-FOUR

THAT NIGHT WE CELEBRATED. The mountain lake turned out to be full of fish, so Saphirra and I (along with the bears and other expert fishermen) set about laying a feast of salmon, mackerel, pike, tuna, cod, eel, and whatever else had been trapped there by the Flood, along the mossy banks. No sooner was a fish out of water than an animal had gobbled it up. For the first time in months, we all ate to our heart's content. Once our bellies were full the games began. Predator and prey alike went racing, wrestling, and frolicking together through the starlit meadow—relishing the sweetness of freedom. It was a beautiful thing to watch (of course, I wound up doing a little more than watching before the night was over). As dawn drew near the party waned, each of us eventually drifting off to sleep. One by one or in groups we scattered throughout the meadow: falling in happy, exhausted heaps onto the silky, cool grass. Even the young ones finally ran out of energy, slumbering wherever they dropped—which for Kahn and Tetiana meant curled up with Womby Jr., the wolf pups, and Eddie's twins. The monkey alone (who never slept as long as there was any chance of fun) stayed awake, and my eyes closed to the sound of him chattering away with a sleepy owl.

* * *

When they opened again they were greeted by a burning, amber light. I blinked and lifted up. Straight ahead—over the hilltops, across the plains, above the distant mountains—the sun was rising in all its radiant glory. I looked away from the heat; the meadow was sparkling with diamond dew, clothed in an array of wildflowers. Actually, everywhere the sunlight hit seemed to sparkle: all over the mountain. The Birds were singing, but otherwise all was quiet—everyone else still worn out from the night's festivities. Even Eddie had succumbed, draped over Bulk's back like a limp rag and snoring away. Nearby, Saphirra lay stretched beside the pile of kittens, pups, monkeys, and wombat: her smooth coat dazzling white against the bright, spring grass. I looked back towards the sunrise. It grew steadily bigger above the line of blue mountains, filling the eastern sky. Watching quietly, I drank in the stillness.

The east.

My mind went back to that morning so long ago on my mountain, when the Voice had come to me out of the fog. I had followed it then, not knowing where it would lead or what it would cost. In the end it had cost me everything I had ever known.

But now...

I looked again at my peaceful family, my unlikely friends, my new mountain home. At last I sighed.

The Voice was right. It was right all along.

At that moment a new smell wafted on the fresh, clean air. A tingling scent: sweet and soothing and smoky. Somewhere a fire was burning. It was then I realized I had not seen Noak or any of the rest of his family since the previous evening. Nathak and Rhia were also nowhere in sight. I stood to my paws and tested the air: the new smell was coming from back up the trail, towards the Ark. My motion stirred Saphirra and her blue eyes opened.

"Do you smell that?" I asked. The lioness yawned and stretched gracefully. As she stood to her own paws I was still poised towards the trail. She chuckled softly.

"Go on," she purred, sapphires sparkling, "I can watch the little ones." My face turned to her and the beautiful creature smiled. That same weak feeling washed over me; no matter how many times I looked at her Saphirra never ceased to be overwhelming.

"I love you," I whispered, rubbing my head gently against hers. Then I moved on, headed for the trail. But just as I started to climb a pattering of small footfalls came from behind.

"Where are you g,g,going?"

It was Womby, standing on all fours: gray fur gleaming silver in the bright sun, black eyes gleaming with curiosity.

Just like the first day I saw him.

"Away," I replied out loud, smiling and recalling a similar conversation on my old mountain. But this time I had no desire to lose him. "Think you can keep up?" I asked with a wink.

My little friend grinned and waddled up beside me. As we climbed the trail together the smell became more distinct. I was able to tell what it was: roasting lamb. The Ark came in sight, as did Noak and his family, along with the wolves. They were gathered around a large pile of stones, stacked symmetrically in the shape of a square, on top of which burned a fire fueled by the left-over lumber of the ship's roof. Their faces were somber and their knees were on the earth. Womby and I stood at a distance—unsure what was happening, but sensing a very sacred moment. The wolves saw us and quietly approached.

"The offerings," Nathak explained, observing our faces, "to thank the Creator for seeing them—and us—safely through." I saw the blood on the stone and realized why everyone was so somber.

"The clean animals?" I asked. An extra one of each kind had boarded the Ark, kept separate from the rest of us in their own holding area. When the ship had emptied they remained on board. I had wondered why—until now.

Rhia nodded and looked at the fire. "When the first man ate the wrong tree and rebelled, the Creator killed animals to make clothes for the humans—to cover them and their sin. Ever since then the Men of the Tree have offered sacrifices to show God they remember His mercy and are grateful: but only of their very best, and only of the animals He has set-apart." The she-wolf's voice was low and soft, "*Never* a human sacrifice, though. Man was made in the Creator's image and He will not take their blood that way: even if they do owe it to Him because of their sin. He is too good—"

Suddenly she stopped. At the same moment the hair on the back of my neck stood straight up. We four glanced at each other, eyes big and mouths empty. We felt it. We all could feel it. Weight. Grandness. Stillness. Awe. Terrifying yet peaceful, sharp yet soft, severe yet full of love, it settled upon us—filling the cradle between the mountains like a waterfall filling a footprint. The humans felt it too and fell on their faces. It seemed like a good idea so we did the same. Soon the feeling turned to something much, much stronger.

A *presence*.

Washing over us like another flood, its incredible strength pressed me to the earth. I felt my throat go dry.

The One that shut the door!

It was the same colossal presence—only even greater. At first I was afraid to look up. But then a breeze started blowing, a strange wind that swirled inside the cliffs as if of its own will. Fierce, yet gentle, it seemed to lift some of the heaviness from around us (or else made us able to bear it). Trembling, my head rose from the ground. The men and women were also somewhat upright, though still with their faces pointed down. At times they glanced at each other, at times they bowed all the way again: almost as if they were listening to someone speak, receiving instructions. The rest of us held our breath, unable to move or whisper. The breeze continued to blow, the presence remained the same, the men kept listening. Something epic was taking place—something incredibly grand—but what we did not know.

Then it came. Soft as a newborn's whimper at first, carried in the sigh of the wind, then growing in volume like the swell of the sunrise. But it was unmistakable:

"And as for Me, behold, I establish My covenant with you and with your seed after you, and with every living

creature that is with you: the birds, the cattle, and every beast of the earth with you, of all that go out of the Ark, every beast of the earth. Thus I establish My covenant with you: Never again shall all flesh be cut off by the waters of the flood: never again shall there be a flood to destroy the earth."

I started trembling uncontrollably. From head to tail my body rocked as shock coursed through me like lightning through my veins.

The Voice!

The Voice from my Dream, the Voice on my mountain, the Voice in the garden, the Voice on the wind, the Voice in the chaos, the Voice in the woods- that was *it!* A fearful reverence overwhelmed me.

But that means...

The Voice continued, *"This is the sign of the covenant which I make between Me and you, and every living creature that is with you, for perpetual generations: I set My bow in the cloud, and it shall be for the sign of the covenant between Me and the earth."*

I felt turned to stone.

The...Voice...is...the...Voice...of...GOD!

My head swam with the revelation. *The Voice of God?* Could it be—was it possible? Yet surely, there was no mistaking it!

But how? Why? And why me?

"Look!" Womby cried. His face was turned upwards, wrapped in wonder. Somehow I managed to look at the sky. My breath caught in my chest. Painted against the blue of heaven, growing out of a towering cloud overhead, a ribbon of color was forming! It rose into the clear air like brush strokes of a paintbrush, brilliant and wide. They were the hues of a prism—like sun through a dew drop—only in perfect layers, stacked and blended together. Violet, indigo, blue, green, yellow, orange, and red, the rainbow shot out of the cloud in slow motion: stretching to arc over the whole mountain. I could not see the end of it.

"It shall be, when I bring a cloud over the earth, that the bow shall be seen in the cloud," the Voice was strong, yet full of compassion, *"and I will remember My covenant which is between Me and you and every living creature of all flesh; the waters shall never again become a flood to destroy all flesh."*

The feeling of fear began to fade. Slowly, still trembling, I stood to my paws.

"The bow shall be in the cloud, and I will look on it to remember the everlasting covenant between God and every living creature of all flesh that is on the earth."

I looked up again. The bow was glowing like a smile in the morning heavens. Beams of sunshine seemed to pour from above—even though the sun had not yet risen over the mountains. It was light of a different kind—warmer, cleaner, and more renewing than any felt on earth—that filled the air around us. I drank in its goodness. For some reason I felt like weeping, but not from sorrow. My gaze turned to Noak and his sons and their wives. They still knelt on the ground, but with faces raised to heaven. Some had tears; some had smiles. Shem and Chenna's had both. Once more the great, awesome, wonderful Voice spoke:

"This is the sign of the covenant which I have established between Me and all flesh that is on the earth."

And then it was gone. We all bowed again with our faces to the dirt as the mighty Presence withdrew to Heaven. The wind died down, but not completely—and in its wake lingered the sweetest fragrance that was ever smelled by man or beast. In a thousand years I could never hope to describe it.

* * *

We stood there for a while in awe, basking in the glory of what had just happened. Eventually I realized the others were stirring. Still I remained planted: almost afraid that if I moved I would realize the whole thing had just been another dream. But a low, gruff voice pulled me out of it.

"It was Him, wasn't it? The Voice?"

I looked at the wolf. He had stolen up beside me: icy blue depths brimming with hidden wisdom. Almost subconsciously I nodded. Something in his gaze filled my heart with even more amazement.

"You *knew?*" I asked.

Nathak's stern face actually smiled. But instead of answering me, his noble silver head turned to look at

A CAT'S TALE

the great ship a moment, peaceful and quiet among the rocky mountain peaks. Then he finally spoke.

"No one comes to the Ark by accident."

He looked back at me with a meaning beyond words, bowed respectfully, and turned to follow his masters. Noak and Marriet, Yeffeth and Nina, Shem and Chenna, and Kawm and Atani were all walking the stony trail, headed down the mountain at last. Rhia was with them, dancing about their heels. Womby looked up at me, that same gullible trust on his little face, and grinned happily. Then he took off to join the wolves. I alone remained in that secluded, sacred place. In wonder I gazed at the altar of stone. It was perfectly clean: no fire, no sacrifice, no blood remained. I looked at the great ship, a thousand thoughts going through my mind. Memories. Promises. Dreams.

But above all gratitude.

The sun rose above the mountain peaks, its golden rays kissing the Ark. My eyes lifted to the sky. Overhead the beautiful bow of color still lingered, perhaps even brighter than before. A breeze stirred, carrying with it the last of the Heavenly fragrance. Closing my eyes, I drew in a deep, deep breath. When I breathed again it was gone.

"Are you coming?"

I turned and saw Shem standing behind me: a friendly smile on his brave, rugged face. The white Tree dangled from his neck by its leather chord, glistening in the brilliance of the morning sun. As if knowing what I was thinking, the man nodded slightly then held out his strong right hand my way.

I didn't hesitate. With one last parting look of gratitude, I left the Ark behind for the new world: heart full of hope, under the sign of God's covenant.

Following the Man of the Tree.

EPILOGUE

THAT WAS ALL A LONG TIME AGO. In some ways things have dramatically changed, and not necessarily for the better: earth after the Flood is a much different place than earth before the Flood. Like a beast still reeling from the shock of an old wound, the world still shakes from trauma—literally, sometimes. Earthquakes, volcanoes, radical changes in temperature, and storms have become the normal way of things. Of all these, the storms are perhaps the most frightening: too graphic of a reminder for me of the horrors of the Flood. Thankfully, however, they pass, always leaving behind a bright, shimmering rainbow.

But it hasn't just been earth and sky; the rest of us—both men and animals—have changed, too. After the morning when God spoke, a strange thing happened: a fear that hadn't been there before began to spread among the animals. A fear of man. Those of us who had had more contact with Noak and his family didn't feel it so strongly, but the rest of the survivors began to shy away from the humans almost as if they were predators. And, as it turned out, they were. The Creator had told the men that now they could eat meat as well as green herbs (they would need it due to the harshness of the new world). So they became hunters. But mercifully (as always) God also gave us the fear so the hunted might have a chance of escape. Yet the Men of the Tree are honorable: they only take what they need.

Truthfully, things have probably been harder for them than any of us. Noak, Marriet, their sons and daughters: they've had to start over from scratch. No other family. No friends but us. No tools, mechanics, or other conveniences they were used to before except for what little they could fit onto the Ark. Nothing but their own ingenuity, a whole lot of natural resources—and each other. Yet they've made it. With their faith in God as a cornerstone, the Men of the Tree have built a life for themselves out of nothing. Noak has become a farmer, planting vineyards and other crops. Yeffeth is a hunter and explorer, though he never stays gone too long from Nina or their many children and grand-children. Shem (not surprisingly) has taken to raising cattle, herding sheep, and working with animals—both for livelihood and pleasure—while Chenna stands by his side and gracefully helps raise their own large family. But Kawm...to his parent's grief the youngest son has turned his back on them. Forsaking the Tree, he has become like the men of the old world: proud and angry, judgmental, stiff-necked, quick to find fault with everyone but himself. Yet, in spite of her husband, Atani still keeps the faith. The wise woman stays true to the Tree and, as much as she can, returns to visit Noak and Marriet, bringing different sons and daughters with her (if Kawm allows). I only hope they take after their mother. One thing I have learned: when men walk with God, they are good—not always perfect, sometimes they can make even big mistakes, but still they are always good. When men do not walk with God, they are evil—maybe not always violent, but always selfish. There is no in-between.

In other ways, however, things haven't changed at all. The sun keeps rising and setting, the grass and trees keep growing and multiplying—and Saphirra is as beautiful as ever. Her form may not be as sleek as it once was (due to the number of young lions she's now brought into the world) but her eyes are as blue and radiant and clear as ever. When they gaze into mine I still can't breathe. Khan and Tetiana are now grown with cubs and grand-cubs of their own, spreading the line of Sengali and Saphirra far and wide under the sun. I couldn't be prouder.

Womby has stayed a little bit closer. Faithful as ever, the good-hearted wombat has remained nearby:

never straying far from either the Men of the Tree or me. Most of the time he and Glori can be found relaxing at Yeffeth's home, keeping Nina company when her husband is gone, while their sons and daughters roam the grassy plains like furry cattle.

Bulk and his mate have settled into a fine territory south of here, re-populating the earth with a strong, healthy stock of bears. He still has that limp I gave him, but it doesn't keep the Champ from teaching his cubs to be some of the toughest fighters on earth. I'm just glad he doesn't hold grudges.

Eddie never stays anywhere very long: between juggling a whole colony of his own, helping Atani as much as he can, visiting Bulk, and checking up on the rest of us, the monkey says he doesn't have time to "Peel a banana or crack a peanut!" Of course, he loves every minute of it.

Nathak and Rhia, on the other hand, never go anywhere else. For them the Men of the Tree *are* home: wherever they go, the wolves go, wherever they stay, the wolves stay. Many of their pups have grown and ventured into the wild while some have followed their parents and remained with the family of Noak. But if you want to find Nathak or Rhia find Shem or Chenna: wherever they are, the wolves won't be far away.

As for me—well, I spend my days doing what a cat my age does best: exactly what I want to. Teaching young ones how to hunt. Exploring new territories with Yeffeth (sometimes Shem and Nathak come along too, and we get into some grand adventure—but that's another story). Patrolling the range of emerald and purple mountains Saphirra and I call home. Escorting Noak as he walks through fields of grain and wheat talking with the Creator. Taking a nap under one very fine tree behind Shem and Chenna's tents. Living life one day at a time. Each morning, with Saphirra by my side, I watch the sunrise from our mountain den, golden light washing over a sea of rich farmland, open country, and green treetops. Each morning I'm reminded that I would be dead if the Voice had not called my name. And each morning, as the burning sphere climbs into the eastern sky, I remember the One who called.

He has been faithful.

In all of the changes and all of the sameness, He has remained.

He has kept His promise.

And for that reason, what thrills me the most is when a young lion—or wolf, or wombat, or any other youngster—looks up at me and says, "Tell me about the Voice!" Before I know it a whole group of them has gathered: eyes shining with curiosity, bright with excitement, brimming with the promise of tomorrow. I look around and smile. Then my gaze turns upwards, towards heaven.

"It all began one particularly hot, still day..."

AUTHOR'S NOTE

THE STORY OF SENGALI IS WHAT I LIKE TO call a "fictional, historical, allegory". "Fictional" because some of it may or may not be true (The Dream, the Tree, the culture of Noah's day, etc.—not to mention a talking cat); "historical" because some of it is *most definitely* true (The Ark, the Flood, the faithfulness of God to Noah and his family, etc.); and "allegory" because the journey of Sengali in many ways mirrors my own (not that I eat raw meat or can take down a dinosaur with my teeth, but I *do* know what it is like to be called, rescued, and delivered). It is my interpretation of what the days of the Flood could have been like and I loved every minute of bringing it to life. However, for the best and *only*, one-hundred-percent-true story of Noah and the Flood check out the Bible, the book of Genesis, chapters 6 through 10 (Matthew chapter 24, verses 37 through 39, and

Hebrews chapter 11, verses 4 through 7, are very good reads, too).

Also, a word about the names: since Sengali (being a cat and therefore unable to read) would only have heard the names of Noah and his family I decided to spell them similarly to how they would be pronounced in the original Hebrew. I did, however, take some liberties in adapting them to English. For example: in the original Hebrew, "Noah" is actually pronounced "Noakh" (with a strong "h" sound at the end). Unfortunately, this wonderful pronunciation was lost when spelled out in English, so I wound up inventing my own spelling of "Noak", hopefully maintaining the same feel of the name. Thus Japheth becomes "Yeffeth", "Ham" becomes "Kawm", "Enoch" becomes "Khanoke", etc. Marriet, Nina, Chenna, and Atani (not having names in the Bible) were all my own invention. As for the rest of them...well, if I were to start telling you their histories now this note would turn into another novel. And since it has already run on quite long enough, I believe I shall end here.

Follow the Voice!
Christis Joy Pinson

ACKNOWLEDGEMENTS

Jesus Christ—You are my "Man of the Tree". I love You with all my heart.

Dad—The first to read *"Sengali"*. Your unceasing enthusiasm and encouragement have been beyond words. As a child you taught me to love Scripture and stand up for what I believe. My prayer is that this book will spark that same vision in a new generation. Thank you for showing me by your life what it looks like to never compromise.

Mom—You are my tireless cheerleader, wise counselor, constant friend, and steady anchor. Thank you for believing in me enough to sacrifice so much to see your little girl's dreams come true. I love you!

Joel— You are my superhero, my most loyal fan since *"Black League of Assateague"* (boiling pits of lava and all)! Thank you for loving *"Sengali"*, for letting your baby sister see your grown-up tears when you finished it, and for bravely escorting her over the treacherous mountains of publishing. "Nathak lives!"

Darlys Warren—You were an answer to prayer! Thank you for taking your wonderful editing pencil and turning my creatively ambitious, grammatically painful manuscript into something other people could actually read.

Denver and Joan Murray—Two of the most generous people I know! Your gift of giving, prayers, and, most of all, friendship have made this book possible. May the Lord bless you a hundredfold!

Mitchell Tolle—Artist, Inspiration, Mentor...your work and legacy mean so much to so many! Thank you for always taking the time to pour into the next generation, including me.

Eric Ludy—By example and the written word you and Leslie have challenged me to follow Jesus Christ no matter what. Thank you for shining as a lighthouse to show me the way—in the world of literary excellence and in life.

All the people who read the first drafts of *"Sengali"*—I wish I could mention you each by name. From ages eight to eighty-two, you have encouraged, critiqued, and breathed life into a very tremulous writer's heart. Thank you *so* much for your support and incredible patience for the finished product. I hope it was worth the wait!

And, finally, to Princess, Sampson, and Esther— The best dogs that ever lived. You would have made Nathak and Rhia proud. I miss you.

SENGALI.COM

Made in the USA
Lexington, KY
03 September 2017